In Bloom

A BRIGHTSIDE NOVEL

Mary butterflies
always be
your guides.
xoxo,
Kristin
Delahanty

In Bloom

A BRIGHTSIDE NOVEL

KATIE DELAHANTY

Entangled Publishing, LLC
2614 South Timberline Road
Suite 109
Fort Collins, CO 80525
Visit our website at www.entangledpublishing.com.

Edited by Karen Grove and Nicole Steinhaus
Cover design by Heather Howland

ISBN 978-1-50038-133-2

Manufactured in the United States of America

First Edition February 2014

To Mum and Da.
And you knew it all along...

OLIVIA BLOOM @BLOOMOLIVIA
SCARED. NO. EXCITED. NO—SCARED. #LEAPOFFAITH

My name is Olivia Bloom and I. Am. Free.

I've given myself a chance to go—to dream—to make something happen. To be *me*. Alone. Just me. I can be anything I want to be, and I hope the world is ready, that it doesn't spit me out. I don't know what will happen; all I know is this is

The
Scariest
Feeling
Ever…
But here I go.

Chapter One

MARK VANCLEER @BRIGHTSIDEBP
OH, YOU DIDN'T ASK HOW THE SI FASHION SHOW IS GOING?
TOO BAD. SWIMSUITINGLY WELL!

PARKER MIFFLIN @ISINDULGENT
@BLOOMOLIVIA IT'S NOT SO BAD, HONEY. IT'S NOT LIKE YOU
WERE WEARING...OH WAIT. NEVERMIND. ;)

Taking a sip of my champagne, I attempt to blend into the potted palm tree I'm standing next to. *Blend in. Clearly I didn't get the half-naked model memo.* I sneak a peek across the after party at Hollywood's current darling, Allie Russo. Still wearing the skimpy bikini from her last trip down the runway, she is at the center of a group of A-listers who are hanging on her every word. They can't seem to get enough, and she's not even the most famous person in the room. *What am I doing here? This is nuts.* I've never seen so many pretty people in one place, and I marvel at how quickly life can change. Last week watching *Project Runway* on TV was the closest I'd been to a fashion show, and now here I am surrounded by household names. Having just moved to LA, I'm a little short on cash, and to help me out, my new friend and neighbor Blair hired me to dress models at the taping of the *Sports Illustrated* Swimsuit Fashion Show that the PR firm she works for is putting on. *This is a huge step in the right direction.* All of these women must have personal shoppers, trainers, and fairy godmothers. I so don't belong... Concentrating on my drink to avoid making eye contact with any celebrities, I slowly become aware of a presence to my right. My skin heats as I glance up, nervously scanning the crowd to locate the eyes I'm certain are examining me. But I find no one. *Don't be ridiculous. You're practically invisible—the girl with nobody to talk to—the help. Who would be looking at you when every one point five seconds a supermodel in a swimsuit walks by?* Despite my all-black ensemble being form fitting, my skin is mostly covered, and I'm certain I look like a frumpy Puritan shadow by contrast. *I should probably go home and spare everyone the snowsuit.*

Making my way through the boisterous crowd, I head toward the exit on the far side of the airplane hangar, in search of the restroom before I leave. The bathrooms are located in a poorly lit, narrow corridor, and I avoid touching the pale blue walls as I squeeze through to the end. Twisting the knob on the door to the ladies' room, I find it's locked.

Sighing, I turn to wait and come face-to-face with the

bluest eyes I've ever seen. Jumping in surprise, I do a double take. The face attached to the eyes is so familiar…perfectly formed jaw…messy dark brown hair…I can't help but look twice before the recognition registers. *Berkeley Dalton.* Lead singer for Berkeley & the Brightside, my favorite band. Sucking in a breath, I tear my eyes from him as my stomach contracts, and I resist the urge to hyperventilate Miss Piggy-style at his feet. I stand perfectly still, sweating and praying to the Restroom Gods to open the door so I can escape. *What is she doing in there?*

"I always wonder why they don't have more restrooms at these things."

OMG. He's talking to me. His voice is smooth and slightly hoarse as though he's been screaming into a microphone all night. Hmm. *Think. Think. Think. Words. Use them.* But it's no use. My brain shuts down and fills with champagne bubbles. *Say something!*

"Yeah. Tell me about it," I say. "You'd think they'd plan it better." I stare at the floor. *Good. So far so good.* And then, for a reason I don't understand, I raise my eyes to his and continue. "So, I'm a *huge* fan. I know you're Berkeley Dalton, and you know I'm—" I try to stop myself. *Where am I going with this? What am I saying?* But it's too late: the champagne is talking now. "Well, actually, you don't know— so let's move on. You're taller than I expected."

What? What kind of crazy talk was that? Why would I say that? What is wrong with me? I want to reach out and pluck back each and every word, but it's too late. Maybe I can just stab myself in the throat with a stiletto—there has to be one around here somewhere.

Berkeley, to his credit, registers only a moment of

confused surprise across his perfect features before he resets his expression and studies me with amusement in his eyes.

Great. He's laughing at me. As well he should.

"Um, thanks? I think?" he says with a hint of a smile that sends my heart straight to my toes. "Maybe I *should* know you?"

Just then the bathroom door opens and I turn to see a scantily clad model towering behind me. Scrambling to get out of her way, I rush to the right, but so does she and I end up blocking her path again. We both scoot to the left. Right. Left again. Finally, with an exasperated glare, she stomps her foot and stands still as I stumble backward against the wall, tripping over my feet in the process, but blessedly out of her way.

"Oh, Berk," she coos, with no further regard to me. "You found me. So sweet." She easily wraps an arm around his waist. "Let's get out of here. I'm starving."

Unable to ignore the body she reveals as she adjusts her tiny dress, I try to console myself. *Enjoy your cucumber slices.*

As the pair turns to leave, Berkeley leans toward me, catching my eye. "It was nice talking to you."

My cheeks hot with humiliation, I grant him a disbelieving half smile before slinking into the bathroom. *Nice talking to you. Right.*

Back home at the Vicente, I slump into a chair in the courtyard and pour myself a glass of wine. The cool night air washes over me as I try to make out the Hollywood sign, barely visible in the hills to the north, and allow the tinkling water from the stone pineapple fountain that dominates the space to soothe my nerves. Behind me an apartment door closes, and I don't have to look to see who has come to join me. I've lived here less than two weeks, but I already know Parker has a sixth sense for cocktails.

"The adorable mistress of apartment one is back so soon?" he asks as he leans down to greet me with a one-armed hug and kisses my cheek. I'm still not used to the kissing thing, and turning my head with an awkward sucking sound, I blow a kiss into the ether. Terrible. After all of those years in junior high practicing kissing my hand, who knew it would be cheek kisses I'd fail so miserably in?

Taking a seat, he pours himself a glass and settles in. With his flawlessly waved hair, knotted ascot, and boat shoes, he looks like he should be sipping champagne on a yacht instead of slumming it with me in our little Spanish courtyard.

"Yes. Another job gone awry," I reply. The costume design job I moved here with has already disappeared. It was on a super low-budget movie and didn't pay anything anyway, but I'd been hoping to make some connections that would lead to future work. No such luck. After my first day on set the film's main investor backed out, leaving me unemployed. I've been applying for jobs ever since.

"I'm starting to think I'm doomed. I accidentally switched two of the models' outfits and one of them had to go down the runway wearing a seashell bra the size of pasties. I'm sure they'll never hire me again."

"Please. It'll probably make the teasers," Parker comforts me. "Wardrobe malfunctions are ratings gold."

The Vicente's iron gate clangs shut, and Blair rushes in. Even after a long day at work, with her brownish-blond hair pulled into a messy bun that is a perfect complement to her smooth, cocoa skin and blue eyes, she is stunning.

"Liv! Thank God. What happened to you? I was worried when I couldn't find you."

"I'm sorry. I should have texted. It was a weird night. I should probably do LA a favor and book the next flight back to Pittsburgh."

"What happened? Did you get abducted by swimsuit models?" she asks, taking a seat and grabbing Parker's wine for a sip. He gives her a dirty look.

An image of Berkeley's charming smile pops into my head, and my stomach contracts. "No. Worse than that. I had a run-in with a rock star."

"Ooh. Who was it?" Parker asks.

"Ugh," I groan, my face heating. "I met Berkeley Dalton."

"Berkeley Dalton!" he says. "That's like hitting the celeb lottery."

"Please don't say that. It makes it so much worse," I say, hiding my face in my hands. "I'm such a huge fan—I listened to Berkeley & the Brightside on repeat all the way to California—it was all I could do to keep from melting at his feet."

"He's super hot," Blair says, fanning herself. "How did you meet him? He wouldn't have been mingling with the regular people—he was on the VIP party list for sure."

"VIP list?" I ask.

"There's a party within every party," she explains. "Full access is reserved for the A-list. Most of the people at that event would have given up Botox for a year if it meant an invitation to the VIP party. We're talking major sacrifice here."

If those were "regular" people, what does that make me? *Insignificant.* "Oh, well, I definitely wasn't in the VIP section—I was waiting in line for the bathroom while he was waiting for the model who was *in* the bathroom, and he started making small talk."

"Wait. He talked to you?" Parker's jaw drops as he stares at me. "You minx!"

"Yes, but I don't even know what I said. I've almost completely erased it from my mind—that happens in traumatic situations, you know. I *think* I told him I knew who he was, and I *know* I told him he was taller than I expected."

"Oh, wow. That violates, like, a hundred rules. I take it back. Not a minx," he says, shaking his head as he turns to Blair. "Didn't you brief her?"

She throws her hands up in defense. "I didn't think I needed to. She was supposed to blend in."

My eyes flit back and forth between them. "Rules?"

Parker studies me. "The rules have been compiled from years of experiences, and many a glass of Cabernet has been spilled in this courtyard during their creation. We don't share them with just anyone," he finally says with a questioning glance at Blair.

She nods her permission.

"But we like you," he says. "We think you have potential, Olivia Bloom, so we're going to let you in on some of LA's secrets. Being with celebrities is an art." He folds his hands and looks at me like he's about to share the long-lost secret of the universe. "Those of us in the industry are not in the business of meeting them from a fan point of view. Instead, we have to strive to be on their level. We may not be famous, but we're still their peers. Celeb inner circles are reserved for the elite, and once you enter the circle, there are certain unspoken rules you must abide by."

"For me, it helps to look at it this way," Blair says. "Celebrities are people, no different from you or me, who are living their dream. That's why we all come here. We're dreamers, and we don't want to settle for ordinary. We'll all meet with varying levels of success; some of us will be great artists whose names will never be known, and others will make it to the level of celebrity. Regardless of where you are in the journey, it's safe to say you probably have a fragile ego. For this reason it's important to remember Rule #1: If you don't know who someone is, just assume they are someone."

"LA is a place where everyone might be anything," Parker continues. "Your barista could have just sold a screenplay, that actor walking the red carpet at a premiere might have had to get his shift covered to attend, the guy working at the Apple store's band might be playing the Staples Center that night. You never know, so Rule #2: Never ask anyone what they do. It's okay to ask general questions until you figure it out, but don't be too obvious. 'What are you working on?' is a good, vague question."

"On the other hand," Blair takes over, "Rule #3: If you *do* know who they are, don't let on you know. You can assume you both know who they are and move on. This is not a time for fans. Be professional. If it gets overwhelming, remember Rule #4: You can always decompress later. Just breathe."

This is getting confusing. "So basically," I clarify, "assume everyone is someone, and if you *do* know who they are don't let them know you know, and if you *don't* know who they are, don't let them know you don't know."

"Right!" they exclaim in unison.

"And," Blair continues, "to take it a step further, keep in mind we are all public until we don't have to be. The people at the lowest rungs of success are the ones who require publicity to fuel their rise to the top. They're the ones who *need* the tabloids and will call the paparazzi any time they leave their house. You don't have to worry about them as much. It's the people at the top you have to look out for. Once a celebrity reaches the top, they become fiercely private, shutting out all the leaches that helped them get there, and keeping only the most trusted around."

"Rule #5: Never breathe a word of what you hear when you're with an A-list celebrity," Parker whispers. "It's suicide."

"Personally, I rarely utter a word about anyone," Blair says, "because if the people at the bottom ever make it to the top, they need to know they can trust you. Unless it's around you guys, of course," she adds. "I trust *you*, and sometimes you've got to tell someone!"

"I think I'm just going to avoid ever talking to anyone," I say.

"That's probably for the best," Blair agrees.

"Especially in restrooms," Parker says. "Rule #6: Never talk to a celebrity in a bathroom. They hate that. Everyone deserves a little privacy now and again."

Of course they do.

My head is spinning with information but I venture, "Technically, he talked to *me*..."

"That's true," Blair says to Parker. "Maybe he was hitting on her."

"Oh no." Waving my hands in front of my face as if they could erase her words, I dismiss that notion immediately. "He definitely wasn't hitting on me—he was probably just being friendly because I looked like such a loser. I'm sure he's benevolent and wonderful and strives to make those of us who fall into the excessively clothed category feel appreciated. I felt *so* frumpy next to his girlfriend."

"Hold on," Parker interjects. "You were wearing *that?*" I look down at my shirt. "Yeah. So?"

"Oh. My. God. Now I *really* can't believe he talked to you. Those aren't your pj's? *What* are you wearing?"

"Blair said I should wear black. It's my 'blend in' outfit."

"Honey, were you trying to be a 1950s beatnik from *Funny Face* or something?" He guesses correctly. "It is one thing to channel your inner Audrey Hepburn, but it is quite another to wear a mock turtleneck and capris to a Hollywood event. This is the big time, sweetheart; you best check your costume at the door."

"But I love Hepburns." I sniff.

Blair and Parker look at each other and a moment passes between them. He shakes his head. "It'll take a lot of work," he warns her. "Accent elimination. She'll need to be able to talk the talk, not just look the part…"

"Yes. But it could be the true test of our spinning ability," Blair replies. "If we turn her into an It girl, it could put us on the map. At the very least it would look good on my resume. I don't want to be an assistant forever, and this could send me on my way to becoming 'the super spinstress'! And, don't you need a project? You'll go crazy sitting around all hiatus."

He considers for a moment. "It *could* be fabulous… as head writer on *The One*, I *am* qualified to craft her into someone worthy of assumption…" *The One is* a reality dating show where either a gorgeous guy or girl must choose their fiancé from a group of attractive singles who live in a mansion together, and Parker is in charge of coaching "The One" on what to say during the lily ceremony.

"What are you talking about?" I ask.

"Operation Loverly," Parker says, seeming to come to a decision. "Your Hollywood initiation."

Chapter Two

OLIVIA BLOOM @BLOOMOLIVIA
TRYING TO PRACTICE BALANCING COCKTAILS ON A TRAY, BUT
@ISINDULGENT KEEPS SAMPLING THEM. I GIVE UP. *SIGH* HOW
MAY I HELP YOU?

"The boobs are real. Good. Don't get fake ones." Parker stands back, examining me. "If, at some point in the future, like after you've had kids, they begin to sag, it's okay to get a lift. But, don't touch them until absolutely necessary."

I've reported to the courtyard promptly at seven this morning for the beginning of "babe boot camp". It took a little convincing last night but, reminding myself that I moved here to take more chances, I finally caved and agreed to let him coach me. How bad could it be?

He leans in, squinting as he continues the inspection. "Teeth: slightly crooked, but could be considered cute. Eyes:

green. Fabulous. Hair: boring light brown, needs color and shape. Body: slim/athletic—passable. Skin: clear except for Mt. Everest on the forehead. A facial should fix that," he mutters as he checks off his list of my features.

"Here's how it is," he says, circling me as I try to stand still and not fidget with my coffee mug. "All the most beautiful girls from every city across the country come to Los Angeles. Almost everyone here was the prettiest or most popular girl at her high school. It's hard to compete. In New York you can get by on sense of humor and killer style. In LA, you need more. You need the bones. That said, there's something for everyone in this city, so let's get to work finding where you fit."

I take a nervous sip of my coffee, unsure I'll ever fit anywhere. *Be brave. It's time to find the new you.*

He comes to a stop in front of me. "This is about creating a look, Liv. No more blending in," he says. "To make it here, it's essential you're recognizable. Embrace what makes you unique. That's what most novices don't understand and they spend thousands of dollars just to have someone else's nose. Whatever you do, don't get plastic surgery. You don't want to look like one of those Runyon Canyon women with surgery face." He shudders. "They all look the same with their frozen foreheads and overinflated lips, strutting around pushing their dogs in baby strollers."

Shouldn't be a problem. I don't have thousands of dollars anyway. "Runyon Canyon?" I ask.

"Oh yes. Thank you for mentioning that. This brings us to your fitness regime. You will hike the canyon every weekend. Everyone does. You will also alternate between yoga and Pilates, with a little bar method peppered in, and you will jog at least three miles twice per week."

"I can do that," I promise. I'm relieved he's finally distracted from examining my pores. *But yoga, Pilates, facials…this is sounding expensive.* "Parker, how much is this going to cost? I'm on a really tight budget." I saved some money after college graduation by waiting tables and living with my parents. My plan had been to move to Philadelphia with my boyfriend, but everything changed when I found out he'd had a one-night stand with his ex-girlfriend. I was devastated at first, but I'm over it now. In fact, I see his infidelity as a gift that changed my direction and set me on the path to following my dreams. Never again will I define my self-worth based on a guy. At any rate, the money I saved from living at home after graduation coupled with what my parents gave me to help with the move is only enough to last six months if I'm careful. If I don't find a paying job, it's back to "da 'burgh" for me, so hopefully something will turn up soon.

"Don't worry. I'm not going to send you to the poor house. Everything here is an illusion," he says, punctuating his statement with jazz hands. "Hiking is free, there are donation-only yoga classes all over the city, and between Groupons and sample sales it's easy to look like a million bucks on a Goodwill budget. I'll show you the ropes."

"Okay," I reply, relieved he's at least considered my lack of funds. "Where do we start?"

"With wax," he says. "I've made you an appointment for a Full Monty at the Queen Bee Salon—with an apprentice bee—they're half price. Unless, of course, you prefer to land your jet on the Heathrow Express. I'll leave that up to you. Let's go."

By the time Blair comes home that night, I already look like a new person. Inspired by style-icon Kay Pritcher's signature California-chic style, my hair is now a rich chestnut color that sets off my eyes and tumbles in soft folds around my face. My eyes are lined in black kohl, and I'm wearing an adorable striped dolman-sleeve T-shirt with pleated black shorts and woven platform pumps that we got at Wasteland, a resale store on Melrose. It's the last "new" outfit I'm going to have for a while so I'm savoring it. I'm hoping my check from the fashion show will offset some of the money I spent today, but I'm on spending timeout from now on.

Parker and I are sipping Sauvignon Blanc in the courtyard when she walks in.

She does a double take.

I widen my eyes and smile at her in expectant triumph.

"Liv!" she exclaims. "I didn't recognize you. You—you're beautiful."

I can see she means it. And that she is startled.

Parker clears his throat and pours more wine. "I deserve this," he says, motioning the bottom of his glass toward me. "I knew the bones were good, but I didn't know they were *this* good."

Just then the courtyard gate opens and a guy walks in. He's skinny, with inky black hair, and he might be wearing more eyeliner than I am.

"Hi, Lance," Blair says without looking at him.

"Hey." He nods at her as he comes to a halt next to us. "And hello, New Girl."

I look up curiously. The Vicente consists of six apartments, and I've met Teresa and Miguel, the couple who lives above me, but I've been wondering about who else lives here. Apparently Jessie, the girl who lives in number three, is constantly traveling for work so I won't be seeing her anytime soon, but this must be the guy from apartment six.

"Lance, this is Liv." Blair sighs.

"Nice to meet you," I say with a small wave.

His eyes travel the length of my body. "I'd say the pleasure is mine."

"Ugh." Blair grunts. "Lance, go away. Leave her alone."

He glares at her but complies, heading to the steps, but not before turning and delivering his parting shot. "See you around," he says, mimicking shooting a basketball.

"See ya," I reply as Parker chuckles. "What was that about?" I ask once Lance is out of earshot.

Blair scrunches up her face and turns to me. "Avoid," she says. "I randomly hooked up with him once and as punishment for going out with another guy the next week he bounced a basketball against the wall we share—which happens to be my bedroom wall—at three o'clock every morning for a month. I'd keep my distance if I were you."

"That shouldn't be a problem. I'm not looking to hook up with anyone," I say. "I want to be alone for awhile."

"Smart girl," Parker says before turning to Blair. "Anyway—I think I've come up with the perfect scenario for Operation Loverly. We'll pass her off as Hollywood royalty at Elton John's Oscar Party."

"Perfect," she says, clapping her hands. "You're brilliant. I'll talk to the guys over at The Lighter Side. They do the lighting for it, and I've been working with them a bunch lately. I'm sure they can get us in. We'll make her the toast of the night."

Oscar party? Elton John? *Are they high?* I must have heard them wrong. At least I hope I did. What kind of freak planet have I landed on where people talk about going to these things like it's normal? *So* not normal.

"Hold on, guys. I know I look like a new person, but under all this hair and makeup I'm still just plain old me. I don't want to let you down, and pretending to be someone else is great and all, but I think I'd rather be accepted for who I really am."

"You've got to fake it till you make it or you'll never get anywhere in this town," Parker says.

"And you'll still be you," Blair adds. "You'll just be a more refined, glorified version of yourself. The *best you.* Think of it as self-improvement."

"Well, when you put it that way…" I do want to fit in, and an adventure is what I came here for…*and maybe they can teach me to form a sentence the next time I'm around a Berkeley Dalton type…*but a vision of me being dragged away in handcuffs while Elton John looks on in disapproval pops into my head. I reach for him, ashamed, pleading my case. He shakes his head, knowing I am guilty, pitying me. I can't think of a worse fate. I love Elton, and the thought of him hating me is crushing. Maybe Blair and Parker will compromise. "What if we pass me off as an It girl at a smaller event?" I suggest. "Like a Bar Mitzvah or sweet sixteen party?"

"EJ's Oscar bash is perfect." Parker dismisses my plea as he swirls the wine in the bottom of his glass. "The Oscars are only five weeks away so we'll need to keep working."

He's talking to himself like I don't exist. And I guess I don't, yet. *Five weeks. At least that gives me time to change their minds about Elton.*

"I'm not sure if I'll have time for training," I say in a last-ditch effort to get out of Operation Loverly. "Hopefully I'll get a job soon."

"Have you heard anything yet?" Blair asks.

"No. I'm really hoping to hear back about the digital artist position I applied for at this lingerie line called Jonquil. I thought my interview was okay, but they had over a hundred fifty applicants so it's probably a long shot."

"Oh. Jonquil's great," Parker says.

"You've heard of it?"

"Please. I'm from Texas. I was born with a Neiman Marcus spoon in my mouth," he replies. "Of course I've heard of Jonquil lingerie. Very beautiful—lacy—vintage-inspired. Expensive. Love it."

"Parker operates under the assumption that anything falling into the 'luxury' category, he deserves," Blair says.

"Well, I work hard. For instance, when the show took all of us writers to Hawaii to celebrate last season, I was getting a massage on the network's dime, and I thought to myself, I deserve this. I *deserve* it after all the work I did to make those people fall in love." He laughs.

"Yes you do," she says, her voice dripping with sarcasm.

"I'm probably not going to get the job," I say. "So I might apply to be a waitress."

Parker looks up in surprise. "You cannot resort to being a waitress unless absolutely necessary," he says. "You'll constantly be asked if you're an actress, which will get old really fast…not to mention you're not, so nobody will understand why you're doing it."

"It's true," Blair backs him up. "The money will be okay and you'll reason you can't do better anywhere else, after all you'll have to take a pay cut to get a real job, not to mention having to work forty hours a week instead of twenty-five. Plus, you'll get all sorts of offers for auditions, and you'll start to wonder if maybe you should be an actress. Why not, right? Then you'll find out all the auditions are in the Valley and the *only* thing shot there is porn. Which will lead to disappointment and self-loathing, and you'll be stuck waiting tables, not moving forward. Why put yourself through that?"

I stare at her in disbelief, certain not all stories end that way. "Believe me, I don't want to wait tables, either, but I might not have a choice."

Parker waves me off. "Something will turn up. You're going to make it here, Olivia Bloom. I know it for a fact. I've seen plenty of people come and go, and I have an eye for the ones who I think have a shot. I wouldn't bother getting attached to you, otherwise. Now, let's work on your accent. That Pittsburgh's got to go. Take the word 'wash', we 'wash' — not 'warsh'. Repeat after me…"

I can tell it's going to be a long five weeks.

Chapter Three

Mrs. Bloom @PsychicMom1
@BloomOlivia Upright judgment card! Judgment is
impossible to avoid but the journey to awakening is
near.

Blair and Parker have called it a night and, exhausted from my whirlwind makeover, I settle onto my couch with my laptop to check my e-mail. My stomach drops as I spy a message titled "Decision" from a Jonquil e-mail address.

For my interview I met with the Jonquil designer, Lillian—a statuesque blonde in her early sixties named after actress Lillian Gish—at the Jonquil home office. Lillian started the label when she was twenty-five and grew it into an international brand before partnering with a larger company to handle the production side of the business.

After I got over my initial nerves at meeting a real

fashion designer, we bonded over Old Hollywood and costume designers like Edith Head and Cecil Beaton—two of my personal style idols. It turned out Lillian's great-aunt was a silent-movie actress, and her grandmother was a fashion illustrator who worked with Edith. *Edith, Cecil, we're practically in the same room!* That's when I started to think I'd found my home.

Unfortunately, I didn't quite have the technical skills they were looking for, but as soon as I got home, I wrote an impassioned thank-you note to Lillian, citing why I thought I belonged at Jonquil, how much I was willing to learn, and enclosing a few sketches.

I haven't heard anything since. Until now.

Shaking, I open the e-mail...

I got the job.

I got the job, I got the job, I got the job, I got the *job!* I do my happy dance around my apartment. Ha! This is the perfect position for me! After all, isn't lingerie sort of a costume? Especially the Old Hollywood-inspired kind! I mean, it's all about dress-up and fantasy, right?

I feel my path level slightly with the knowledge I can stay and see this out a little longer.

I'm so excited; I can't wait to tell everyone. The first person I call is Boots.

Boots, aka my cousin Amanda, is a couple years older than me, but we've always been best friends. When we were little and I had trouble saying "Amanda," I nicknamed her "Boots" when she wore a pair of bright red rain boots to the Ice Capades, and the name stuck.

She picks up on the second ring, sounding groggy.

"Boots!"

"Hi! I'm so happy it's you." She wakes up a little.

"Who were you afraid it was going to be?"

"My chief resident on trauma surgery. I think I've only slept five hours in the last three days. I swear he's a cyborg and doesn't understand the concept of sleep. Or food. Or friends. Or laughter."

Boots is in her fourth year of medical school. Sometimes I wish I could be more like her—that I, too, should have a selfless dream that could actually impact people's lives. Mostly I try not to dwell on it, though. I'm clumsy and squeamish with a negative sense of direction. Choosing *not* to operate on people is impact enough.

"That sounds miserable."

"This is what I always wanted right? I swear if I have to do another rectal exam in the trauma bay I'm going to shove something up *his*..."

"Ew."

She laughs. "How are you? What's new in La La Land? Meet any celebrities yet?"

The blood rushes to my face as I recall the run-in outside the restroom. "OMG. Yes. You'll never believe it. I met Berkeley Dalton."

"What? That is *huge*. Is he gorgeous in real life?"

"You have no idea. He's beautiful. And of course I made a total ass of myself. You know me, I can barely talk to an attractive UPS man let alone a rock star. I was super tongue-tied and told him he was taller than I expected. I'm a total idiot. But that's not why I'm calling. I got a job!"

"You did? Where? Doing what?"

"It's at a lingerie company called Jonquil, and I'll be assisting the designers with illustrations for department store presentations."

"Awesome. Does this mean I don't need to clear the cadavers off my couch for you to crash?"

"Not yet. Fingers crossed I'll be here for a while."

"Good for you. Now enough about work. Tell me more about Berkeley. How tall *was* he?"

I laugh. "Well, he was tall enough that a model could wear heels and still be shorter than him—which is a bonus in my book." Having reached my full 5'8" height at age thirteen, I'm still self-conscious about towering over people. Especially guys. "He has the most amazing eyes I've ever seen," I muse on in a starstruck daze, "and he was so nice..."

"Do you think Psychic Mom saw that one coming?"

The mention of my mom sobers me, and I frown. "If she did I don't want to know about it."

My mom's a free spirit, but not in an acid-induced sort of way—in more of an I-think-it's-cool-my-dental-hygienist-sees-dead-people way. She and her clairvoyant hair stylist Esme are determined to tell me my future, but I don't believe in that stuff and go out of my way to avoid hearing their predictions.

"You never know, maybe she summoned a celebrity spirit guide for you..." I lose Boots for a minute and hear muffled voices in the background. "Liv," she comes back to me. "I have to go—my stupid pager is going off again. Call you later?"

"Go—yes—call me later. Just be sure you wash your hands first."

"Ha ha. Bye."

Hanging up the phone, I sink into my couch, smiling. *Hollywood, I'm here to stay.*

Chapter Four

PARKER MIFFLIN @IsIndulgent
@BloomOlivia You must have an opinion on all things
fashion. Pop Quiz: Defend Cate Blanchett's gown last
night.

Olivia Bloom @BloomOlivia
@IsIndulgent Can I do it later? SOME people have to
work!

PARKER MIFFLIN @IsIndulgent
@BloomOlivia I'm insulted. Believe me, sweetie, YOU
ARE WORK! Fine. We can do it after yoga during our
martini break.

After spending the remainder of the week with Parker at

my side constantly coaching me on my speech, my walk—
posture posture posture!—and all things pop culture, my first
day of work dawns.

I arrive on time and, after filling out some paperwork, I'm
shown to my office. *My own office? Whoa. Wasn't expecting
that!* It is a windowless room that contains two chairs, an
L-shaped desk, a computer, a dress form, and a rolling rack.
Wire grids adorn the walls, and the two nighties that hang on
them lend the only color to the room. Even though it is small
and lackluster, it has an actual door and a ceiling, and is far
better than the cubicle I was expecting. Taking a seat behind
my desk, I resist the urge to put my feet up and call Boots.
Guess where I am?

As I turn on my computer, a girl with jet-black bangs
that cover one eye walks in. Wearing a tight black lace top
and bright pink lacquered lipstick that shocks against her
pale skin, she looks like she belongs on a gallery wall, or at
least on the cover of *Nylon* magazine, as her petite frame
teeters forward on too-high heels.

"Hi." She thrusts her hand forward to greet me. "Are
you the new girl?"

"Yeah, I'm Liv." I shake her hand, with a glance down
at the short-sleeve, burgundy Isabel Marant dress I've
borrowed from Blair, feeling I belong on the cover of
Reader's Digest by contrast.

"I'm Gemma," she introduces herself as Lillian pops her
head into the room.

"Hi," she says. "Welcome, Olivia. Are you getting
settled?"

"Yes, thank you," I reply.

Lillian takes a seat in a chair across from my desk

and gestures for Gemma to do the same. Spine straight, she appears regal as she elegantly addresses us. "February market is coming up in New York and next year's spring Jonquil line must be finished in a couple days, so we'll need to complete the line sheets," she says. "We'll require prices on everything before Liv can do that, so we'll have to labor and yield the line." She directs this at Gemma.

I begin scribbling notes, realizing this is my official to-do list.

"Gemma is our assistant designer," she explains to me. "She'll show you what the line sheets are supposed to look like and will bring you the line to sketch as it's ready."

I acknowledge Gemma with a smile, but she doesn't reciprocate. Her expression is as hard to figure out as Mona Lisa's as she focuses on her notes and the list continues.

By the time Lillian finishes explaining everything, I have nine projects to work on, and I can't remember the details of the first one. They all run together, and I begin to hyperventilate.

She moves to leave. "So happy to have you, Liv. If you need anything, my office is down the hall. Come in any time."

I manage a small "thank you," as I stare at my list, trying to figure out where to start.

Gemma stands as well. "You can start sketching those chemises," she says with a nod at the two garments hanging on the grids, before she follows Lillian out.

Happy to be alone, I exhale relief, despite being unsure if "Gemma the walking art installation" is pleased about my presence. Opening Illustrator on my computer, I get to work. Drawing the outline of each chemise is easy enough—after my interview I made sure to learn how to do that—but when it comes time to drop in the print and add the lace I come to a halt. These are things I didn't anticipate, and I spend fifteen minutes trying to Google how to do it. Frustrated, I decide this is taking too long. I need to figure this out fast because based on my list there are at least a hundred more sketches to go.

Gemma reappears with a mound of sleepwear and a stack of papers. "Okay," she says as she plops the lingerie on my rolling rack and slides the stack of papers toward me. "This is what the line sheets are supposed to look like. All the cost sheets and style names are here. Show me the line sheets as you finish. I'll check them before we show Lillian. She can be pretty particular, and I can probably save you from redoing them a million times."

"Thanks, Gemma," I say in a normal tone before I whisper, not wanting to be overheard, "but can you help me? I'm not sure how to get this print or lace onto the sketch..." I have no reason to believe she'll come to my aid, but I'm desperate.

Just then Lillian walks in. "Liv, can you sketch this gown and mock it up in the raspberry/blood orange and the hibiscus/sea foam colorways for me? I have a meeting in ten minutes with Bloomingdales, and I need you to e-mail it to the buyer before the conference call."

"Um, sure," I say, panicking. Ten minutes? I have no idea what I'm doing. Maybe I could figure it out if I had two hours, but there's no way I'm going to be able to finish this in time for the meeting.

"Things have changed; yeah they've changed for good. I guess all along I knew that they would... With every promise, a new heartbreak, with every moment of perfection, a new

mistake."

My phone lights up, blaring Berkeley & the Brightside's song "House"—my ringtone and touchstone—the song that gave me the courage to take a leap and follow my dreams to California. I scramble to silence it, noticing the name on the display reads "Michael". My ex-boyfriend. I haven't spoken to him in months. *What does he want?*

I don't have time to think about it. Lillian is waiting for me to begin as I stare blankly at my computer screen not knowing where to start. I wonder if they'll pay me for the few hours I've been here or just tell me to get lost?

To my surprise, Gemma hobbles to my rescue. "Do you know where all of the files are in our system?" she asks me before turning to Lillian. "I'll show her. The system is a little confusing if you've never used it before."

"Of course," Lillian says as she turns to leave. "Just let me know when you've e-mailed the buyer."

"Okay. All of the prints are on the company drive. We have a bunch of laces already scanned in, too," Gemma says, hovering over my shoulder.

I watch her click through files, furiously taking notes as she walks me through dropping in the print and applying the lace while giving me tips about what Lillian likes and doesn't like as she goes. I note this as well.

Gemma finishes in record time and e-mails Lillian and the Bloomingdales buyer.

She saved me. "Thank you, Gemma. You didn't have to do that," I say. "You could have just let them fire me. I have no idea what I'm doing!"

She considers me before answering. "You'll learn." She shrugs. "If you have questions, just ask me."

"You might be sorry you offered. I already have a list of questions a mile long, but thank you again."

"It's no problem…besides, Berkeley & the Brightside is my favorite band." Her eyes light up as she smiles at me conspiratorially, transforming her face. She no longer seems so untouchable.

I smile back, relieved that we have something in common. "They're my favorite band, too."

"I was devastated when Berkeley broke up with Christina," she says, sinking into one of the chairs across from my desk. "Berkstina was the perfect couple."

"I know. I loved them together," I say, leaning forward eagerly. I religiously followed their fairytale love story along with the rest of the world. From their chance meeting on an airplane that changed him from bad boy to boyfriend, to him hiding secret notes in her dressing room to surprise her when they had to be apart, to her turning down roles to tour with him—I've hung on every word. "I'm still finding it impossible to believe they won't live happily ever after."

"Me, too." Gemma sighs. "If Christina Carlton can't hang on to a guy, there's no hope for the rest of us."

"Seriously," I agree. "It's interesting, though. My friend Blair works in PR, and she says Berkstina has the best publicity team in the business. I guess her company put on an event a couple months ago that Christina attended, and to keep her happy they had to have a makeup artist and manicurist on staff to follow her around in case she got smudged, pay her thousands of dollars, supply her with an Academy Award-worthy gift bag, and have special chrysanthemum green tea flown in from China because the stuff from Trader Joe's wasn't green enough for her."

Gemma nods. "She's a huge star. I'm sure she gets special treatment, but every time I hear her interviewed she seems so down to earth. She's perfect."

"Yeah. I find it hard to believe, too. Blair said for sure the breakup was Christina's fault and they're just making Berkeley out to be the bad guy, but I've always thought she seemed nice. Like the big sister—albeit gorgeous big sister—I always wanted."

"Totally. You'd think even Berkeley Dalton would hold on to that and never let go, but I guess it must be hard for him to avoid temptation. Women must throw themselves at him all the time."

"Women who are capable of speaking in front of him probably do," I agree, starting to feel comfortable enough with Gemma to confide in her. I lower my voice. "I met him last week. He was really nice, but one look at him and I practically turned to stone."

"You met him?" Gemma squeals. "Oh my gosh. I have to know everything."

Just then Lillian pops her head into my office. "I think some samples just came off the machines, will you run and grab them?" she says to Gemma.

"Of course," Gemma replies, composing herself as she stands and heads toward the door, but not before turning back to me. "I need details. We're eating lunch together."

Chapter Five

Mark Vancleer @BrightsideBP
@SuperSpinstress Making our way back to CA. You up for some Santa Barbara "bowling"?

Blair Hamilton @SuperSpinstress
@BrightsideBP Ummm…are you asking what I think you're asking? Been on the road too long and can't wait to hit the lanes, right? ;)

Mark Vancleer @BrightsideBP
@SuperSpinstress Nah—I'm afraid I'll break a finger. I have a better idea: Two tickets await you at Will Call.

Blair Hamilton @SuperSpinstress

SOMETIMES I THINK MY FAVORITE WORDS ARE "YOU'RE ON THE LIST."

Blair is deep in thumb-versation on her cell phone as we are enjoying cappuccinos outside our local coffee shop, Paper or Plastik, on an unusually warm February evening. It's a week before I'm to meet my inevitable demise during "The Spin"—as Parker and Blair refer to it—at Elton John's Oscar party, and they have been busy putting the finishing touches on their "project." I've spent every moment I'm not at work being "groomed" and I now speak flawlessly, without the slightest hint of Pittsburghese peppering my vernacular. In addition, I can recite random facts about every movie in the AFI Top 100, have procured a fabulous wardrobe (thanks to the new job and Blair's hand-me-downs from her work), and have become something of a local on the Silver Lake music scene.

"Oh. This is perfect!" Blair exclaims, not taking her eyes off her phone as she continues to type.

"What's perfect?" I ask, a little annoyed at her lack of focused attention.

"Hold on…ummmm…" Her fingers fly as she texts.

"BLAIR! Come on."

"Okay. I'm done." She tosses the phone aside and takes a sip of her coffee. "I've just secured a final practice outing before the big day."

Great. "Now what? Are you going to pass me off as the Queen of Bulgaria or something?"

She gives me a pitying stare. "Don't be absurd. "We"— she pauses for effect—"are going to the Berkeley & the Brightside concert at the Santa Barbara Bowl Sunday night courtesy of Brightside bass player, Mark!"

I almost fall off my chair. "We're not going to meet the band, are we?"

"Maybe." She shrugs.

"BLAIR! This is *the most* uncomfortable thing you could possibly do to me. Don't you remember what happened last time I met Berkeley Dalton? That *he* is the reason I've come home every night for the past month and recited the alphabet with marbles in my mouth? That because I acted like such a *freak* in front of him, you and Parker decided I wasn't fit for Los Angeles civilization?"

I'm almost crying. Maybe I'm overreacting, but it's partly because I'm stretched to breaking from Operation Loverly exhaustion, not to mention just hearing Berkeley's name has slashed open the place where I've buried the embarrassment over meeting him at the fashion show. I have no intention of reliving that night.

"And it's a Sunday," I babble on. "In Santa Barbara. I have to work Monday morning. I can't go traipsing off to Santa Barbara."

"I have to work, too," she says. "And I don't know if we'll go backstage or not. I've only met Mark in person twice—once briefly at the fashion show, and then again when they played at the Mona Foundation event my firm planned at Rainn Wilson's house—but we've been texting all week setting up the next event they're going to play. He's really nice and offered to leave tickets at Will Call, but no promises on backstage or even talking to him. It won't be a crazy night, and Santa Barbara's not *that* far away. Besides, I thought you *loved* Berkeley & the Brightside."

"I do," I say reluctantly. "I'd love to go to the concert—I

saw them once in college and it's one of my favorite memories—but I'm terrified of seeing *him* again. I can't even hear them on the radio without getting embarrassed."

"Well, I think it'll be fun. I mean, it's *free*."

"No, you're right," I concede as the phrase "No Regrets" inserts itself in my brain. It's a value my mom has instilled in me from birth. "We should go. Even if we do see him, I'm sure he meets so many people, there's no way he'd remember me, right?"

"Definitely, no way," she agrees. "But you should look cute, just in case."

"Well, so should you. Maybe Mark really wants to see *you* and that's why he's giving you tickets."

She scrunches up her nose. "I don't think so. He's cute, don't get me wrong, but rule number ten: Don't date guys in bands. They are *drama*."

"There's got to be an exception to every rule."

"I guess. At least he's the bass player; they're usually the safest—the peacemakers."

"You never know…"

"I don't think we need to worry," she says, shaking her head with a smile. "He's just being nice."

Chapter Six

PARKER MIFFLIN @IsIndulgent
@BerkeleyBrtside There's someone I'd like you to meet.
Again. @BloomOlivia

OLIVIA BLOOM @BloomOlivia
@IsIndulgent PARKER! I CANNOT BELIEVE YOU
DID THAT. Take it back!!! #hate.

PARKER MIFFLIN @IsIndulgent
@BloomOlivia Nope. You're welcome.

Sunday morning breaks across a crisp blue sky over a glittering ocean, and Blair and I turn up "When You Need Me" by Berkeley & the Brightside as we drive up the coast. Parker has started back to work and is away on location this weekend so he isn't joining us. I'm relieved he will now be spending his twenty-hour days coaching "The One" instead of me, and I'm grateful Operation Loverly will be over soon.

"All this longing to be free has got the best of me. Now I'm tied so tightly to this love. Baby, you've got to give me a break, I've got my own smile to fake, Got enough on my plate, Without the lines you want to feed me..."

Deciding to take advantage of the beautiful weather, we pretend we're on vacation, even if it's only for a day. We eat clam chowder on the Santa Barbara pier and spend the afternoon shopping on State Street. I buy some new sparkly hoop earrings that are on sale, and we have dinner at Stella Mare before heading to the show. As we dine, I can't help but notice the restaurant is full of what I assume are other concertgoers. Glancing at the table to my left, I'm shocked at the amount of cleavage on display.

"Jeez. Where do these girls get those?" I whisper, leaning toward Blair and glancing down at my own completely contained and covered breasts. I've opted to wear the new-to-me black-and-white Alexander Wang dress that was abandoned by its original owner at Crossroads Trading Company.

She giggles. "What do you mean? The boobs or the hooker shirts?"

"Both, I guess. Look—I don't think that one is wearing a bra. Gross. It's really not attractive."

"I bet they're hoping to get backstage."

"Well if that's what it takes, you and I are definitely not making it back. We're way too fashionable."

"Agreed."

We clink glasses.

After dinner, we wind our way through a sleepy neighborhood on our way to the Santa Barbara Bowl. The crowd is just starting to pour in.

"I have a bad feeling about this," I say. "I guess we can always scalp tickets if they didn't leave us any."

"We'll be fine. I have Mark's number, so worst-case scenario, I'll text him."

We are next in line for Will Call, and the large lady in the booth ahead waves us forward, the soft skin folds hanging from her arms echoing the motion.

"We're on Berkeley & the Brightside's list," Blair says as we step forward.

"Name?"

"It should be under Blair Hamilton."

"Spell it?"

"First name, B-L-A-I-R, Last name H-A-M-I-L—"

"It's not here," the lady cuts her off.

Great. We drove *all* the way up here on a Sunday for nothing. I knew I had a bad feeling about this.

"Can you double-check? It should be there," Blair urges, pulling out her phone. "Let me make a phone call…"

"Yeah," the lady grunts, "you go ahead and make your phone call. Just get out of my line."

Everything about her says "nice try."

We walk to the other side of the ticket booth as Blair texts Mark.

"She wasn't very pleasant," I state the obvious. "Well, it was fun to see Santa Barbara, anyway. And this way we'll get home at a decent time."

"Let's just give him a few minutes to respond, okay? He doesn't seem like the type who would forget to leave us tickets."

"Okay. I'm sure he's busy. I mean, he *is* about to perform in front of five thousand people." I should be disappointed, but the truth is I'm relieved my chance of a Berkeley run-in is diminishing.

Blair's phone buzzes.

"Aha!" she exclaims, shooting me a superior look and reading the text out loud. "Sorry about that. We've been having problems with our list all day. Sit tight. I'm bringing the Rover." Smiling up from her phone, she bats her eyelashes at me.

Crap. I close my eyes and take a deep breath.

Five minutes later, a black Range Rover comes barreling down the hill and halts directly in front of us. Mark leaps out of the passenger seat and opens the back door. Known for being the most laid-back Brightside member, he's wearing a white T-shirt, worn gray pants, ratty white Chuck Taylors, and I'd recognize his longish brown hair anywhere, having obsessed over all of their music videos. "Blair! Jump in," he says, giving her a quick kiss on the cheek.

I can't believe this is happening.

We scramble into the backseat as he gets into the front, and we take off as quickly as they came. Mark turns around and offers me his hand, his eyes welcoming. "Hi. I'm Mark."

"I'm Olivia," I say, trying to keep my hand from melting in his as he grips it. *I'm touching a member of the Brightside!* The Rover bounces up the hill around the side of the bowl. It's almost like we're off-roading, and I struggle to stay in my seat.

"Here. Put these on," he says, handing both of us "all access" backstage stickers. "I'm so glad you could make it. This is gonna be fun."

So, this is pretty much the most exciting thing that's ever happened to me. All access backstage at Berkeley & the Brightside? *Gemma's going to flip.* I know being a fan is a violation of the rules, but I can't help it; my weeks of training forgotten, I succumb to my own private fangirl moment. Looking to Blair, my eyes shining with wonder, she raises her eyebrows at me in response, silently pleading "be cool."

The Rover stops outside a slew of buses and vans, and I try to pull myself together for Blair's sake. My body is humming with adrenaline, and a drip of sweat rolls down my back as we step out of the car.

"Let me give you a quick tour," Mark says. "These are the semitrucks that carry all of our equipment and lights. This is the bus Berkeley and I share, and that's the bus Jeff and Ted share." He points at two massive buses, one metallic blue, one raspberry, and both with heavily tinted windows.

We walk over to the blue one, and as he opens the door, I immediately tense up. Oh no, we're going in. I hope *he* isn't in there.

"Watch your step."

I don't have a choice, and Blair and I heave ourselves up the steps and past the driver's seat, taking in cream-colored leather benches, a mounted flat-screen TV, and a shiny wood parquet dining table as we step inside.

"This is the bathroom, the kitchen, and these are the bunks," he says, leading us down the length of the vehicle past cozy-looking cubbies hidden by curtains. "And this is our game room." We come to the end. The last room in the bus is filled with overstuffed couches, TVs, and every gaming system imaginable. It is boy heaven.

As we head back to the front of the bus, Mark pops the seat off one of the benches. It turns out to be a cooler. "Beer?" he offers. *Very clever, bus, very clever.*

"Sure, we'll take a couple," Blair answers for us.

We descend out of the bus. "Do you want to lock the doors, Olivia?"

"Sure!" I say as an overwhelming sense of relief washes over me. *I made it out of the bus alive!*

"Just punch the code 0-8-2-3-7-8 into the keypad, then press the two outer buttons at the same time."

I follow his instructions and feel the entire bus suck in its breath and go into a thunderous lockdown mode. It's quite satisfying.

We hurry after Mark toward the backstage area. As we walk, we briefly meet Jeff, the lead guitarist, who is deep in conversation on his cell phone. Backstage, we walk past a door labeled THE BRIGHTSIDE TREADMILL AND YOGA ROOM before we are introduced to Ted, the drummer, who is warming up in a little room off to the side. "Ted, this is Blair and Liv, friends of mine from LA."

"Great to meet you." He pauses his drumming and half stands, extending a good-natured hand to each of us. "You girls should hang out after the show—it'll be less crazy around here then," Ted says. He is the friendliest of the crew we've met so far, except for Mark.

"Speaking of the show," Mark says, "where do you want to watch it from?"

Blair and I look at each other. "I don't know. Where will

we not be in the way?" she asks.

"Hmmm. Let me ask. HAYNES!" He beckons a red-haired guy toward us. "Haynes is our manager."

Haynes walks over. "These are my friends Blair and Olivia," Mark says. "Where can we set them up to watch the show?"

"Nice to meet you, ladies," Haynes says in a thick Cockney accent. "I'll give you two options. Follow me." We trail behind him single file down a narrow hallway lined with dressing rooms. As we walk, a door up ahead swings open, and out steps Berkeley Dalton. Upon recognition, my heart stops, and the hallway begins to sway. Dressed in his full ensemble for the show, he is wearing a tuxedo jacket with shiny lapels. His sleeves are rolled up, and underneath the jacket he wears a slim red-and-white T-shirt, skinny black jeans, and black leather, lace-up ankle boots. His hair is standing up at all angles, and I can see his blue eyes smoldering even from this distance. He is larger than life and pure magnetic energy, and he is heading directly toward us.

Time moves in slow motion as our eyes meet over the distance.

For my part, I'm pretty sure I look like a hopeful puppy while he, for some reason, looks scared to death. What could he possibly find intimidating?

I don't have time to think about it, and my lungs seize as he approaches. *Please don't remember, please don't remember, please don't remember.*

"'ey, B," Haynes greets him.

"Hey, man. Mark." Berkeley gives an imperceptible nod to each of them, and his vibe seems to say "I can't do this now." He keeps walking past us without so much as a further glance in my direction.

He really is taller than I expected.

Time speeds up as he passes and wind rushes in my ears as I force myself to concentrate on what Mark is saying.

"Yikes," he says, once Berkeley is out of earshot. "Sorry about that. I totally would've introduced you if he didn't look so nervous. He's actually the nicest guy in the world—he's just a total perfectionist, and he never wants to let anyone down. He gets pretty freaked out before shows. It's a lot of pressure being the front man."

"And 'e's 'ad a bug up 'is arse since last night—we played Vegas," Haynes says. "I don't know why; 'e's the only one 'ew didn't lose."

"Oh, that's okay," I say as I stave off a nervous breakdown. I don't know what I would have done *had* there been an introduction. This is best-case scenario as far as I'm concerned. "We're just excited to see the show."

Blair gives me a knowing look, but I can see she's a little shaken, too. Maybe now she can empathize with the effect he has on me. After all, how can anyone be expected to maintain their composure when *that* is talking to you.

Mark and Haynes lead us to the wings of the stage just as the opening act, The Remainers, are finishing their hit song "Some Rules."

"Tonight I'm at the end of my rope, but since I'm still alive, I guess there's still a little hope, when you told me we could still be friends, that's when I knew some rules are made to bend…"

"You can watch from 'ere, or you can watch from down in the front row," Haynes suggests. "Ef you want the full show experience wiff all the lights, I recommend going down front. Ef you prefer a be'ind the scenes take, I can set you up 'ere. Et's up to you."

We don't have to consult each other. "Here's good!" we say at the same time.

"Great. You can 'ave a seat on this." He pulls over a large black trunk. "I'll grab you some more drinks, but no liquid past that electrical tape line on the floor—there's too much expensive equipment over there to risk et."

He runs off as we take our seats.

"I've got to go get ready for the show," Mark says. "Is it okay if I leave you here? Haynes will take care of you."

"Of course," Blair says. "Go! We'll be fine. And thank you. This is way more than we expected."

"No problem. Have fun," he replies. "I'll see you after the show."

Haynes returns a few minutes later with beers and a set list so we can follow along, and then he leaves with a second reminder about the tape line.

"This is amazing," I say once he's gone, trying to play it cool as the guitar techs and sound guys work around us, and I snap a quick picture of the stage for Boots. "I can't believe it's real."

"I know," Blair whispers. "It's crazy. And Mark's so nice, but B.D.," she abbreviates, "how intimidating was that?"

Blair isn't afraid of anything so I'm glad she can feel my pain, if only for a moment. I acknowledge her with my best I-told-you-so glance.

The bowl goes dark, and the crowd erupts in a fervent cheer. Thousands of chesty girls scream to be noticed as the band walks on stage, only their silhouettes visible to the crowd against the crush of the lights.

My heart pounds as Berkeley takes the stage and picks up his first guitar. Without saying a word he busies himself studying the strings, double-checking the tuning. Behind him, Ted starts drumming the opening beats to their most recent single, "Up All Night."

Off to the side of the stage, a musician who is not an original member of the Brightside starts the opening piano notes and Jeff kicks in on guitar. The music swells until it reaches a feverish pitch. Finally, the lights focus, fully revealing Berkeley as he saunters to the microphone and begins to sing.

"You can take it all with a grain of salt, you can take it downtown, show 'em what you got, take it to the top, take another chance 'cause you know the dance better, change your plans up, put your hands up, tell 'em what you need, you're bustin' at the seam..."

The crowd loses it.

I can't take my eyes off him. Every fiber in his being oozes charisma. Every movement is personified charm. It must be impossible for anyone in this amphitheater not to have a crush on him. As I watch I can't help but drift into the memory of our last meeting. Remembering his expressive eyes and the control he possesses over the muscles in his face, I blush. I still can't believe he talked to me. I allow myself to rerun the entire conversation in my head and marvel.

As the song ends, he removes his guitar strap from his shoulder, and instead of putting the instrument back on its stand, he lays it down on the floor in the middle of the stage and turns to greet the crowd. A frantic guitar tech gives an I-know-he-does-that-just-to-mess-with-me eye roll and inconspicuously runs out on stage to save the stranded piece of equipment, then places an acoustic guitar on the stand.

"Hello," Berkeley greets the crowd as they erupt in deafening noise. From my vantage point, I watch as the lights illuminate the thousands of faces before us. Girls swoon while their boyfriends try to appear unaffected. Berkeley looks over at Mark, for whom "going to get ready" apparently meant putting on a navy-blue sweater with elbow patches over his T-shirt. They smile at each other in a shared moment, seeming to know the other so well they can communicate without words. Berkeley turns back to the crowd. "We're going to take you back in time, with a little tune off our first album," he says into the microphone, his voice revealing a slight accent I've never noticed before as he picks up the acoustic and strums a few chords. I remember him mentioning in an interview once that his mom is from South Africa… Maybe that's where he gets the accent from.

His shoulders hunch forward as he launches into "Love Again," the second single from their first album. *You don't like this song.* Even though he performs it beautifully, I can tell from his posture he isn't confident in it. The crowd doesn't seem to notice and sings along with unabashed abandon while, with this knowledge, I begin to feel intimately connected to Berkeley, like we share a secret.

The show boulders on, and Berkeley works the stage, throwing his entire body into every motion. He is an exemplary performer; he pulls out all the stops. As a band, the Brightside is in perfect sync. Their group energy is contagious, and they move as one, dancing around the stage and encouraging the crowd. In between songs, however, I notice them exchanging confused looks and glancing into the wings.

They quake into the grand finale, lights blazing and drums crashing in a final crescendo. Ted throws his drumsticks into the crowd, and the band exits the stage as the masses cry for more. As they thunder off, Blair and I leap to get out of their way. In my frenzy, I knock over my beer. Liquid pours over the case we are sitting on, and I hysterically try to mop it with my dress. Crap. Leave it to me. I did *not* just do that. I'm probably ruining thousands of dollars worth of equipment, not to mention my Alexander Wang. "Help!" I implore Blair. "What should I do?"

"Paper towels?" she says, throwing her hands up, also at a loss.

I run. Should I go to the bus? What's the code again? I hurry in that direction, but come to a crashing halt when I see the band huddled outside.

"We're *not* doing the second encore," Berkeley says. "One and done."

"What was up with them?" Jeff asks. "Terrible crowd. No energy. Why were they sitting down?"

"I don't know. There must be a lot of people from LA—they're always harder to please. Let's get this over with," Berkeley says as they move back toward the stage—and toward me.

I turn and run in the opposite direction. The bathroom, that's it!

"Now you know what a crappy show looks like," Ted calls out with a good-natured smile as they pass me.

"I thought it sounded amazing," I yell back, but they are gone.

I spend the encore hunting for the bathroom and finally

return to the wings, a roll of paper towels under my arm, as the song ends. The mess has already been cleaned up. "Should we get out of here?" I ask, not wanting to linger at the scene of the crime.

"Probably a good idea," Blair agrees as she dodges a flying light fixture. The roadies are already dismantling the stage. "You've made enough of a statement, I believe. We should go before something knocks you unconscious."

We walk down the stairs from the stage and help ourselves to some coffee in the cafeteria.

"I'd like to say good-bye to Mark, and then we can get out of here," she says. "If we can find him…"

We stand waiting for the band to show up. Scanning the room, I notice we aren't alone. Several groups of people are milling about, also waiting. Out of the corner of my eye, I spy the braless girl from dinner sitting in a corner pouting. Like many of the others, she is wearing a yellow wristband, and she looks impatient.

After what seems like eternity, Mark finally makes his way through the crowd. He walks right up to us and I feel braless's eyes bore into the back of my head.

Get stared down by a groupie. I can check that off my bucket list, now.

"Hey—sorry to keep you waiting," he says. "What a show, right? We've been telling our label we'd rather play a bunch of small shows instead of these big venues. We feed off the crowd's energy, and smaller stages are more intimate and a better experience for everyone. They never listen to us, though. Berk's pretty pissed. He's dragging his feet coming out for the meet and greet." He glances at all of the yellow wristbands, resigned to being the bearer of the bad news that they will have to wait.

This information has the power to devastate the room, but it's the best news I've heard all day. Relief floods my veins. The weird girl from the bathroom will officially survive unrecognized! *If we get out of here soon.*

"Well, if that was a bad show," I say, my voice sounding chipper, "I can't imagine what a good show would be like. I was blown away. Oh, and sorry about the beer," I add, wincing as Blair's elbow jabs my side.

"We had a fabulous time." She cuts me off before I can dig myself into a hole. "I can't thank you enough. Really— we won't forget it. We should get going, though, and let you get to work…"

"Yeah, we're going to be getting on the road pretty soon, too," he says. "And it's probably a good idea to run away before I tell them he's not coming out yet." He smiles with a nod toward braless and whispers, "That one looks really scary."

Chapter Seven

PARKER MIFFLIN @ISINDULGENT
YOU'RE NOT GOING TO STAY THERE FOR LONG. I WON'T LET YOU.
RT @BLOOMOLIVIA I LIKE IT HERE—UNDER THE RADAR.

"How'd she do?" Parker asks, referring to last night's test.

A rare rainstorm has chased us into Parker's apartment, and we are lounging in his living room. We're all running on empty; Blair and I from our late-concert adventure, and Parker because of issues on set.

"Only some minor spillage. Vocally, she performed perfectly. I don't know what we can do about the accident proneness." Blair sighs. "I mean, you'd think all that yoga and Pilates would have taught her some balance by now."

"I'm right here," I remind them. "I'm not some live doll that can't hear you. I actually possess superior levels of comprehension, thank you very much."

They ignore me.

"Favorite venue to see bands," Parker quizzes.

"The Satellite." I yawn. "But it is still acceptably known as Spaceland. In fact, even though the new name is the Satellite, everyone who knows anything still calls it Spaceland. So, Spaceland. I mean, the Satellite. Spaceland. Whatever."

"Correct. Highest-grossing film of 1998," he throws out.

"Titanic."

"What comes wrapped around the morning newspaper?"

"A Gum-ban."

Parker glares at my Pittsburghese.

"I'm just kidding, jeez. A rubber band." I enunciate each syllable.

"Who are you wearing?"

I look down at my T-shirt. "I think it's H&M?"

"You're testing my patience," he says, his voice cool, but I notice he bites back a smile.

I smile back. "I don't know. I can't decide." Blair has borrowed several dresses from the fashion closet in her office for me to choose from.

"Well, you better figure it out soon. We only have a week, and all of the good tailors will be swamped. We want to make sure there's enough time."

"I think I'm going to go do that right now," I say, heaving myself off the couch. Truthfully, I'm beat, and I'm over being quizzed. Operation Loverly and The Spin can't be over soon enough. "See you guys tomorrow." I let myself out and walk over to my apartment to enjoy some coveted time alone, pondering my dress.

Chapter Eight

The workweek flies by. The previous week all the designers were away at New York market so Gemma and I had the office to ourselves. She used our free time to teach me how to computer-illustrate, and this week, now that the designers are back and we are busy again, I'm feeling far more adept at my job. Lillian even pops her head into my office occasionally to ask what I think about a certain print or a lace. I'm flattered she respects my opinion and love having some design input.

Even better, though, Gemma and I have become good friends. I've told her all about Operation Loverly and The Spin, and she's offered to help style my final look. When I walk into my office Friday morning, I find Gemma has wallpapered the room in red paper adorned with cutout Oscar statues. A HAPPY OSCARS! sign hangs across the front of my desk, and my computer is playing Elton John's "Tiny Dancer." At first I think I'm going to get in trouble for defacing my office, but when Lillian walks by she smiles. "Fun! Happy Oscars!"

"We paper each other's offices for birthdays and anniversaries," Gemma explains. "It means I'm happy you're here."

"I'm happy, too," I reply.

Finally the day I've been dreading/waiting for arrives. My final test is here. EJ-day dawns and my morning begins with oatmeal. It's the first solid food I've had all week, and I hope it will stay down. I can barely eat it anyway. LA is buzzing: who will win, what will they wear, what will they say? The Oscars are all anyone can talk about as the city prepares to shut down for its most glamorous night. I wish I could escape. I wish someone, anyone, would talk about something else.

The Spin is imminent and I withdraw, overcome with anxiety. It's no use begging Blair and Parker to let me stay home and watch the awards on TV like a normal person;

they're beside themselves with excitement. The evenings leading up to the event have been filled with facials, yoga, and a nearly liquid diet to ensure I'll be at my leanest and meanest. Parker hired the makeup artist and hairstylist from *The One* to polish me into the final rendition of their project; Gemma is on board to make last-minute decisions regarding shoes and accessories; and Blair secured a list of possible designers every best-actress nominee might be wearing to guarantee I don't accidentally show up in the same dress. Personally, I don't think there is any danger of that as my dress is from last season, but I don't interrupt her analysis.

"Gwyneth will probably wear Calvin Klein or Tom Ford, so we should be good there." Blair is studying her notes as the hairstylist winds my hair around a fat curling iron. Mia Dalton will probably have some cool vintage thing going on…"

"Mia Dalton will be there?" I ask. Mia is Berkeley's gorgeous indie-darling actress sister. I can't seem to escape this family.

"No. She won't be at Elton's. She's nominated for best supporting actress—she'll have to go to the Governor's ball." Blair dismisses her, and I'm relieved. "Meryl Streep— probably no danger of the two of you wearing the same thing…Christina Carlton, she's a presenter, likely wearing Armani or Balenciaga…"

I leave Blair to her devices and scroll through my phone, checking tweets. They are all, of course, about the Oscars.

BLAIR HAMILTON @SUPERSPINSTRESS
GOING TO BORROW SOME FABULOUS JEWELS FROM NEIL LANE,
BUT NOT IN A LOHAN SORTA WAY. #TRADINGFAVORS

CHRISTINA CARLTON @CELEBRIGHTLY
THANK GOODNESS FOR THE ULTIMATE #OSCARS CLEANSE!!! AT
LEAST THE TOXIC PEOPLE ARE OUT MY LIFE...

OLIVIA BLOOM @BLOOMOLIVIA
FEELING RESTED, AND FULL OF OATMEAL. OH WELL. AT LEAST
THE BUTTERFLIES HAVE SOMETHING TO EAT.

CHRISTINA CARLTON @CELEBRIGHTLY
AND THE FINAL FIT IS PERFECTION! MY OSCARS DRESS IS
A DREAM COME TRUE...

I shoot a quick text to Boots, thinking of all the times we've gotten ready for parties together. If she were here, she'd be running around cracking jokes and teasing me about how my mom saw a vision of me tripping on the red carpet in her crystal ball. I know her presence would lift my spirits, and I'm missing her today. She doesn't respond. I'm not surprised—she's probably somewhere saving lives.

As the makeup artist applies her finishing touches, showering me in a rosewater mist, I put down my phone. Parker, Blair, and Gemma are oohing and aahing over me, but I can barely hear them as dread clouds my ears. The Spin draws near. How am I going to do this? Who in their right mind would go through with it? Nobody, that's who! Fear renders me immobile as Blair sweeps through the room, carrying my gown. I imagine what Boots would tell me right now, and I try to talk myself down. *Just do your best, Liv. It's all you can do. You gave up fear in favor of taking chances, remember? Be brave.* Yes, I must be brave. Swallowing my nerves, I concentrate on my dress, trying to enjoy the details leading up to the imminent catastrophe. I've never worn anything as beautiful—or expensive—and a thrill shoots through me as I slip it on.

Half an hour before we are to leave, I stare at the creation reflected in the mirror. I still feel like me, but the girl staring back is me on alpha-hydroxy-oids. My face has been painted to accentuate my eyes, and they appear catlike and green. The asymmetrical coral chiffon Matthew Williamson gown falls to the floor in soft folds, skimming my body. Sixteen thousand dollar carnelian and diamond earrings sparkle at my ears. It hits me. I look like I belong on TV, and I make a decision: the only way I'm going to get through this night is to pretend I am someone on TV. Sucking in my breath, I let normal Olivia take a backseat and allow the Olivia that goes with this face to take over. With a glint in my eye and confidence in my step, I emerge from my apartment and step down into the courtyard for final inspection.

"Liv," Blair says. "Wow."

"Gorgeous," Gemma agrees.

"Thanks. I couldn't have done it without you," I reply. "And you two look great." I admire Parker, standing starched in his perfectly altered tux, and Blair, wearing a strapless, beaded mini dress that hugs her figure and shows off her legs. We're a pretty good-looking trio, I think.

Parker begins to circle me, clipboard in hand.

"Teeth: slightly crooked but could be considered cute. Eyes: green. Fabulous. Hair: loose waves of chocolaty perfection. Body: to die for. Skin: flawless. Accent: eliminated. Boobs: real. Bones: excellent. Inspection: pass." He turns to me. "You have my seal of approval. Are you ready for your test drive?"

"As ready as I'll ever be."

Gemma snaps our picture before Parker, Blair, and I walk out the Vicente's gate.

"You don't look like no riffraff!" a shaky voice calls from the depths of a dilapidated front porch across the street. Willis, our ninety-year-old one-man-neighborhood-watch, waddles into the sunlight and squints at us.

"We better not look like riffraff," Parker exclaims. "I didn't get my nails 'did' for nothing!"

"Well, if you're needin' some sec-ur-ity," Willis says, drawing out the syllables, "Betty and I are happy to oblige. We protected some pretty fan-cy off-ici-als in our day." He holds up "Betty"—the gun he keeps in his pocket at all times. *If the twenty-two don't get 'em, the forty-five will!* I'm not sure if Betty's loaded, but Parker promises Willis is harmless. *Hasn't shot one yet.*

Blair laughs. "Maybe next time."

"Suit yourselves," he replies, splashing us with a giant toothless grin.

With a final wave we slide into Parker's Mercedes and drive up the hill into Hollywood. Blair secured our tickets through her friends at The Lighter Side, and to ease our qualms about crashing a charity event, we've each made a significant donation to the Elton John AIDS Foundation. Parker guides the car into a parking structure rather than using the valet so I can make my entrance alone, as planned.

"Remember, this is all about timing. Follow behind us to the front of the building," Blair instructs. "We'll go in before you; just don't let on you know us. Outside the entrance, you'll notice the paparazzi; this is your first test. They have a sixth sense for celebrity, and they won't photograph just anyone. You have to own it. We're going now. You count to one hundred, then follow."

I nod my understanding as they slip out of the car and start walking.

Parker looks over his shoulder. "Remember everything we've practiced," he calls out. "You look amazing. You're IT!"

I am an It girl, I think as I count slowly, trying to psyche myself up. One hundred arrives too soon, and I check my appearance in the car window before beginning my walk. With Berkeley & the Brightside's "London" playing in my head, I walk to the beat, reminding myself to be the girl that belongs to this face, trampling butterflies with each step.

"There's plenty of time for you, to get where you're going to. Recover everything you've lost or burn every bridge you've crossed…"

Ahead of me, Blair and Parker arrive at the Pacific Design Center. Handing their tickets to the guard at the velvet rope, they begin their descent down the white carpet. The paparazzi don't budge. Blair slips a stealth note to the press escort, a girl she knows from previous events, before leaning over to Parker and saying loudly in her best starstruck voice, so she is sure to be overheard, "I think that was Olivia Bloom back there."

"Really?" Parker responds, with a sly glance over his shoulder, "She's *so beautiful!* And such a party girl. I heard she's being considered to play the love interest in Brad Pitt's new movie. She's been kind of under the radar, and they want an unknown for the role…"

That's all it takes. Even if it isn't true, the potential to spoil something for a star like Brad Pitt could pay millions. By the time I reach the white carpet moments later, the photo-hungry paparazzi are in a frenzy. "This is Olivia Bloom," the press escort validates me after a peek at her note. They begin calling my name, "Olivia, over here!" "Olivia! Olivia!" This is it. My moment has arrived.

The screaming photographers go silent in my head, and all I can hear is Parker's voice as I take a deep breath and step forward. I don't allow myself to get overwhelmed. We've been through this so many times, my body automatically responds to each instruction. Stepping forward, I hit my mark. Cross legs at the ankles. Hands rest delicately on the hips. Arms straight back so the yoga definition shows. Shoulders down, elongate the neck so there are no wrinkles. Chin out and down. Eyes look up directly into the camera; a hint of warmth and amusement behind them. Closed mouth, half smile in place. Look left. Look right. Look center. Walk five steps. Repeat. Walk five steps. Repeat. Do not stay too long, leave them wanting more.

With a slight wave, I glide inside the tent, as they cheer and beg me to stay. My fate is sealed. Despite the lack of personal recognition, those who have witnessed the paparazzi's reaction to me begin to whisper, and before long people are wondering telephone-style exactly who I am.

Once inside, relief washes over me. Feeling the worst must be over, and having far exceeded my own expectations, I momentarily relax and take in my surroundings. The party is breathtaking. It is a tiffany blue and white ball. The decorations are sparse and clean so as not to distract from the real eye candy: the guests. Simple centerpieces comprised of twinkling tea lights and white plumeria adorn the tables, and soft blue bulbs cast a glow on the walls. At the center of the tent, large television screens are broadcasting the red carpet from the Oscars on Hollywood Boulevard while the A-list crowd who has chosen to watch this year's broadcast with Elton mingle and talk about what their friends on the screens are wearing. Feeling out of place, I begin to search for my table. Blair, Parker, and I will be seated together for dinner and the viewing party, but we are to pretend we don't know one another. Forcing myself to move, I find my way to table eighty-one.

I watch from a safe distance as Lisa Greene, who I'm to be seated next to, greets Blair and Parker with hugs and cheek kisses. Lisa is an actress on the TV show *Cosmic Companions*, and I've met her a couple times at various events during my training, each time beaming my friendliest smile and looking her directly in the eye. For her part, each time she meets me, she looks right through me like I don't exist, making me feel beyond insignificant. The table seats twelve, and according to Parker's research the other guests are all executives from Relativity Media, the company that produces *Cosmic Companions*. Like me, Lisa is attending the party alone—no doubt as a gift to make the execs happy—and tonight I am counting on her to, as usual, not recognize me. The hope is she will find me slightly familiar, causing her to assume I am somebody, thereby validating me to everyone at our table, and hopefully the room. This is my second test, though it is a mini one. In the event Lisa does recognize me, I will still come across as her peer. The real exam is to come, though it is unclear to me who I will have to convince for Blair and Parker to consider the Spin complete. Having made it past the paparazzi is enough for me to deem the night a success.

Blair and Parker take their seats as I approach.

"Is it okay if I sit here?" I ask, pulling out the chair next to Lisa.

She is petite—barely five feet tall—and her long, black hair hangs in a shiny mane halfway down her back. I tower above her, and she looks up at me, focusing on my face. For a second recognition shimmers in her dark eyes and I think I'm done for, but it passes quickly. I'm on the other side of the game, now. "Go ahead," she motions and adjusts the skirt of her canary yellow dress so I have room to sit. "I'm Lisa," she presents her hand.

Smiling, I take her offering. "I'm Olivia. Nice to meet you." I resist peeking across the table at Blair and Parker, who I know are pretending to be deep in conversation but are really watching the scene before them. Test number two: pass. They must be ecstatic.

"So, what are you working on?" Lisa asks.

The perfect vague question. She thinks I'm "someone" and is trying to find out who I am. Parker has carefully crafted my answer for me, and I recite my line without hesitation. "I'm actually not working on anything right now," I say. "I'm taking some time off. I might try moving in a new direction, but for now I'm enjoying some free time. I mean, it's so nice to be able to sleep in every once in a while!" The perfect vague answer.

"Oh, I know," Lisa agrees. My answer doesn't satisfy her curiosity, but it gives her an opening to talk about herself. "Call times to set can be *so* early, and then they keep you there *so* late. I don't know about you, but I find it impossible to nap in my trailer. I'm always exhausted when I'm working.

Thank God for hiatus."

"Yes, breaks are nice," I agree.

To my left a man and woman have joined our table and having overheard our conversation, will naturally assume I'm an actress. This is going perfectly. They begin chatting with Blair and Parker. From their conversation, I gather they are lawyers at Relativity.

The first course is served, and Billy Crystal appears on the screens at the center of the tent. The party erupts in applause as he begins his opening routine. I laugh along with everyone else as he acts out the Best Picture nominees via a giant song-and-dance number. Turning from the screens to take a bite of my salad, I notice a thirteenth chair has been added on the other side of Lisa. I don't think much of it, as Rhea, the woman on my other side asks me to pass the pepper. I reach over Lisa to obtain the shaker as the final member of our table arrives.

My hand begins to shake uncontrollably as Berkeley Dalton takes his seat.

Chapter Nine

MRS. BLOOM @PSYCHICMOMI
TONIGHT THE STARS WILL ALIGN UNDER THE #SUPERMOON
@BLOOMOLIVIA THINGS ARE GOING TO CHANGE. YOUR STARS
ARE BURNING BRIGHTER THAN EVER.

OLIVIA BLOOM @BLOOMOLIVIA
@PSYCHICMOMI OK. WE'LL SEE. RIGHT NOW THE ONLY
THINGS BURNING ARE MY EARS. THANKS, FELIX.

Snatching my hand away as if it's been scalded, I hand off the pepper, and my gaze shoots to Parker across the table. The tent might not be big enough for his grin, and he casually tilts the tip of his champagne glass toward me in acknowledgement. He *knew* Berkeley would be here. *This is your last Oscars, Mifflin.* My daggers take aim.

"Berkeley!" Lisa squeals. "You made it."

"Yeah," Berkeley says. "I just came to say hi. I need to go back soon to finish warming up." He's dressed for the occasion in a tailored tuxedo, and I concentrate on not finding those blue eyes as he slings his arm across the back of Lisa's chair. She leans into him, resting her hand on his chest as she whispers something in his ear.

It shouldn't bother me—Berksa or Greenton or whatever they'll be called—they don't make a difference to *my* world, but for some reason their togetherness bugs me.

I turn my attention back to the rest of the table, trying to ignore them. The Oscars are on a commercial break, and everyone is chatting.

"What did you think of the opening number?" Rhea asks me.

All my weeks of training should have prepared me for this moment, but my mind goes blank, only finding focus in the burning presence next to Lisa.

"Ummm," I falter, racking my brain to remember *anything* else that has happened tonight. "I really liked the part where he did the routine to the Bruno Mars song."

"Bruno Mars?" Rhea looks puzzled.

"Yeah—I'm not going to sing it—but where they were all dressed as sailors for the *Popeye* movie?"

One of the lawyers on the other side of the table erupts in laughter. "That wasn't Bruno Mars," he says. "That was 'Message in a Bottle' by the Police." He shakes his head at Rhea as if to say "kids these days!"

My eyes hit the table. *Of course it was. I knew that. I'm an idiot.* Another tune jumps into my head. *This face is on fire!*

Rhea frowns at me, shrugging her shoulders with pity.

As I endure the laughter across the table, I venture a peek at Berkeley, certain he finds my musical chops lacking.

To my surprise, he is staring at me with curiosity, but he looks away as soon as our eyes connect.

Standing, he excuses himself. "I need to get back to warm-ups," he says, his voice hinting that adorable South African accent. "But I have to say, I prefer the Bruno Mars version, myself."

The table goes silent.

My eyes widen as his words impact, sending a rush of warmth and gratitude through me. I look up to thank him, but his back is already turned. Without another word, or even a good-bye to Lisa, he walks off.

Lisa is busy picking onions out of her salad and doesn't seem to notice him leave.

He didn't have to do that, but I'm grateful he did.

For an instant my eyes meet Parker's. He casually raises his eyebrows and takes a sip of his drink. I resist acknowledging him. If I had superpowers, I'd freeze that smirk on his face forever as punishment, but instead, I reinstate my composure. With Berkeley on my side, my confidence is restored, and with him gone I can concentrate again. I find the courage to rejoin the conversation, which turns to the Best Picture nominees. All my studying pays off as I am able to maintain my composure and articulate my opinion on each film. I consider myself a success as I win back the respect of the table.

An hour into the party, Elton and David make their royal entrance. They parade around the tables, shaking hands and greeting friends as the awards carry on. I try to fade into the crowd, feeling more like an imposter than I have all evening, but to no avail. Eventually they arrive at our table. Elton takes my hand and looks me directly in the eyes. I almost pass out and fight the urge to tell him I'm a fake. I saw him in concert when I was twelve, and I've been a fan ever since. Mesmerized by his talent and over-the-top performance, he became one of my idols. When everyone else was listening to 'N Sync, I was listening endlessly to "Madman Across the Water," imagining a black-and-white video shoot filled with dramatically made-up models. I practiced the makeup on myself, heavily ringing my eyes in black and pretending I was the slightly mad star of said video. (Yes—I've always had an overactive imagination.) Nonetheless, this is real. Elton has long been an inspiration, and here he is, the legend, shaking my hand.

"Charming, quite charming," he says.

Gripping the only reality I know (the Rules), I am speechless and grant him a delicate smile. He grins back, showing the gap in his front teeth, and moves on. I exhale, realizing I've been holding my breath. I can die happy.

Thinking now that I have Elton's approval surely the test should be over, I look across the table for Blair and Parker's endorsement, but they are gone. The awards have ended, and the concert is beginning as crooner Samantha Shelton takes the stage in the center of the tent. Excusing myself from the table, I follow the crowd, scanning for Blair and Parker. Instead, I find Felix Sheridan. As the face of the gossip empire *TMI*, he is notorious for knowing the dirt on everything celebrity. Standing in the center of the room, his suit is precise and his olive skin stretches over surgically altered cheekbones. He is smaller in stature than he appears on *TMI* (despite his pompadour giving him a few extra inches) but his presence is huge. He has the power to make or break anyone in Hollywood. He knows everybody, and everything about everybody. But he doesn't know me, and he's out for blood. *Oh boy.* I forget Blair and Parker and start searching for an escape route, but it's no use.

"Hi. I'm Felix," he says, staring me down. His eyes are swift as he assesses me, and I get the feeling he will pounce on whatever I say next.

"Hello, Felix," I offer him a polite smile and look away, pretending to be enthralled with the show.

He won't let me go. "And who are you?" he flat out asks me.

I'm sure he can hear my heart pounding as I turn back to him and answer simply, "I'm Olivia Bloom. Nice to meet you."

"Olivia Bloom. Any relation to Orlando?"

I smile as if I'm asked that all the time. "No."

"What do you do, then, Olivia Bloom?" Leave it to Felix to break all the rules.

I pretend to think for a minute, struggling to remain in character and silently thanking Parker for the flashcards, before answering with a mischievous shrug. "I go to parties."

He's not fazed. "Are you enjoying this one?"

"Oh, yes. Very much."

"Who are you here with?"

"I came with some friends. They're around."

He fires the questions in rapid succession, and the answers fly from my tongue just as quickly, due to the constant repetition with which I've practiced them. I refuse to let him stump me.

"What are you doing after this?"

"I don't know, yet. I usually just see where the night takes me."

He throws his fastball. "What's your relationship with Brad Pitt?"

"I'm not at liberty to say," I reply, truthfully.

The song is ending and we both know he can't keep quizzing me without it getting awkward. "Well, it was nice meeting you, Olivia," he says. "I'm sure I'll see you around."

"I look forward to it," I answer with a tiny wave as I move away from him, deeper into the crowd and closer to the stage.

He moves in the opposite direction, his hypothesis already formulating.

I have no idea if I've passed Felix's inspection, but I'm ready to leave. Certain I cannot handle another conversation like that one, I continue searching for Parker and Blair, finally spying them huddled across the room, whispering with a woman I don't recognize. At that moment, all three of them look over at me, and as the woman leaves, Blair and Parker burst into fits of laughter. Parker tugs on his left ear, our signal it's time to go.

As planned I let them get a head start. I'm about to slip quietly out a side door and start toward the parking garage when Berkeley & the Brightside take the stage.

Curiosity gets the best of me; I can afford to watch for a few minutes. Blair and Parker can wait.

Like Berkeley, the Brightside are dressed in tuxedos. In contrast to the last time I saw them, they all look rested and pressed. As I observe them, somehow my eyes connect with Mark's, and he gives me a minute wave of surprised recognition.

Flattered he remembers me, I wave back.

Berkeley looks first to Jeff, then to Ted. They nod their readiness, and Berkeley leans into the microphone. "We thought we'd switch things up tonight," he says as the room erupts in cheers. "Let's have a little fun." He looks at Ted, who clicks off three taps of his drumsticks and they launch into a song.

My jaw drops as I recognize the notes. They're covering Bruno Mars' "Locked Out of Heaven", the song we were just talking about. No wonder Berkeley defended me. What a crazy coincidence.

My eyes are glued to him, and I'm positive the Brightside's version of the song is better than the original. I watch the intensity in Berkeley's eyes as he lives out every note, and it's like I'm the only girl in the room—like he's singing straight to me—though I'm instantly reminded I'm not alone as the crowd pushes me forward. Allowing myself to be momentarily swept away with the current, I come to a halt as the song changes, and he starts singing "Message in A Bottle". Standing motionless against the dancing bodies surrounding me, I stare at him in shock. What are the chances? This is surreal. It's like a mash-up of my most embarrassing moments being played out for all of Hollywood's elite. I can't begin to comprehend the strangeness, so I start to laugh, certain he has *no* idea what he's doing to me.

As the song ends, I again try to find Berkeley's eyes to thank him for his help, but he's in another world. The band starts playing "Margaritaville", and with a whoop the audience joins in, singing along. I would love to stay and watch the rest of the show, but I know Blair and Parker are dying for a recap, and I've made them wait long enough. Reluctantly, I make my way out the door.

Chapter Ten

PARKER MIFFLIN @IsIndulgent
WELL HELLO, CHOCOLATE CROISSANT. WHAT'S THAT? I DESERVE
YOU? I KNOW.

I'm bursting with words—I can't wait to tell Blair and Parker what they missed. But united once again, we stay in character and stealthily get into Parker's car. We remain silent until we are safely out of Hollywood, though we can barely contain ourselves.

Finally, Blair erupts, "We DID it! That was amazing!"

"I can't believe it!" Parker cries out. "I almost died when that woman came up to us and said she heard it from Felix that Olivia is *not* a movie actress at all…that she's a fraud."

"'She's too perfect,'" Blair quotes Felix. "'Her answers too flawless, and I can't find anything about her on the Internet—she doesn't look like any of the Olivia Bloom's that show up on Google. It's probably not even her real name. She obviously comes from money, probably from some foreign oil dignitary in Dubai.'"

"And he declared her an *ingenue.*" Parker triumphs.

"We did it. We spun it!" Blair chimes in. "I can't believe we did it."

"I'll start fielding the scripts," Parker says. "I wrote the character anyway."

"Can you believe it? Felix Sheridan?" Blair says. "Nobody puts one over on Felix. This is huge. If we can fool him, we can put a spin on anybody. We're in business."

I sit waiting for acknowledgment that doesn't come, my excitement in telling them about Berkeley and the song dissipating. Invisible, I slump, silent in the backseat, listening to their glee. They rattle on about their night and how they made it all happen. *I'm an outsider.* Spying on their revelry, it's like I don't exist, like I wasn't part of this whole scheme. I did all of this so they would accept me, but I've never felt so alone. *This was only about the Spin and validating themselves, never about helping me. I'm a pawn. Insignificant. They never wanted to be my friends. It was all a game. A test of their abilities, and they won.* A lump rises in my throat, and I fight the tears that crowd behind my eyes. *I don't have any friends in this city.* I am achingly on my own.

Pressing my lips together, I remain silent as we arrive at the Vicente, and I follow them into the courtyard. Parker runs into his apartment and emerges seconds later with a bottle of celebratory champagne and three glasses. Popping the cork, he and Blair go on and on, clinking glasses, congratulating themselves on "The Spin of the Century." Standing aside in solitude, still unnoticed, I take a sip of my champagne, and the hurt that is simmering inside me boils into rage. I stop feeling sorry for myself. They're completely ignoring the role I played in this. I'm the one who stands to be made a fool in this scheme, and I have the most at stake. Had we failed, it would have been my face splashed across the gossip columns as the loser who crashed Elton's party. Plus, on top of feeling taken for granted, I'm exhausted from the long weeks of practice. The enormity of it all finally gets the better of me. I pick up the abandoned champagne cork, then throw it at Parker, interrupting his mirth by landing it square on his forehead.

"Ow!" he shrieks, sloshing his champagne as he swats at the offending object. "Careful, Olivia Bloom, you almost made me spill champagne on my tux!"

"Good," I reply, taking the borrowed diamonds from my ears and pelting Blair with them.

"Liv! What's gotten into you?" She leaps back in surprise before hitting the ground on her hands and knees to retrieve the expensive jewels.

"I don't appreciate being ignored, and I think I deserve some credit here," I say, fighting tears as I unclasp my bracelet and launch it across the courtyard. "I'm not some character you invented. Maybe I played a role tonight, but I'm done with her. I'm tired of being taken advantage of. My life is not some story you get to write. I'm real, and I have feelings, and I did all of this because I wanted you to like me."

Blair and Parker stare at me, mouths gaping. I've never stood up to them before.

"I'm sorry. I'm not your ingenue. I'm just me. And you don't hafta like it…" The tears are flowing now and I take a ragged breath. "I mize well go back to Pittsburgh for all you care — "

Parker gasps. "Have to. Might as well," he corrects me.

I glare at him as I descend into a fresh round of sobs. "Enough," I manage to say through hiccups. Needing to be alone, I turn on my heel and run up the steps to my apartment, slamming the door behind me. Safely on the other side, I slide down into a heap, letting my tears flow free. Ignoring the *thumps* on my door and gentle calling of my name, I sit and sob. It is a relief to let go.

At some point I manage to find my bed, and I awake the next morning, still in my dress, mascara caked on my tear-stained face, to knocking at my door. I crawl out of bed and try to look out the peephole but am unable to discern the fuzzy image on the other side through my puffy eyes. Having cried everything out, I am calm as I open the door. Blair and Parker stand before me, armed with orange juice, coffee, and an ivory cardboard box from La Maison du Pain.

"Hi," I say quietly.

"Can we come in?" Blair asks, her voice solemn. She holds up the box in offering.

"Sure." I shrug, unmoved.

They hurry into my kitchen and set up shop, pouring orange juice and opening the pastry box to reveal buttery croissants inside. Handing me a coffee, Blair begins, "Liv, we feel really bad. We want to apologize for last night."

"You were right," Parker says. "You were perfect. It all worked because you're *you*. I'm sorry we got carried away."

"We did pull off something pretty incredible, though," Blair continues. "But with your help — nobody else could have done it."

"And we wouldn't have *wanted* to do it with anyone

else," Parker adds.

"I guess what we're trying to say is, we love you," Blair says.

Their words begin to chip away at some of the armor I've layered on through the night. My lower lip begins to quiver as my sorrow lifts, and I start to believe maybe I'm not alone.

"And we think we're going to be *best* friends, if you can forgive us," Parker says.

"And from now on, no more training or spins. We love you for you," Blair finishes.

I stare at the two of them looking so hopeful, and I allow the rest of my anger and hurt to melt away. I'm not one to hold a grudge, and I have to admit, being an ingenue for one night is not something I could have accomplished on my own. It was unforgettable.

"Well…I guess it all depends," I waver. "Did you get any chocolate croissants?"

"Only one," Parker answers.

"I guess we can split it, then," I say. "On one condition. You owe me a *huge* apology for not telling me Berkeley Dalton was going to be there."

"Oh my God. How fabulous was that? He's even hotter in real life," Parker says. "I don't know what he's doing with that hag Lisa Greene, but the way he defended you… Swoon! I think something's going on there. First the fashion show, now this?"

"It wasn't fabulous, and he doesn't remember me from the fashion show," I say. Last night I was dying to tell them about the song, but now I want to keep the moment to myself. I don't need them jumping to conclusions over a coincidence. "He was being nice—unlike you, who set me up to fail by putting me at his table. You *know* I can't talk in front of him!"

"Listen, missy, don't get so huffy. I would *never* do that to you. I knew Berkeley & the Brightside was playing the party, but I didn't know he'd sit at our table. That was just an added bonus. And I didn't tell you because I didn't want to make you more nervous."

"It was the ultimate test, though, if you think about it," Blair says. "I think you've redeemed yourself."

"If looking like an imbecile is the same as redemption, I guess so," I reply, picking up a croissant and dropping the subject. I tear the croissant into thirds, covering my fingers in chocolate.

"Here you go," I say, wiping chocolate onto Parker's face. "You deserve this."

Chapter Eleven

MRS. BLOOM @PSYCHICMOM1
RUNNING LOW ON PYRAMID WATER—ANYONE KNOW A GOOD
OCCULT SUPPLY STORE IN LA?

Following Elton's party, no papers pick up the "Olivia Bloom" story, perhaps sensing our attempt at deception. For three days Gemma and I scour the Internet at work for any sign of me, under the guise we're looking at Oscar fashion for inspiration. No mentions turn up, which is fine with me. My mom is flying out for a visit this weekend, and I'm kind of relieved she'll be greeted with ordinary me and not an It girl.

I'm too new at work to take any days off, so I'm only going to be able to spend two days with her, but she's staying for four. LA is full of psychics and lunatics, and it's not unusual for your next-door neighbor to have a PSYCHIC

ADVISOR sign in their front yard. In fact, our neighbors two doors down from Willis prominently display their psychic sandwich board, promising to "put an end to all of your problems—one visit will convince you!" I've seen the people who live there: an elderly woman who wears flowing skirts and walks with a cane and her deranged son (the "psychic") who chain smokes in his BMW while listening to hip-hop. I'm not convinced. But with no fewer than 2,119 psychic advisors living within a one-mile radius of the Vicente, I'm not worried that Mom will find a good one to keep her busy.

I pick her up at LAX Friday evening after work.

She greets me with a big hug. "Liv! You look terrific. Namaste." She long ago adopted "namaste" as her favorite salutation, and she uses it every chance she gets. "What a transformation. Esme was right…"

"Mom," I complain, giving her my best don't-start-with-me look. "You promised. No voodoo."

"You know I don't practice voodoo," she says with mock shock as we head to my car.

"I know. Let's drop it. I'm happy you're here."

We stop in Culver City for a casual dinner at the Father's Office before heading back to the Vicente.

"Your apartment is adorable. I love the mint tile in the bathroom. It has so much character," she declares after the six-minute grand tour. "Is it safe, though? All of the windows on the east side open to the street. Anyone could climb in."

"It's a pretty safe neighborhood, Mom. I know it looks a little different than Pennsylvania, but the people are good. Look." I stick my head out the door and wave at Willis. From his porch, he responds with a flourish and a giant toothless grin. So worth it. "Proof," I say as I gesture toward him.

"Well, your father and I are proud of you. You've done a *great* job for yourself." She's starting to mist up. "Not everybody would be brave enough to try this on their own. It's hard to leave what's comfortable and take a risk. But you're doing it, and I think it's great."

"Well, I haven't conquered this city, yet. But, thanks. I like to make you proud." I'm getting a little misty myself.

We look at each other through our tears. "Stop it."

"You stop it."

"Stop it!"

"You started it!"

We giggle. "Come on, let's watch a movie," I say, opening a drawer of discs. "What sounds good?"

"Something scary."

Shocking.

I pick up *Wait Until Dark*, one of our old favorites, and turn in time to catch her staring intently at the flame on a lavender-scented candle.

"Ma—"

"Shhhhhhh!" She waves me off and continues her trancelike gaze. "All clear," she reports a few moments later. "If the flame flickered, that would mean there are spirits present, but from the looks of it, this is a very clear space."

"Well, that's a relief."

I'm glad I closed the windows.

We spend the next day exploring the most haunted places in Hollywood—I'm positive Mom would be more starstruck by seeing a ghost than a celebrity and am thankful none choose to materialize—before we head back to the Vicente to cook dinner for Blair and Parker.

After dinner, we are all sitting, stuffed, finishing another bottle of wine. The air is cool, but we're warm from good food and good conversation.

"Thank you for dinner, Mrs. Bloom. That was fabulous," Parker says. "Liv, I'm officially crowning you head chef at the Vicente. I had no idea you could cook."

"I actually love cooking, so if you ever need a night in, just let me know," I reply, thinking I wouldn't mind a few nights at home now that I don't have to worry about Operation Loverly anymore.

"You're welcome, Parker," Mom says. "I'm just so happy Liv has found such nice friends. I knew she would, of course, but the two of you are even better than we anticipated."

"Mom." I give her a warning look. Thus far she's been on her best behavior and hasn't peeped a word of her latest readings with Esme, but give her a few glasses of wine and the namastes start flying…

"What do you mean 'we' anticipated?" Blair asks, opening the door to the flood.

Oh boy. Here we go.

"Well, once Olivia chose the path that led to LA, Esme, my advisor, had a vision of Liv walking down a red carpet, and there were two brightly colored butterflies with her. She seemed to be following them, and they were looking out for her. Esme said the scene had an overwhelming sense of peace and safety about it, and she felt these butterflies were Liv's guides and they would lead her to great happiness."

Blair and Parker are hanging on every word. I roll my eyes.

"How does Esme see these visions?" Blair asks. "Can she do it for anyone?"

"Sure she can. She has many different methods: cards,

crystals, tea leaves. It usually helps if she has a piece of the person, and I always keep a lock of Liv's hair in my purse, just in case, but this particular vision came to Esme in a dream. It's interesting, she usually doesn't dream, so when she does, the messages are clear and strong and not to be taken lightly."

My elbows are on the table, and I'm resting my face in my hands, praying for the conversation to take a different direction.

"Did she see anything else?" Parker asks.

"Oh, well, I left out the best part. Liv doesn't like it when I talk about these things, but I've been dying to share—she was holding hands with a very attractive—"

"Enough!" I jump to my feet and slam my hands to the table. "You're right. I don't like it when you talk about these things. We're done." I begin stacking the dishes.

"Aw, Liv. Come on," Parker begs.

"Yeah—how can you not want to know? I wish someone would tell me something like that—that I was going to be holding hands with a hot guy on the red carpet," Blair says. "Then I wouldn't have to work so hard to meet someone. It would be a relief to know it's going to happen."

"But you wouldn't know it's going to happen or when. And maybe it won't happen because you'll stop trying and you won't make the choice that leads you to him," I argue. "And then you'll always be wondering if you missed the opportunity, and you'll drive yourself crazy. No thank you. Besides, Mom didn't finish her sentence; I could have been holding hands with a very attractive orangutan for all we know."

Blair shakes her head at me.

"Party pooper," Parker complains.

"While I'm pooping on the party, why don't you two flutter on into the kitchen and start on some dishes." I slide a stack of plates toward Parker.

"What? And get my wings dirty? I don't think so." He pours himself more wine.

"Come on." Blair drags him out of his chair, nearly toppling his glass. "They cooked. We clean up. You can bring the bottle." They head into my apartment, leaving Mom and me alone at the table.

"So, have you heard from Michael at all?" she asks.

I shake my head. "I missed a call from him recently, but he didn't leave a message. It must have been an accident. I haven't talked to him since I left, and I hope you're not trying to get at something here…"

"No, I'm curious is all. But Esme *has* seen a few other things—"

"I'm sure she has." I stop her. "But please respect I really don't want to know."

"I know." She nods with a sigh. "I won't tell you. I don't need to. The impression has already been made." She grins.

"Mom." I groan, standing up and kissing her on the forehead. "I'm removing myself from the situation so you won't be tempted." Grabbing the remaining dishes, I head to the kitchen as well.

The next day Mom has her first celebrity sighting. We've just sat down for dinner at an ocean-view table at Geoffrey's in Malibu, when I notice Jonathan Stanley sitting two tables away from us.

"Hey, Mom," I whisper, leaning toward her so we won't be overheard. "Look over there. That's Jonathan Stanley. Do you recognize him from the show *Devil May Care*? I've actually met him before. He'd never remember who I am, but it's kinda cool, huh?"

"Oh my gosh. Yes! I love him. Should I go over there?"

"No. No, you should definitely *not* go over there. Leave him alone. He's trying to enjoy his dinner," I reply. "I'm sure people bug him all the time. Really. It's best to pretend you don't see him. What looks good on the menu?" I ask, trying to distract her.

"Oh, come on, Liv. I think I should go over there."

"Please don't. *Please!* That's not how people do it here."

"But I may never get this opportunity again," she says, getting out of her seat. "What have I always told you? No regrets."

No regrets for her, but what about *me?* I hide behind the menu, praying for this to be over quickly. I give it what feels like an eternity but is probably only one minute before I peer over the menu. Jonathan is standing next to his table and Mom is doing all the talking. I close my eyes, realizing I should break this up before she tries to read his palm or something.

Sighing, I stand and walk over to Jonathan's table.

"Hi, Jonathan, I'm Liv," I interrupt the conversation. "I met you a few weeks ago at the Baldwin Hills Overlook with Blair?" I say, trying to apologize with my eyes.

"Oh, yeah… Hi!"

He is pleasant enough, and I can't tell if he remembers me or not, but at least he pretends to.

"My mom's a big fan, but we'll let you get back to your dinner. Good to see you," I say, trying to initiate an exit.

"Yes, it was very good to meet you," Mom says. And then she does the unthinkable. She breaks rule number seven. It happens in slow motion right before my eyes. Gathering him in a full embrace, she hugs him. Over her shoulder, his eyes widen as his body stiffens. I feel his look reflected on my own face, and we share a moment of disbelief. I think I die a little inside.

Rule #7: Never initiate physical contact beyond a handshake/air kiss combo with a celebrity. Celeb personal space is coveted. It is a no-contact zone.

Back at the table, I scold her, "Mom. Why did you hug him?"

"I'm a hugger."

"That's fine with people you know, but you don't go around hugging strangers, do you?"

"He's not a stranger. You know him."

She is impossible. "I *do not* know him. I've met him once, and he doesn't even remember me. We're barely acquaintances."

"Well, I think I made a good impression," she says, pleased with herself. "So he'll probably remember you now."

That's what I'm afraid of.

"Let's order," I say, resigned and shaking my head.

The rest of her trip passes uneventfully enough, and I take her to the airport on Tuesday during my lunch break. As we are saying our good-byes at the curbside check-in, she hands me an envelope.

"I almost forgot to give you this."

I'm immediately suspicious. "What is it?"

"It's a picture I took back in Pittsburgh. I thought you might like to have it."

I'm on to her. "You never give up. I'm not opening this," I say, waving the envelope at her before I throw it into the backseat of my car.

"Suit yourself." She shrugs. "I love you, sweetie."

"I love you, too, Mom. Have a safe flight." I hug her good-bye and get back into my car, the envelope already forgotten.

Chapter Twelve

BERKELEY DALTON @BERKELEYBRTSIDE
@BRIGHTSIDEBP SO I HAVE SOME LEFTOVER SCREENERS…
THINKING WE MIGHT NEED TO PLAN A LITTLE GET-TOGETHER.
YOU GOT ME?

MARK VANCLEER @BRIGHTSIDEBP
@BERKELEYBRTSIDE BTW, AT FIRST I READ THAT YOU HAD
SOME LEFTOVER "SCREAMERS" AT YOUR HOUSE. MUCH MORE
ROCK 'N' ROLL.

Still exhausted from the Spin followed by having my mom as a houseguest, tonight I purposely turn off my phone and sneak out of work an hour early. I can't wait for a normal night at home. Alone. After the gym, I'm looking forward to a hot shower and a spaghetti dinner (yum…carbs!) in my pj's in front of the TV.

My pasta water has just started to boil when Blair bursts into my living room.

"What are you doing? Get dressed," she demands.

"Get dressed? Uh-uh. I'm in for the night."

"Seriously, hurry up. You do *not* want to miss this."

"Blair. It's six thirty on a Wednesday night. What could be so amazing?" It would take nothing short of an Everything for $1 Chloe Sample Sale to move me out of my pj's right now.

"We have been invited to Berkeley Dalton's house for movie night," she reveals, pleased with her news.

My heart skips a beat. Okay. So this *is* big. Definitely out of the ordinary. But there's no way I'm going and risking him recognizing me as the dumb girl from Elton's. Reliving that moment is definitely not pj-removal worthy. I fix her with my best blank stare. "Blair. We don't *know* Berkeley Dalton. Yes, we've seen him in passing a few times, but that doesn't mean he knows who *we* are. Why are we being invited to his house? I highly doubt he wants two random girls hanging out at his movie night. Plus, I'm *in* for tonight."

"Really? How could you pass this up? Do you know how many people would *kill* to go to Berkeley Dalton's house? Mark invited us. He said he thought of us because he saw you at Elton's party?"

"After you left I watched some of Berkeley & the Brightside's performance," I admit. "Mark and I randomly made eye contact. I forgot to tell you."

"See, at least we know Mark. Besides, he said it's super-chill—only ten people or so watching some screeners. It won't be weird, I promise. He really wants us to come."

"Mark is super-nice, but ten people? Nope. No way. That

means I might actually have to *talk* to Berkeley. I can't risk that."

Maybe I'd consider it if it was a big party where I could get lost in the crowd. This sounds way too intimate, though. Not happening.

"Blair," I complain, "I'm so tired. Really. Can't we stay here in our pj's and have our own movie night? We can eat spaghetti and have a glass of wine…" Even as I say it, my stomach churns, and I know I'm going. It's too crazy an invitation to pass up, no matter what awaits. This is a rare event that tests the limits of my mind and leaves me wondering how I got here. I can't believe this is my life.

"Liv. You did not move all the way out here to sit on your couch and eat spaghetti. Just think, at the very least it'll be a great story to tell your friends back home."

"Tell my friends? Rule number five. I believe Berkeley Dalton falls under the category of A-list celebrity? *Maybe* I can tell my mom." I roll my eyes. "But she probably already knows."

"Well maybe I need a wingman and I don't want to go alone."

"Really?" I ask, suddenly feeling selfish for not being available to my friend. "Is there something going on between you and Mark?"

"There's only one way to find out," she says.

I shut off the stove. "Okay. I'm getting dressed."

Forty-five minutes later we're parking Blair's car on a narrow side street in the Hills outside Berkeley's house. Darkness has fallen and the city lights twinkle against a black sky as we walk up to a heavy iron gate. Tension tightens my jaw and neck with every step. We have to be buzzed in, and I think this is the part I dread the most. Well, that and having to enter a room full of people that includes one A-list celebrity without looking awkward.

"Are you sure they know we're coming? Can't Mark come get us? I'd feel better about this whole thing if we could walk in with someone we know. You know, that way it would validate our presence?"

"Would you calm down? It'll be fine. They *want* us here! Rule number four."

Rule #4: You can always decompress later. Just breathe.

"You press the buzzer. I'm scared."

"You're ridiculous," she mutters as her finger compresses the button.

"Hello?" crackles a faraway voice.

"We come bearing popcorn!" Blair sings into the speaker.

If I wasn't so panicked, I would be appreciating her charming ease. Instead, I'm hoping the buzzer short-circuits and we can't get in.

"Come on in," the voice welcomes.

No such luck. The gate slides open. Access granted. Here we go. Deep breath in through my mouth and out through my nose. I'm so intent on breathing out and breathing in, I hardly notice the thriving landscape and panoramic city views as we descend the hill toward Berkeley's house and what is sure to be one of the most uncomfortable evenings of my life.

The front door looms before us. "Now what?" I ask.

"We go in," Blair replies.

"We can't just walk in to a stranger's house. How will we know where to go?" My nerves are preventing my mind from processing the informality of this event. This is a casual everyday occurrence for everyone except me.

She sighs and opens the door. "Just follow me. And relax."

Smoothing the silk on my Jesse Kamm tie-front shorts, I follow close behind her toward the sound of voices in the next room, unable to acknowledge my surroundings. If I were able to see past my fear, I would be admiring the white-washed walls, clean lines, and reclaimed wood floors that comprise Berkeley's house. It isn't as large as I expected an A-list celebrity's home to be, but it's uncluttered and peaceful in the evening light that filters through floor-to-ceiling windows.

Eventually we appear in the doorway of a dimly lit library. Eight pairs of eyes turn our way, but blessedly there is no break in the conversation.

"Hey, guys! Grab a seat," Mark welcomes, standing to greet us with hugs and cheek kisses (which, I have finally mastered under Parker's tutelage). "Everyone — this is Blair and Liv," he announces to the room.

Validation. Whew.

He runs through the names in the room, "You've met Jeff, our guitar player, and that's his wife Alexandra; this is Jeff's sister Kim and her boyfriend Kelvin. You remember Haynes, our manager, that's his wife Carly, and of course that's Berkeley. Everyone waves hello and returns to their conversations as I put on my winningest smile, greeting and scanning the room without really focusing on anyone. I feel *his* presence somewhere to my right and manage a glance and a wave in his general direction as I find my way to a couch.

Relieved, I sink back into the cushions as Blair and Mark chat about the next Mona Foundation fund-raiser they're working on. The worst part is over. Now all I have to do is try to be invisible and concentrate on the movie.

Blair leans over. "Hey, Liv, why don't you grab us some drinks?"

"Oh yeah, help yourself. There's beer in the fridge—take whatever you want. The kitchen is through that doorway," Mark offers, gesturing back toward the way we came in.

They can't be serious. They're sending me to the kitchen alone? I want to vomit.

"Sure." I feign a smile, swallowing my anxiety as I slide off the couch, reluctant to leave Blair, my security blanket. "What sounds good? Something Corona-ish?"

"Perfect," Blair responds in a proud-that-her-little-bird-is-leaving-the-nest sort of way.

Somehow I walk across the room without tripping, and I'm pretty sure without notice. I find my way to the kitchen easily enough and quickly scan the fridge for the least expensive beer I can find. Grabbing three Pacificos, I shut the door and secure a lime. Relishing the moment alone, I turn to the marble island in the center of the room and hunt for a knife.

"Third drawer on your right," comes a smooth voice from behind me.

Aw hell. Instantly recognizing the voice from the slight accent on the letter "*i*", I freeze, briefly closing my eyes. This is not happening. Abandoned and trapped, I force myself to move, and steeling myself as best I can for the onslaught of those eyes, I turn.

It's comical to think I could have prepared for the jolt of

energy that rushes through me as our eyes meet. If it's at all possible, his eyes are brighter and bluer than I remembered. His hair is perfectly messy and his skin is lightly tanned, as if he's just rolled up from an afternoon relaxing in the sand. Intoxicated and suffocated, I take a sharp inhale.

"Thanks. I really wasn't trying to rummage through your drawers," the words come out in a rush. *OMG.* I bite my cheek at the implication.

"No problem," he says, pulling out a cutting board and sliding it my way. "Everyone's getting hungry. I was going to order us pizza."

Stars! They're just like us! They order pizza! *Focus, Liv. Focus.*

"Oh—well, you have the fixings for guacamole in your fridge—I could make some to satisfy everyone in the meantime... Not that I was rummaging through your fridge," I add. Where am I getting this? Did I just offer to make guacamole? That's like the equivalent of carrying a watermelon.

"That'd be great."

As he finds the Cheech's Pizza menu and begins to order, I curse the bizarre form of Tourette's that commandeers my tongue whenever I'm around him. After gathering ingredients from the refrigerator, I walk back to the island and begin mashing avocados.

He orders pepperoni, mushroom, and olive. *Eats meat and is okay with mushrooms.* Noted.

Pull it together, I tell myself as I stir. *Be normal. Be friendly. Breathe. Here it goes.* Turning toward him as he hangs up the phone, I bravely extend my hand. "I'm Liv, by the way."

A slow smile spreads over his face as he accepts my outstretched hand. He studies me and his eyes light up, intensifying his beauty.

"I know."

You know? A thousand butterflies burst from their cocoons in the pit of my stomach and my brain scrambles for it to make sense. I'm concluding that Mark *did* just introduce me to the room as Berkeley steps closer, dizzying me with his proximity.

Holding my gaze, he grins. "And I'm taller than you expected."

What? Heat floods my cheeks. Mortified. I'm mortified. Why? How could he possibly remember that? I want to die. That's it. Strike me down right here. It can't get any worse than this.

Seemingly enjoying my blush, he grabs a chip and dips it in the guacamole. "Mmmm…" He chews for a moment. "This is really good. You know, I think I should come to dinner."

It just got worse.

Disbelieving and reminding myself of rule number four, I eek, "You want to come to dinner at the Vicente?"

"The Vicente? Sounds exotic." He laughs, expertly raising one eyebrow. "Friday at eight?"

"S-sure." I'm so confused. "Do you have any food allergies?" Curses! *Stupid tongue.*

"Nope. It's a date. I'll bring the wine." With a wink, he grabs the chips and guacamole and heads back toward the living room before I can spout another word.

Just like that the whirlwind is over. I wait for my breathing to return to normal and for my heart to start beating again before grabbing our drinks and following him. Entering the library in a daze, I make a beeline for the couch, careful to keep my eyes focused on my destination.

"Where have you been?" Blair whispers as I hand her a beer.

"Do not talk to me. Do not look at me. I've been making guacamole, and I hate you," I whisper back.

I sink back into the cushions and stare at the TV.

"What happened?" she asks.

"Please. Please leave me alone. I'll tell you later."

"Okaaaaay." Blair nods, probably assuming the worst.

I sneak a glance across the room in Berkeley's direction. He's deep in conversation with Jeff and Alexandra. Good. Two more hours and this horrible night will be over.

The movie plays on and the pizza arrives, but I can't eat. My jaw is locked. As everyone helps themselves and chats between scenes, I steal the occasional peek at Berkeley. He is always preoccupied. It is as though our kitchen conversation never happened, like I don't exist. Perfect. Maybe it didn't happen. Could I have slipped into an alternate reality? I must have. I'll have to consult Psychic Mom on the possibilities.

As the final credits roll, Kim leaps up from her chair. She stumbles, seeming intoxicated as she announces, "Enough watching TV. Let's play Celebrity!"

My heart catches in my throat. Celebrity is a charade-like game where everyone submits celebrity names into a drawing and then acts them out for their teammates. We used to play all the time in college so I'm familiar with the rules, but as far as I'm concerned playing Celebrity with actual celebrities is my worst nightmare. I picture having to act out "Berkeley Dalton" and clam up in fear. "Blair." I moan, squeezing her arm. "Please, my night has been weird enough—we need to *go.*" She doesn't know what I'm talking about, but I hope she will sense my urgency.

With a sigh she leans toward Mark. "We actually have to go—we both have big days tomorrow."

I knew I could count on her.

In a loud voice, Mark responds, "Of course, don't worry about it. I'm glad you could make it," and I can't help but notice he looks to Berkeley for confirmation, like he's asking permission for us to be dismissed. Berkeley's eyes connect with Mark's, and then for the first time since we spoke in the kitchen, he looks at me.

I develop a fascination with the rug.

"Yeah, I have a big pitch meeting in the morning," Blair explains, looking at me sideways. I can tell she doesn't want to leave, but whatever. I blame her for putting me in this situation, and now she has to get me out of it.

We rise to leave, and Blair begins her good-byes. She's taking her time as I uncomfortably stand by. Remembering seeing a restroom near the front door, I decide it might make sense to visit it. With a whisper to Blair that I'll meet her there, I make a grand gesture to the room, saying a bulk "good-bye" and "nice meeting you" to everyone as I exit.

I make it to the bathroom without incident, and realizing I don't need to go, I fidget for a few minutes, fixing my hair and washing my hands. The bathroom's decor is sparse and it seems unused. Without much to look at time passes slowly, and hoping I've been inside long enough for Blair to be ready to go, I head back out into the hallway. As I close the bathroom door behind me, I turn and am startled to see Berkeley leaning in the hallway's doorframe.

My stomach drops, and I don't think before I blurt, "We

have to stop meeting like this."

He laughs, and a little thrill shoots through me. I just made Berkeley Dalton laugh.

Taking me in, he steps forward. "Well, I don't know where the Vicente is," he says. "And maybe I was too presumptuous before—I'll only come over if you want me to."

I feel those eyes on me, and I struggle to hold it together. If I want him to? Does he think I have a choice? For a second I imagine saying no, but it's not in me. It's my nature to try to make him feel comfortable even when I'm *so* uncomfortable. "Of course you should come over if *you* want to. It'll be fun," I lie. *If by fun you mean us staring at each other in painful silence while we both wonder why the heck you came over in the first place and maybe alternate between electrocution and water boarding. Sounds great.*

"Okay, let me give you my number, then. Text me your address, and then I'll have your number, too," he says.

"Sure," I say. Right. As I fumble for my phone and add a new contact, Blair comes around the corner and halts upon seeing us.

I punch in our address. "I'm texting you right now," I say. "Friday at eight?" I confirm, looking up at him.

"See you then," he says with a half smile before turning down the hall.

Blair, having regained her wits, is headed toward us.

I stand still, nodding after him as he retreats, my mind a jumble as Blair reaches me. She stares, eyes wide.

With a glare, I drag her out the front door. We are silent for the walk back up Berkeley's driveway in an unspoken pact that explanations can wait until we are sure there are no excess ears to hear them. The cool air sobers us as we struggle to open the gate. My head is spinning, and I can't think, so I leave it to Blair to produce the correct equation that will facilitate our escape. She prevails, and as soon as we are safely in the car, she pounces.

"What was that about?"

"Apparently it's impossible for me to be in a building with Berkeley Dalton and *not* end up alone with him," I answer. "That was the worst! My jaw hurts so bad from not being able to relax for the last few hours. My entire body is in rigor mortis."

She doesn't take pity. "Aside from that. Friday at eight?"

"He wants to come to dinner."

"Berkeley Dalton is coming to the Vicente?"

"Yes." I briefly recount the guacamole-making episode as Blair hangs on my every word.

"He remembered you from the fashion show and he's coming down from the Hills to the Vicente. Unbelievable."

The people who live in the Hills rarely grace us lowlanders with their presence. The higher you live on the hill, the less reason you have to leave your nest. Everything— and everyone—comes to you.

"Tell me about it. This is crazy. You know me… I'm going to have a nervous breakdown for sure. What are we going to talk about? What are we going to eat? What are we going to *do*? I hope he cancels."

"No you don't. And he won't. I've tasted your guacamole," Blair teases as she parks the car.

"Hate." I toss the word at her, my skin heating at the memory. "Besides, what about Lisa Greene? Isn't she his girlfriend? What does he want with me when he's got her?"

"You know celebrity relationships. They're so on again/

off again. Maybe they broke up...if they were even together in the first place. There didn't seem to be many sparks flying at Elton's," she says as she opens the gate to the courtyard. "He barely looked at her. In fact, from where I was sitting, it seemed he was way more interested in looking at *you.*"

"It's hard to look away from a train wreck," I reply.

"You're impossible."

"What about you and Mark? You seemed to be having a good time."

She purses her lips. "I don't think there's anything there. He's sweet, but he seems really young...he's too much of a guy. I like them more sophisticated."

"But maybe we could double date? It could be fun. Four 'just friends' hanging out?" I'm not giving up on her saving me from having to be alone with Berkeley.

"Ha-ha. You're on your own with this one. Besides, I have a feeling Berkeley would mind the extra company."

I thrust out my lower lip and look to her with pleading eyes in a last effort to get her to give Mark a chance—at my place. On Friday.

She doesn't take pity. "You'll be fine. Nightcap?"

I shake my head. "I'm going in. I need to call my mom for some recipe advice."

With the time difference it's too late to call my mom so I call Boots instead, thinking she might still be up with her crazy school hours. As much as I love Blair, I need to talk to someone who will understand how abnormal this night was—someone who can help me off this cloud. The phone rings four times before she picks up.

"Hi! Sorry I almost missed you—I was cutting my fingernails."

"That sounds important," I tease.

"Oh it is. After my chief resident made me "manually disimpact" a constipated old lady last night, I realized they can never be too short."

"Eew! Boots, that sounds awful," I say, resisting the urge to gag.

"Sadly, I'm getting used to it," she replies. "Fortunately she wasn't as 'impacted' as we thought…"

"Ugh," I groan. "Well, it sounds *almost* as horrific as my night."

"What happened?"

"I don't know where to start. I'm having the weirdest night ever." I take a deep breath and put it out there. "You'll never guess where I watched a movie tonight."

"At Paramount Studios."

"Not even close." I can't contain it any longer and my words gush. "At Berkeley Dalton's house."

Boots is silent. For a moment I think I've lost her, but then I hear her breathing.

"Boots?" I ask. "Are you still there?"

"Yeah—sorry. I'm just trying to wrap my head around what you just said." Her excitement sounds forced as she continues, "That's crazy! Was it a big party?"

"It was only ten of us, actually." Now I'm worrying I sound like I'm bragging, which is the last thing I want.

She sucks in her breath. "Wow, Liv. You definitely travel in different circles than I do." We are both quiet. I think about her day-to-day—the sleepless nights, the stress and pressure she is under all so someday she'll be a brilliant doctor who will save lives—and compare it to how stressed I am about cooking dinner for a rock star, and I feel small. I don't want to tell her the rest.

"Did you talk to him?" She breaks the silence.

"Yes. Never mind," I say, not liking the uncomfortable feeling mentioning Berkeley has caused. "Let's talk about something else. It doesn't matter. Tell me about your craziest patient today."

"Oh no. You're not getting off that easy. I would much rather talk about Berkeley Dalton and those gorgeous blue eyes than the guy who showed up with a knife sticking out of his cheekbone today. I don't know how it missed his eye."

"Yikes," I say, feeling a little better despite the visual. "You were so quiet, I thought maybe you didn't want to hear any more."

"To be honest"—she sighs—"I'm a little jealous. Your life sounds so glamorous, and I'm up to my elbows in blood and bone chips all day. The closest thing I've had to a date lately was with this resident who took me to the pathology lab to show me some specimens and compared each one to food. Like, rotting lung is called caseating necrosis, and it looks like cream cheese—I swear I'm never eating again. Besides, it's nice to be able to focus on something fun for a change. I'll get over it."

"Boots, first of all, ditch the resident, and second of all, I feel the same way. The grass is always greener. I wish I could have your dedication and purpose. Sometimes I feel like my life is so frivolous—I mean, I illustrate G-strings all day! That doesn't do anyone any good."

"I'm sure the entire male population would disagree with you," she replies. "Besides, people need entertainment. I need entertainment to escape how hard my job is every day. Getting a break now and again keeps me sane and helps me focus when it's important. So start talking, and please tell me you at least put your foot in your mouth—it'll make me feel better. Did you remind him that he's taller than you expected?"

"Worse," I declare, feeling better now that we've leveled with each other. I'm determined to play up my lack of composure for her pleasure. "*He* reminded *me* that he's taller than I expected, and then he invited himself to dinner at my apartment on Friday. Just the two of us."

"WHAT? Liv! What did you say?"

"What could I say? I told him okay." I groan. "I don't get it. Why would he want to come over? Do you think it's because I was the weird girl not really talking to anyone and he felt sorry for me?"

"Liv, he wouldn't want to hang out with you if he thought you were the 'weird girl.' He probably thinks you're cute and wants to get to know you better, silly."

"No, that's not why," I dismiss her, refusing to consider the possibility. "It didn't seem like he was hitting on me." I shake my head even though she can't see me. "Maybe he just wants a home-cooked meal. I'm sure he eats out a lot."

I can almost hear her eyes roll. "Well, what are you going to make?"

"I don't know. I'm so stressed."

"I don't blame you... I take it all back. I'd rather remove infected bone from some old lady's butt than be in your shoes."

"Me, too." I laugh.

I fill her in on the whole impossible story, and we talk into the night. Promising to call her as soon as Berkeley leaves and to have her paged if she doesn't answer, we hang up and I drift into a fitful sleep.

Chapter Thirteen

Mrs. Bloom @PsychicMom1
Oh shoot. Missed the Festival of Carna, the Roman
goddess of bodily organs. Next year.

"I'm so hungover," Gemma says, plopping down on the
chair in my office as I am sleepily reillustrating a babydoll/
thong set for the fourth time. Wearing a black minidress with
a white lace collar and her hair held back by a double crystal
headband, she must be the only person a hangover looks
good on.

"What did you do last night?" I ask.

"I went to happy hour with a bunch of girls from the
denim company I used to work at. They're crazy. We ended
up singing Journey at a karaoke bar in Koreatown until two
in the morning. I have no clue how I got home." She takes
a sip of her coconut water. "I'm going straight to yoga after

work. Wreck and repair." She smiles. "What'd you do?"

"You don't want to know." I grimace. I know she's going to freak, but after Boots's initial reaction last night, I prefer not to talk about it.

"Oh, tell me a story, anything to get my mind off this headache," she pleads.

"Oh, it's a story all right," I say, excitement getting the best of me as I give in. I haven't been able to concentrate all morning; all I can think about is him. Besides, the way Gemma looks, I'm sure she's no stranger to guys cornering her in kitchens. "I was randomly invited to Berkeley Dalton's house for movie night," I say.

"What?" She sits up straight in her chair.

"Oh, it gets stranger." I tell her the whole story.

When I finish, she stares, not sure what to make of me. "Liv, that's insane."

"I agree."

"What are you going to do? How can you be so calm? I would be losing it."

"Cook, I guess?" As I shrug, I feel a sense of pride. If a girl like Gemma would crack, I'm impressed I've held it together this long.

Just then Lillian pops her head into my office. "Good morning."

Gemma pulls herself out of her slump. "Good morning!" She tries to be cheery.

"I need to meet with both of you in the conference room in ten minutes," Lillian says. "Gemma, can you bring the artwork we just bought?"

"Of course."

Lillian leaves as Gemma moves toward the door but

not before turning back to me. "Does he have any single friends?" she asks.

"I'm sure he does." I laugh.

Ten minutes later, I join Lillian and Gemma in the conference room. The table is covered in fabric swatches, laces, and prints.

"Have a seat, Liv," Lillian says, and I choose the chair next to Gemma.

"I asked you girls here because I'd like your help on a project. Nordstrom has asked us to design a bridal collection aimed at young brides. It should be fun and flirty—but tasteful—something not embarrassing to open at a bridal shower. I'm flying to Seattle next week to present concepts to them, so we'll need to make boards, and I'd like you to make them for me. You girls are the customer, so I want to know what you'd like to wear. Take some time this week and go through prints, draw up some bodies, pick out laces and trims, tear out trend inspiration—basically design me a little collection that you and your friends would want to wear. Do you think you can do that for me by Friday?"

My skin erupts in goose bumps, and Gemma and I look at each other before turning back to Lillian, nodding eagerly. She wants us to design a collection for Nordstrom? Insane! I immediately start daydreaming about walking into the lingerie department and seeing *my* design prominently displayed on a mannequin.

"We can definitely get that to you by Friday," Gemma says, snapping me back to reality.

"Absolutely. We'll start right now," I add.

"Wonderful. Let me know if you have any questions," Lillian says as she stands to leave.

As soon as she's gone, Gemma and I dive in, draping each other in silks and laces, imagining the nighttime version of our wedding dresses.

"I think I'm going to wear a tight, short, stretch-lace chemise trimmed with pearls," Gemma decides.

"I'm thinking a chiffon babydoll/thong set with molded cups and pale blue satin bows," I say.

It's a dream come true, playing dress-up with endless fabric and lace at my disposal. *Edith! Cecil! I've arrived!*

And, added bonus, for a few hours as I concentrate on the project, my mind is a Berkeley-free zone.

That all changes as soon as I get in my car to go home. The previous night comes flooding back and I start to panic about dinner. Time to call Mom.

"Hello?" she answers.

"Hi, it's me," I announce to the car as I drive. (Hands-free!)

"Hi, sweetie! How are you? I was just thinking about you!"

Of course she was.

" O h h h h h h h m m m m … O h h h h h h h m m m m … Ohhhhhhhmmmm…"

"Mom? What's that noise? Are you in a room full of ghosts?"

She laughs. "No, it's my Clairvoyant Certification Course. We're learning to connect to our True Selves."

Oh brother.

"Well, I don't want to interrupt. I just needed some recipe ideas for this dinner I'm cooking Friday night. If you have some ideas, maybe you could e-mail them to me? It's a dinner for two."

This spikes her interest. "Really, what's the special occasion?"

"I'm celebrating the anniversary of my most embarrassing Hollywood moment," I say in my best blank voice. "It's a theme, really, so like I said, if you have any ideas…"

The phantoms continue their gothic dance. "Ohhhhhhhmmmm…"

Distracted, she responds, "That's nice, honey."

"Okay, Mom. I'm going to let you go," I offer, sensing her diverted attention.

"No! Wait. I forgot to tell you. I was working a Chakra Cross Tarot Spread on you the other night, and this is very interesting…"

I wish I could mute her. I've decided it's inappropriate to hang up on my mother without so much as a Namaste, but that doesn't mean I want to subject myself to her predictions. I try to tune her out.

"The Wheel of Fortune card was upright in your Universe," she explains. "The upright Wheel of Fortune represents good luck, destiny, and fate—a turning point—and having it in your Universe means it's all completely out of your control. But, what's really interesting," she continues, "is that Death is before you."

I snap back to her after that one.

"What does that mean?" I ask, letting my annoyance show.

"The Death Card means transformation. It's like changing from the physical body to the spiritual being. It can represent changing something as simple as an attitude, but for the most part it means change is on its way. The best part, though, is because it's combined with the Wheel of Fortune in your Universe, good changes are coming, and there's nothing you can do about it!" She is triumphant.

"That *is* great news. Hey, if your cards tell you what I should make for dinner, let me know." I'm driving into my usual dead zone and I know my phone will drop her soon.

"No problem, Love!"

"Namaste."

"Namaste."

She e-mails me the next day:

Mom's Best Love Potion

1/3 cup lemon blossoms, gathered in moonlight

3 tsp. honey (use a copper measuring spoon)

3 cloves

3 cups black tea (preferably imported from Tibet)

3 mint leaves (crushed with a marble mortar & pestle)

Light 3 votives and brew in a copper kettle until potion is the desired darkness. Before pouring, stir the potion clockwise with a wooden spoon while chanting,

"By the Light of the Moon, our Love will Bloom

May the Powers that Be Hear my Plea

And See that Forever Entwined, our Lives will Bind."

Cook's Note: This is best prepared during a full moon.

Right. I can see I'm on my own here.

Chapter Fourteen

PARKER MIFFLIN @IsIndulgent
A certain so & so is coming to the Vicente! What will I wear?!?!

OLIVIA BLOOM @BloomOlivia
@IsIndulgent You will wear your invisibility cloak. You promised. No interruptions.

PARKER MIFFLIN @IsIndulgent
@BloomOlivia The courtyard is public domain, sweetie. And I happen to LOVE lounging there in my Vilebrequins.

Friday night arrives, misty and gray. My hope Berkeley will cancel proves futile when he texts me "see you tonight."

Resigned to getting the evening over with, and with no thanks to my mother, I've opted for a French theme. I'm putting the finishing touches on the French onion soup when I hear the knock at my door. My nerves are stretched to a breaking point, and I have no idea if my stomach will allow me to partake in the feast I am preparing. With my luck, I'll take a bite and immediately regurgitate it on the table, thereby sealing my fate as Miss Awkward Universe.

Wiping my hands on the floral-print apron I wear knotted at my waist, I walk grudgingly to the door. Turning up the music on my iPod speakers as I pass them (I've chosen a mix of Motown and classic rock—hopefully that's safe), on an inhale I open the door. Exhale, our eyes meet. Inhale, ignore the cold goose-bump shower. Exhale, open the door wider. Inhale, away we go. Exhale, "Hi. Come on in."

I can't believe he's really here.

Berkeley crosses the threshold into my apartment, taking in the whole expanse in about twenty seconds. "It smells good in here," he says, standing uncomfortable but beautiful just inside the door. He is casually dressed in slim jeans and a button-down shirt. His hair is disheveled and a faint scruffiness that indicates he hasn't shaved highlights his strong jaw. He is perfect.

He hands me the bottle of wine he's brought and self-consciously gives me the hug/cheek kiss combo. Having never touched him beyond a handshake, this seems way too intimate, and I'm stiff as a board as he puts his arm around me. He comes in for the cheek kiss too quickly and I panic, turning my head the wrong way so he ends up grazing my hair somewhere around my ear. Cheek-kiss fail. Is it possible that I've met my match in the awkward cheek-kiss competition? I doubt it.

Forcing myself to focus, my peacemaker sensibility kicks into overdrive and I set my mind to putting us both at ease.

"Thanks. I may need a little help, if that's okay," I say, thinking if our hands are busy it will give us something to focus on other than how out of the ordinary this is. Well, it's unusual for *me*. I can't vouch for Berkeley. Maybe he invites himself over to random girls' apartments all the time.

"Sure," he replies, his eyes never leaving my face. "Just tell me what to do."

Blushing under his scrutiny, I hold up the wine. "Maybe we should start with opening this. It'll take the edge off," I suggest.

His eyes light up with an intoxicating smile. Who needs wine? "I think that's a good idea," he agrees.

I lead him around the corner to my little yellow kitchen, gathering my wits along the way. "We're having French onion soup and steak frites… I hope that's okay," I say as I hand him the wine opener and pull down two glasses.

"Sounds fabulous," he says, seeming like he means it as he checks out the room. "Great apartment. I'm really into 1930s architecture. I love all of the arches and exposed wood. This place has good character."

I nod, knowingly.

"How long have you been here?" he asks as he opens the wine and fills our glasses. I can't help but notice how strong his hands are, no doubt from years spent playing guitar.

"I moved from Pittsburgh a couple months ago," I answer, trying to keep my mind on the conversation.

"Cool. Pittsburgh's fun. We had a day off there during our last tour so we got to see the city a little. It has a great vibe. Very artsy.''

"It does. I liked it there. Did you eat at Primanti Brothers?"

"No. What's that?"

"Just try it next time you're there. It'll change your life." I hand him a knife. "How are your mushroom-slicing skills?"

"Probably not as good as yours, but I'll give it a shot." He grins.

We stand next to each other in the tiny kitchen, slicing mushrooms in silence, and I realize it's now or never. Taking a sip of wine, I gather the courage to ask the question that's been plaguing me since guacamole night. "So why are you here?" That came out wrong.

He looks at me long-ways, eyebrows raised, as I flounder. "I mean, not *why are you here*, but why did you want to come to dinner? I'm a little confused," I confess. "I guess it caught me off guard you would remember me from the fashion show…and you would still want to talk to me after I was such an imbecile."

He lets out a little laugh. "I appreciate your honesty," he says, "so I guess I should be honest with you." He hesitates as if unsure how to put it. "I thought you were charming at the fashion show. You had kind of a *Roman Holiday* thing going on, but that's not why I invited myself over." He pauses. "You may recall I've seen you since then… For starters, you ruined my show."

My stomach drops and my cheeks burn. I truly think he's going to ask me to pay for the equipment I destroyed. "You're right. I'm so sorry about that. I don't know how I can make it up to you. I didn't think the beer made it over the electrical tape line. I don't have very much money…

what can I do to fix it?"

He looks at me like I've just sprouted fangs and rabbit ears. "*What* are you talking about?"

Just call me *Bunnicula*.

"I spilled a beer at your show and it got all over the trunk we were sitting on. I thought we cleaned it up in time…"

His eyes assault me with their full force and he grabs my arm. "No," he says. And more to himself he whispers, "You funny girl." He drops my arm and turns back to the mushrooms. "I meant before the show. I saw you and I got nervous," he reveals. "You looked so pretty; I was afraid to talk to you." He turns back to me and his eyes search my face. "Then I was anxious about performing in front of you. I kept seeing you in the wings. It's always strange when someone catches your eye when you're performing, but when you recognize the person it's even more distracting. I was too focused on you and hoping you were having a good time, and it ended up being a bad show."

Hold on. *I* make *him* nervous? What is he talking about? The words refuse to sink in.

"I think that's giving me a little too much credit," I murmur. "You were incredible."

His eyes hold mine. "I wanted to apologize for being rude," he says.

"You don't need to apologize. You more than made it up to me at Elton's Oscar party." I don't know if he equates me with the girl who put her foot in her mouth, seeing as that was TV Olivia, but this is my opportunity to thank *him*.

"Did you like the song?" he asks, his lips stretching into a smile as his eyes search my face, like my answer is important to him.

That answers that. *So he did recognize me.* "The song?" I repeat.

"The Bruno Mars/Police mash-up."

"Yeah. I *loved* it. It was so original. It's pretty crazy you picked those songs. Did you know Billy Crystal was going to sing over the Police?"

"No." He laughs. Apparently my ears and fangs are growing. "Liv, that was for you. I didn't know we were going to play it until I left the table."

"You wrote it on the spot?" *For me?*

"Well, we had three hours. The Oscars are pretty long and boring, and there's almost nothing I'd rather be doing than playing music. You inspired me. Besides, that guy who was laughing was being a dick. You were right, those songs are really similar. It just takes someone with a good ear to pick up on it."

I have no words so I stare at him blankly.

"I'm glad you liked it," he says. "And I was hoping to talk to you after the show, but I guess you'd already left. That's why I had Mark throw movie night."

Again, his words meet a wall. Can this get any more insane? "You staged a movie night to meet girls?" *To meet me?* "Is that normal?"

"Well, to meet *a* girl," he confirms. "And, yeah, it's normal. Mark throws parties all the time so girls will come over—but so they can meet him, not me. My house is the bait. This is the first time I've tried it."

"Wow, that's bizarre." I laugh, deciding just to go with it. I'll ponder this information later. "Then apology accepted. I'm sorry about the beer. And thank you for the song."

He laughs with me. "You're welcome. More wine?"

"I'll try to refrain from spilling it on you." *Seriously.*

The timer on the oven goes off and I bend over to retrieve the soup while he pours. Setting the soup on the counter, cheese bubbles over the sides of the crocks, and I hand him a spoon. We stand and eat as I put the fries into the oven and adjust the timer. Now that we've cleared the air, we ease into a more comfortable rhythm. I'm even able to swallow a couple bites of soup.

"This is really good," he says, polishing off his bowl. "Better than in France."

"Thanks." I smile, dismissing the compliment as I put steaks into a cast-iron pan to sear them. I have Berkeley start chopping shallots, and looking down at his forearms below the rolled cuffs of his shirtsleeves I notice his skin is smooth and clean.

"You don't have any tattoos," I say. "That's unusual for a musician."

"They're so permanent—I guess I've always been a little afraid of forever," he replies. Then, stopping to think for a minute, he elaborates. "When I was younger, I always planned on getting one when my first album came out."

"But that was four albums ago. What happened?" I ask, not bothering to hide my intricate knowledge of his discography.

"Well, it all happened kind of fast. I thought I'd have to fight to make it for a lot longer than I did, and when the first album came out, it wasn't what I'd envisioned it to be. The record label was really involved, and I felt like it wasn't mine anymore," he divulges. "The label was right, though. We were a huge hit. Those first few years were exhilarating. The moment you're on stage in a city you've never been to before and the crowd starts singing your words back to you is like nothing else. It's a high you can never feel again. You chase it, and the thing is, once you define a sound it's hard to reinvent yourself. The fans make you, so you owe it to them to give them what they want, even if you've moved on as an artist. Before I knew it, we were working on the second album so, I guess, in a way I'm still waiting to write *my* first album."

"I'd love to hear it when you do."

"I look forward to playing it for you," he says, the corners of his mouth hinting at a smile.

The air around us thickens and seems to shimmer. The kitchen is getting warm.

"Blowtorch time," I announce, breaking the tension as I add brandy to the pan on the stove. "Could you reach into that drawer behind you and pull out the lighter? We have to ignite the sauce."

He turns toward the designated drawer, and I lean over his shoulder to look for the lighter. As he tugs on the swollen drawer, it sticks with age, forcing him to yank harder. This time, it gives way more easily than he anticipated, and his right elbow thrusts back and nails me in the left boob.

"Oooh." I double over, giggling and in pain. "Ouch."

Caught off guard and seemingly uncertain of how to react, his immediate reaction is to grab me and pull me into his chest. Locking me in a full embrace, he holds me for a moment longer than necessary. His skin smells clean, like he's just stepped out of a spa, and I can feel the strength in his chest through his thin shirt. It's nice here, I think, enjoying feeling his arms around me. I allow my head to lie against his shoulder and let myself go. *See ya later rule number seven.*

It's strangely comfortable in his arms; like I belong here. My heart pounds at the thought.

"I'm so sorry. Are you okay?" He releases me.

"I'll survive." I smile, my legs unsteady. Our eyes meet and I take an awkward step back, turning and trying to compose myself. I light the sauce and shake the pan as blue flames flare in front of us. "Ready to eat?"

We fill our plates and head into my little breakfast nook. It is intimate, our faces close across the tiny table, and there is a momentary silence as neither of us knows what to say. The silence stretches on, and I rack my brain for something to fill the space, finally blurting, "So how did the Brightside meet?" I already know he and Mark have been friends forever, but it's the first thing I can think to say. Besides, I want to hear the story straight from the source.

"I've talked enough." He smiles, the tension breaking. "Tell me about you. What do you do?"

"Well, the first thing you need to know about me is I'd rather talk about you," I reply. "So please tell me. And I'm an assistant lingerie designer."

"That sounds far more interesting to me," he says.

I don't respond. Instead I pick up a fry and make a show of biting into it, staring at him expectantly as I chew.

"Fine." He laughs, cutting into his steak and swirling it in the sauce. I notice he eats like he's European, keeping his fork in his left hand as he takes a bite.

"I've known Mark since second grade and Jeff since high school—he was in a band called Star Shoes then. After graduation Mark and I lived together at UCLA and Ted was our roommate our freshman year. We started the Brightside, and Jeff joined later when his band broke up."

"That's cool you've known each other so long. And you were an overnight success?"

"Hardly." He swallows. "Being in a band is a lot of work and there's tons of rejection—it's almost impossible to be successful. We got lucky. Haynes found us and got us our first record deal. We were turned down by every label in the US, so we had to move to London to get someone to sign us. That's why we spend so much time in Europe. We have a big fan base over there. In fact, I'm headed to Spain tomorrow. This is amazing by the way." He gestures at his plate and looks at it in comparison to mine. I haven't touched my steak. "You should try it," he suggests.

"That sounds fun," I say, scrunching my nose and slicing off a miniscule bite, fearing the scene should it get stuck in my throat. I'm not relaxed to the point that swallowing steak is a good idea yet.

He sits back, watching me pick at my food. "I'm not looking forward to it, actually," he says. "Being on tour can be lonely." His eyes move from my plate to my face, sending a jolt through me. "I always get homesick."

"But you do it anyway?" I ask, my stomach twisting and officially choosing to ignore the meat while his eyes are on me.

"Getting to play music makes it worth it," he says, seeming to accept my inability to eat by diving back into his meal. "Even if it was only for ten people, I'd still be playing somewhere. As long as one person is connecting to the song—as long as it means something to someone—it's all worth it to me. There's no greater feeling than being able to creatively share your truth with someone else—for them to be touched by it enough to make it their own is the ultimate reward."

"That's beautiful," I say, thinking about all the times I've walked the streets with his music in my ears—how many times his words have guided me through tough times. My right arm erupts in goose bumps as I search his face and muse out loud, "You've always done that for me. I remember when I bought *Dear Rose,*. I was sixteen and ran upstairs and closed the door and listened to it on repeat for hours. It was the first album I listened to in my car when I got my license—I loved it—and everything ever since. Your music is sort of my soundtrack."

He puts down his knife and fork as our eyes lock. "Thank you."

The words hang in the air and the tension mounts. Awe that I'm sitting here with him washes over me in waves as I realize I've admitted too much. Afraid I sound like a stalker superfan, I close my eyes, breaking the connection.

When I reopen them, he's still staring at me.

I blush at the concentration reflected on his face and move to divert his attention. "What was your major at UCLA?" I ask, picking up my plate and carrying it into the kitchen.

He narrows his eyes, looking like he wants to say something, but holds back and succumbs to my line of questioning. "Economics." He picks up his now empty plate and follows me to the sink.

"Econ? Not music? Not writing?"

"No." He shakes his head. "My dad was adamant I have something to fall back on." He rinses his plate and picks up a sponge while I scrape my dinner into a container. "I'm glad he forced me into Econ, though, because at the end of the day the band is a business, and it's good to be able to look at it that way."

"I never thought about it like that," I say. "You don't have to do that." I point to the pile of dishes he's started washing.

"You cooked, and I don't mind. Now it's your turn. What about you? What was your major?" he asks.

"Journalism."

"Journalism, not fashion?"

"I would have loved to major in fashion," I say, grabbing a towel and drying. "But to be honest, I've always been a little embarrassed about having such a frivolous dream. Part of me always thought people would laugh if I told them what I really wanted to do, so I kept my dreams a secret and majored in something sensible."

"I get that. I used to feel that way, too, but I promise your dreams aren't frivolous. There's nothing frivolous about doing what you were born to do."

"I wish it was easy for me to see it that way—but I can't help but compare myself to people like my cousin Boots, who's in medical school. She's going to really help people someday, and I can't see how pursuing fashion can have impact like that."

He nods his understanding. "I guess I'm lucky. Growing up in LA, people are making their dreams come true all around you, and I've seen how much following your own passions gives you the power to make other people's dreams come true. It makes it easier to believe it's possible. Had I grown up somewhere else, maybe I wouldn't have had the courage to try—to pick up and move here and risk everything." He looks at me out of the corner of his eye. "I admire people who are brave enough to do that."

My face heats, and I turn my back on him, busying myself putting dishes away.

Knock, knock, knock. The sound comes from the front door. I ignore it.

That's odd. Blair and Parker promised me *complete* privacy, even though I'm pretty sure they're camped on the balcony waiting to catch a glimpse of Berkeley on his way out.

Knock, knock, knock. The sound grows more persistent as I become more annoyed. Why won't they leave me alone?

"Do you want me to get that?" he asks.

"No." I sigh. "I'll get it." I jog to the door. Expecting to see Blair and Parker on the other side, I stick my head out and sternly say, "What do you want?"

Oh shit.

My eyes go first to the flowers in his hand before traveling up to his face in disbelief. I'd recognize the eyes behind those glasses anywhere; I spent three years gazing into them.

Startled, my ex-boyfriend Michael takes a step back from the doorway.

Chapter Fifteen

Mrs. Bloom @PsychicMom1
@BloomOlivia The fortune cookie never lies: A
traveler waits for you.

No no no no no no NO! Not happening. Not now. If ever there's a time for an ex-boyfriend to *not* show up on a doorstep, it's now. My instinct is to slam the door in his face, but that won't do any good. I need to get rid of him. Quietly, I slip outside, pulling the door shut behind me, guiding him into the courtyard. "What are you doing here?" I ask in an urgent whisper, silently pleading for the sick joke to end.

"I thought I'd surprise you."

"You succeeded."

"I can't believe it's you. You look really pretty, Liv. Prettier than I remembered."

My face flushes. "Thanks, you look—" I notice his

pants are a little too baggy and he's wearing outdated running shoes. His style hasn't evolved since college, and the sharpness of my observation alerts me to how much I've changed. "You look good, too, Mike," I say. "Do you mind if I ask how you found me?"

"I took a cab," he says.

"All the way from Pennsylvania? I mean, how did you get my address?"

"Your mom gave it to me."

That figures. Apparently the moon currently isn't in her house of timing.

"Why are you here?" I ask for the second time tonight. "You couldn't have called first?" *You can't come inside! I have a secret—I'm hiding an A-list celebrity in my kitchen!*

"I wasn't sure you'd let me come over," he admits. "I'm in town for work, but I came in a couple days early. I thought we could talk."

"We don't have anything to talk about, and it's not a good time," I plead.

Just then, the door opens behind me and Berkeley steps into the cool night air.

Michael's face goes white with recognition, and I close my eyes. During the course of our relationship, we enjoyed plenty of Berkeley & the Brightside albums. We even drove to New Jersey once to see them play. He's as much a fan as I am, and I can't imagine what he's thinking in this moment. I just hope he doesn't ask for an autograph.

"Hey, man," Berkeley acknowledges Michael with a brief nod as he steps into the courtyard and turns to me. "I should probably go. It's getting late, and I should finish packing."

A pang shoots through me. I don't want him to leave. "Are you sure you have to go? This is my friend Michael." I rush an introduction. "But he was just leaving."

Michael is staring at us, lips parted, as his eyes flit back and forth between Berkeley and me. I wish I had a magic wand to shoot at him and make him disappear. *Poof!*

Berkeley smiles down at me. "Yeah, I think I should go."

"Can I at least walk you to your car?" I know I can't hold him hostage, but I'm not ready for the night to be over. Not giving him a chance to refuse, I start walking him to the gate. "I'll talk to you later, Mike," I toss over my shoulder, suggesting he, too, should go.

"Sure," Mike mumbles, not moving. At least the shock of seeing Berkeley has rendered him somewhat speechless.

"I'm sorry," I apologize to Berkeley once we're on the other side of the gate. "He's an old friend. I wasn't expecting him."

Our short walk ends as we reach his Audi. Standing between Berkeley and the car, I turn to face him.

"I think he likes you," he teases, his eyes searching my face.

"Oh no. No, he doesn't. I promise. No chance," I reply.

His eyes darken. "I don't blame him," he says, his voice gravel. My insides constrict as energy reverberates around us. Berkeley reaches out and runs his fingers through my hair, leaving heat imprints on my scalp as they pass, and I don't resist as he cups the back of my neck. It's like a silver chord ties me to him as our eyes lock. My breath catches in my throat, but I tilt my head back to connect further with his gaze. I want nothing more than for him to kiss me. Inches from touching, we are tight with tension. He leans toward me as I sink back against the car ready to accept him.

"BOOOOOW   OWWWWWW   BOOOOOOW

OWWWWW- BOOOOOOOW OWWWWW- MEH-MEH-
MEH-MEH-MEH-MEH- EEEEEEEE OOOOOOOOOO
-EEEEE OOOOOOOOOO…"

I close my eyes in disbelief as the world rights itself.

Amused, Berkeley lets go of me and inserts his key in the door lock, turning off the alarm. "I'll call you when I get back from Europe?" he asks once silence is restored.

"I'd like that. How long will you be gone?"

"Two weeks. It's just a few spot dates."

"What's all that racket?" Willis's front door bangs shut behind him as he waddles onto his front porch.

"Sorry, Willis," I call as I wave him off. "It's okay. We accidentally set off the alarm. We're fine."

"Oh! Okay. Just makin' sure no riffraff was botherin' you!" He eyes Berkeley, tapping Betty in his pocket.

"No riffraff here," I reply.

"All right. All right," he says with a cheery wave before shuffling back inside.

"Friendly neighbors." Berkeley smiles, raising his eyebrows.

"Hmmmm…you could say that…"

He steps forward, and in an instant his arms are around me, igniting my body with his heat. "I had a nice time, Liv," he says into my ear.

"Me, too," I whisper back. *Too nice.*

He releases me to the cold night and, rubbing my arms, I step back as he gets into his car.

"Bye." He nods, closing the door.

"Good-bye." I grant him a sad half smile, and with a tiny wave, watch him speed away.

Turning my back on fairy tales, I walk slowly toward reality.

Chapter Sixteen

BLAIR HAMILTON @SUPERSPINSTRESS
@BLOOMOLIVIA MEANING?!? RT @BERKELEYBRTSIDE
HAVE A FEELING IT MIGHT BE HARD TO STAY FOCUSED.
HOPEFULLY A TRIP TO MADRID WILL DO THE TRICK.

OLIVIA BLOOM @BLOOMOLIVIA
@SUPERSPINSTRESS OMG. WOULD YOU CUT IT OUT!?! HE CAN
SEE THAT YOU KNOW. I'M QUITE SURE THAT WAS IN REFERENCE
TO JET LAG. #HATE

I take my time walking back to my apartment, trying to wrap my head around everything that happened tonight and collect my thoughts. The shock of seeing Michael hasn't worn off, and even though I was rude to him, I don't feel bad. What, he thinks he can show up on my doorstep after not talking to me for three months and I'll welcome him with open arms?

Letting myself back into the courtyard, I'm disheartened to find him still waiting for me.

"Hi," I say.

Seeming to have regained his composure, he doesn't return the greeting. "Was that the real Berkeley Dalton?"

Here we go.

"It was. The real, live, authentic Berkeley Dalton," I reply, coming to a stop across from him and folding my arms across my chest.

"Crazy. What was he doing here?" he asks, trying to sound innocent.

How can I explain this without going into too much detail? Well, I made an ass out of myself in front of him at a fashion show, which he somehow found charming, and then he ignored me at a concert and felt bad about it, so he threw a party to meet me and I made some guacamole, which he liked, so he invited himself over for dinner—Right.

Instead, I respond lightly, as if things like this are common, "Oh, we had a misunderstanding a while back, and he came over so we could clear it up."

"Wow. The last time I saw you, you were waiting tables in Pittsburgh, and now here you are getting in fights with rock stars." He looks impressed. "Isn't he dating Lisa Greene?" he adds, offhandedly.

"Is he?" I pretend he didn't just stab me in the heart. "I hadn't heard. I try not to read the tabloids." I lie. "And, for the record, it wasn't an argument, just a miscommunication. We don't know each other well enough to argue."

Michael seems relieved. "Well, for the record, I don't read the tabloids, either. I just came from the airport, is all.

That stuff is hard to miss — "

My teeth are chattering, and I want to go inside to rehash this evening's more pleasant events so I cut him off. "What do you want, Michael?"

The Vicente's gate slams shut behind me and I turn to see a pretty girl struggling with an oversized suitcase. This must be Jessie, the girl from apartment three getting back from the crazy trip she's been on for the last couple months. Having yet to meet her, I hate that her first impression of me is a domestic dispute in the courtyard.

"Hi." I greet her. "I'm Liv. I moved in to number one. Do you need help with that?"

"No, thanks." She smiles. "I'm Jessie. It's great to meet you. I'm in three." She glances at Michael, expectantly.

"This is my friend Michael," I supply.

"Nice to meet you," she says as she rolls her suitcase toward her apartment, seeming to not want to interrupt. "I just got back from a really long trip and am dying for my own bed," she explains her quick exit. "But I'm sure I'll see you around."

"Yeah, I hope so," I say as she unlocks her door and steps inside. "Have a good night."

"You, too."

"You're freezing. Why don't we go inside and talk there?" Michael says after her door closes.

"I'm fine," I whisper. I don't want Jessie to overhear us, but I'm afraid if I let him in, he'll never leave. "Just say what you came to say."

He takes a deep breath. "Okay. I've been doing a lot of thinking. I've missed you, and I wanted to see if I could take you to dinner while I'm in town. Just as friends."

Looking at his hopeful eyes, I consider the offer. He came to LA early to see me, and I'm afraid disappointing him will make me feel guilty. I don't have feelings for him anymore—seeing him again tonight has made me certain of that—and it might be fun to spend time with someone from home who knows me so well…but it feels like a giant step backward. When he cheated on me he released me from the "safe and expected" path I was on, and made me hear the tiny voice begging me to follow my dreams that had been roaring inside me for years. I'm not going to stop listening to it anytime soon.

"I don't think it's a good idea," I decide.

"Please, Liv. If we could sit down and talk, it would mean so much to me." His voice cracks in desperation and I start to waver—I don't like hurting his feelings. *Maybe I should hear him out*…but that little voice flares up inside me, reminding me I've cried over him enough.

"There's nothing left to say, Mike."

"Yes there is," he says. "Guilt has been eating away at me since you left. I need to know you forgive me."

"I forgave you months ago, you know that," I reply. "I've moved on and you should, too. Why do you want to reopen old wounds?"

He runs his fingers through his hair as his shoulders visibly tense. Taking a step toward me, his eyes are pleading for me to hug him—to make it all better. It seems unfair for him to be putting this on me, like it's *my* fault *he* feels guilty, and I refrain from consoling him.

"Don't you believe in second chances?" he asks.

"Yes." I sigh, stepping away from him toward the security of my apartment. "But we've been through this,

Mike. I already tried, and I don't think your second chance is with me. I know you won't make the same mistake again, and I hope for you loads of happiness with whoever the next girl is." I've never been able to make him understand that it wasn't his infidelity that made me leave—that it was *me* not him—and I can't devote any more energy to explaining that we're not meant to be. It's something he needs to come to terms with on his own. Opening my front door, I prepare to go inside.

"If you leave right now, I'm never talking to you again," he says, his grief turning to anger over not getting his way and confirming for me I'm doing the right thing.

"Maybe that's for the best," I calmly reply. "Enjoy the rest of your trip." I close the door behind me, making certain to lock it. Safe on the other side, I exhale, my head spinning, shocked that I was able to stay so cool. Three months ago I would have been crying along with him, trying to make him feel better—heck I probably would've let him stay the night! *Backbone? Where'd you come from?*

I avoid looking into the courtyard to see if Michael has left and finish putting away the dishes, missing Berkeley. He took the apartment's warmth with him, and it echoes with emptiness. Hyperaware of my aloneness, I put on my pj's and crawl into bed to text Boots.

"Mayday, Mayday! Intruder alert!" I type. "You'll never guess who showed up at my apartment tonight."

My phone lights up with her response. "Berkeley Dalton, I hope!"

"Him, too."

"Too? How'd it go?"

"He was wonderful. It was oddly comfortable, once I got

past how hot he is."

"Wow! He's nice?"

"*So* nice. It was perfect until...Michael showed up."

"NO! WTF? Michael, Michael?"

"Yes. Michael, Michael."

"What did you do? What did *he* do?"

"I freaked, Michael almost passed out, Berkeley left— he's leaving for Europe tomorrow and will call when he gets back."

"OMG."

"Yep." My fingers are tired and I sign off. "Will call you with details later. Must lay in bed and rehash. ☺ Good night!"

Lying back, I push the Michael incident out of my head, and start at the beginning of the night...

Chapter Seventeen

BERKELEY DALTON @BRIGHTSIDEBP

PARIS. NOT SO ROMANTIC WHEN SHARING A BUS WITH @
BRIGHTSIDEBP. IT'S WORTH IT FOR THE AMAZING CROWD AT
THE TRABENDO, THOUGH. SEE YOU TONIGHT!

MARK VANCLEER @BRIGHTSIDEBP
@BERKELEY BRTSIDE BRO, NO MORE FOOT MASSAGES FOR YOU
THEN.

I promise myself I will forget Berkeley and focus on work,
but I know I'm lying. It may not be healthy, but my mind finds
it easier to contemplate the inner musings of a certain lead
singer than to think about what width bra strap elastic goes
on a molded-cup babydoll. I try not to obsess, but before
long, my lunch breaks are devoted to reading past *Rolling
Stone* and *Interview* articles starring Berkeley, and the more

I read, the more distracted I become. I try to avoid clicking on the images tab in Google because the first four pages are all pictures of Berkeley and Christina Carlton: images of Berkeley and Christina on the red carpet, images of them holding hands running through LAX, images of them deep in conversation at a tapas bar in London, images with "Not yet!" and "Engaged?" splattered in fluorescent colors across them are peppered in with more recent tabloid shots of Berkeley and Lisa Greene drinking coffee and shopping. The photos serve as a glaring reminder that I don't belong in his world and further justify my confusion as to why he would make time to talk to me in the first place. How can I compete with this? I can't. I know I should force myself to look at them, to keep my feet on the ground, but I don't want to. Instead, addicted to the emotions he inspires in me, I keep reading.

My favorite piece is a *Los Angeles Magazine* Q & A from several years ago, published just after the release of the first Berkeley & the Brightside album, *Dear Rose,*. It is becoming my routine to reread it over my morning coffee after I get to work, trying to glean from the article every possible insight into Berkeley's psyche.

In the midst of his band's slew of recent Grammy nominations, a media storm seems to follow Berkeley Dalton wherever he goes. Fortunately, we were able to catch him at King's Road Coffee for a quick chat about his LA upbringing, what inspires him, and what it's like to suddenly be so famous.

Talent seems to run in your family. Your father is a major real estate developer, your mother is a famous

novelist, and your sister is an up-and-coming actress. What made you choose music? *I guess music has always been a part of my life. My parents started sending me to piano lessons at a very young age. I hated practicing back then. It was torture being forced to play the same progressions over and over. They wouldn't let me quit, though, and I'm grateful they didn't. My grandfather gave me a guitar the summer I turned fourteen and it opened up a new world to me. I began writing my own music and eventually I started a band with a couple of guys at UCLA.*

You grew up in LA. Are you glad you did, or do you wish you'd had a less glossy upbringing? *I wouldn't exactly call my upbringing glossy. Yes, I grew up in Beachwood Canyon, but my parents were totally against things like private schools and trust funds. I went to public school just like everyone else, and I never had an easy ride. If I wanted something, I had to earn it. I love LA, though. My mother grew up on a winery in Stellenbosch, a Dutch settlement just outside Cape Town in South Africa, and we used to spend a couple of weeks every summer visiting my grandparents there. It's beautiful, of course, but it could never compete with the feeling the first glimpse of downtown LA would give me on our drive back from the airport. It has a spark, you know?*

Your debut album, *Dear Rose,* has been both critically and commercially successful. How has that changed your life? *I guess it's a little harder to run out and grab a bite to eat <laughs>, but truthfully my life doesn't feel that different. I just feel blessed I'm lucky*

enough to get to do what I love every day.
Your lyrics are very emotional. Many critics have commented on your ability to provoke a variety of reactions, from intense joy to tears, through your words and phrasing. Why do you think that is? *I don't know. I guess I try to be as honest as possible with my lyrics. I couldn't sing them with conviction, otherwise. The songs are sometimes based on personal experiences and sometimes they are just trying to tell a story—either way I have to believe what I'm singing in order to connect with the audience.*
Do you feel different now that you've made it? *<laughs> I wouldn't exactly say I've made it. I'm not sure I ever will. Yes, we are unbelievably lucky Dear Rose, has received such an amazing response, but it's just the beginning. I'm not the sort of person who can exist without having a goal. I always want to be working toward something, and when I think of all the possibilities in this world, I know I'll never run out of opportunities to grow. If I ever get to the point where I think I can sit back and relax because I've made it, well, I might as well be dead.*

I'm beginning to pick apart the article line by line when, sensing a motion outside my office, I scramble to click the Illustrator tab at the bottom of my computer screen. A sketch of a pink floral-print nightgown quickly fills the screen, barely covering the article in time as Lillian steps inside.

"Liv," she says. "Did you hear Tina paging you?"

"No," I reply.

"She wants to see you in the production office. I think

it's about the Nordstrom order."

In super-exciting news, Lillian's trip to Seattle was a success and Nordstrom chose one of the styles Gemma and I designed to test. It's a small order and the styles will only be sold in their best-performing stores, but if it does well, they'll order it as an all-store buy for a later delivery. Beside ourselves, we took each other out for a scorpion bowl at Trader Vics to celebrate, musing over seeing our design on Nordstrom's floor. We decided it's not the same as having your name in the label—we won't be given credit that way—but it's a validating start in that direction.

Gemma is training me to see a style through the production system in our office from concept to completed garment, and I turned in my first tech-pack yesterday. The tech-pack contains all the information—from pattern measurements to technical sketches to color standards needed for the factory to create a garment.

I've never been called into the production office before. It's on the other side of the building, and I don't want to keep them waiting, so I'll need to hurry. Jumping out of my chair, I assure Lillian, "I'm going now."

As I approach, Tina looks up from a round table where she's sitting with two of the production girls. She doesn't greet me. Instead she puts me on the spot. "Olivia, I see you did the tech-pack for the SBS1859?"

"Yes," I say, slowly. They are all three staring at me, and I start to get warm.

"What color rings and slides does the blue colorway have?"

"Ummm, I don't remember off the top of my head. I'd have to check."

"Well, you've only put in the tech-pack the need for ivory rings and slides, but you say here the blue babydoll has blue straps." She presses her finger into the paper stack in front of her without looking down, her gray eyes piercing me. "Do you want ivory rings and slides on blue straps or should they be dyed-to-match blue?"

"Probably dyed-to-match blue," I admit.

The production girls look away, seemingly embarrassed for me, which makes it worse. "That's what I thought," Tina says. "Please be more careful in the future. You're lucky we caught this. If a mistake like this gets through and thousands of babydolls arrive in our warehouse with the wrong color rings and slides, we have to fix them here—which takes time and money—and if we're late with the order, Nordstrom might cancel it."

My nose is burning and I want to cry as my dream of seeing my design on a mannequin at Nordstrom shifts to seeing it on a clearance rack. "I'm sorry, it won't happen again," I promise.

"I hope not. You can go."

Hanging my head, I walk back to my office. I hope Tina doesn't tell Lillian—I don't want her to know how dumb I am. Back at my desk, I bury my face in my hands, still smarting from the encounter. Clearly my obsession is beginning to infringe on my work. Enough is enough—something has to be done. I take an oath. *Starting now, I vow to only Google Berkeley once a day—from home—just to make sure he hasn't been in any accidents on tour. When I'm at work, I will focus on work alone.*

Effective immediately I follow him around Europe from the safety of my living room. Vicariously, I play the Paradiso in

Amsterdam, the Trabendo in Paris, and La Riviera in Madrid. In the evenings I allow myself the indulgence of walking the streets of LA as I listen to his albums on repeat. Walking the city he loves with his words in my ears leaves me feeling attached to him. *So this is what it's like inside your head...*

Oh, and I secretly hope he notices when I start following him on Twitter, though I'm mildly disappointed when he doesn't follow me back.

One evening Blair and Parker accost me as I am deep in thought strolling down Wilshire in front of the El Rey. I don't notice the black Mercedes inching along next to me until I move to replay my favorite song from the *Dear Rose*, album, "Out There."

"There's no way for us to know how far we have to go, how long we have to wait..."

Out of the corner of my eye I finally notice their exasperated faces staring at me. Caught, I blush.

"Liv, what planet are you on?" Parker says from the driver's seat. "We've been calling your name for five minutes! You should be more careful; you could get mugged and not even notice!"

"Sorry. I'm sorry. I guess I'm a little distracted..."

"Well, stop being sorry and get in the car," Blair orders. "You're coming to dinner with us. It's about time you focused on something real for a change."

"Oh, I'm not dressed okay, am I?" I glance down at my jeans and striped off-the-shoulder tunic as I open the back door and slide into the car.

Blair gives me a once over. "You'll be fine."

"Where are we going?"

"Downtown. To Bottega Louie," Parker says, meeting

my eyes in the rearview mirror. "It's Jonathan Stanley's birthday."

Inwardly I groan as I remember my mom hugging him in Malibu. I haven't seen him since the incident, and I hope that impression of me isn't burned into his psyche. "Will there be a lot of people? Are you sure it's okay I come?" I ask. I would enjoy a relaxing dinner alone with Blair and Parker, but am a little disheartened at having to converse with strangers.

"You're always invited," Blair says.

We ride the rest of the way in silence, and before long we pull up to the valet outside a large white building with Gothic lettering. Inside it is packed. Everything from the marble floors to the subway-tiled walls in the wide-open space is bright and white. Expertly lit glass cases command one end of the room, highlighting an array of the most beautiful macaroons and desserts I have ever seen. Far at the other side of the crowded restaurant we spot Jonathan and make our way toward him through a series of bistro tables. He greets us with warm hugs and cheek kisses, thanking us for coming.

"You remember, Liv, right?" Parker double-checks.

"Of course." He smiles. "The girl with *the mother*."

Great. Just how I've always wanted to be known. I know my face is bright red as I apologize, "Oh my gosh. I'm so sorry about that. I…I couldn't stop her!"

He laughs. "It's fine. She was great. And it's good to see you again." He moves to greet another friend, and Parker, Blair, and I claim some empty seats at the far end of the table as another member of our party arrives.

"Parker! Blair! Hello!" a voice cries out from behind us.

Turning to the sound of the voice, I see Lisa Greene

clacking toward us on dangerously high heels, her dark hair swaying in a perfect cascade behind her. Well, this just got interesting. I've purposely pushed her out of my Berkeley-haze, finding comfort that, despite the previous gossip about their relationship, there have been no recent mentions about the two of them. In fact, her presence here in LA is somewhat consoling. At least I know she isn't paying him any visits!

As usual, I stand directly in front of her, my most genuine smile plastered on my face, waiting for her to acknowledge me as she embraces Parker and Blair.

Releasing her hold on Parker, her eyes graze my face without the slightest hint of recognition.

Blair jumps to my rescue. "Lisa, you remember Liv, right? From Elton's Oscar party?"

I extend my hand to greet her, widening my smile.

It seems to take Lisa a moment to focus, "Hmmmmm? Oh! It's so good to see you guys. Let's sit down and catch up," she replies, as though she never heard the question.

Right.

Parker gives me a knowing look as the four of us sit down. For the next two hours, I don't have to say a word as Lisa briefs us on the many auditions she's been on recently, her new organic cupcake recipe that the boys on set can't get enough of, and how embarrassing it is when fans yell her catch phrase at her and she responds "hell to the yeah!" out of habit.

She rambles on, and I listen with rapt attention, waiting for her to make some mention of our common "friend." I'm somewhat grateful to her for ignoring me; I don't feel up to making small talk anyway and am content to enjoy the incredible food while listening for any words that start with the letter *B*. His name never passes her lips though, and even as we make our exit and my pleasant wave and, "Good-bye, Lisa!" meets with a blank stare, I consider the evening a victory.

Upon our return to the Vicente, I say a quick good night to Blair and Parker, feigning sleepiness and bowing out of our usual courtyard nightcap. Alone in the sanctuary of my own room, with girlish giddiness I succumb to replaying my few precious Berkeley moments over and over in my mind. I've memorized every detail, and the visions have a soft, worn-in glow about them. Reliving the feel of his fingers in my hair and the magnetic pull that tugged me toward him, the amused look on his face after I set off the car alarm—I lay awake, dreaming. In a few days he will return. I can't wait.

After what seems like eternity, the Internet says he's back. With insatiable diligence I check my phone, searching for any sign of life. It doesn't ring. Maybe he's jet-lagged and needs a few days to recover? Maybe he doesn't want to look too eager? After all, we haven't spoken in two weeks, I shouldn't expect calling me will be the first thing he'll do upon his return. If guys normally impose a two-day rule after a first date, what's the rule after a two-week European tour?

A week later, I still haven't heard anything when my daily allotted Google search delivers a crushing blow to my ego. There it is plain as day: a candid shot of Berkeley and Lisa Greene enjoying a late-afternoon lunch at Dough Boys. It's official. And I can't justify any more excuses because the Internet always tells the truth. I'm forced to admit he isn't going to call, and worse, he's made his choice.

Chapter Eighteen

MRS. BLOOM @PSYCHICMOM1
@BLOOMOLIVIA OOH. NINE OF SWORDS. ROUGH WEEK. BAD
NEWS/GOOD NEWS: SWORDS = SAD AND LONELY. NINE = THE
FINAL PHASE. IT WON'T LAST FOREVER!

I don't know why I thought he'd call. Clearly I've been living in a one-sided dream world for the last couple weeks. What was I thinking? His world is so different than mine; there certainly isn't room for silly, ordinary me in his life. I try to convince myself over and over I'll never fit with him. Deep down, though, I'm blindsided. Maybe I'm being irrational, but this isn't how it's supposed to be. It isn't what I expected. Where's happily ever after? All of that buildup and tension for nothing? I can't comprehend it. How can I be so wrong?

As evidence of my tortured brain, a rash of Psychic Mom nightmares begins plaguing me every night. They are all more or less the same:

We meet at the top of a snow-capped mountain, the wind whipping our hair.

"Do you want to hear my prophecy?" she asks in an ominous tone.

"No. I do not want to hear your prophecy," I respond icily.

Her: "Namaste."

Me: "Namaste."

Then she turns and skis down the side of the mountain (which is odd because she's not really the athletic type).

Or:

We meet on a deck surrounding a tree high in a rainforest, our skin sticky in the humid air.

"Do you want to hear my prophecy?" she asks in an ominous tone.

"No. I do not want to hear your prophecy," I respond icily.

Her: "Namaste."

Me: "Namaste."

Then she turns and zip-lines across the jungle. (*Definitely* out of character)

Or:

We meet on a bridge high over a waterfall, and for some reason we're wearing yellow raincoats and burlap booties in this one, the mist raining around us.

"Do you want to hear my prophecy?" she asks in an ominous tone.

"No. I do not want to hear your prophecy," I respond icily.

Her: "Namaste."

Me: "Namaste."

Then she turns and bungee jumps off the bridge. (I actually kind of enjoy this one because the sight of her rebounding on the bungee cord in her yellow raincoat with her arms folded across her chest is pretty funny.)

And so on.

I'm sure she's found a new trick to make me listen to her predictions.

"Mom, did you learn how to insert yourself into people's dreams in your Clairvoyant Certification Course?" I ask her one morning.

"You can do that?" she astounds.

"I don't know! You're the psychic here. Don't you have all the answers?"

"Well, I'll ask Esme if it's possible, but, no, I'm not inserting myself into your dreams. Maybe it's your True Self trying to tell you something by taking the form of me. Maybe you should listen to your mother!"

I can see this isn't going to go anywhere.

"Never mind. Forget I mentioned it." I sigh. "I love you. Namaste."

"Namaste."

To top things off, it seems to be a slow news week, so the papers are playing up the Berkeley–Lisa connection. Even though they never seem to do more than have a cup of coffee or a salad, it still irks me that I can't turn on the TV without seeing Lisa staring blankly at me while newscasters speculate on the details of their budding romance. Maybe I'm more in tune than most with any news Berkeley related, but to me they are everywhere, and I am sick of hearing about them.

One evening, I sit slumped in a chair wearing the same faded pajamas I've been wearing for a week straight. Blair, Parker, and I are sipping sangria in the courtyard while passing around an *US Weekly* article featuring my favorite duo.

Blair puts down the magazine and stares at me, shaking her head. "I'm tired of seeing you so gloomy. Why don't you *call* him?" she asks.

"We've been over this before. I can't. It's not my place. He said he'd call. He didn't. It's that simple." I sigh, familiar tears forming behind my eyes.

"You have to go after what you want," Parker says.

"Not when what I want is completely unattainable. No. I can take a hint. I'm not going to be the girl who makes a fool out of herself just because some guy paid her the slightest attention."

"Well, I think that's stupid," Blair says. "I don't think he's so unattainable. *He* invited himself over. That doesn't happen!"

"Yes, but *he* is the one being seen all over town with Lisa Greene. Besides, maybe he does just invite himself to people's houses. Maybe that's normal for him," I argue. "Who knows—I probably made up all those feelings. While I was feeling gravity, he could have been thinking about a breakfast burrito."

Blair grimaces at me. "Well, if it were me, I'd make sure I *knew* what he was thinking. You can't leave things to chance in this city. Sometimes you have to *make* your dreams come true."

"She's right, honey," says Parker. "It's never just about luck. There's a lot of hard work behind the scenes, and sometimes you have to risk it all."

"Not this time." I shake my head. "I completely agree with you both about making your dreams come true, but I've been doing a lot of thinking, and Berkeley is not the dream I came here to pursue. It was never my plan to get caught up in Hollywood drama. I came here to work, and that's what I intend to do. All work and no play: the new me." I nod.

"Well, *that's* boring!" Blair tsks. But she is smiling as she continues, "I guess you've got to do whatever your heart tells you, though, and if it will get you out of those ratty pajamas, I'm all for it! I mean, are those Old Navy? Don't you work for a lingerie company?"

I want to glare at her for the lingerie comment, but instead, for the first time since Berkeley's return, I laugh. "My heart is definitely telling me to protect it. Final answer," I confirm.

With my renewed focus, my mood improves. And after my "rings and slides" mistake at work, I'm determined to prove my worth.

One day, I approach Lillian at lunch.

"Do you mind if I join you?" I ask.

"Not at all," she welcomes. One thing I admire about Lillian is her ability to take constructive criticism. She believes in being open to all concepts and the word no isn't in her vocabulary. She doesn't put her ideas above anyone else's, but instead feels it's the collaboration of opinions that yields the best product. She never forces her hand, but takes into consideration other people's views. I'm hoping her open-mindedness will work in my favor right now.

"How are you doing, Liv? Is everything going well?" She immediately strikes up a conversation.

"It's good. I'm still learning a lot, but everyone's been so helpful." Gemma says my Tina run-in was nothing compared to the berating she would have received for the same mistake at her last job. I'm still embarrassed by it, so I'm glad it wasn't worse.

"Everyone here is very nice. It's rare in this industry," Lillian says. "My first boss threw a hamburger at me. I quit on the spot."

I look at her graceful posture and tapered suit and can't imagine anyone throwing a hamburger at her.

"I feel really lucky to be here," I reply, gathering my courage for the next part. "But lately I've be wondering what else I can do. I think I've mastered CAD designs, and I'm learning tech-packs, but I really enjoyed the Nordstrom project and would like to do more creative projects like that, but I'm not sure how."

"You have to make yourself valuable," she advises. "Bring ideas to the table. Don't be afraid to voice an opinion. We'll give you a chance."

"Well, actually, I've been thinking… I know you guys need to do a Jonquil photo shoot soon, and I have some ideas for it…"

"I'd love to hear them," she says.

"Really? Can I put together a presentation?"

"Of course. Does Thursday afternoon give you enough time?"

"Yes. Plenty of time. Thank you."

Excited for the opportunity, I rush home that night to

begin my preparations. This is cake for me. I've been tearing out layouts from *Vogue* photo shoots since I was three when my mom discovered I'd slipped the September issue into her grocery cart. Viewing my deception as an omen, she subscribed in an instant.

Whenever my new issue arrived, I would savor it, carefully removing my favorite shots and filing them away for safe keeping. I still have binders of torn magazine pages in my closet. For some reason I can't bear to part with the beautiful images: Kate Moss wearing a sparkling Oscar de la Renta evening gown in Vietnam, Linda Evangelista wearing a gold bikini on the back of a boat in the French Riviera, Amber Valletta posing in Versace in a cobblestone corridor in Malta, all tucked away in my closet so I can visit them anytime. They evoke a momentary getaway. A snapshot of beauty. It doesn't matter what was really going on when the picture was taken; I always imagine it was beyond glamorous. In real life everyone was probably hungover, exhausted, and sweaty, but you'd never know it from the pictures. I love them. They can be anything.

I spend the next few days poring over images, finally choosing a select few to provide the backdrop for the mood boards I'll combine with sketches from the line to present my vision. When Thursday morning dawns, I meet the challenge with confidence and my presentation is a smashing success. Photo-shoot stylist is added to my list of duties, and I'm to get to work casting a model and scouting locations.

I feel like my career path is moving in the right direction. Now, if I can get my personal life in order, maybe I can become whole again.

Chapter Nineteen

Blair, Parker, and I are huddled outside CJ's Diner, eating *chilaquiles* as I recount having survived yesterday's model casting. The shoot is coming together. I spent the week location scouting, ultimately securing a 1930s Spanish estate in the Santa Monica Mountains, and devoting a glorious day to photographing potential shooting spots there. It felt like I was cheating on my day job, getting to be outside imagining instead of inside chained to a desk, and I hope there are more days like it in my future.

After analyzing the pictures, I settled on three different editorial stories ranging from dancing the Tango in front of the arches on the pavered patio, to sunbathing Brigitte

Bardot-style by the pool, to film noir glamour in a bedroom. Everything was coming together nicely until I started searching for a model. Lillian and I went through hundreds of photos from agencies before narrowing it down to the select few girls we wanted to see in person. It was interesting seeing the girls through her seasoned eyes. She pointed out things I never would have noticed—she's too posed, doesn't know how to move; her hands aren't graceful, she doesn't know how to hold them; her face doesn't draw you in—all valid observations that can make or break a photo, but by hour nine I was starting to worry nobody would be good enough.

"So you found a girl?" Parker asks as he swallows a bite of his breakfast.

"I think so, but I officially hate model casting. Especially for lingerie models. It's *so* awkward to have to ask a girl to turn around so you can look at her butt in a G-string."

"I'm sure they're used to it," Blair says, scrunching up her nose.

"Oh *they* definitely are, but *I'm* not. I usually try not to judge people—especially not based on appearance—so it was hard to eye them critically. I'm probably a freak for caring. The models were all very comfortable with their bodies, but I wasn't. I had them changing in an office nobody uses and I wanted Lillian to come to them to make the final call, but every time I went to find her, the model would leave the room and start walking through the building wearing nothing but a bra and underwear! I kept chasing them down, trying to throw robes over them—I mean, it's an office not a strip club—but the girls didn't seem to care."

"Hey, free show. I'm sure nobody minded," Parker says.

"I don't know. I totally got yelled at by one of the sales reps for not putting a CAUTION NAKED MODELS sign on the door when he walked in on one who was pouring herself a drink in the kitchen. But I didn't know she was in there. Believe me, I would have followed her with hazard lights and herded her back to her closet had I known." I pause to take a sip of my mimosa, which I feel I deserve after all of this. "And then Lillian kept seeing things I didn't notice — probably because I felt bad for looking. 'But are her boobs too small—is she too old?—are her legs too skinny?'" I do my best Lillian impression, mimicking her stately voice, every line delivered as though addressing the queen.

"Casting isn't easy. It's like dating. It's hard to find the person you want to stare at for the rest of the year. Believe me, you have no idea how many weeds we have to pick through to find the lilies for *The One*," Parker says. "Why don't you be the model, Liv?"

"No way." I look at him like he's delusional (and clearly he is). "I could never endure being picked apart like that, not to mention these are every guy's dream weeds I'd be competing against. If they're dandelions, I'm crabgrass. They *do* get paid more in a day than I make in a month, but I'm still not sure it's worth it."

"I think you're too hard on yourself," Blair says. "You could totally do it."

"Believe me." I shake my head. "I've seen enough perky model rear ends to know I don't have a chance. Besides, we finally picked someone everyone is happy with. I'm not rocking the boat."

"That's a load off, right? I feel the same way. I'm *so* glad this season is done shooting," Parker says. "There's still tons of work to do, but at least I don't have to console the deflowered anymore. Some of those girls are horrifying. I'm glad next season is *The One-ette.* I much prefer offering up my shoulder to those poor, dejected boys."

"Speaking of boys," Blair says, "maybe there will be some cute ones at the party tonight."

Parker is invited to a party at the house of a producer from *The One,* and Blair and I are his plus two.

"I don't know," I say. "I'm not getting my hopes up. There's lots of cute ones, but they're always so into themselves."

"I hear you," Blair says. "Some people say it's a jungle out there. But I think it's a cave—a cave full of men."

"I'll toast to that," Parker says. He *would* probably enjoy a man cave. I put the mental image of Parker dancing with a bunch of guys in caveman costumes out of my mind as soon as it appears. "But don't worry, Liv. All is not lost. We'll find you someone worthy."

"I'm not in any hurry." I shake my head. "I'm supposed to be focusing on work anyway. I'm better off without the distraction. What are you going to wear tonight?" I ask, changing the subject.

"Probably a bikini," Blair replies.

"A bikini? Isn't it a little chilly for that? It doesn't feel like spring, yet."

"Oh, didn't I tell you? It's a pool party," Parker says. "Actually, it's more of a hot-tub-toga party. I plan to wear my bathing suit under my toga."

Hot-tub-toga party? Weird. Maybe someday I'll get used to this...

"I guess I should hunt down a swimsuit, then," I say. "Shopping?"

Chapter Twenty

Mrs. Bloom @PsychicMom1
Waning crescent moon! It is time to purge negativity,
eliminate clutter, and purify! #callingthehousekeeper

We valet Parker's car outside the producer's midcentury mansion in the Hills. Wearing our toga-bikini combos, Blair and I wait at the top of the steps that lead down to the house as Parker gives our names to the massive man wearing a black suit and earpiece who is standing guard at the door. I have opted to wear a royal blue L*Space bikini with gold binding under my toga. While shopping I'd fallen in love with two suits, one sporty, one sexy, and Blair, having an uncanny gift for justifying any purchase—especially if it results in a giant credit card bill for me—convinced me to buy them both. Allowing my hair to fall in loose waves around me, I've accessorized with a gold leaf headband across my forehead, a gold cuff bracelet, and Cleopatra-style eye makeup. Enjoying my costume, I feel I'm in my element.

"Parker Mifflin plus two," Parker says, peering over the doorman's shoulder as he ruffles through the booklet that comprises the list.

"Here you are," the man replies, crossing us off with a black Sharpie. "Wrists!"

We extend our left arms and wait as we are shackled with florescent bands announcing our acceptance at the party. I'm not sure I'll ever get used to wearing a wristband to go to a friend's *house* party. I mean, how amazing can it be?

As we descend the stairs to the mansion I realize some parties *are* extraordinary enough to warrant the secret service keeping the wannabe's out. They've spared no expense. Luminescent white paper lanterns sway in the surrounding trees and *Animal House* is being projected across the front wall of the home's facade. Waitresses clad in tiny togas pass drinks and appetizers while gourmet food trucks representing delicacies from around the world are lined up on the expansive lawn. Walking through the front door, we are greeted with sparkling city views from every angle. The house is completely open to the outdoor balconies that surround it. Stepping out onto a terrace, I can't help but love this city.

My eyes follow a spiral staircase down to the pool. It has been covered with a clear dance floor, and topped with DJ and a bar. All around it, extra hot tubs have been brought in, their jasmine-scented steam creating a mystic fog while nearby pits blaze.

"Shall we make the rounds?" Parker asks.

"Definitely," Blair answers as she adjusts her tiny toga to reveal a bit more of her bikini.

We wander around the balcony level of the party, mingling with friends and acquaintances. As I make small talk and nibble on the bite-size appetizers that pass my way, I realize I'm feeling oddly free and comfortable. I don't have any expectations for the evening except to enjoy myself.

"Do you guys want to go in the water?" Parker asks as the couple he's talking to leaves to hunt down drinks.

"Not, yet," Blair replies. "I don't want to get my hair wet." She pats the perfectly tousled bun piled on the top of her head.

"We should go down and check it out, though," I say, training my gaze on the mass of dancing people below. "It looks like fun."

"Yes. Let's go."

Parker leads the way down the cascading staircase to the pool level. DJ David Bullock is spinning, and beats thump in the background. As we reach the pool deck, I'm scanning the scene for a place to camp for a round of drinks when my eyes find his.

Berkeley is sitting with a small group of people around a fire pit, his toga revealing his lean, muscular build. I recoil as I notice that perched on his lap, wearing a miniscule half sheet, is Lisa Greene. With a sharp inhale, I alert Blair and Parker to my discomfort and they follow my gaze.

"Uh-oh," Blair says under her breath.

"Are you okay?" Parker, in meltdown-prevention mode, tries to steady me.

Shaken, every inch of my being wants to run and hide. Though I've convinced myself I've moved on, the physical reaction to seeing him again stuns me. The longing is almost more than I can bear. I have to fight it. "No! I mean, yes." I bite my lip to be strong. Resisting the fresh surge of pain at him not calling, I resolve I'm not going to let him affect me. I'm done with silly fairy tales. The reality is he prefers Lisa Greene, and I have to accept it. Burying that sad truth, I remind myself I've moved on and Berkeley and I don't have anything to say to each other.

"It's fine. I'm fine," I say, determined not to let him ruin my night. Tossing my hair over my shoulder, I prepare to ignore him. (I'm secretly pleased I've chosen the sexy swimsuit, though.) "Drinks?" I ask.

Equipped with glasses of champagne from a passing tray, my wolf pack gathers around me. We attempt to act normal and chat, but it's proving difficult for any of us to ignore the presence behind me. As it turns out, we don't have to avoid him for long.

"Parker! Blair! Liv!" a shrill voice rings out over the crowd. Raising my eyes skyward, my temples pound with disbelief. Of course. Twenty times I've met her. Twenty times she's refused to acknowledge my existence. Why in the name of Hollywood Boulevard would she choose this moment to birth my name from her lips?

"I think she wants us to go over there," Blair says through her teeth while she smiles and waves at my betrayer.

"Nope," I declare in a voice steadier than I feel. "Not happening." Mad Max glints in my eyes. "I'm fine right here if you guys want to go."

"It's okay, we'll stay with you," Parker promises. *Wolf pack. Unite.* "Oh no. She's coming over here," Blair whispers the play by play, "and she's bringing him."

"What should I do?"

It's too late. I try to look natural as they close the short distance separating us.

"Hi, guys," Lisa purrs, inserting herself into our circle so she stands wedged between Berkeley and me. Frozen with fear, I attempt to remain unaffected as Lisa winds her fingers protectively around his biceps. "You know Berkeley," she says to Blair and Parker. I'm back to nonexistent as far as she's concerned. If only that were true for both of them. I can feel his eyes on me.

"We've met," Berkeley confirms, a slight edge to his voice as he shifts his weight away from her.

I can't stay for this. Being this close to him is overwhelming. My only chance at escape is to meet the challenge head-on. Channeling every last ounce of inner strength I possess, I smile at him innocently, pretending I haven't given him a second thought since the last time we saw each other. He's grown the beginnings of a beard since I saw him last, and somehow it serves to make his blue eyes brighter. "How was Europe?" I ask, with confidence I don't feel, meeting those eyes directly. Familiar tension holds me spellbound and gravity begins its usual tow. I fight to hide the emotions that crowd my eyes, but I'm sure he sees right through me.

"It was good," he says softly. "Grueling, though. I'm glad to be back." His voice hints promise, and his eyes never leave my face. My body temperature rises under his scrutiny.

"He'll be in town for a little while," Lisa says. "I'm working on a new pilot that just got picked up by NBC." She turns the conversation to her, and I'm relieved to have a new focus for everyone's attention. Tearing my eyes from

Berkeley, I busy them with a thorough pedicure examination as Parker takes Lisa's bait.

"So exciting! Tell me about it. What's it called?"

Lisa launches into an endless description of the new series, and I'm okay tuning her out. My part in this dialogue is done, and I begin to plan my exit strategy as Lisa rambles on. "I'm going to run to the restroom," I whisper, with an imperceptible lean toward Blair. "Meet me by the food trucks when you're done?"

She nods as I back out of the circle, mumbling an "excuse me." Without so much as a peek at Berkeley, I head back up the stairs toward the house, trying to shake the feeling he's watching, and worse, trying to stop hoping he is.

Sequestering myself in the bathroom, I attempt to prevent the physical reaction my body has to being near him. Letting my forehead rest against the door, I allow the energy to course through me and wait for my goose bumps to subside. *Get over it, get over it…pull it together!* My head is swimming in a fog, and I hate that he has this power over me. I want to kick something.

Several minutes later, my thoughts begin to clear. There's probably a line of togas waiting to use the facilities. I shouldn't hide out any longer. Making sure my features reflect inner peace, I open the bathroom door and slip out the front of the house toward the food trucks.

It's almost impossible to recognize anyone in the sea of dancing white sheets around me, but my eyes go straight to him. He's standing alone in front of the Kogi BBQ Truck. Pretending I don't notice him, I continue to search the crowd for Blair and Parker as my heartbeat accelerates. Midscan, my eyes catch his, and I know I've been spotted. I turn on my heel and start walking away from him as he quickens his pace.

In the distance, I spy Blair and Parker examining the crowd. With frantic relief I wave, and they beckon me toward them. Breaking into a full sprint, I run toward Parker and Blair, my toga billowing behind me. "Let's get out of here!" I yell.

And we are gone.

Safely back in the car, Parker turns to me. "You were amazing, Liv. I've got to give it to you. 'How was Europe?'" he mimics, a bit breathless after our jog. "Well played."

"And the way he was looking at you," Blair says. "That energy... You guys are magnetic. We could all feel it. The two of you shouldn't go near power lines; you'd cause transformers to explode."

"He was out of there so fast after you left, I'm surprised he didn't catch you," Parker says.

"I'm glad he didn't; I don't think I could have handled it." I shake my head. "This is self-preservation. It was too hard to get over last time, and I'm tired of games. I'm done," I resolve. "I hope I never have to talk to him again."

It's not true. He's the only person I want to talk to. But I'm determined to convince myself otherwise.

Chapter Twenty-one

OLIVIA BLOOM @BLOOMOLIVIA
FEELING GREAT. DON'T THINK I'LL NEED TO ATTEND THOSE
CYBERSTALKER ANONYMOUS MEETINGS ANYMORE. #MOVINGON

We lose Blair the next week. On Monday she starts working on an event celebrating the opening of a new Geisha House location and meets one of the Dolce Group owners. He sweeps her off her feet, treating her to late-night private dinners, VIP treatment at his clubs, and flying her out to his place in Vegas for the weekend. She's head over heels.

Parker and I spend our evenings entertaining each other and become maybe a little too addicted to eating pizza while watching *Dancing with the Stars*. Our pack is decidedly less full with just the two of us, and by Thursday, Parker starts to feel restless and decides to put a stop to our couch time. Launching his Thai takeout container across the room, he announces it's high time we celebrate our return to "the scene."

When I get home from work the next afternoon, he greets me in the courtyard. "Guess what I have in my hand," he says with a sly grin, his hands hidden behind his back.

"Do I really want to know?"

"Yes. You really want to know."

"A bottle of wine."

"You're so unoriginal. Try again."

I think for a moment. "Well, it can't be two eligible bachelors who want to show us a night on the town…"

"Closer! Try five plus a bench."

"Huh?"

"I scored us floor seats to tonight's Lakers–Nuggets game!" he says. "One of the producers on my show gave them to me. They're his seats, but his wife's family is in town so he can't go."

"Ummm. Yay?" I come off sounding underwhelmed. Of course I know how fanatical this city is about the Lakers, but I've never been to a professional basketball game. Pittsburgh doesn't have a team, so it's not a sport I grew up with. To be honest, I'm not sure what all the fuss is about.

"Liv. Have I taught you nothing? The floor of a Lakers game is *the* place to be seen. It's second only to the—" Stricken, Parker falls silent.

"What. It's second only to the what?"

"*What* are we going to do?" he asks himself, sweating as he paces. He's close to the edge. This I've never seen; he's always so pulled together. "It will never work," he decides.

"*What* will never work?"

"Your car. We have to take your car. Mine's in the shop."

Parker's pimped-out black Mercedes is his pride and joy, and he took it in this morning for its monthly spa treatment.

"So what? I don't mind driving."

"Liv." He shakes his head. "Perhaps there are two rules to living in Los Angeles that we forgot to mention. Rule #8: All people need two cars: one to drive, that you don't mind getting scratched or dinged when you parallel park, and one to *valet*." He pauses to let that marinate.

"Well, if you don't want to valet my Volkswagen, we can take a cab."

"A cab!" He stares at me as if I just suggested we go on a shopping spree at Sears. "Oh no. What are you thinking? Rule #9: The only place more significant than being seen on the floor of a Lakers game is being seen in the *valet line* of a Lakers game." He rests his case.

"Parker. That's absurd."

"No, it's not. Just you wait. You'll see. Everyone who is anyone is in that line. Jack always gets his car first because he's royalty, but the rest of us have to wait."

"Jack Nicholson will be there?" *OMG.* "Well, why don't we go to the end of the line, then? That way we'll have more time to mingle and nobody will have to see us get into my car," I offer.

"I knew I raised you right."

It's settled. My car it is.

We arrive at the Staples Center valet early and deposit my Jetta so as not to be seen. Parker is right. I swear the valet driver holds my keys between his thumb and forefinger in disgust.

As we walk into the arena, the paparazzi are already lining up. They ignore us. It never ceases to amaze me how they can tell with barely a glance who is photo worthy. They are right, though—it definitely isn't us.

Once inside we make our way to our seats. I have to say I feel pretty privileged as we enter at floor level and walk along the court. If the paparazzi didn't wonder who we are, the fans already gathered in their seats sure do. I'm convinced more of them are here to people watch than to see the Lakers play. That's certainly what has me mesmerized at the moment. Parker wasn't kidding about the amount of celebrity at the game. *Everyone* is here. As we settle into our leather folding chairs, our feet on the court, I observe the crowd. Oscar-winning actors, musicians, athletes, reality stars, talk-show hosts—everyone crams together as music blares out of the sound system and the Laker Girls begin to dance. The energy in the room thickens as the anticipation builds. Scanning the faces in my row, my eyes come to rest on a familiar one. *Ah. That makes sense. That explains the energy increase.* It isn't just the crowd; along our row at the other end of the court, sit Berkeley and Mark. Berkeley lounges casually in his chair, wearing black jeans, a charcoal T-shirt, and a dark gray zip-front hoodie. I look away, determined to ignore his presence. *At least he's not here with Lisa Greene.* And at least we're sitting parallel to one another so the chances of him spotting me are slim.

The game gets started, and I'm immediately captivated by the size and speed of the athletes as they dribble back and forth along the length of the court. I don't really know what's going on, and Parker is no help (*look at his biceps!*), but I can't resist getting caught up in the excitement of the contest. Watching with rapt attention, I completely forget about Berkeley until halftime. As the teams retreat to their locker rooms, Parker wants to go to the Chairman's Room for a drink. The Chairman's Room is the exclusive club in the belly of the Staples Center where those with "court" seats mingle at halftime.

"Come on, Liv, it's part of the experience. You can't miss it!"

"Parker, I *have* to miss it. I can't risk seeing him, and I'm pretty sure he'll be in there," I say. "You go. I'll keep our seats warm."

He can tell I'm not going to budge and doesn't want to waste precious time trying to convince me. "Are you sure?"

"Go," I assure him. "And hurry back so you can tell me all about it."

Twenty minutes later, Parker returns full of stories about standing between Penny Marshall and Al Pacino. Berkeley was there, so it's good I wasn't. He babbles on, ecstatic, while I half listen.

The game begins again and, as it continues, I begin to relax, certain I'm going to remain unnoticed. That is, of course, until the inevitable occurs. In the last few minutes in regulation, as the crowd's insistent "we want tacos!" chant rings in our ears (I learn it's home-game policy that if the Lakers are able to hold their opponent to less than a hundred points, while scoring over a hundred points themselves, everyone in the crowd gets a free taco), a missed pass sends the ball and two huge basketball players hurling through the air, straight for me and Parker. We leap out of the way, but not before our fearful faces are plastered all over the big screen. If a ball is flying through the air...it never fails. As I regain my composure and climb back into my chair, I'm positive my cover is blown.

As luck would have it, the Lakers win, and I figure the crowds of celebrating fans will make it impossible for Berkeley to close the gap between us in the arena. With this in mind, I stall in our seats as long as possible. Parker, understandably, can't wait to get to the valet line, so I send him ahead, claiming I need to stop in the ladies' room. In stealth mode, I allow myself to be absorbed into the crowd as I head to the top deck of Staples, knowing Berkeley won't venture up there for fear of being recognized.

I lock myself in a ladies' room stall, taking my time, fiddling with my jeans, waiting for the coast to be clear. *Just a few more minutes*. I dig through my purse for my lipstick, ignoring the frustrated shuffling of the waiting women outside. What am I doing in here? Will he really be looking for me? Do I really think I matter that much to him? Who am I kidding? I'm probably making up this entire game of cat and mouse. I'm nobody! Here I am, hiding in a stall at the Staples Center, having deluded myself into thinking Berkeley Dalton would give me a second thought, while Parker's having the time of his life in the valet line. I'm being ridiculous, and I can't spend the rest of my life hiding in restrooms.

Convinced I'm a fool, I leave the stall and head back down to floor level. As I approach the corridor that leads to the valet, I spot Parker through the doorway. He's hanging at the back of the line talking to someone I don't recognize, our valet ticket in hand.

"Parker!" I call out, starting to head his way. As he turns

to beckon me forward, his face lights up with surprise and I feel a feather touch from behind me run the length of my arm. The trap slams shut, and I stop as familiar warmth engulfs me. *Maybe I do matter after all.* Happiness threatens to overtake me, but I try to stifle it. *I guess there's no reason to put this off any longer. Time to get this conversation over with.* He has me cornered.

"You're hard to catch up with," he says, his fingers softly circling my arm as if he's afraid I'll make a run for it. "Long line at the bathroom?" he teases.

"Am I that obvious?" I ask, turning to face him.

"Well, I'm starting to figure out your patterns. I feel like all I've been doing lately is chasing you."

"Really?" I murmur, raising my eyes to his. *Down, lightning bolt, down!* "I'm sorry about that; I guess I've been busy," I say with strength I don't feel as I look away. "Is there something you wanted?" I return my eyes to his face and try to sound unaffected.

His eyes search mine, and I wonder what they're searching for. "I'd rather not do this here," he says, with a fleeting look toward Mark who is close to the front of the valet line. "But" — he pauses, seeming to make a decision as he leans closer to me so as not to be overheard — "I wanted to say I'm sorry I didn't call when I got back from Europe." His breath brushes my ear during his revelation, sending a delighted shiver through me as my face flushes.

I don't want to talk about this, either — to have it out in the open that he stood me up and I was hurt. It's embarrassing. I shrug and manage lightly, "It's fine. I didn't expect you to anyway." At least it's partially the truth. By now, I've convinced myself I shouldn't have expected it, but I can't deny I *wanted* it. "And you seem to be pretty busy yourself."

A small crowd is forming around us, and out of the corner of my eye I notice a camera flash.

Berkeley flinches and pulls me forward. Wedging me against a wall and shielding me from the swarm with his body, he lowers his head close to mine. "It's not fine. It's complicated and I don't expect you to understand," he whispers. "I know the way it looks—and please don't breathe a word of this—but I want you to know Lisa's a publicity stunt. It's not a good excuse for not calling, I know, but the truth is…" He trails off, seeming to struggle with the words. "You scare me, Olivia."

His voice reverberates through me when he says my name. Before I can comprehend or respond, Mark waves Berkeley forward as his Audi pulls into the valet. Rushed, Berkeley grabs both of my hands. "I'm having dinner with some friends tomorrow night. Come as my date."

"I don't think I—"

He cuts me off. "Please say yes. Let me make it up to you. Meet me in front of Joan's on Third at eight o'clock. Please come. I won't take no for an answer." He has to go. Holding my eyes a moment longer he says, "I'll be waiting," before he jogs off to join Mark at the front of the line. I let him go, but my eyes follow him as he takes his keys from the valet. He glances my way one last time, a question in his gaze, before he slides into the driver's seat.

Watching him drive away, I let my heartbeat return to normal before I inch toward Parker. I try to push the conversation with Berkeley out of my mind with each step, determined not to fall for his charm.

I reach Parker in line.

"How'd it go?" he asks, innocent.

Realization dawns. "You set me up."

"No!" he responds with mock surprise. "The fast is over, sweetheart. Welcome back."

"Did you know he was going to be here? Was this whole night a ploy?"

"No," he assures me. "I didn't know he was going to be here, but when I saw him in the Chairman's Room, I seized my opportunity. I told him you'd have to show up at the valet line eventually..." He hands our ticket to the runner.

I'm annoyed, abandoned by my own pack. "Well, I'm sorry you went to all that trouble."

"What did he say?"

"He apologized for not calling, which was totally embarrassing, and he invited me to be his date at a dinner party tomorrow. But I'm not going. I finally feel okay with being alone. I can't risk it." I don't want to dwell on the other things he told me. Besides, rule number five...

The valet pulls my Volkswagen to a stop in front of us.

"HURRY!" Parker screams as he scans the line's remnants for anyone noteworthy. "Pick it up, Olivia Bloom!"

We make a beeline for the car, slamming the doors shut behind us in a panic.

"Step on it before someone sees us!" he yells.

I press the gas pedal, and the Jetta takes off with surprising speed. We roar down Olympic Boulevard and onto the freeway, enjoying the rush. Rolling down the windows, I let the wind wash over me as I push the car faster, allowing the adrenaline to leave my body. "Another Moment Like This" by Berkeley & the Brightside happens to be on the radio, and I turn it up and drive, taking the long way home.

"Another moment like this, it would pull me apart, it would break my heart in two, All my limitations, all my expectations, I don't ever want to have another moment like this…"

As we pull up to the Vicente, I am calm and firm in my decision not to meet Berkeley.

"What's this?" Parker asks, picking up an envelope that must have flown forward from the backseat during the drive.

Before I can stop him, he opens it.

Confused, he stares at the picture in his hand. "Why do you have this random picture of him?"

He turns the picture toward me, and I look at it. Sure enough, it's Berkeley. Actually, it's a picture of The Point in Pittsburgh where the three rivers—the Ohio, the Monongahela, and the Allegheny—meet. It appears as though Berkeley inadvertently walked in front of the camera just as my mom snapped the photo.

"Look. There's a note on the back," Parker points out.

"I accidently took a picture of this guy, and he's so handsome, I thought you'd like to have it. No regrets—Namaste, Mom."

Tears crowd my eyes as I stare at the words. Curse my mother's tricks! "This is *exactly* why I don't want to *know* this stuff!" I cry. "It taints my decision process. I was settled. I was fine. I wasn't going to dinner!" I'm crying real tears, not caring that they drip onto the photo in my hand. "Now she throws this at me? No regrets? It's the one thing she's instilled in me my entire life. Now I *have* to go."

"You still have a choice, here," Parker suggests.

"No. No I don't. What did she just say to me? 'Maybe you should listen to your mother?'" I stop, take a breath, and quietly resign, "I'm going."

Chapter Twenty-two

OLIVIA BLOOM @BLOOMOLIVIA
DISTANT, ALOOF, FARAWAY, UNTOUCHABLE... I'M APPARENTLY
REALLY BAD AT ALL OF THESE. #FALLING

My plan is simple. I'll obey my mother by attending dinner, but I'll keep the evening distant and polite. It's going to be difficult, but I vow to remain strong and not fall victim to his charm. Feeling the need to look my best, I take extra time getting ready, enlisting Gemma for reinforcement. She helps me straighten my hair into a shiny cascade and apply smoky-eye makeup. I choose to wear a printed silk V-neck dress that has the shoulders cut out of its bell sleeves and a strappy T-back. To complete the look, I opt for nude ankle-strap pumps and tiny gold-stud earrings shaped like doves.

Parking at a meter a short distance away, I arrive outside Joan's on Third promptly at 8:05, my stomach a bundle of nervous energy. I've timed it this way because I don't want to seem too eager (which I'm not), and I want him to sweat a little bit (which I hope he is)—but I don't want him to go in without me.

He's leaning against a light pole in front of the restaurant, examining his phone, and he looks up as I approach. A slow smile spreads across his face. He seems pleased. "You came." Is that a touch of relief I detect? "I wasn't sure you would."

"I wasn't sure, either," I admit, my resolve already wavering at the sight of him in his slim black pants, perfectly faded T-shirt, and structured gray jacket.

"I'm glad you did." His eyes hold mine as he takes me in.

"I'll let you know if I'm glad, later," I say softly with a half smile, effectively breaking the spell.

Laughing, he reaches forward and pulls me into his chest, hugging me hello like we're old friends. So far, this is not going well. A chill races down my arm at his touch. *Distance, Liv, distance.* I try to pull away, but his left arm refuses to leave my waist.

"I'm not going to run away," I say, avoiding his eyes.

"Hmmm. I think you'll understand if I make sure." He smiles. "Shall we?" He gestures away from the restaurant with his right hand while pulling me closer with his left.

We start walking. "I thought we were going to dinner?" I ask, attempting to ignore his body's proximity to mine and how much I enjoy the feel of his arm around me.

"We are. But not here. I thought we could walk for a minute before I subject you to my friends. You know, ease you into it."

"I appreciate that," I say. And I do. "Good game last night," I offer, trying to keep the mood light.

"I'm glad that ball didn't mess up that pretty face of yours," he says.

I can't help it. I laugh. "Great. I've been trying to block that out for the last twenty-four hours. Thank you for reminding me."

"Anytime."

We walk on a moment longer in silence, neither of us wanting to venture into more serious subjects. The night is chilly, and we can see our breath in front of us as we stop before a random door in the middle of a stucco wall. "Here we are."

I look around for a sign. "Where are we?"

"The Little Door," he reveals, opening said door for me as he shifts his hand to the small of my back and guides me forward.

As I step inside, I'm transported to Greece. We're standing in a bazaar under a canopy of trees, stars peeking through their leaves, surrounded by flowers and flickering candlelight. Outdoor fireplaces blaze and waterfalls gurgle over the chatter of the other guests. The air is heady with exotic spices as the maître d' leads us across a cobblestone path, then through a set of heavy curtains to the piano room, where an intimate table is set for ten by a roaring fire. Glass balls filled with candles hang at varying lengths from the rattan ceiling, creating dancing shadows on the stone walls, and the long wooden table is laden with wine bottles. It's the most romantic room I've ever seen.

A familiar pang of nervousness shoots through my stomach as eight curious sets of eyes focus on me.

Berkeley takes my hand. "I've got you," he murmurs so only I can hear, before greeting the table. "Everyone, this is my friend, Liv. Liv, this is everyone." One by one he introduces me to comedians, writers, actors, and photographers as we ease onto the bench against the wall. I recognize Haynes, the Brightside's manager from Santa Barbara, and his wife Carly from movie night, and each person welcomes me warmly to the group. A screenwriter sits to my right, and Berkeley is to my left. He pulls me closer to him with his right arm, letting it fall to rest loosely around my waist. I wish he would stop touching me. My breathing is becoming labored with his nearness, and the distance is beginning to melt. He isn't making this easy.

A waiter pours us some wine, and we settle in for a long dinner.

"So how did you two meet?" Kevin, the writer next to me asks. I can almost hear the ears perk up across the table, and I freeze. Oh no. I haven't thought of this question coming up. A recollection of the awkward meeting outside the restroom darts through my mind and I feel my cheeks glow.

Before I can utter a word, Berkeley fields the question. "We met backstage at the *Sports Illustrated* Swimsuit Fashion Show. Liv's a stylist, and I couldn't resist watching her work."

"Tough gig," Kevin says, smiling. "I don't blame you."

"Actually, that was a freelance project," I say, finding my tongue. "I really work in lingerie."

"Even better," an actor from across the table says.

"Lucky, man, Berk, you're a lucky man!" a director from the other end of the table calls out.

Everyone starts laughing and toasts to lingerie.

I take a big sip of my wine, raising my eyebrows at

Berkeley over my glass, happy to have the intros over with. He winks at me, and to my surprise, I start to relax, knowing he's looking out for me.

Before long, I feel like part of them. Kevin keeps asking me lingerie questions, and everyone makes sure I'm included in the conversation, even as it turns to remembering nights at a place called the Franklin House, where the Brightside attended late-night jam sessions in the basement long before they "made it." Delighting in their stories and becoming privy to long-standing jokes, I feel accepted. Plus, having so many interesting people around takes the pressure off Berkeley and me, and for the first time I'm able to observe him for who he honestly is. Stripped of his rock-star persona and relaxing among friends, he's down-to-earth, witty, and earnest; he's real. He never turns the conversation to himself; instead he intuitively keeps everyone else talking and seems genuinely interested. I feel myself losing the distance battle as I realize (curses!) I actually *like* him.

Several hours later, as the evening draws to a close, we all stand to leave. Flushed and warm from the heat of the fire and Berkeley's closeness, I join in the good-byes and Berkeley leads me to the door. I'm sad to leave.

Stepping back through the magic opening, we're spit out onto a stark, cold Los Angeles street corner. The contrast is startling. It feels as though we've just returned from another world, and a shot of fear rips through me as the thought crosses my mind: it's all a dream. Berkeley quickly banishes the thought, however, with a shot of his own magic as he puts his arm around me. We begin to walk back toward our cars, the air cool against our rosy cheeks.

"Thank you for inviting me. I had a wonderful time," I

say. "Your friends are great."

"They are," he agrees. "I try to do this as often as possible. It's too easy to get caught up in the pressure of everything else, and they always bring me back to the ground. They remind me what really matters." His voice catches on the last word, and I'm suddenly conscious of how close our bodies are.

We reach my car. "This is me," I say. Unsure of the next move, I take a step back and look up at him, a question in my eyes, remembering the last time we stood next to a car and the almost kiss. My heart pounds as the heat between us grows.

He seems uncertain as well, and he searches my face, considering. Finally he asks, "Do you want to come back to my place?"

Hesitating, I think about the perfect evening, not wanting it to end. Picturing us in his kitchen, though, I have the uncanny feeling that if I go home with him, it will result in a distance-FAIL. I'm already struggling to resist the tension that is pulling me toward him.

"No," I decide. "I think I should go home. I had a really great time, though."

He nods his understanding and folds me into his arms. "Can I call you?" he asks into my hair.

Can I stay here forever?

Being in his embrace overwhelms me with a sense of belonging, and it takes all of my willpower to pull away. Doing my best to lighten the mood, I laugh as I step back and look up at him. "You'd better." It comes out sounding flirtatious. That does it. So much for remaining aloof. Shame on me.

I walk around to the driver's side of my car. "Good night," I say as I step inside.

"Good night." He gives me a small wave and watches me drive off.

On my drive home, I replay the evening in my mind. The farther I drive, the easier it is to push Berkeley away. I turn up the radio, and the warmth of the evening subsides in the chill of the car while I concentrate on forgetting his easy laugh and how sincere he seemed by reminding myself how difficult he was to get over the first time.

Once I'm safely at the Vicente and have finished washing my face and brushing my teeth, my walls are almost rebuilt. I'm crawling into bed to indulge in the solitary rehashing of the entire night that I will allow myself, when my phone begins to buzz.

"Hello?" I answer in a slight fog, expecting Boots.

"You said I could call you. I couldn't wait," a smooth voice replies. That accent is so darn intoxicating! The butterflies immediately alert me to their presence.

"Apparently," I reply in what I hope is a light voice, blushing as I try to hide my pleasure. I'm glad he can't see me.

"I kept thinking how lucky I was to be at dinner with the most beautiful girl in the room."

Oh. He's good at this. I remind myself I'm in protective mode and therefore immune to his charisma. Thinking quickly, I try to fend him off. "You had dinner with Jessica Alba?" Jessica had been sitting in a secluded corner of the restaurant having dinner with a girlfriend. "She's probably pretty ticked you didn't talk to her all night."

Berkeley bursts out laughing. "*No!* I mean *you*, Funny."

"Good." I smile. *Hang on, don't fall.*

There is a momentary awkward silence before we both start talking at the same time. We giggle. "You first," I say.

"So how have the last few weeks been for you?" he asks, as I wiggle my way under the covers.

"Honestly? Sort of a roller coaster."

"Yeah? It didn't seem so bad from your tweets."

"You read my tweets?" I squeak. He doesn't follow me, and I can't imagine him looking me up. Apparently I'm not the only cyberstalker among us. My cheeks burn as my brain scrambles to recall anything incriminating he might have read. Oh no, oh no, oh no. As far as I remember, he was the topic of more than a few of my tweets. #mortified. "How many did you read?"

"Pretty much all of them." He laughs at my obvious discomfort. "I found them very entertaining."

"I'm sure you did…" I grit my teeth, making a mental note to privatize my account first thing in the morning.

"Have you read mine?" he asks.

Of course I have. I probably read through them a hundred twenty times during the height of my cyberstalking. Though I'm still trying to recover from the Twitter-revelation, I somehow manage to answer in my most nonchalant tone, "Well, I do follow you, so yeah, I've seen a few."

"Well, then we're even. I usually try to keep my private life to myself, but somehow you keep sneaking in…"

He doesn't give me a chance to contemplate his exact meaning before he continues.

"Anyway, I hope you don't think not calling you was easy. I thought about you more than I'm going to admit while I was in Europe."

You are made of steel, Olivia. Don't forget it.

"But the real reason I didn't call is I wanted you to have a chance at normal. I saw you with that guy after dinner at your place and he seemed safe for you."

"I did date him in college," I admit. "But trust me, he isn't good for me. After you left that night, I knew for sure I'd moved on. He was part of the reason I moved here. If he hadn't cheated on me, I may never have found the courage to give my dreams a shot. I can't imagine what my life would be if I stayed," I say, marveling again at the gift Michael bestowed by freeing me.

"I don't know if my world is any better—it's so complicated. Sometimes I think it's selfish to bring anyone into it. It's like living under a magnifying glass, and I thought it would be better for you if I left you alone." He pauses. "That's why I usually date people in the industry. They're used to it."

"Yeah. I noticed. You and Lisa are kinda hard to miss."

"Tell me about it. I hate that nothing is private, but Lisa really is just a friend, and everything you've seen or heard is part of a bigger scheme."

I can't help but wonder about his definition of friendship and the benefits it entails. The thought makes me sick to my stomach, and I push it away, reminding myself it's none of my business. It's not like Berkeley owes me an explanation—he barely knows me—but I do hope whatever their agreement is, it requires him to keep her at arm's length.

"It's a long story, and I'm not supposed to tell anyone this, but I trust you," he says.

"I won't tell; I promise."

"Thank you. Basically, my publicist thought Lisa was

necessary to divert the negative attention I was getting as I was going through a pretty bad breakup myself. The band supports a lot of people, and my reputation directly impacts sales. Market research says Brightside fans prefer me in a relationship, and more importantly the massive, influential "Berkstina" fans needed to think I left for love, so enter Lisa. I promise I'm not interested in her romantically; she was my publicist's idea. In fact, I've always thought she was an odd choice. She's so…vacant."

This makes me feel a little better. "Wow. That's a lot of pressure."

"It is."

"So the bad breakup was Christina Carlton?" I ask, hinting at Berkstina's very public demise. "What happened? If you don't mind me asking." *I can't believe I just asked that. Who am I to be flirting with the exquisite Christina Carlton's ex-boyfriend? I'm like some sort of ugly stepsister.* "I don't mean to pry."

"No. It's fine. I liked her—liked her a lot at first." He sighs. "She's very driven, and in the end I felt like she was only with me because of where our relationship could take her career-wise. All she cared about was getting press. She was constantly baiting me in public so we could play out some sort of drama for everyone to see, and she started to seem two-dimensional. She wasn't who I thought she was, and in the end she made it look like I broke her heart even though that's not what happened. It was the other way around—she was plotting behind my back with a costar."

He sounds sad, and I feel for him. I've never looked at the situation through his eyes before—never thought about how many people must try to use him to get ahead.

"I'm sorry," I say. "I never thought about it that way. It must be hard for you to know if someone likes you just for you—to find Team Adventure."

"Team Adventure? What's that?" he asks after a curious pause. He sounds amused.

"It's my dream," I answer, beginning to get drowsy. It's getting late, and after all the wine at dinner my guard is weakening. "I just want to find that person I can't stand to be without. Where I don't want to be independent anymore, and regardless of where I'm going or what I'm doing, I know it will be more fun if they're with me, and vice versa," I mumble, my eyes getting heavy. "I want to be part of a team that knows no matter what…we're in it together…it's our adventure…and we wouldn't have it any other way."

I fight to see through the slits, as I whisper, "Us against the world."

"I like the sound of that," he says with soft sincerity, and I smile, sleepy and content. "Hey—before I lose you—what's the verdict? You promised you'd tell me later." His voice is quiet, almost a whisper, as if he doesn't want to disturb me. "Are you glad you came?"

"Mmmmmmhmmmmmm…" I'm almost asleep. "Very glad," I drift. "So glad…Berkeley…"

Chapter Twenty-three

PARKER MIFFLIN @IsIndulgent
@BloomOlivia Mwahahahahaha…

Someone is knocking at my door. The sound pounds me into consciousness, and I hazily crawl out of bed. Not pausing to check my appearance, I make my way toward the noise. As usual, I assume Blair and Parker are here for their debriefing. Swinging the door open wide, I motion them in as I rub my eyes.

"Morning," I yawn.

"Good morning," says an unexpected voice from my dreams.

I snap to attention. Oh no. The previous night comes rushing back to me as I look down at my ancient sweat shorts and paper-thin Penn State T-shirt with a sick feeling in my stomach. My hair falls around me in complete disarray, and

I try to push it out of my face. "Hi," I say, unable to hide my surprise. "Come in."

"Sorry if I woke you." Stepping just inside the door, he removes his sunglasses and watches me as I fumble for a response. He's wearing a soft gray T-shirt and jeans and looks far more rested than I feel.

"No…I…I'm usually up by now. What time *is* it…? I guess I was up kinda late… Can I get you something? Coffee?" I complete the scattered string of thoughts.

He smiles. "I'd love some, but I can't stay long. I'm actually on my way to the airport. I have some press to do in New York over the next couple of days, but before I go, I wanted to ask you something."

"Go ahead," I urge as I sink onto the couch, confused as to what could be so important he'd show up unannounced on my doorstep.

"Well, I was sort of wondering if you wouldn't mind going on a little adventure with me," he says, fixing me with his sparkling gaze in that way that makes me feel my heart pounding in my toes. "I need a wingman."

What is he talking about? "Sure," I say slowly. "Where are we going?"

"To the Grammys?" he asks.

I'm glad I'm sitting down because I almost fall off the couch. Taken aback, I stare at him, my brain refusing to process his question. "You want *me* to go to the Grammys with *you*," I say, finally finding my tongue. The enormity of what he's asking is overwhelming.

"No, with my friend, actually, I already have a date." Apparently my reaction is entertaining because he's laughing at me. "Yes. I want *you* to go with *me*. That's why I'm here."

"Are you even allowed to go with me? I mean, aren't you supposed to show up with some sort of supermodel or something? Or Lisa?" I ask, purposely stalling to buy some comprehension time. My mind flashes back to the swimsuit model who'd interrupted our initial meeting near the restroom. Even she would be a far more appropriate choice. I'm nobody.

He considers for a moment as he leans against the doorframe before he gives me his full attention. "To be honest, that's probably what I'm *supposed* to do, but for once I don't care. This is what I *want* to do."

Want? I don't even try to process it. "Ummm... This may sound forward, but does this mean we'll be walking the red carpet? That we'll be seen together?" *And that the whole world will be staring at me? Gulp.*

"Why?" He smiles. "Do you mind being seen with me?"

I flush. "No. Not at all—I—"

"I'm teasing you," he says. "There are so many people at the Grammy's it's pretty easy to keep a low profile. We'll be walking the carpet in a group with the rest of the band and sitting with them at the show so it won't be obvious who is there with whom."

"That doesn't sound so bad..." *No regrets.*

"And we're only nominated for 'Best Rock Performance'—which is a sore subject—but it works in our favor because the press will want to spend more time with bands that have more nominations. I *am* presenting 'Best New Artist' so I'll have to do interviews alone and leave you with the band while I'm backstage—I hope that's okay—but you won't have to be photographed unless they do sweeping overhead shots or something. It's pretty easy to blend into the crowd if you want to."

I search his face. "You've really thought this through."

"I've been up thinking about it all night," he confirms. "I can't think of anyone else I'd rather go with, Liv... Will you come with me? Please?"

The earnest look in his eyes is making it impossible to say no. "I'd love to," I answer in a quiet voice, still trying to decide if I'm awake.

"Good." He nods. "I'll pick you up next Sunday at two." And with a pleased raise of his eyebrows, he makes his way out into the sunlight.

As the door closes behind him, I pinch myself to make sure I'm not dreaming. Lying back against the couch cushions, I cover my face with my hands. It's not real. No way it's real! I am on the verge of hysteria, but deep down I know this is really happening. Officially forgetting that I ever tried to stay away from him, I bolt upright. What am I going to wear?

Finding my phone, I dial Boots. She's not going to believe this.

She picks up almost immediately and answers in a hushed voice, "Hi, Liv, how are you?"

"Crazy. I mean it. I think I've officially gone mad. You are not going to believe what just happened."

"What happened?" she whispers.

"Are you okay to talk?" I ask. "Where are you? Why are you whispering?"

"I'm observing a liver transplant. I miss you, though. I feel like I haven't talked to you in forever, and we have exams coming up so I may not be able to talk much in the next couple of weeks."

"You can answer the phone while you're in the middle of a liver transplant?"

"Well, I'm not actually *doing* the transplanting. No, we're not supposed to, but these things take forever. Sometimes you gotta do what you gotta do. So what's new?"

"Well, the strangest thing just happened." I can't hold it in anymore and burst, "Berkeley Dalton just invited me to be his date at THE GRAMMYS!"

"ARE YOU FUCKING KIDDING ME?" Boots shouts. I hear a clatter in the background before she whispers, "Oops. That's insane. Wow... Uh-oh. I think I better go..."

"I'll tell you more later." I giggle. "Good luck."

Ending the call, I lay back on the couch, trying to steady myself. *This isn't happening.* Saying it out loud didn't make it reality. I don't deserve it... I haven't done anything worthy of such a gift, and part of me is afraid to believe—afraid that if I accept this as truth, it will disappear in a poof of fairy dust.

I don't have time to contemplate it. I'm scheduled for a recap brunch at the Nickel Diner with Blair and Parker, and I'm thankful I have them to lean on. Realizing I'm going to be late, I hurry to get changed.

"So? How was it?" Blair asks as soon as we slip into Parker's car.

"Incredible." I can't help but blush. "Dinner was great. He's so...so real. I can't explain it. I mean, I guess I expected him to be this powerful superstar and he *is*, but last night, I forgot about all of that. He's actually quiet and considerate and sweet…"

Parker smiles at me in the rearview mirror. "You like him."

My flush deepens. "Yes," I admit. "I like him. A lot. Oh, you guys, the craziest, scariest thing happened." My words spill out in a breathless rush as I recount last night's dinner and the phone conversation, minus the Lisa information. Even though I know they'd keep their mouths shut, and Blair would die to have the inside scoop on Berkeley's publicist, I made a promise and I will keep it.

We arrive at the restaurant, valet, and make our way inside. I'm just getting to this morning's surprise visit as we are seated in a back corner booth.

"…and I opened the door, expecting it to be one of you guys, and instead was surprised to find *him* standing on my doorstep."

"What? He was at the Vicente? This morning?" Parker asks. "I can't believe you didn't call me."

"I can," Blair says, glowering at him. "You probably would have shown up wearing your bathrobe and nothing else."

"Never. You know how shy and modest I am."

She rolls her eyes and I laugh; picturing Parker mixing us mimosas in his bathrobe makes this morning's events even more surreal. "Well, he didn't stay very long," I continue, lowering my voice. "He was on his way to the airport, but he just wanted to, you know, stop by and see if I wouldn't mind being his date for the Grammys…" I don't look at them as I say it, preferring to contemplate the menu. Again, I am struck with the fear that saying it out loud will make it all go away.

When I finally look up, Blair and Parker are staring at me in stunned silence. The quiet stretches on until Parker starts clapping, breaking the stillness. "Well done, Olivia Bloom."

At the sound of Parker's applause, Blair snaps out of her daze and her eyes sparkle as she says, "Liv, this is unbelievable. It's so romantic. What are you going to wear?"

"I have no idea. Help?"

"We have so much work to do." Blair takes charge. "The Grammys are on Sunday... We only have a week!" She's already digging through her bag for her phone as the waitress comes to take our order.

"Oh, I think we need a few minutes," I say, having yet to decide what I want for breakfast, other than the diner's famous maple bacon donut, that is.

"We're ready," Parker interrupts me. "She'll have an egg-white tofu scramble with roasted vegetables. No cheese. And fruit. And I will have the brioche French toast with butter and jam."

I stare at him as Blair places her order.

"What?" he asks, innocent.

"What if that's not what I wanted?" I reply.

"Honey, we only have a week to get you back in shape. All of that broken heart couch time has made you a little soft."

"Ouch!"

"I don't mean physically," he says. "You look great. I'm just saying maybe we need some refresher courses."

"It's true," Blair jumps in. "This is a big deal. We're going to need to pool our resources to pull this off and get you Grammy-ready." She is already busy texting. "Fortunately we just put on the Beverly Hills Fashion Festival honoring Halston, and we still have a bunch of the dresses at work — I'm sure I can borrow one."

"I'll see about hair and makeup. *The One* team will probably do it again, if they're available," Parker says.

"What about accessories?" Blair asks.

"I can see if Gemma will let me borrow some things. She's the queen of accessories. She rents a two-bedroom so her shoes can have their own room."

"Perfect," Blair says. "Parker, can you be in charge of appointments? We'll need wax, hair color, mani-pedi, a facial, a massage, teeth whitening…"

"What am I supposed to do?" I ask.

"Pilates, yoga, gyro-anything that will stretch you out and keep you as relaxed as possible. Work on your posture. Make sure you get up at work and walk around — we can't have you looking like a hunched-over computer curmudgeon," Parker says. "Get lots of sleep and drink only tea and water. Oh, and no solid foods. I think a juice cleanse is in order. Enjoy your last meal."

"Great. Thanks," I say, salivating as Parker slathers butter on his brioche French toast that has just arrived. "It's going to be a long week."

"Yes," Blair agrees. "But it's worth it. Aren't you excited? This is *huge*. You'll be the talk of the town."

"No," I say. "I'm petrified." The enormity of what is about to occur is hitting me. How am I going to ever fit in? Even with Berkeley & the Brightside by my side, I'm sure everyone will wonder what little old nobody me is doing there. "I don't want to be the talk of the town. I hate being the center of attention. I can't even walk into a room of ten strangers without clamming up. How am I supposed to walk into the Grammys? What if I end up on a worst-dressed list or something?"

"Impossible," Parker says, insulted. "You'll be the mysterious girl everyone wants to know more about. But don't worry about it too much. There will be so many stars to look at I'm sure nobody will worry too much about you."

"That's comforting. I hope you're right." I'm imagining the worst. "So, Blair, how was *your* date last night?" I change the subject. We'll be spending enough time focusing on the Grammys and Berkeley this week, it will be nice to talk about something else for a while.

Blair launches into the play-by-play of her boyfriend's birthday party at one of his clubs and how he brought in caged white tigers just for the event.

I listen, savoring my tofu, happy for the distraction.

Chapter Twenty-four

OLIVIA BLOOM @BLOOMOLIVIA
BASED ON MY MOST RECENT FOLLOWER, I GUESS THERE'S NO
REASON TO MAKE THIS THING PRIVATE.

MESSAGE FROM BERKELEY DALTON @BERKELEYBRTSIDE
@BLOOMOLIVIA HA-HA…DEFINITELY NO REASON

The week flies by, filled with beauty treatments and yoga classes. I secretly stray from my liquid diet and devour pita chips and hummus every night before bed in the privacy of my kitchen. I can't help it. I'm starving.

On Tuesday night I watch Berkeley perform on Letterman and struggle to equate the image on my TV screen with the guy that stood in my apartment a couple days ago. Watching him work feeds my neurosis that I made this whole thing up. Did it really happen? I know it did, of course, but I'm starting to wonder if everyone is going to all this trouble and he isn't going to show up. I begin to doubt him, remembering he said he'd call when he got back from Europe and never did; I'm having trouble trusting the same thing won't happen again.

I don't tell anyone about my fears, not wanting to worry them. Every evening Blair brings me Halston dresses she has lifted from her office, and I model them, trying to determine which is "the one." I can't decide. And I'm not enjoying myself. They're all beautiful, and I could never have imagined I'd be choosing a dress to wear to the Grammys, let alone having vintage Halston to choose from, but am I really going to the Grammys?

My paranoia eats away at me, but I try to push it aside and concentrate on work. The photo shoot is on Thursday and organizing samples and tying up loose ends keeps me occupied.

When shoot day is finally upon me, I arrive at the estate early to set up breakfast, which no one eats. I watch as the makeup artist transforms the model into a statuesque Brigitte Bardot for the first look. *She's gorgeous. What would it be like to look like that? People must fall all over her.* Berkeley should be taking someone who looks like her to the Grammys. I'm like a squat troll by comparison.

It doesn't help that the model, who is probably my age, if not younger, seems to think I'm her personal assistant rather than the person who set up this whole thing. She sends me off to do her bidding: can you carry my shoes?—I'm gluten-free, when you order my lunch make sure there's no starch—when you hand me a change, hand it to me hem first—don't you know anything? Sweating in the Santa Monica sun, I trudge along behind the crew, dragging endless wardrobe changes, trying to keep my head up and not think about how lackluster I am.

Lillian makes me feel a little better, asking my opinion about accessories and seeming pleased with the locations I've chosen, but I almost lose it when the estate owners yell at me for allowing the model to walk around topless in front of their teenage son. Why does she hate tops?

Needing a break, I excuse myself to a shady corner of the front porch, meaning to text my frustrations to Boots, but instead I see an alert that there has been a response to one of my tweets.

OLIVIA BLOOM @BLOOMOLIVIA
CAVALLI OR HALSTON? IF ONLY I HAD TO ASK THAT QUESTION EVERY DAY! I BETTER NOT GET STOOD UP.

BERKELEY DALTON @BERKELEYBRTSIDE
@BLOOMOLIVIA NOT A CHANCE. PROMISE.

He tweeted at me? I stare at my phone in shock, relief flooding my veins that I didn't make up the Grammys, though a new fear overtakes me as my in-box indicates my twenty new followers. What if Christina Carlton saw that? It is unfathomable that I'm going to the Grammy's with her boyfriend. *I mean ex-boyfriend. This is insane.* Not wanting to share our conversation with the world, I reply via direct message.

MESSAGE FROM OLIVIA BLOOM @BLOOMOLIVIA

@BerkeleyBrtside You cannot tweet @ me. You're going to give me a heart attack.

Message From Berkeley Dalton @BerkeleyBrtside @BloomOlivia Sorry. Can't help it. But I meant to direct message. Already deleted.

Message From Olivia Bloom @BloomOlivia @BerkeleyBrtside This is still tweeting. You obviously want me dead.

Message From Berkeley Dalton @BerkeleyBrtside @BloomOlivia I wouldn't say dead…

OMG. Running away, now.

Buoyed by the interaction, I'm able to suffer through the rest of the day doing the model's bidding. Besides, doesn't she know the rules? Assume everyone is someone? The lowly assistant on today's photo shoot may be going to the Grammys this weekend with Berkeley Dalton!

As the sun begins to set, Lillian thanks me for all my hard work, saying she can't wait to see the pictures and she thinks it's the best shoot Jonquil's ever done. I'm over the moon. *Yeah, it was a tough day on set, but the shoot came out great. Now I need to go home and try on some more Halston for the Grammys this weekend…* How is *this* my life?

Sunday morning dawns and I try to wake up. All the

anticipation and tension leading to today has led to many sleepless nights, and I hope the makeup artist can paint some life onto my face. The team, including Gemma who is armed with a steamer trunk full of shoes and accessories, is assembled in my apartment by nine. I bathe, and they set to work, masterfully plucking, plumping, and pruning. I'm more nervous than I was for Elton's Oscar party, even though this time I will have Berkeley & the Brightside at my side, and therefore, automatic validation.

Once the hairstylist is done tousling my hair to obtain that just-rolled-out-of-bed look, coaxing it to fall around me in a mass of perfectly distressed waves, I slip on the vintage cocktail dress we've settled on, and Gemma appears with gold chandelier earrings and black ankle-cuff Jimmy Choos.

The finishing touches complete, I step out from my bedroom in full dress. I'm the culmination of everyone's hard work and creative spirit, and I'm grateful to them.

"OMG! Seriously, I'm going to have to go dip my eyeballs in cold water, now," Parker declares as I make my entrance.

Everyone laughs.

While I was dressing, they repacked the abundance of tools that crafted my look, and now they all take leave, having decided it's best for me to be alone when Berkeley arrives. I'm ready. Bond girl-inspired TV Olivia is in place and, as promised, a large black Escalade with heavily tinted windows, carrying a tuxedo-clad Berkeley, arrives at the Vicente promptly at two o'clock. I answer the door on his second knock.

The sight of him clean shaven in his slim retro suit leaves me winded. As usual, he is just *so* handsome. I'm inexplicably happy to see him. *Is it possible I missed him?*

"You're stunning," he compliments.

"It took hours, and a lot of paint," I say with a lopsided smile. "You're not so bad yourself, you know."

"You need to learn how to take a compliment, but flattery will get you everywhere," he says, offering me his hand. "Shall we go?"

We step into the courtyard and are greeted with camera flashes as Blair and Parker take pictures of us on our grown-up prom date. All that's missing is the corsage.

I shake my head at them. I should have known better than to think they would stay hidden in Parker's apartment.

"Berkeley," I introduce him. "These are my friends, Blair and Parker whom you've met, and this is Gemma."

Blair smiles and waves hello while Parker steps forward, hand formally extended. "Nice to see you." He shakes Berkeley's hand, staring at him through narrow eyes that travel the length of his body, sizing him up. I'm almost surprised he isn't toting a shotgun with the scrutiny he's applying, and I widen my eyes at Parker, begging him to stop. Ceasing his examination, he finally smiles through tight lips. "Take care of our Olivia," he says, his voice implying there will be hell to pay if Berkeley doesn't return me in one piece.

"Of course," Berkeley answers graciously, unfazed, as he turns to Blair and Gemma. "Good to see you again." He hugs Blair hello as she mouths "oh my God!" at me over his shoulder. "Gemma, nice to meet you." He extends a polite hand, and I can see Gemma is having trouble standing, and it's not just because of her impossible platform boots. Her hand is limp in response, and she smiles a dazed hello. I know exactly how she feels.

"We should probably go." He places his hand at the small of my back and nudges me toward the gate. "Have a good night," he bids to the sendoff crew.

"You, too," Blair says. "Have fun, you guys. We'll be watching!"

We make our way out of the courtyard, but not before Gemma regains her faculties and grabs my arm. She leans into me, stealthily whispering in my ear. "If you're going to be late to work tomorrow for any reason, I'll cover for you." She winks.

I stare at her and stutter out a thanks as Berkeley pulls me forward onto the street.

The chauffeur opens the back door of the Escalade when he sees us coming. With a wave to Willis, who is wearing an impressive rainbow-colored umbrella hat and his bathrobe while watering his front lawn, I climb into the backseat of the car. It's like no car I've ever been in. With its wide, cream leather seats and wet bar, it looks more like a private jet.

Berkeley settles in next to me as the chauffeur closes the door on our private sanctuary.

"Are you nervous?" he asks.

"I'm always nervous around you," I reply. The butterflies threaten to fly me away.

He looks at me directly, and the vortex begins. Energy seems to reverberate around us, ricocheting off the walls of the car. "I mean about the red carpet," he says as the car lurches forward.

"Oh. That. It's so outside my frame of reference I can't even think about being nervous," I reply. "I went down a white carpet at Elton's, but otherwise I've never done anything like it. And I wasn't really being me that night; I was pretending to be someone else. Ordinary Olivia has definitely never done the red carpet." I'm rambling. Apparently, even though I'm able to have the occasional normal conversation with him, his presence continues to infect my tongue. "What about you, are you nervous?"

"Yes. Always. I hate this stuff," he answers. "It used to be fun when I was trying to make it—when I had something to prove. Back then I could walk down the red carpet and feel like I killed it, like I got myself out there. It was a huge victory when the press would finally notice me. It was great. Now, I'm under so much scrutiny, I just feel let down, like I let everyone down. I can never be good enough."

"I think you're beyond good enough," I say, staring him straight in the eyes. "And so does everyone else. Don't you notice how people look at you?" I pause for effect. "It usually goes something like this…" I glaze my eyes over and allow my jaw to hang open in a state of total zombie awe.

He laughs and gives me a playful shove. "She's not just beautiful; she's a comedienne to boot."

"It's my defense mechanism," I admit. "I find the easiest way out of an uncomfortable situation is through laughter."

"Well, I like it. Thank you." He smiles as his arm circles my waist. "Does this make you uncomfortable?" he asks with a glint in his eye as he pulls me closer to him.

I feel my body warm in response, and I can't help but inch closer still. Unable to resist, I am being drawn in to him. "You know it does," I say softly into his eyes as my breath catches in my throat.

Tipping my chin up with his free hand, he runs his thumb across my lips. "I'll have to work on that," he murmurs, his eyes never leaving mine as the car slows to a stop behind a line of black luxury vehicles outside of LA Live.

Our faces are inches from each other, and I'm having trouble breathing. In this moment he is my world and time ceases to exist elsewhere. "You're doing well so far," I whisper. Just then the chauffeur comes around and opens the door, blasting us with cool air and breaking the spell. Instantly composing my features, I jump away from Berkeley and turn toward the open door, trying to put as much innocent distance between us as possible. *Nothing happening here, Dad!*

Berkeley laughs at my overreaction but plays along with my routine. "I have to warn you, this can be pretty overwhelming," he says. "Are you ready?"

"I guess I have to be." I take a deep breath and swallow my nerves as he takes my hand and we step out of the car. "Just don't let me go," I murmur, holding his hand tighter to try to steady the quaking in mine.

"Never," he whispers in my ear, sending shivers down my spine. "All you have to do is smile and look pretty—which you're already doing. I'll do the talking. I'm going to try to talk to as few people as possible, but when I do you can just stay back with the band—I'll come right back for you, I promise."

Smile, look pretty, and not fall flat on my face, you mean. Got it. Even my knees are shaking. Out loud I say, "I think I can handle that."

"Here we go."

Hand in hand, we step onto the red carpet.

Chapter Twenty-five

The crowd erupts in a deafening roar, and my heart stops. I've never had so many people staring at me at once, and I start to hyperventilate a little, trying to keep my face a facade of calm. Overwhelming? This is like storming Normandy! There are people everywhere, and flashes explode all around us. It's chaos. Unsure of where to look first, my eyes focus on the disapproving face of a woman holding a clipboard in one hand and a Chanel clutch in the other. Her strawberry-blond hair is pulled back in a severe chignon and her nude strapless gown almost blends with her alabaster skin. I have the distinct impression she is angry with me, her wide-set eyes scalding.

I don't have time to consider the bizarre woman's reaction,

though. Behind us, Mark, Ted, Jeff, and his wife, Alexandra, emerge from another Escalade and join us. Berkeley re-introduces me, and as a group, we step slowly forward.

The crowd erupts as Berkeley & the Brightside are announced. Taking it all in, I look from Mark to Berkeley to the endless line of reporters, and a strange thing happens. The throngs of photographers and fans surrounding us go silent in my head and the moment engulfs me. As I stare down the red sea, it's like looking through a fish-eye lens. The crowds become a giant blur of sparks and faces as a drumbeat begins to pound in my head, and I walk to the rhythm. I look around and everything moves in slow motion, "*Da da da duh da. Da da da duh da…*" It's extraordinary to have so many people howling and cheering us on. An imaginary wind machine picks up and blows our hair around. We are caught in a swirl of cameras and color. "*Da da da duh da. Da da da duh da…*" I am inundated with confidence and adrenaline. So this is what confidence feels like! We smile, they wave, slow motion flashes blaze.

I mingle with the Brightside as Berkeley charms reporters, taking Mark with him occasionally, and always returning to my side as soon as possible. We make it down the carpet in record time, as he selects only a few reporters to talk to, pretending not to hear when the others frantically call his name. As we come to the carpet's conclusion, the imaginary music fades and my vision sharpens into focus. I snap out of my euphoric daze.

With the bulk of the celebrities still on the carpet behind us, it's less chaotic here near the entrance to the Staples Center. It almost feels private.

Berkeley pulls me aside and leans toward me, whispering, "You made it."

Exhilarated, I turn to him and exclaim, "How can you not love that? That was incredible. I want to do it again! It's like being caught in the middle of a happiness storm—having all of those people cheering you on—adoring you—sharing this joy with you—" I'm giddy with energy so it catches me completely off guard when Berkeley cuts me off midsentence.

Out of nowhere, he ambushes me. Seizing my face in both of his hands, he leans into me and without warning his lips are on mine. My eyes widen as he eases my lips open. Instantly lost, I succumb, closing my eyes. His mouth is full and his skin is smooth as he kisses me. Enveloped in his clean scent, and helpless to resist, I kiss him back. His hands move behind my neck and he pulls me closer to his chest in a full embrace, deepening the kiss.

What was I saying about incredible? I'm so dizzy I'm almost to the edge of consciousness. We kiss for what feels like eternity until I start to become aware of flashbulbs sparkling in my periphery.

Opening his eyes, Berkeley breaks away and rests his forehead against mine, ignoring the cameras, his focus solely on me. Still holding me close, he whispers, "So much for keeping a low profile...do you want to get out of here?"

I can only nod and hope my legs can carry me.

We take off through the crowd, holding hands as we run, frantically dodging photographers, musicians, and models. We skirt around power cables and barriers until we find the parking lot of waiting limos. Back at the Escalade, Berkeley tells the driver to get lost.

"We may need to hide out in here for a few minutes to let the photographers find something more interesting to look at," he says as we scramble into the back of the car.

"Fine by me," I say, a bit breathless. I'm filled with adrenaline, the kiss having unlocked a long buried longing that Berkeley seems to be feeling too.

He closes the door behind us and urgently pulls me on top of him, his mouth instantly finding mine. I can feel his hard strength beneath me as I fold my legs on either side of him and he moves his hands up my thighs and under my dress.

A vision of what exists under my dress—a full, thigh-sucking body-shaper suit and duct tape—darts through my mind and terror strikes as I realize I can't let him discover this. *Spanx! Is there anything less sexy?* Thinking fast, I snatch his hands away from my thighs and direct them to my back, outside my dress, as I deepen our kiss and move my hands to his chest. I know where this might be going—and I *want* it to keep going—but I have to stop it. Of all the lingerie I could have worn…

I come up for air, tearing my lips from his and finding his eyes. "We can't." I moan, not believing my own words. "We shouldn't…"

He throws his head back and takes a deep inhale as his hands run the length of my body from my waist up to my shoulders, and he pushes me down harder into his lap. He kisses me again, and I am lost in his insistence. His hands are everywhere, and I'm starting to think maybe Spanx aren't so bad—I mean, they're crotchless—when his kisses start to slow and become more tender. His fingers move to my face and through my hair before he finally pulls away, seemingly at a loss himself.

"You're right," he whispers as he pulls me into his chest and holds me there. "I shouldn't have. But I couldn't help it."

I can feel my heart beating against his as I try to calm myself, to comprehend his meaning. My head isn't clearing, though, and once I begin to catch my breath, I crawl off him and lean back in the seat, my eyes on the Escalade's ceiling.

Peeking out the corner of my eye, I find him watching me, his eyes burning. Fighting for distance, I close my eyes, trying to compose myself. He is overwhelming.

With a groan he tears his eyes from me and pulls himself upright. "We have to go now, or else I'm not going to let you leave this car," he says.

I nod, not totally opposed to staying here, as I try to straighten myself. Thankfully I have sex hair anyway, so I don't have much rearranging to do.

"Are the photos going to be bad for you?" I ask as he throws open the door, allowing the cool air to sober us.

"It'll be fine," he promises. "My publicist can fix it."

Best in the business, Blair's voice reminds me.

Looking only slightly rumpled, we head back into the Staples Center, careful to keep our distance from each other as if nothing happened, while he sends a quick text.

Once we're inside, we find our row. I am to be seated between Mark and Berkeley and Mark grins at us as we sink into our chairs. "Where have you been?" he asks.

"Forgot something in the car," Berkeley replies, narrowing his eyes at Mark.

"Ah," Mark says as he averts his eyes to the stage, but he is still smiling.

Sitting back, I peek at Berkeley's perfectly symmetrical profile, my thoughts turning to the near escapade in the Escalade. That was so *almost* rock 'n' roll. He catches me looking. We share a conspiratorial smile, and he reaches out and squeezes my hand.

Hook, line, and sinker, I'm in love.

Chapter Twenty-six

PARKER MIFFLIN @ISINDULGENT
I SHOULD HAVE BEEN BORN ROYAL. I WOULD LOOK
FABULOUS IN A CROWN. #JUSTSAYIN

BLAIR HAMILTON @SUPERSPINSTRESS
@ISINDULGENT YOUR HEAD WOULDN'T FIT IN A CROWN.

PARKER MIFFLIN @ISINDULGENT
@SUPERSPINSTRESS MODESTY IS FOR PEASANTS. #SHUDDER

Berkeley doesn't leave my side the entire evening save for
when he has to go to present the Best New Artist award. A
seat filler arrives and I smile at the guy, who is likely a USC
student. *I probably look like I belong with him more than a
superstar like Berkeley.*

Berkeley stands. "Take good care of her for me," he says as he turns to leave.

The kid goes pale, seemingly stunned that Berkeley is talking to him. "Umm...sure. Oh-okay."

I'm glad I'm not the only one Berkeley has that effect on.

The seat filler sits, offering me a weak smile before turning to the stage, apparently afraid to look at me again.

In Berkeley's absence, I use the time alone wisely, stifling the hysterical urge to giggle, while tweeting at Blair and Parker and texting Boots. Reality smacks into me, though, when he walks onto the stage with Beyoncé. Observing him as a spectator once again, I sit riveted by his powerful presence, trying to place the Berkeley who was with me in the Escalade with the Berkeley I am watching now. It's almost impossible to believe they're the same person, and like the rest of the audience, I'm unable to tear my eyes from him.

In a daze, I watch him banter with Beyoncé and read the nominees' names before he hands the gold gramophone to his friends, The Remainers. Watching it all unfold before me, I begin to question my role in all of this. What am I doing here? There has to be some mistake. I've just about convinced myself I'm out of my league and should head back to the Vicente and get comfortable in my faded Penn State T-shirt when he slips back into the seat next to me. He catches my eye with a sidelong glance and an imperceptible hint of a smile. My heart skips, and I feel myself connect with him on the most intimate levels. I know exactly what he's thinking—and I like where he's headed. Inching closer to him, I smile softly back, finally comprehending the difference between the larger-than-life Berkeley I've just witnessed on stage and the Berkeley that sits next to me now. This one is for my eyes only.

Even though Berkeley & the Brightside doesn't win the Grammy for "Best Rock Performance," they don't seem bothered, and the night progresses in an endless round of after parties. We're separated from the rest of the band as Berkeley has different parties to attend, but he introduces me to everyone who is anyone, and I'm content to observe as he captivates each room. I even manage to remain cool and collected as I try to decide who is more charming, Berkeley or George Clooney. (I have to give Berk the slight edge on this one, but maybe I'm biased).

The only scar on the perfect evening occurs at our last stop on the party circuit. I'm relieved to finally be talking to someone familiar as we are reunited with Mark. The three of us are standing in a dark corner in The Spare Room lounge at the Roosevelt Hotel when across the bar Lisa Greene appears. As usual, I pass completely under her radar as she spots Berkeley and makes a beeline for him.

"I thought you'd never get here." She pouts as she approaches us, seductively wrapping herself around his arm. "You know I don't like to be kept waiting." She's wearing a skintight strapless dress, the hemline barely grazing the top of her tiny thigh.

Taken aback by her blatant come-on, I try to give her the benefit of the doubt, figuring that having never seen Berkeley and myself together before, she's made the incorrect assumption that I'm here with Mark. I take a step back, shifting uncomfortably away from her.

"Oh, hi, Lisa," Berkeley says, attempting to disentangle himself. "You remember Olivia and Mark, right?"

"Of course." Her eyes gloss over me without the slightest hint of recognition before they fully focus on Mark, and she moves to hug him. "Mark! I miss you. We need to hang out. You boys should to come to my place for breakfast and try my organic granola. Tomorrow?" She lets go of Mark and fixes Berkeley with her wildcat stare.

I silently applaud as he notices me trying to slip away and catches me around the waist with his free arm, pulling me back to his side. "Ummm…it's getting pretty late, actually, and I have a feeling I'm going to want to sleep in…" He punctuates his sentence with a sly glance in my direction.

"Oh. Right. It *is* pretty late," she agrees. "Time flies when you're waiting…maybe the day after tomorrow, then?" Cocking her head to the side, she adds, "I'll call you." She trains her sights on Berkeley before slinking away, seemingly unfazed by my presence, her eyes full of promise.

"Pleasure as always, Lisa!" Mark calls after her, laughing and shaking his head as he raises his glass toward her in mock sincerity. I'm glad to know I'm not alone. Lisa's either a really good actress or really dense. Either way, she's irritating. I'm trying to decide which of the two is more likely, when Berkeley's breath brushes my ear, "Ready to go?"

"I thought you'd never ask." I smile.

Once we're back in the Escalade, he doesn't offer me the option to go back to the Vicente—which is fine with me. Instead he directs the driver to his house as he tucks me into his side. We are silent for the ride, both happy for a moment of peace after the whirlwind evening. His arm is around me, his fingers tracing a shape on my bare arm, and I sit with my legs curled up on the seat and my head against his chest as we wind our way to his house. For the first time,

I'm completely comfortable with him.

"I'm sorry about earlier," he says, breaking the silence. "I should have had more control."

"You don't have to be sorry. I'm not," I say, looking up at him as the memory of the kiss unleashes a small flutter in the pit of my stomach.

He frowns as his fingers stop moving and, gripping my arm, he pulls me up to face him. "You don't know what you're getting yourself into," he says. "And it's not fair to make you decide this now. I owe you more time."

"Decide what? I'm not sure I understand what you're talking about."

"I know." A sad smile twitches the corner of his mouth as he studies me. The car pulls to a stop behind the gate in Berkeley's driveway. "It's just that I like you, Liv, and I don't want anyone to hurt you. Being seen with me comes with a lot of baggage—you need time to see if it's worth it."

"Berkeley, I don't think anyone could hurt me as long as I'm with you," I reply, looking him directly in the eye, trying to convince him he doesn't need to worry—that I already think it's worth it, but even I am surprised at the conviction in my voice.

"Thank you," he says, his eyes lighting up as he smiles, sending warm shivers through my body. "But I'll still do my best to give you time. I made a mistake tonight, kissing you in front of the cameras, but I promise I won't let it happen again—until you're ready."

The driver opens the door, and giving my arm a small squeeze, Berkeley helps me out of the car.

"I don't think we should worry about it anymore tonight," I say, trying to lighten the mood as we walk to his front door. "Your publicist is taking care of it anyway, right? It'll be fine."

"She is," he says, opening the front door and ushering me in.

I find this entrance far less intimidating than my previous foray into his space. He abandons his jacket and tie and loosens his shirt while I kick off my shoes and excuse myself to the restroom. Once inside, I text Gemma that I'm pretty sure I'm coming down with "flu" and ask her to spread the word at work tomorrow, before wiggling out of my under armor body suit and ripping off the tape. Stuffing the "lingerie" remnants into my handbag and stowing it behind a plant near the front door, I make my way toward Berkeley. He's in the kitchen, and I take a seat on a bar stool on the other side of the now notorious island where I once made guacamole.

"Hungry?" he asks.

"Starving."

We fall silent as I watch him navigate the space, preparing a cheese, cracker, olive, and mustard feast.

"Thank you for tonight," I say, suddenly unsure of what is going to happen next after our intimate conversation in the car, and feeling the need to fill the quiet. "I had an amazing time. I'll definitely never forget it."

"I hope not," he replies. "It was certainly out of the ordinary. I don't make a habit of kissing girls on the red carpet."

I blush.

He shakes his head, concentrating on slicing before peering up at me from under his eyebrows. "I don't know about you, Olivia Bloom…"

I open my mouth to defend myself, but it's too late. He's already come around to my side of the island, and his face is dangerously close to mine. He doesn't hesitate as he does the one thing certain to disrupt my argument: he kisses me.

This kiss is slow and penetrating; I feel its effects all the way to my toes as my skin catches fire and my head whirls. He runs his hands up my thighs, and this time I don't stop him. Moaning in soft surprise as his fingers find my hip and connect only with skin, his kiss becomes insistent as he pulls me closer to him, and his hands move to cup my backside as I wrap my legs around him. I cling to the back of his neck and his lips linger on mine as he picks me up and carries me to his bedroom. Reaching the bed, he disentangles our limbs and throws me onto it. Giggling, I bounce away as he crawls playfully on after me and catches me around my waist, pulling me toward him, picking up where he left off. His lips are soft, and his breath is warm as he navigates my mouth. He's impossible to resist, and I get to work removing his shirt, tossing it aside as I run my nails down his bare back before feeling my way across his strong chest and lower, to his pants. Managing zipper and buttons, I discard his pants while he reaches into a drawer and finds a condom.

I want to feel every inch of him, and my hands are free to explore. I can barely contain myself, but with tight control, he takes his time, tantalizing me. Kissing my eyes, my face, my forehead, my ear before concentrating on my neck. He slips my dress over my head and works his way down to my breasts, and I arch into him, urging him to keep going.

His flesh rubs my flesh, his skin searing me as he comes up for air.

"You're beautiful," he whispers, resting his forehead

against mine as we lock eyes and his fingers trace the shape of my waist and come to rest on my hips.

I shake my head and my response is lost as his mouth finds mine again. The next thing I know, protection in place, he is filling me, taking up all the swollen spaces inside, exploding my mind in bliss. My eyes widen, and all I can see are his blue eyes. A soft cry escapes my lips, my body rhythmically responding to his as we move together. All I know is him. He is everywhere, moving me, engulfing me, leading me to the edge, until together we climax.

He holds me close while we slowly flutter back to earth, taking our time, savoring the moment. His lips brushing my forehead, he rolls us over, never letting me go, allowing my head to rest on his smooth chest as he wraps his arms and a sheet around me, tucking me in. We don't talk, and I don't care. We don't need to; this is where we belong. I'm sleepy and dazed and utterly content. The tension and buildup and sleepless nights leading to this moment are erased as Berkeley quietly plays with my hair. All I know is that I never want to let him go, and I cling to him, allowing a whispered, "*You're* beautiful," to escape my lips as I succumb to sleep.

Chapter Twenty-seven

Mrs. Bloom @PsychicMom1

@BloomOlivia Your palm's fate line has always been deep—Trust—it is out of your hands. #nopun

The shrill bell cuts through the silent air, and from somewhere deep in my conscious I will it to stop. What *is* that?

As I come to, I realize it's the phone. Covered in the thin sheet, I'm laying on my stomach. Forcing my heavy eyelids open, I try to push my hair off my face as the noise subsides.

Attempting to focus, my bleary eyes open and meet Berkeley's. He's propped on one elbow, staring at me. The lower half of his body is covered in my same sheet, exposing his lean, muscled chest. He reaches out to help me with my hair placement.

"Good morning." He smiles as he tucks a strand behind my ear.

"Good morning," I reply before burying my face in my pillow to hide the delighted grin that is permanently affixed to my face. *I can't believe this is happening!*

"Hey, no hiding. Come back here." He moves to pull me toward him, but the shrill ringing begins again, halting his progress.

I look up from the pillow. "Are you going to get that?"

"I don't really want to." He sighs. "It's not going to be good news. The only reason someone would be calling this early the morning after the Grammys is to tell me I did something wrong."

The phone goes silent.

"Well, I'm going to have to disagree with that," I tell him. "In my estimation, you definitely did everything *right* last night." I slide across the bed until my body is pressed against his and accost his lips with a seductive kiss. Caught off guard, he kisses me back, running his fingers down the length of my body, igniting me in chills. I understand his surprise because I've just shocked myself. I'm not usually this aggressive, but the longing to touch him at all times is more than I can bear.

"Is that so?" he murmurs, pulling his face away from mine so he can see me. "Well, I'm not so sure about that. I think there *might* be a thing or two I could perfect." His fingers trace the shape of my hip. "Maybe?"

"If you think you need more practice, I'm happy to oblige." I smile.

The ringing starts again.

He groans. "I'd better get it. She won't leave us in peace if I don't." He climbs out of bed and crosses the room to a small desk that holds a phone and a laptop.

I can't help but wonder if "she" is Lisa Greene as I

admire him from behind. He turns to face me as he picks up the phone, and I avert my eyes.

"Hello, Shar," he says into the receiver, his tone flat. Before he can complete her name a female voice begins to screech on the other end of the line. He holds the phone away from his ear.

I can't quite make out her words, but her pitch is definitely unhappy.

Pulling the phone back to his ear, he yawns. "No, I haven't seen it. It's seven fifteen the morning after the Grammys; sorry if it's not exactly prime gossip site surfing time for me." He pauses. "Okay. I'm going."

Cradling the phone between his ear and his shoulder, he opens the laptop and types in a URL. A moment later, he smirks at whatever is revealed to him on the screen, his eyes lighting up as they flicker to me and back to the screen, a small smile forming on his lips.

"It's not that big of a deal, Shar."

The voice on the other end of the line seems to feel differently and continues its grating dialogue.

"No, I haven't considered that... I don't know."

Shar's voice squawks in response.

"It's not what you think. It's different. I don't expect you to understand."

He listens to her before stating in a voice that is final, "I just know, okay." After allowing her to speak for a few seconds longer, he cuts her off, his voice lacking its previous control. "Listen. I know you've been working hard, and I'm sorry her publicist let you have it, but can I remind you I asked you several times to put a stop to the rumors about me and Lisa? You wouldn't listen, so now maybe I have your attention."

I've never seen him angry before, save for those brief moments following the Santa Barbara concert, and even then it was somewhat good-natured. This is something else. His eyes burn bright and his steady voice has an icy edge to it as he continues, "I've met someone I actually like and I can't be seen with her because it looks bad? Fix it, Shar. I don't care how you do it, just fix it. It's not fair." He slams down the phone and runs his fingers through his hair before turning to me, his sweltering eyes giving me their full concentration.

"I'm sorry you had to hear that. That was Shar, my publicist," he says. "Clearly she's a tough lady and we don't always agree on what's best…but something strange is going on. She couldn't erase the pictures, and she thinks," he pauses, and I tense with anticipation, "that you've been hiding something from me."

My stomach drops. I'm certainly not hiding anything, but this Shar lady is one of the biggest publicists in the world—who knows what she has the power to plant. She obviously isn't happy about whatever is on the computer screen… What did she tell him? "What could I be hiding?" I ask tentatively.

"Well," he says as he turns the computer toward me, a smile tugging at the corners of his mouth. "For starters, you didn't tell me you were an It girl…"

I fly out of the bed, taking at least four steps before I notice my lack of attire and scramble back to the bed to tie a sheet around myself before I confront the computer screen.

Amused, Berkeley watches my hijinks and makes no move to assist me.

The screen is set to FelixSheridan.com, and the majority of the page is captivated by a large image of Berkeley and me lip-locked in an intimate embrace at the end of the red carpet. My eyes take in the massive headline "Berkeley Ditches Lisa for Liv." I can see why Lisa's publicist is upset. Further down on the page is a smaller picture of me standing in my coral Matthew Williams dress on the white carpet in front of the white wall stamped with black Elton John Oscar Party logos. The stark white surrounding me makes my bright coral dress pop out of the picture. I'm impossible to miss. This headline reads, "Who Is She?" and is followed by two short sentences that identify me as "the newest It girl, well known in Hollywood party circles, rumored to be the lead in Brad Pitt's top-secret feature." Even though he didn't post them at the time, Felix must have saved his insight and pictures from Elton's party should the need arise and will be credited as the first to break the story.

I finish reading and look up at Berkeley, who is studying the horrified expression on my face.

"I'm so sorry," I attempt to explain. "I'm definitely not an It girl. This is from an experiment Blair, Parker, and I performed at Elton's party. We never meant for it to show up anywhere. To be honest, I'm not that much of a party girl. I'd rather have a glass of wine in the courtyard at the Vicente than be seen at the newest club, if that's any consolation..."

Berkeley laughs. "Well you must have made quite an impression on Felix Sheridan because even Shar can't get him to take the story down, and he's usually at her beck and call."

I stare at him, feeling sick to my stomach. "I don't know what kind of impression I made. It was all a ploy to get the paparazzi to take my picture, and apparently it worked," I admit. "I'm so sorry. This looks really bad for you."

"It's okay." He smiles. "Believe me, I've been through much worse than suddenly being romantically tied to the newest ingenue in the business. I have to ask, though, how do you know Brad?"

My cheeks bloom red. "I don't. Oh my gosh, is Brad going to be mad at me, too?"

"I wouldn't worry about it too much. He's pretty easy going...and nobody's mad at you."

"Except for Shar."

"Not even Shar," he says. "She's mad at me. It's not your fault—it's mine." He looks back to the screen. "The paparazzi took your picture, though. That's impressive. Those guys recognize celebrity; they don't photograph just anyone. You've got presence, Liv." As proof, he scrolls down the page and the screen fills with pictures of us kissing and running through the crowd—even pictures of us scrambling into the Escalade. They are endless, and the only thing I can focus on is how handsome he looks in every scene. He's a star; his image jumps off the screen and screams "look at me!"

Even though I can hardly believe it possible, my blush deepens. "Look who's talking about presence," I interject in an attempt to dodge his compliment. "You captivate women all over the world, Mr. Dalton." My eyes flash at him in defiance.

He looks at me and softens. "I'm not captivating—far from it, actually. I'm just honest. And to be honest, I've never met anyone I liked more than you. *And*, for once in my life, I don't care who knows it."

My attempt to make sense of his words is squashed as he snaps the computer shut. "Breakfast?" he asks, as if he hasn't just revealed his undying love for the rumpled girl standing before him wearing only a sheet.

"Ummmm…I don't have anything to wear," I say with a fleeting peek at my sheet.

"I don't have a problem with that." He grins. Planting a kiss on my forehead, he leads me to the kitchen. "Come on, I'll make you some eggs."

Fortunately/unfortunately he's out of eggs.

Chapter Twenty-eight

AMANDA CONRAD @BOOTSMD
PROUD TO SHARE A BLOODLINE WITH @BLOOMOLIVIA. GURL,
YOU WORKED THAT RED CARPET!

After "breakfast" Berkeley offers to drive me home to the Vicente to pick up some clothes.

"If I drive you down there, you have to promise you'll come back with me, though," he says as he hands me a pair of his sweatpants and an undershirt. "It's probably best we stay together for a little while—that way I can help you avoid the cameras," he reasons.

I smile as I pull on his shirt. "That's fine with me, if it's fine with you." I can't imagine a more appealing scenario.

"It is definitely fine with me," he says, grinning at the sight of me swimming in his clothing. "We have to be discreet, though. Follow me."

He pokes his head out the front door and scans the yard before guiding me stealthily outside and around to the side of his house where he keeps his cars. Silently we creep along, alert to even the slightest noise that might indicate a member of the paparazzi has infiltrated his abode. His house sits below the main street, and it's nearly impossible to see beyond the gates surrounding the property at street level, but I suppose it's better to play it safe.

We reach the carport, and he opens the back door to his Audi. "I know this is going to sound ridiculous, but if you wouldn't mind lying back here on the floor and covering yourself with this blanket, it'll make things a lot easier." He hands me a blanket identical to the car's gray interior.

"Do this often?" I ask, unable to prevent the question from slipping out. It comes off sounding accusatory. I didn't mean it to.

He looks at me head-on. "No. I've never done this before."

I feel the heat from the intensity in his eyes, and I know he means it. "I'm sorry," I apologize, looking away. "That wasn't fair…"

Cutting me off, he wraps his arms around me. "It's a totally fair question. I've been portrayed a million different ways in the media, and not all of them are flattering, so you should feel okay to ask me anything. I promise I'll always be honest with you." He releases me. "As for the blanket, it was a gift from my sister. I've never figured out a use for it until now. She's more paranoid than I am—you'll see when you meet her."

Meet her? An image of Mia Dalton, Berkeley's gorgeous, Oscar-winning sister and indie-film darling, materializes in my brain. I've always enjoyed her films, often delighting in the characters she chooses to play—from a showgirl in Paris, to a 1960s rock star, to a flapper-mafia wife—I mean, the costumes alone are enough to make me want to grovel at her feet. I hope Berkeley is kidding. I'm just getting comfortable around him—I can't fathom how tongue-tied I'll be around his sister. She's going to hate me, for sure.

My eyes are wide as I crawl into the back of the car and try to make myself comfortable on the floor. "I hope you'll give me some advance warning before you go making any introductions."

"We'll see." He laughs as he covers me with the blanket before shutting me in and settling himself into the driver's seat. He obscures his eyes with his Ray-Bans and turns up the radio as he maneuvers the car to the top of the driveway. I hear him murmur as the gates part, "Wow, Olivia. You've made quite an impression," then louder, "Here we go!" The car lurches forward, and I am vaguely aware of a commotion outside and fists pounding on the deeply tinted windows. I know they can't see me, but I try to make myself small. We inch forward for a few moments longer, clearing a path in the paparazzi before Berkeley breaks free and steps on the gas. He expertly maneuvers the winding turns in the canyon as we speed out of the Hills and toward the Vicente.

Once we're out of Hollywood and less at risk of being noticed, Berkeley allows me to climb into the front seat with him. I attempt to look dignified as we pull up to the Vicente and am relieved to find the courtyard appears to be empty. Not that this is a walk of shame, or anything—I just don't much feel like explaining to Blair and Parker that I'm not going to be around for a few days. With Blair gone so much, part of me feels like I am abandoning Parker. I'm pretty sure he'll survive, though. Our world-traveling neighbor Jessie is in town this week so at least he has her.

"Do you want me to come in with you?" Berkeley asks.

Conjuring an image of him sitting alone in the car, I'm suddenly terrified he won't be waiting for me when I come back outside. An overwhelming need to keep him near overtakes me—I've never felt anything like it before and it startles me.

Thus far he seems to always tell me exactly what he's thinking so I decide to try his tactic. Moving my eyes upward from my lap to meet his, I take a deep breath and answer, "This is going to sound crazy, but I think I'd miss you too much if I was away from you for that long." It doesn't make any sense. Yesterday I spent my entire life, save for a few hours here and there, away from him. It is unfathomable how quickly my emotions have changed.

His face lights up in response. "It's not crazy. I'm pretty sure I know exactly how you feel."

After pulling the car keys from the ignition, he follows me into my apartment as I promise to make it a quick stop.

Two distracted hours later my apartment has been devirginized, and back in my own clothes with my bag secured in his trunk and me secured under Mia's blanket, we make our way up the hill.

On this drive, instead of turning up the radio, Berkeley starts to hum a melody. "I love driving," he says. "Whenever I'm writing, I always get the best ideas when I'm on the road. Sometimes I drive for hours, winding around on Mulholland, getting lost in canyons. I guess in a way the hum of the tires and the motion of the car is meditative. I don't know. Anyway, this song just popped into my head. Can I sing it for you?"

"I'd love you to sing me a song," I answer, my voice muffled by the blanket, feeling like the luckiest girl in existence.

He begins to sing, his voice tender.

"*I could spend all day, tucked in a hideaway, with my lovely little Liv, laying low, laying low, We're headed for somewhere, a place all the dreamers can do as they dare, we're headed for somewhere...*"

Feeling my eyes well up, I chide my pathetic tear ducts and the ease with which they overflow as I giggle and cry under the blanket. "You just made that up?" I ask, hoping my voice doesn't betray my emotions. "You're pretty good. You should write songs more often," I tease, thankful he can't see my face and how touched I am.

"I have to say, I'm feeling particularly inspired today for some reason." I think I hear him smiling. "Honestly, I haven't felt this relaxed in a long time..." He trails off as we slow to navigate through the paparazzi outside his gate, and he turns serious. Listening as he mutters his frustration, I try to imagine what it's been like for him to have to put up with this for so many years. For me it's all new and exciting, but I'm sure for him the shine has dulled.

The pounding fists and screams fade away as the gate closes behind us, and Berkeley drives down the hill into the carport. Turning off the car, he's silent and still. I remain hidden, wondering if there's a reason for his solitude. A moment later, I feel cool air as he leans into the backseat and pulls the blanket down to reveal my face. He stares down at me swaddled in my cocoon and smiles. "Thank you, Liv."

"For what?"

"For putting up with this craziness. For putting up with everything I've put you through. You must think I'm insane—throwing parties for you, sending you Lakers tickets, showing up on your doorstep, kissing you at Grammys, hiding you under blankets, forcing you to stay with me... I'm not usually like this, I promise." He takes a deep breath. "It's just I've never met anyone like you before. I can't resist you."

I can't deal with his words or their implications and I put up a wall, instead focusing on the most comprehensible part of his statement. "You sent me Lakers tickets? How? Parker said he didn't know you'd be there..."

Berkeley's eyes have a mischievous twinkle in them as he replies, "Parker didn't know. I have my ways..."

"Are you magic?" I ask, at a loss.

He smiles and shakes his head. "No."

His earlier words are starting to sink in, and again the need to touch him overtakes me. This feeling, this longing, this fullness in my heart—the meaning behind what he just confessed scares me, and I do the only thing I know how to do when my emotions overwhelm me.

"No? Me, neither." I sigh. "If I was, I would have levitated out of here by now. Can't a girl get some padding down in this piece?" My back is aching from the uncomfortable car floor that I am wedged on, and Berkeley laughs as he races to my rescue.

As we walk back to his house, hand in hand, I try to forget his compliments because I know if I accept them, I'll be putting everything on the line—and I will not recover from the disappointment if he changes his mind.

The only thing I know for certain is being with Berkeley is *intense*.

Chapter Twenty-nine

BERKELEY DALTON @BERKELEYBRTSIDE
SO THIS IS WHAT IT'S LIKE TO BE HOME FOR THREE DAYS. I
SHOULD DO THIS MORE OFTEN. #NEVERWANTTOLEAVE

As soon as we're safely back inside Berkeley's house, I sneak away to a secluded corner of his balcony to call Gemma. If Berkeley thinks it's best for me to stay with him for a few days, I'm not going to argue, but I'll need to get out of work. I dial her extension.

"Gemma, it's Liv," I whisper.

"Liv!" she squeals before lowering her voice. "Oh my God, Liv. Where are you? Are you freaking out?"

"No. I'm perfectly calm and in control. Why do you ask?" I try to play it off, but it's no use. I can tell she's not buying it. "Yes, I'm totally freaking out. I'm at Berkeley's, and he thinks it's best for me to stay for a few days, that way he can protect me from the paparazzi."

She exhales a soft "Ohhhh…"

"Do you think I should call in sick?" I ask.

"After that kiss? Impossible. Liv, you are the talk of the planet right now."

"We are?"

"Haven't you seen the Internet? You're everywhere."

"Well, I guess I've been a little distracted," I admit. I haven't given much thought to what rumors might be spreading; I've been so wrapped up in Berkeley. It seems like it was a week ago that I read Felix Sheridan's page, even though it was only this morning.

"What do you think I should do?" I ask. "If it's as bad as you say it is, probably the only way anyone will believe I'm sick is if *US Weekly* prints an article about Berkeley contracting the flu after kissing me."

"And even then you'd have to ask them to write in you're waiting on Berkeley hand and foot wearing a Jonquil chemise or something," Gemma jokes. "You could call in lovesick, maybe."

"Gemma, you're brilliant," I say, her joke striking a chord. "Can you put me on the phone with Lillian?"

"Sure," she says. "Oh, and make sure you get some rest, stay in bed…" she advises before putting me on hold and transferring me.

Lillian answers her phone right away. "Liv," she says. "How are you doing?"

"Pretty good," I reply, remembering I'm supposed to be ill. I hate lying, and I'm guessing she knows why I didn't come in today. "I sort of had to take a personal day today."

"Understandably. We were all so shocked to see the

Grammy coverage. We had no idea you're dating Berkeley Dalton! It's thrilling."

"I'm not *dating* him, exactly..." I realize I'm not quite sure how to describe our relationship. I guess last night was our third date, and technically it hasn't ended, but everything has been so spread out, and dating implies sequential outings and the promise of more to come. We haven't discussed that, and frankly I'm not sure I'm ready to. "It's very new," I hesitate. "I guess you could say we're figuring it out." I'm nervous to ask for time off, especially when I have all the photo-shoot images to go through. Having my name on that shoot is such a big step for me, I hate to push it to the backseat, but at the same time...it's Berkeley. As much as I don't want to be the girl who gives up everything she has going for some *guy,* I do it anyway. Taking a deep breath, I continue, "And that's why I'm calling. I might need a few days to let the dust settle."

"Of course, take a few days," she says. "Just let us know when you're ready to come back."

Well, that was easy. "Thank you, Lillian. That's really nice of you. And hey, I was thinking this could be good for Jonquil—maybe we'll get some press mentions out of it?"

"That would be wonderful," she says. "But no pressure. When I was your age, I spent a glorious weekend in a cabin in Carmel with one of the members of The Doors—not Jim Morrison, so he was no Berkeley—and *we* were probably on LSD..." She trails off, perhaps remembering. "But it was one of the best weekends of my life. This is a special time. Enjoy it."

What? I scramble to picture poised Lillian as a drugged-out hippie groupie. This does not compute. I want to know more, but now isn't the time. "I really appreciate it," I reply. "And it will only be a few days, I promise."

"We'll see you soon. Have a good night."

"You, too." I end the call and turn to open the French doors that lead to Berkeley's living room.

He's sitting just inside at his piano, staring at the keys as if they're telling him a secret. I try to tiptoe by, not wanting to interrupt.

Looking up with a good-natured smirk in his eyes, he catches my wrist as I pass and pulls me onto the piano bench with him. "So you're not exactly dating me, huh?"

A blush spreads over my face, even though his comment is flippant. "Eavesdropping does not become you," I say, pretending to glare at him, but then I relent. "I didn't know what to say, but whatever I said worked. I got my permission slip signed."

His eyes warm. "You can stay?"

"Yes. For a few days, anyway."

"Perfect. I haven't had a day off in over a month. We've been so busy touring, and even when we're in town we're still promoting the album so there are interviews or shows almost every day. I could use a break."

"I'm sure you can," I agree. "Want to start now?"

"I have the perfect spot," he says as he stands and walks to the kitchen. Pulling the plate with last night's untouched cheese and crackers out of the refrigerator and tucking a bottle of wine under his arm he asks, "Will you grab those blankets off the couch?"

"Sure," I reply, gathering the soft cashmere throws in my arms.

He guides me out the French doors and along the terrace

that runs the length of the backside of his house. Opening a little gate at the end, we step onto a dirt path that leads through a grove of fruit trees. The sun is beginning to dip into the sea and a golden sky is visible through the branches rustling overhead. On the other side of the grove, the path opens to a grass knoll where two Adirondack chairs and a small table sit in front of a panoramic view of the valley and the sweeping sky beyond. It's a quiet spot, isolated and private, surrounded by hills and invisible to prying eyes.

Directing me to a chair, he arranges the blankets around me as the valley lights begin to sparkle at my feet.

"It's breathtaking," I say as I sit back and he opens the wine.

"Yeah. This place is what sold me on this house," he says. "I love looking out over the city and imagining all the people and what they're doing. It inspires me. I don't come here very often, though."

"Why not? I think I'd be out here all the time."

"Unfortunately, I'm not alone much. Usually there's a ton of people over here, and sitting in solitude admiring a view isn't exactly high on their entertainment list."

He pours me a glass and hands it to me.

"Point of Grace," I say, referring to the wine label as I take a sip. "That's the same wine you brought to dinner at my house. Is it your own blend?"

"Sort of." He pours himself a glass and takes a seat.

"I was kidding. You're a winemaker, too?"

"No." He smiles. "Point of Grace is my grandparents' winery in South Africa—where the heavens meet the vines. They make sure I have a constant supply."

"South Africa," I venture. "I've noticed you sometimes

have an accent…"

He takes a big sip. "Yeah. My mom grew up there, and when we were little, Mia and I both had strong accents from being around her all the time. It was fine until I started school and realized I sounded different than everyone else. I worked really hard to learn to talk 'normal' whereas Mia embraced being different and tried to learn more accents. It's probably why she's such a good actress. For me the South African inclination is still there, but I'm pretty good at hiding it." Swallowing another sip, he stares at the city. "Except when I'm nervous."

"*That's* pretty interesting." I grin, thinking back on all the times I've noticed his voice slip.

"Well don't count on hearing it again." He looks at me, innuendo in his eyes. "You've seen me naked, so there's not much left to be nervous about."

My stomach tightens with anticipation, but I'm not ready for him to take me to bed yet. I want to keep him talking, so I change the subject. "Do you hang out with the guys in the band a lot?"

He looks disappointed, but he answers my question. "Yeah. We're like a family; we love each other, but it's good to have some distance once in a while. We usually take some time apart after a tour, but then we start missing one another."

"I was on your bus once; I can see how things might get a little cramped."

He looks at me, curious. "When were you on our bus?"

"In Santa Barbara. Mark gave Blair and me a tour. And the bus gave us a beer out of the seat cushion," I add.

He laughs. "So then you know. It's not so bad at the start

of a tour—we're always excited to have new material and a new experience. By the end, though, usually someone is not talking to someone else and another person is quitting the band...it never lasts, but the final few days are an eternity."

"Why does it end up like that?"

"Lots of reasons. Not sleeping, living on top of one another, crazy hours, creative differences. The road wears you down. It's funny, though, even with all that, I'm always a little let down when a tour ends because I know when we start again the next time, we'll have changed a little bit without one another. It'll never be the same. And I always wonder if maybe that was our last show."

"Why?"

"Sometimes I think we'll eventually go our separate ways. Everyone wants to try new genres and collaborate with other artists—we love music, that's why we do it—and it's frustrating having to stick to a sound you crafted when you were twenty."

"Can't you try something different but still be Berkeley & the Brightside?"

"I wish it was that easy. If it's too different the fans won't buy it," he explains. "So we have to be true to the sound we established eight years ago. It's our brand."

The impact of what he's divulging hits me. "You can't stop! You're my favorite band." For a split second I revert to fangirl and am devastated at the thought of them breaking up. "I don't know what I'd do without your music. I'd be lost." The fan in me wants to grasp some small piece of memorabilia to remember them by, and I look around frantic, trying to memorize every aspect of my surroundings.

"It won't happen anytime soon, don't worry," Berkeley

says, amused. "We still have two albums left on our contract, and like I said before, the band's a big business—it supports a lot of people—we're not going anywhere."

"Well, that's a relief. You scared me. I was about to ask if you wouldn't mind autographing my bra so I'd have something to remember you by."

He takes his time responding, his eyes slowly looking me up and down. "But you're not wearing a bra," he finally points out.

"Well, I figure what's the point of putting one on if you're just going to take it off?" I reason, with a mischievous flash of my eyes.

"I'm a big fan of your logic, Liv."

"Well, I'm a big fan of yours." I smile back.

He stands and leans over my chair, lowering his mouth to mine in response. The kiss is gentle at first, and I lean back, allowing him to coax my lips open, demanding more as he takes us deeper, and the rushing world spins.

Slowing the kiss, he murmurs against my lips, "I think I better get you back inside."

I don't disagree.

Pulling me to my feet, he wraps the blanket tighter around me, and we make our way back through the orchard to his house, where Berkeley verifies I am, in fact, not wearing a bra.

Chapter Thirty

OLIVIA BLOOM @BLOOMOLIVIA
THIS MIGHT JUST BE THE PRETTIEST DRESS I'VE EVER WORN,
SUCH A SHAME THAT I'M GOING TO SWEAT ALL OVER IT.

As the first rays of Tuesday morning light peek through Berkeley's blinds, we're jolted from our slumber by the sound of the front door slamming shut, followed by a screeching voice.

"BERKELEY! I know you're in here!"

Berkeley groans and rolls onto his side. "Damn it. I never should have given her a key." He rubs his temples as though willing her to go away.

"Who is it?" I ask. Unnerved by the intrusion, I cower under the blankets.

He climbs out of bed, pulling on a pair of jeans and a white undershirt while he calls out, "I'm coming, Shar!"

Turning back to me, he whispers, "You stay here. I'll take care of this… And don't worry!" He kisses my forehead before he leaves the room.

As soon as he's gone, I leap out of bed and slip into a comfortable maxi dress. I wash my face, brush my teeth, comb my bangs forward, and braid my hair to the side. After a quick mascara application and a swipe of lip gloss, I feel refreshed. This Shar woman scares me, and if I do meet her, I want to be presentable.

Moving to the bedroom door, I press my ear against the wood, straining to hear the conversation coming from the living room.

"I can't believe you cut off all communication for two days after that stunt." I hear Shar say. "I should have known something was up after you tweeted at her, but I wrote her off as some fan you were being nice to. It's all so unlike you…"

"I know," Berkeley says simply. "I can't believe you barged into my house."

She ignores him. "Me, neither. I never thought I'd have to resort to such a thing; you're always so well behaved. This is shocking. It can't go on any longer. You have commitments. It's starting to look bad," she says. "Lisa's publicist is having a field day with this, and it doesn't help when you're a no-show to events and you won't even talk to me."

I can't make out Berkeley's response, but from his tone it doesn't sound like he's apologizing.

Shar's booming voice is loud and clear. "Of course you deserve a break, but I've never seen you like this. Who is this girl?"

"I'd rather not bring her into this." His voice is muffled,

and I struggle to make out his words.

"Well, you should have thought about that before you allowed yourselves to be photographed by every photographer in the free world. What were you thinking?"

I crack the door open slightly in order to hear his response.

"I wasn't, for once. I don't expect you to understand."

"This is bad, Berkeley. You're risking everything we've been working for. They're dragging your name through the mud and they'll take her down with you. I guarantee they're finding any dirt they can on her, and what they can't find, they'll make up."

"Lisa's people will do that regardless," he says, his voice tinged with regret.

"Listen, the way I see it, you have two choices," she says. "Call Lisa and go out with her immediately—we'll spin this Olivia Bloom person as a momentary misjudgment on your part and Lisa's people can have fun with all the ways you'll make it up to her. I can erase Olivia, make the world forget about the kiss. Felix owes me one if he wants to get back into my good graces. I'll get him to plant a story and she can go back to her normal life. *Or* you can start being seen with her. She'll lose all of her privacy, of course, and Lisa's people will rip her to shreds, but maybe we can make her the new Lisa. It'll be tough, though."

Berkeley's laugh is bitter. "What a selfish decision to have to make."

Erase? It's like the wind has been knocked out of me.

The room goes silent.

Finally Berkeley speaks, "It's not fair to Liv to put her through this—either way—maybe I should call Lisa and see if—"

Before he can finish, I recover my faculties. Realizing I find it extremely irritating he's considering me in all of this when *he* is the one with everything to lose—not to mention the last thing I want him to do is call Lisa—with courage I don't know I possess, I throw open the bedroom door and march into the living room.

"Don't you dare!" I cry out, ignoring Shar and setting my sights on Berkeley. My bravado wavers as they both stare at me. "You can't…" My voice cracks pitifully as it trails off.

Berkeley's eyes warm me and he smiles, shaking his head. "No. I can't." He moves forward and takes my hand. "I wanted to keep you for myself, but I guess I have to share," he whispers to me before turning to Shar. "Shar," he says, pulling me forward, "I'd like you to meet Olivia Bloom."

I recognize her in an instant as the alabaster woman from the red carpet. She makes no move to greet me as her wide, staring eyes examine me. She must be able to see every cell in my body she's staring so hard. I try to remain unaffected, but I cringe as I imagine what I must look like to her. After all of the brilliant beauties Berkeley has dated, I must seem insignificant.

With a grimace she tears her eyes from me and speaks to Berkeley as if I'm not present. "This is your decision, and there's no turning back after this. Are you sure you want her?"

"Positive," he replies, his eyes never leaving my face.

"Then I guess she'll have to do," she says, adding to herself, "she's not much of a seductress, but maybe that will work in our favor."

Before Berkeley can admonish her insult she transfixes

me with her eyes again. "I just hope you're media trained."

Recoiling from her bite, I prickle against her obvious judgment of me. *Does she doubt my intelligence? What does she know? She just met me!* Besides, after all the time Blair and Parker spent honing my skills, I do consider myself "trained." Feeling the need to prove myself to this woman, I silently vow to survive anything she throws at me—it certainly couldn't be anything worse than The Spin. "I'll do my best," I say in quiet defiance.

"Your best might not be good enough. You have to be better than that," Shar says before turning to Berkeley. "You have the premiere of the new Bond movie tomorrow night and you *will* attend," she says. "After all, you wrote the theme song. It would be a major misstep not to give it its due."

"Of course," Berkeley answers. "I had every intention of attending."

"Good," she says. "We need to plan our attack. Your friend here needs to look perfect—elegant—regal even. It's our only hope to dispel the rumors Lisa's team is spreading." She takes a deep breath. "What a mess. I'm going to call my friend Kay to style her," she says as though I will need to repay her kindness with my firstborn.

Part of me hopes she means Kay Pritcher, my favorite stylist, while at the same time I hope she means another Kay entirely. I've watched her reality show on Bravo religiously since it started airing last year and have tried to mimic her signature California style since day one. I can't fathom she would drop everything to come dress me for a movie premiere. How did I get here?

Shar retreats to make our wardrobe arrangements while Berkeley pulls me into a quiet corner of the kitchen.

"Is this okay, Liv?" He leans over me, his voice hushed. "I'm sorry to drag you into this. You can still change your mind."

"It's fine. I don't mind, really. How different can it be from the Grammys?" I ask.

"Not much in procedure. The difference is now people know your name. And they'll have opinions and make comparisons. I'll shield you from as much as I can, but it's impossible to hide from all of it. Some of the bad stuff always trickles in, and it's hard not to let it affect you, at least on some level. Do you think you can handle it?"

I try to comprehend what he's telling me, but I truly don't understand how this is any different than going with him to the Grammys. "I'll be fine. I'm stronger than I look." I flex my arm to prove it.

He doesn't grant me the smile I'm eager for, and the joy is lacking from his eyes as he shakes his head. "I hope so."

"All right, we're all set." Shar comes around the corner into the kitchen. "The team will be here at eight o'clock tomorrow morning to prep you. I'd appreciate it if you would do me a favor and stay here where you won't be photographed until then."

She's just sentenced us to life in heaven, and as the corner of my glance meets Berkeley's in heated anticipation, we make an unspoken agreement that sends a tickle down my spine.

"We'll be here if you need us, but I can't imagine you'll be needing us," Berkeley says, leaving no room for misinterpretation as he guides her to the door. "We'll see you in the morning."

"Get some rest," she prescribes, as she steps out the

door. "I need you at your best tomorrow."

"I promise I'll put her to bed right away."

"Oh, Berkeley!" I hear her exclaim as she walks off, muttering something about insane celebrities.

He closes the door behind her. "Well, this is a surprise," he says, turning to me. "Another day off... What would you like to do?"

"I'm sure we can think of something." I saunter over and push him back against the door, leaning my body into his as I rise on my toes and persuade his mouth. "I thought she'd never leave." I breathe into him.

"Me, neither," he murmurs, his hands raising the soft folds of my dress. Finding my thighs and running his hands along them, he hooks the corner of my underwear and rids me of them.

He picks me up, whips me around, and slams me back against the door, wedging me there. His mouth moves from my lips to my neck, sending delighted sparks through me, igniting my body with need. I can't undress him fast enough. My fingers fumble with his jeans until I reveal him, and we slide down the door. He tries to roll me onto my back, his teeth grazing my collarbone, his tongue moving lower, but I push him to the floor, wedging my leg between his as I struggle to dominate. Underneath my dress his hands are everywhere, coercing me, and I lower my face to his, trying to subdue him with my mouth. He emits a low groan as he rips my dress straps from my shoulders, forcing the bodice down until it's around my waist. I pull up to hover over him, letting him look as I rip open a condom and roll it onto him (I keep them on me at all times now). My legs on either side of his body, I slip onto him, allowing just a taste before sliding off. I taunt him until need overtakes us both and he bursts through my walls, filling me. Throwing my head back, I dictate the ride, letting his hands explore, before leaning over him, urging him deeper for the final act. My mouth finds his again as his arms tighten, clutching me as the pressure mounts, and we crash into a splintered mass of shivers.

He holds me close as our breathing returns to normal, and I kiss his forehead and cheeks, waiting for my mind to solidify and resume cognition. He doesn't make it easy, just his nearness obscures the path.

Slowly my synapses begin firing again, and I climb off him. "Thanks," I say, trying to keep my voice casual. "I needed that."

Narrowing his eyes at me in a seductive smile, he catches me around the waist and pulls me back toward him, not letting me escape as he penetrates me with a kiss that turns my mind to ether. Breaking away, he asserts with dashing poise, "Thank *you*. So did I."

He wins.

Leaving me in a bewildered heap, he stands, putting himself back together before he offers me his hand and pulls me up. Guiding me to his bedroom, we crawl onto the bed, and he gathers me into his side. Turning on the TV, we stay in bed all day watching movies, alternating between sleeping, snacking, and sex, not necessarily in that order. It's perfect.

When we awake the next morning, we're refreshed and ready to face the public. Shar arrives with her team to prep us (mostly me) promptly at eight. Her entourage includes a pale, waiflike assistant named Eden and a robust makeup artist named Nancy. They are followed fifteen minutes later by Kay, who turns out to, in fact, be the Kay I've been hoping for/dreading. In person she is petite and her face shows its age, lined from too much sun, but her eyes are energetic.

She and Shar embrace, revealing a side of Shar I've yet to see. They hug, jumping up and down, chattering a mile a minute in lighthearted chirps. Had this been the side of Shar I was first confronted with, I'm sure I would have reacted differently to her. I have trouble equating this chipper chipmunk with the icy albatross she has thus far presented and wonder how many personalities exist behind her frigid stare.

Introductions are made as Kay rolls into the house, her rack stuffed with gowns for me and suits for Berkeley. The dresses are an array of designers that range from Marchesa to Balmain and are accompanied by suits by D&G, John Varvatos, and Armani. I am in awe of the spread displayed before me as she unwraps her wares.

"All right. First things first." She looks us over, sounding like a playful drill sergeant. "Berkeley, let's get you out of the way." She thrusts a stack of hangers toward him. "Try these on for me, sweetie."

Berkeley good-naturedly models for us—looking impeccable in everything he puts on. He is decisive, and it's clear this is just another day at the office for him. "I like this jacket," he tells Kay as he admires a black John Varvatos with leather buckles ornamenting it. "I don't think it's right for tonight, but I'd like to buy it."

"I'll put it on your tab."

It's not lost on me that the price Berkeley just paid for

that jacket could probably pay my rent for a month.

His wardrobe is determined fairly quickly, as Kay decides he will wear a deconstructed suit consisting of skinny black jeans and a fitted white shirt with the sleeves rolled to his elbows. A tailored gray vest, slim black tie, and soft gray leather high-top sneakers complete his look. She pins out some of the space on the vest, assuring him that the alterations will be made before we need to leave.

Now that Berkeley's wardrobe is settled and things seem to be running smoothly, Shar excuses herself, claiming calls at the office, and prep at the theater. She promises we're in capable hands and that she'll see us at the premiere before taking leave.

"All right, Olivia. Your turn." Kay beckons me toward a spare bedroom.

I look to Berkeley for permission. "I guess I'll just go?"

"Is that okay? Will you be all right if I leave you with them for a little while?" he asks, sounding concerned. "I wouldn't mind getting some writing done, and you'll probably take longer to dress than I will." He winks.

And debrief. "Of course. Go write. Don't worry about me. I'll be fine. You don't have to watch me get ready; that would be so boring for you."

"I disagree. Watching you do everything fascinates me. But I think writing will be more productive." He leans in and kisses me softly. "I'll see you in a little bit," he whispers before heading toward the living room and the piano.

I turn to Kay and she fans herself with her hands. "You two are adorable. Everyone is going to *love* you. Come with me, Olivia." She takes my hands and leads me to a spare bedroom. "We're going to find you the perfect thing to wear.

And it should be a surprise." She smiles as she closes the door behind us.

Kay is much warmer than I expected her to be. Having watched her on TV, I know her cunning and sharp tongue. She likes things her way and is passionate about her vision. I don't expect her to be accommodating or to take my opinions into consideration—which is fine with me. Having always held her in esteem and trusting her instincts, I'll do anything she tells me to.

She begins laying dresses across the bed and goes to work, pairing shoes, jewelry, and handbags with each look. She steps back often, considering her work and glancing back and forth between the bed and me before she rearranges the pieces, sometimes tussling everything into a jumble to see how it lays, allowing for unexpected surprises. I watch her method, enthralled, while I thrill to the fact that she, too, spreads everything out magazine-layout style, as I do. She finally narrows the options to three looks.

"You need to look polished," she tells me. "To dispel the temptress rumors Lisa's team is spreading. Let's try all of these on and see how you feel. I want you to wear the dress, not for it to wear you. It's important you're comfortable."

I take mental notes, memorizing everything she is saying in case I ever get to play the role of stylist. "They're all beautiful," I tell her. "I'm sure any one of them will be perfect. I love them all. I can't decide."

"Try them on," she urges.

Soft strains from Berkeley's piano drift into the room as I slip each dress on, and I wish every day could be like this— me trying on designer dresses while Berkeley Dalton plays the piano in the next room. I could never have dreamed this for myself.

The dresses are all made with precision, their tailoring expert. I finally understand why people spend this much money on designer clothing. This fit and attention to detail cannot be mass produced.

I step out in the third and final piece, a couture Sachin & Babi dress with a nude sequin bodice, black sash, and pale green satin skirt accented with pleated ruffles creating style lines over the princess seams.

Kay sucks in her breath. "That's the one, sweetheart. It was made for you. Here, put these on." She hands me a pair of lace Louboutin sling backs. "Perfect," she says. "Now all we need are accessories."

I study myself in the mirror. The dress is a fantasy. It is refreshing and elegant, the sash accentuating my waist while the neckline lies in a perfect scoop, revealing just enough. She gives me diamond earrings and a pale gray clutch to complete the look. Turning to Kay, I tell her, "I love it." But as I stare at myself I start to worry the look is too elegant. Berkeley's a rock star, and I feel like I need to have a little edge.

"What is it," she asks. "Something's bothering you, I can tell."

I'm afraid to tell her what I'm thinking. Having seen her TV show, I know she berates clients, bullying them into believing she knows best. I'm afraid if I offer a suggestion she'll yell at me, but I really believe I have a valid point. Taking a deep breath, I go for it. "Well, I was thinking maybe the look needs a little edge? Maybe I could paint my nails really dark and wear a bunch of different rings or something."

She considers for a moment, nodding to herself, and I brace myself for the tsunami. It doesn't come.

"I think I have the perfect color," she finally says as she turns to dig through a bag.

"Really?" My shoulders go slack as the tension releases. "You're not mad?"

"Aha! Burnt Plum," she announces, pulling a tiny pot out of the recesses of her bag. "Mad? Why would I be mad?"

"Well, I've seen your show on Bravo, and I thought you didn't like other people's opinions," I admit.

"Oh." She dismisses the notion with a wave of her hand. "That's just for the cameras. If I walked around being nice to people all the time, it would be so boring they'd probably cancel the show. The truth is, I *love* it when a client has ideas. I think it's ideal to have them wear something of their own—something that's their signature style—that way they feel confident in the look. And *confidence* is what great style is all about. It takes a lot of effort to look effortless, and it's impossible to pull off if the client isn't behind the look one hundred percent. That's the true secret to being a good stylist."

My mental notes are turning into a novel.

"Besides," she says as she finishes pinning some minor alterations on my dress, "I can tell you have good instincts. I trust your opinion, and I'd be happy to work with you again, anytime."

The compliment warms me. I needed to hear that. "Thank you. I'd love to work with you again, too. I'm a huge fan," I say. I don't know what the rules are anymore.

We try the dress with the rings I've chosen: a stack of simple chains, a dove with delicate wings, a twisted snake with tiny diamonds for eyes, a delicate Egyptian scroll, and a large moonstone.

"Love it." She smiles, then calls Nancy in to paint my nails while they discuss my hair and makeup.

Eden appears as well.

They decide to arrange my hair in soft waves while leaving my bangs straight and angled off to the side. For makeup, they will concentrate on my eyes, painting my lips a pale pink.

Nancy sets up a chair for me in front of the mirror and rolls out her brushes as I change into a fluffy white bathrobe. She begins by cleansing and toning my face as we make small talk. It turns out she's been working with Berkeley for the last six years, and she quickly becomes a favorite of mine as she chats effervescently in a charming Irish lilt.

Seemingly out of nowhere, without any pleasantries, Eden launches into my briefing and I jump, having forgotten she's in the room.

"Things you cannot discuss," she begins, reciting her list in a bored voice as Nancy falls silent and massages a hydrating cream onto my cheeks, "Lisa Greene, obviously, your relationship with Berkeley—we can sell the exclusive rights to that story later—politics, not that anyone would ask you about that anyway, your opinions on movies, TV shows, music, books, or art. Basically, you can't have thoughts on anything."

I marvel at how the tables have turned. If the rules Blair and Parker laid before me seemed extreme, the rules on this side of the camera are even more ridiculous.

"We need people to like you, and Lisa's people are not making that easy," she continues. "Her people are portraying you as the other woman right now—the vixen who stole Lisa's man. Combine that with your party-girl image and we've got our work cut out for us. We need to make you look as innocent as possible."

"They are?" I ask. Berkeley has cleverly been diverting my attention from the media since I arrived, and I've yet to read anything that has been written about us.

Eden hands me a tabloid, and I look at the cover as Nancy rubs foundation into my skin.

A large, particularly sultry image of me from Elton's Oscar party is paired against a picture of a wholesome Lisa looking adoringly at Berkeley as they walk casually along Robertson, coffees in hand. The headline reads "Olivia's Seduction Secrets: How She Bewitched Berkeley" and goes on to paint me as a conniving, evil, seductress who plotted to steal Berkeley from the winsome, unsuspecting Lisa.

It's a shock to see myself portrayed in such a light, and it stings me to the core to be judged by people who have never met me. My instinct is to fight their assumptions, and I wish they'd stop talking about me. I can't be that interesting. I'm nobody, and right now I wish everyone would remember that and I could go back to being nonexistent. *How does Berkeley deal with this all the time?* I'm not sure I can handle being as famous as he is. Hopefully this will all blow over soon.

"It doesn't seem fair that Lisa's publicist can spread these vicious lies without giving me the opportunity to defend myself or make a first impression," I say, indignant over the article. "It's so far from the truth. Nobody has ever considered me a vixen before—and I can't imagine anyone will believe it."

"That's what we're hoping," Eden says, her voice monotone. "You'll get used to it, but we do have our work cut out for us—people definitely believe it. You should see what they're saying about you on Twitter."

"What do you mean?" I ask, fear leaping into my throat. "Will you hand me my purse? I'd like to see my phone."

She shrugs and leaves to find my bag, returning a moment later and dumping it in my lap. Locating the device, I check my in-box and am shocked to find hundreds of Twitter mentions. Incredulous, I scroll through the insults that are being dished out in one hundred forty characters or less. The majority of the tweeters seem to side with Lisa and are calling me names like "tramputee" and "slutapotomus."

CHRISTINA CARLTON @CELEBRIGHTLY
ALWAYS NICE TO SEE AN EX TRYING TO MOVE ON. IT'S HEALTHY.

LISA GREENE @THEGREENEGODESS
WHO IS THIS LITTLE GIRL WHO STOLE MY FAVORITE ACCESSORY?
#IWEARITBETTER

LISA GREENE @THEGREENEGODESS
SO THAT'S WHAT IT TAKES… #SERIOUSLY?

TEAM BERKSTINA @BERKSTINAFANS
DIE @BLOOMOLIVIA! @BERKELEYBRTSIDE AND @
CELEBRIGHTLY 4-EVER!

Ouch. Biting back tears, I keep scrolling. "Whatever

happened to 'if you can't say something nice'?" I wonder aloud. People are ruthless. The next tweets I see make me smile, though.

PARKER MIFFLIN @ISINDULGENT
@SUPERSPINSTRESS HOLY HOTNESS @BLOOMOLIVIA IS DELICIOUS…JUST ASK @BERKELEYBRTSIDE *FANS FACE* #SWOON

BLAIR HAMILTON @SUPERSPINSTRESS
@ISINDULGENT I KNOW. OUR LITTLE @BLOOMOLIVIA IS ALL GROWN UP. LIV, COURTYARD MIMOSAS ARE READY WHEN YOU ARE! #DETAILS!!!

AMANDA CONRAD @BOOTSMD
@BLOOMOLIVIA ALL THE HATERS CAN BUZZ THE <BLEEP> OFF. THEY'RE JUST JEALOUS. IF THEY MET YOU, THEY'D ALL WANT TO BE YOUR BESTIE. #LUCKYME I GOT YOU FIRST!

Grateful, I tweet back.

OLIVIA BLOOM @BLOOMOLIVIA
@ISINDULGENT @SUPERSPINSTRESS I MAY NEED A REFRESHER COURSE ON #THERULES LOVE YOU! XOXO

OLIVIA BLOOM @BLOOMOLIVIA
@BOOTSMD NO, #LUCKYME. XOXO

Eden returns to her list of instructions as I try to defeat the gnawing dread the tweets have left me with. I put my phone away. "You are only to talk about what you're wearing. That's it. I'll be giving the press a list of off-limit topics as well, so you shouldn't have to worry much."

"And I *wouldn't* worry too much," Nancy says, probably noticing my furrowed brow as she lines the inside of my eyes with a shimmery white cream. "At least they're talking about you—people pay a lot of money for this kind of publicity—it's not a bad thing. Ask Berkeley. He's been through it all right, and he's turned out just fine. Don't forget there are people saying nice things, too. The nice things are just harder to believe."

"I definitely didn't see any strangers saying anything nice," I reply, struggling to keep my brimming eyes from overflowing.

"Your fans are out there. You'll see. They just haven't met you yet. After tonight, they'll see what Berkeley sees, and they'll love you. I just know it."

"I hope you're right," I say, blinking away my tears. "Thank you for believing in me."

"Welcome to fabulous show business," says Berkeley from behind me. "Isn't this fun?"

"It *is* fun," Nancy replies for me as she dries my eyes and finishes sweeping mascara across my lashes. She steps aside as Berkeley comes around and stands in front of me. A surge of happiness courses through me at the sight of him, stamping out the negativity. I've missed him. Over the last couple of days I've become accustomed to my Berkeley, and seeing him dressed for the cameras startles me at first. Magnetism emanates from him, and I'm reminded of when I watched him perform in Santa Barbara. His face is smooth and his eyes are bright—he's pure, massive charisma, and I can't tear my eyes from him.

"Wow, you're beautiful," he whispers, taking the words from my lips.

"Get out of my head," I rebound the compliment back to him with a glint in my eye, instantly relaxing as I glimpse *my* Berkeley shining in his. As long as he's by my side, I'll be invincible.

He smirks, eyes dancing, as he leans in to kiss me. Before he reaches his destination, though, Nancy swats him away.

"I just spent twenty minutes painting those lips—don't you mess them up!" she scolds.

He stops short, his face hovering inches from mine, and glances up at her with a good-natured glare.

She laughs and drags Eden out of the room. "Your dress is hanging in the bathroom, Olivia. You guys have fifteen minutes. And Berkeley, I'm serious," she says, wagging a finger at him. "Don't you dare smudge her. I'll blame *her* if you do."

He groans and backs away from me. "Not fair."

"I know you," she admonishes. "And I like her, too." Nancy smiles her approval as she closes the door behind her.

I stand and tighten the belt on my dressing robe. "I guess I should get dressed."

"Not my preference, but it's probably for the best." He grins.

I head to the bathroom and with a deep breath start wiggling into my Spanx.

Berkeley leans against the doorframe next to the bathroom door, his back to me. "Thank you for doing this," he says. "I know it's pretty scary putting yourself out there—allowing the world to judge you. I can't tell you how much I appreciate it."

My stomach drops as I'm reminded of the scrutiny to come. I already feel like the world hates me, but I don't want to alert him to what is being said on Twitter because I know it will upset him. I don't want him to feel more guilty than he already does for putting me in this position. "It *is* pretty scary," I admit, trying to keep the quiver from my voice as I zip up the dress and start sliding on my rings. "I don't know how you do this all the time. I promise I'll try to be perfect for you." More than anything, I want to live up to his standards. I know how important this is to him and how hard he's worked to get here—calculating every decision from what shows to play to what reporters to talk to along the way. I don't want to let him down.

"You *are* perfect for me," he answers. "And don't worry. Team Adventure, right?"

My lips tremble as I smile to myself, thrilling to the sound of my dream on his lips. I walk out of the bathroom, and then come around the corner to stand in front of him. "Team Adventure." I nod, conveying more confidence than my jumbled insides are feeling right now.

He lets out a low whistle. "You definitely have nothing to worry about. Looking like that—they won't be able to ask you any questions anyway. They'll be speechless."

His lips are on mine before I can utter a deflection, and then I'm so dizzy I forget what I was going to say.

He pulls away from me. "Just say thank you," he whispers.

"Thank you," I repeat, feeling heat in my cheeks.

"Good job. You've just accepted your first compliment."

I laugh and drag my eyes away from him. "I guess I did. But at what cost?" My wide eyes return to his, solemn.

"Nancy is going to kill you."

"No she's not." He smiles. "It's your fault for being so beautiful. I couldn't help myself."

I roll my eyes as we head to the door. "Tricky, Mr. Dalton. You're very tricky."

"Berkeley!" Nancy exclaims as soon as we step into the next room. "You never listen. You'd think you could manage to leave her alone for five minutes... Come on. I'll fix this in the car. We've got to go."

Eden joins us as we climb into a waiting limousine.

"I don't usually have an escort," Berkeley murmurs as we settle into the leather seats and Nancy repairs my lips. "After I sprung you on Shar at the Grammys, though, I think she's afraid of what I'll do next. Apparently we need a chaperone." With a nod toward Eden, he sighs as the car rolls forward.

The premiere is being held at the Fox Theatre in Westwood and we ride in silence, my stomach muscles becoming increasingly tense as the car sails along Sunset Boulevard. We are just turning onto Westwood Boulevard when Eden's cell phone breaks the silence. "Hi, Shar," she chirps with more animation than I've seen out of her all day. "Yes. We're just pulling up." She listens for a moment. "Yes. They've been prepped... Okay. We'll wait for you."

The car comes to a stop around the corner from the premiere as she hits the end button on her phone and acknowledges us for the first time since the beginning of the drive. "Our instructions are to wait here for Shar. She wants to walk with you."

Berkeley's eyes widen. "She hasn't walked with me in years. We don't need to be on a leash—I think we can handle it."

"She won't take no for an answer. You guys are big news. Apparently they're saving your entrance for last—even the stars of the movie are going in before you. There's a lot riding on this."

My mouth goes dry. I'm not sure how I am going to survive this. Taking a few deep breaths, I concentrate on not sweating on my dress.

Thirty seconds later, a fist raps on the window. The chauffeur walks around and opens the door on Berkeley's side, and Shar slips into the seat across from him.

Berkeley narrows his eyes. "Shar, you don't need to walk with us. We'll be fine. Everyone has been instructed to only talk about the song... We'll be on our best behavior—"

She silences him with an arctic look. "There's no way you're going without me. I never thought I'd be saying this to you, Berkeley, you're always so polished, but I don't trust you can control your emotions right now, and it's imperative you do."

"I'm in perfect control. In fact, I've never done anything this deliberately in my life," he argues.

Shar disregards him as she raises her hand to the earpiece she wears in her left ear and listens intently. "Discussion over. They're ready for us." She knocks on the partition separating us from the chauffeur, indicating he should drive us to the red carpet.

I can feel Berkeley smoldering next to me and speak up. "I'd actually feel better if Shar came with us," I whisper. "I'm pretty nervous, and I think I'll be more comfortable if she's there to help direct the interviews."

He glances at me and yields. "Okay. But if we make it

through this, Shar"—he directs his voice to her—"you have to promise to leave us alone on the next one."

The car pulls to a stop. I hear the crowd swell with anticipation as Shar's pale eyes examine him. "Fine. If you make it through this, she's all yours." Her voice is ice. The chauffeur opens the door, and Shar steps out before Berkeley can respond. "Let's go."

Briefly meeting my eyes, Berkeley squeezes my knee before he follows her, and I hear girls begin to shriek as he emerges from the limo. His persona in place, he waves to the crowd before extending his hand to help me out of the car. "Team Adventure," he whispers, tightening his grip on my hand as I emerge next to him.

Right now, I'm quite certain it's us against the world.

Chapter Thirty-one

OLIVIA BLOOM @BLOOMOLIVIA
CLUMSIEST: DONE AWKWARDLY OR WITHOUT SKILL OR
ELEGANCE. #ME

I huddle close to him. Am I supposed to wave? Even with all of the day's preparation, nobody has mentioned what I should be doing at this exact moment. Unsure of where to look, I concentrate on following Shar as I plaster a smile on my face to mask the sheer terror that engulfs me. Busying my hands by holding onto Berkeley with one and clutching my handbag with the other, I try to fade into the background, praying nobody cares who I am anyway.

Bleachers filled with screaming fans run the length of the street, and in front of them, separated from the red carpet by metal barriers, stands an endless line of cameras and microphones. The carpet itself is sandwiched between the media line and a white cardboard wall with *007: Spy Another Day* etched all over it. Shar guides us forward to the start of the line and *Access Hollywood*, our first interview. She has barely finished giving our full names to the show's producer before the correspondent speaks.

"Hi, Berkeley," she says into her microphone. I can't help but notice the invitation in her eyes before she continues. "Love the title song to the movie tonight. It's so romantic. What inspired it?" She thrusts her microphone toward him, expectant.

"It was actually inspired by being given the opportunity to work on this film," he says without flinching. "It's a dream come true. I'm a huge fan of all the films; it felt like a tremendous gift to get to write a song for one. I incorporated that feeling into the music—the whole thing was sort of like falling in love—it was a once in a lifetime experience."

"That's sounds incredible," she says. "What do you think of the song, Olivia?" she guides the microphone to me, challenging me by asking a question not on my safe list.

"Sorry," Shar interjects, prodding us forward. "That's all we have time for."

Having never heard the song (prep FAIL!), I shoot a grateful glance Shar's way. I really am happy to have her here.

The correspondent looks annoyed until Berkeley catches her eye and says, "Thank you for your time." He smiles at her politely.

"Yes, thank you," I echo, following his lead.

Shar shuffles us forward a few feet to the next reporter, and we repeat the scenario on down the line. She makes sure I never have to say more than "Sachin & Babi," and I begin to relax, feeling confident I can remember my line.

Forty-five minutes later we arrive at the final obstacle: the podium, a raised platform in the middle of the premiere that is viewable from all sides. Situated at the top is E! Entertainment Television, our final interview.

We climb the short flight of stairs leading to the platform and are greeted by an intimidating camera, a producer, and the premiere's host, Jillian Raney.

"Well, hello, Berkeley Dalton and Olivia Bloom," she announces into her microphone as soon as we arrive. The crowd's cheers raise a decibel, and the noise grows in a ripple effect as the sound delay causes her voice to echo over the bleachers. Berkeley waves, and I smile. "We've been waiting for you. We have so much to talk about!"

Shar shoots her a warning look.

Jillian ignores her. "Let's start with you, Olivia. You look adorable. Doesn't she look adorable?" she squeals into the microphone. The crowd screams, and I feel myself blush.

"What are you wearing?"

At least I know the answer to that. "A Sachin & Babi dress and Christian Louboutin shoes," I deliver my line into the mic.

"Love it," she says. "Now, you're a lingerie designer, right? I bet you've got some exquisiteness going on under the dress, too." She winks.

If only she knew. Spanx! I pause, faced with having to think on my feet for the first time tonight. *The question is still sort of within the topics I'm allowed to discuss...* My approval-seeking gaze finds Shar.

She nods.

I'm being given a test. Trying to ignore the camera that

is giving my face a thorough examination, I answer honestly, "Oh, I'm not exactly a designer, but I do style the photo shoots for the lingerie line Jonquil."

"Of course you're a stylist, I should have known. I love all the rings you're wearing—what made you think to do that?"

"Well, I love really feminine clothes, but I never want to look too prissy-pretty," I explain. *This is going okay. So far so good.* "I like a little edge, so I always try to add an element like a belt or some unexpected jewelry—you know—something to funk the look up a little."

Perfect. Except that's not what I actually say. The worst thing that could possibly happen, happens. In my nervousness, my voice catches on the "n" in funk and the letter ends up not being vocalized.

"You know—something to fuk the look up a little."

It is as though a wind sweeps across the crowd and takes with it their voices. Silence. Crickets.

"Oh my God," the producer says.

"Oh my God," the cameraman mutters.

"Oh my God," Jillian whispers.

Shar just stares at me, speechless.

OMG! My face gets hot and I close my eyes, fighting the nervous laughter bubbling in my chest as the crowd erupts around me and sound rushes back into my ears. I don't know what to do. Overwhelmed with giggles, I bury my face in my hands and pray for death—this is beyond mortifying. "I didn't mean it," I say to no one in particular. It's not that I've just said the F-word on national television that is making my insides recoil in horror; it's that I said it in front of Berkeley. He probably thinks I'm a complete idiot, and worse, I've totally let him down.

I don't have much time to revel in my embarrassment as Shar springs into action, hissing at the producer to turn off the camera or move on to the next question. In the same moment, Berkeley's arm slips around my waist and turns me toward him. Vaguely aware the camera is still rolling, I don't want to look at him. I squeeze my eyes shut before I open one and peek at him. He's laughing at me.

"That was amazing," he whispers, pulling me forward and kissing my forehead. "I told you they'd be speechless." He saves me, turning us both back toward the camera and speaking into the microphone. "I guess I'll have to learn to share the spotlight from now on," he jokes. "It seems my girlfriend here likes to make headlines."

Girlfriend? Gulp.

Shar forces a laugh. "Yes, our Olivia is quite the delight."

Jillian laughs with them. "Don't worry. We're not live—we can edit that out," she tells me kindly before moving the microphone back to her lips. "I think I speak for all of us when I say you guys look great together. We'd better let you get inside, though…the movie is about to start!"

I do my best to thank her with my eyes while Berkeley waves to the cheering crowd and Shar herds us off the platform and toward the theater entrance.

"Unbelievable," I hear her mutter once we're out of the camera's range. "Go watch the movie—that way you won't be able to do any damage for at least a couple hours. I'm going to go make sure this doesn't end up on YouTube." She hurries off to talk to the E! producer before we can respond.

"I'm so sorry," I whisper my apology to Berkeley as soon as she's out of earshot. "I'm such an imbecile!"

"No. Don't say that. It's a lot of pressure being up there. I'm sorry I put you through this. Most people wouldn't have performed half as well as you did." He guides me to a discreet corner in the theater and leans toward me so we won't be overheard.

I stare at my feet, willing myself not to cry. "I was terrible. I feel like I let you down."

"Hey—" He tips my chin up, forcing me to meet his eyes. "You could never let me down. Yeah, your voice slipped—it happens—but your reaction was so genuine and endearing that every single person in that audience was on your side the minute you started talking. They were rooting for you— they loved you. I promise they did."

His focus is intent on my eyes as his hand moves to the back of my neck and he leans closer. "It would be impossible not to…"

My heart skips a beat, and I lean into him, lost.

"Do you need help finding your seats?" an usher interrupts us.

Berkeley straightens and the moment passes. "Thank you, I think we can manage," he says, snapping back into character.

"Shall we?" he asks, taking my elbow as he leads me to our row.

"Yes," I reply. "It'll be good for me not to have to talk for a few hours."

He gives me a knowing look and takes my hand as we find our seats and the room darkens. Grateful for a few moments out of the lights, I attempt to escape into the movie and forget the last hour.

The film is entertaining and moves quickly, but I can't

help reliving the mortification leading up to it. I'm glad it is dark so no one can see my cheeks glowing. Before I'm ready, Berkeley's song fills the theater and the end credits roll as the crowd applauds.

"Are you ready?" He leans over to me.

"Don't you want to hear the end of your song?" I ask, surprised.

"Not really. I've heard it before—I'd rather get to the after party so we can be seen and leave."

"That sounds perfect." I'm practically out of my seat before he can finish, longing to be alone with him in his house where we can shut out the world, occupying our mouths with uses other than talking.

As we exit the theater, he takes my hand. "What did you think of the movie?" he asks.

"I liked it," I reply. "I might have to see it again, though. I was a little distracted by my eff-up. I couldn't stop thinking about it." I feel myself blushing even now.

Berkeley smiles and squeezes my hand. "Don't worry about it. Really. Shar will fix it."

"Do you think she can?"

"I know she can. She's gotten me out of some jams I thought were impossible. This will be easy for her—she's really talented. And even though she pretends to be annoyed, deep down she loves the challenge. I know she seems tough, but she does have a sympathetic side. I hope she shows it to you someday; it'll transform her for you."

I'm silent as I digest this information. "She makes me feel like I'm a bug she's trying to squash, but she doesn't want to dirty her Manolos with the likes of me, so she's hoping if she stares at me hard enough I'll explode."

"I'm sorry she's been so hard on you," he apologizes with a laugh. "Don't take it personally, though. She's like this with everyone. I think sometimes she forgets we're not all as hard as she is. It's just her way."

"I can't imagine her ever being nice to me," I admit. "But I know she's looking out for you, so I'm glad you have her."

He smiles a thank-you at me and tries to give me some insight. "She's never been very lucky in love," he says. "She's been divorced a couple of times, and I think the failed marriages really hurt her. Things never seem to work out for her in that regard, and to keep from feeling lonely, and from having to feel in general, she throws herself into work. It's her defense. She doesn't want to let anyone get too close."

This makes me sad. I don't like the thought of anyone feeling lonely or not finding love. Even Shar.

We arrive at the limo. Nancy, Shar, and Eden are waiting for us. This time Berkeley doesn't complain about the entourage as we climb into the backseat. The after party is being held at the Bazaar in the SLS Hotel, and Nancy gets to work refreshing my face as the car navigates out of Westwood and onto Wilshire Boulevard.

"E! finally agreed to edit out our little moment," Shar says. "*That* was certainly an unexpected hiccup I'm sure we'd all rather forget." She speaks to the car in general, but I know her words are intended for me. "I had to make some pretty hefty promises to get them to agree, though." She sets her sights on Berkeley. "I had to consent to let them do an exclusive interview with you at your house."

Berkeley looks irritated. "*You* had to consent? When do *I* get to consent?"

"You don't. You made this mess; I'm cleaning it up. You

aren't giving me much to work with, here, you know."

Her statement stings. I already feel terrible that I messed things up for Berkeley, and now he's going to have to do an interview he would never normally do to make up for my mistakes. Tears gather behind my eyes as I stare at my hands, struggling to prevent my emotions from overflowing. In an effort to keep control, I shift my concentration to Nancy. She's just finished touching up my makeup, and I refuse to let my tears ruin her work.

"That's unnecessary, Shar. And it's not true," Berkeley jumps to my defense. "She's a star and you know it. She's effortless."

I throw up a force field, and his words ricochet away from me. A star? Effortless? *Who* and *what* is he talking about?

Shar's eyes flicker to me and back to Berkeley. She remains silent.

"I'll think about the interview," he continues. "*If* I do it, I'll want full approval over the final edit, though." It's clear from his tone that he's had enough of this conversation.

Shar doesn't back down. "I'll see what I can do." Folding her arms over her chest, she stares out the window.

The car sinks into silence before she gets back to business. "I should prep you for the after party," she says, her voice ringing out over the quiet. "It's a short walk into the hotel. We won't be doing any interviews—I'll make sure to hustle you through. Once you're inside, just remember there are cameras *everywhere*. You will always be watched, so best behavior, please."

"We're not planning to stay long," Berkeley informs her. "Can you send someone to the house to bring my car?"

Eden goes straight to work, arranging for the limo to take her and Nancy back to Berkeley's house before returning for Shar and herself. Eden will drive Berkeley's car to the hotel and will text him when she arrives.

"That's fine," Shar says. "The less I have to worry about you two, the better."

The limo turns left onto La Cienega and left again into the hotel's half-moon-shaped driveway. A small group of photographers wait next to a miniature red carpet. It's far less intimidating than the earlier junket, and we easily exit the vehicle to the sound of cameras clicking. As we stop to have our picture taken, I attempt to bury my emotions and be professional, making a silent pledge not to make things worse for Berkeley.

True to her word, Shar ushers us through the hotel doors without us having to speak.

Entering the Bazaar is like falling through a rabbit hole. All around us frosted-glass tables filled with multicolored lights are topped with glorious spun-sugar confections. Black-and-white tile floors, oversized furniture, and distorted glass artwork turns the lounge into an eclectic wonderland. Music thumps in the background, and even though we're early, the party is in full swing. Seemingly out of nowhere, pisco sours appear in our hands and we smile for a passing camera.

I look around in wonder, trying to take it all in as Berkeley smiles his thanks to a few passersby who compliment his song. He seems to be trying to avoid getting stuck in conversation and leans in to get Shar's attention.

"See you later, Shar," he says, indicating her presence is no longer required. "I think we've got it from here."

She thinks for a moment, examining the room. "Just

remember you're being watched," she says before shrugging her acceptance and letting us go.

Without another word, Berkeley tucks me under his wing and leads me through the hotel's lobby to a bank of elevators. "It'll be much quieter up here," he explains, nodding to a security guard who lifts a velvet rope and allows us to pass before following us into the elevator.

Tapping a card on a sensor on the wall, the security guard presses a button labeled roof and we begin our ascent. "Two coming up," he speaks into a microphone hidden in his sleeve.

I have no idea where we're going, but I have the sense to keep my curiosity to myself. I'm sure the elevator has ears.

The elevator slows to a stop, and the guard motions for us to follow him. He leads us through a small anteroom and out a set of double doors to the rooftop pool and another velvet rope. "Enjoy your evening," he says as a different guard allows us to pass. The party on the roof is subdued in comparison to the thumping scene downstairs. Soft music blends with the sound of water. A warm breeze, twinkling lights, and swaying palm trees add to the tranquility. Other partygoers recline on wide white lounges, sipping cocktails and admiring the city views.

We are inside the party for less than a minute before Berkeley pulls me down into the shadowy corner of a cabana, his insistent lips finding mine. My eyes widen in surprise, and I try to pull away. "Best behavior!"

He laughs. "Sorry. I've wanted to do that for the last three hours. We should be pretty safe up here—they're usually good about keeping people out."

Scanning the pool, I spy Christian Bale sipping a drink

in a corner along with Megan Fox and a few others. I don't see any cameras, but my stomach contracts when my eyes connect with Lisa Greene's. I squeeze Berkeley's arm. "Uh-oh," I whisper.

Following my stare, he narrows his eyes. "It's a trap," he mutters. "Her publicist must have finagled this. She'd never get up here on her own."

"What should we do?"

Berkeley shrugs and takes a sip of his drink. "Ignore her, I guess. Don't give her any reason to strengthen the case her people are trying to build against us. I wish they'd lay off. This was a business relationship from the start, and she got what she was promised."

"What was that?"

"Publicity. And a role in a movie. You coming along actually works out better for her," he says. "She's shuffling the Shuffle."

"The what?"

"The Shuffle," he repeats, looking up at me from under his eyes. "Shar's plan to make sure Christina and my breakup didn't hurt either of our careers—she's Chris's publicist, too."

Blair is going die when she hears she was right.

"It's ridiculous that I went along with it for so long, but basically Shar wanted to protect Christina's I'm-every-girl's-best-friend image by painting her as the sweet, scorned lover while making sure I didn't start looking like a womanizing asshole again. She thought it was best if it looked like I left for love, fell head over heels for a gorgeous temptress who I felt meant to be with. Christina started playing the victim who rises above and finds inner strength, gaining sympathy, and Shar started staging meetings for Lisa and me. We'd only hang out long enough for us to be photographed."

I would like to know more about his "womanizing asshole" time, but I refrain. "Wouldn't you have to 'break up' with Lisa at some point though, too?"

"The plan was to let it fizzle out and have Lisa move on first, essentially breaking up with me, but in a small way. By then we would have led Berkstina fans to believe Chris had moved on and we were still friends, thereby protecting Christina's box office draw because her true personality wasn't revealed. I would end up looking like a guy who's been unlucky in love so Brightside sales are safe, and Lisa's celebrity status is raised for having dated me. Plus, with her new seductive image, a larger variety of roles are open to her. Everybody wins."

I nod along as he talks, marveling at the complicated cover-up as realization slowly hits me. "But then I came along and ruined everything."

His eyes flash to mine. "The only thing that's your fault is being so adorable at the Grammys I couldn't resist kissing you," he promises, pulling me toward him and kissing my forehead before lowering his eyes to mine and holding them there. "That was *my* mistake." After a beat, he sits back and takes another sip of his drink. "I thought I could get away with bringing you in Lisa's place because Shar said it would be easy to avoid being photographed together that night. In one respect by bringing you—the girl I *wanted* to be my Grammy date—I was proving a point to Shar. But I should have known better. I'd wanted to kiss you since the fashion show and my resistance was worn thin."

My memory flashes back to the restroom, and it's inconceivable he wanted to kiss me that long. I wrap myself in a protective layer, refusing to believe it.

"Besides," he continues, bringing me back to the present, "the Shuffle was messed up from the start because unbeknownst to me, Shar had promised Lisa the same film role Christina had already signed a contract for."

"Why would she do that?"

"I guess she had trouble finding someone willing to take on the Berkstina fans—or Christina—she's pretty powerful. Most actresses want to stay on her and her fans good side, so Shar sweetened the deal. She promised Lisa a coveted starring role even though she knew in the end the role would remain Christina's—she just figured she'd have the publicity she needed by then and would deal with Lisa later. It was a mess, but eventually Lisa settled for a smaller role in the same movie, and I started begging Shar to put a stop to the Shuffle. She said she was, but Lisa kept showing up. Like at the toga party." He meets my eyes again. "That was the worst."

"You certainly had me fooled," I admit, recalling seeing Lisa perched on his lap and not liking the sickness the memory conjures in my stomach.

He looks at me in shared disbelief. "Unbelievable timing on her part. Toga parties aren't exactly my thing. Shar talked me into going because she wanted me to meet a producer about an upcoming project. I took Mark and Haynes and we ended up around a fire pit talking to some guys we've toured with before. Mark saw you come down the stairs first and was trying to get my attention when Lisa randomly showed up and made herself comfortable on my lap." He shakes his head. "From the look on Mark's face, I knew something weird was happening. It was ironic—we'd just been talking about you on the car ride to the party, and suddenly there you were."

"You were talking about me?" I ask. *He hadn't seen me in weeks—I can't believe I'd still be on his mind.*

He looks away. "Yeah…Mark wanted me to call you."

I wait for him to elaborate, but he doesn't, so I prod, "Were you surprised when Lisa called out my name?"

"I was shocked," he says with a wry smile, returning his eyes to mine. "But I was kind of grateful. It gave me an excuse to talk to you, even though I was pretty sure you hated me at that point, and if by some off chance you didn't, then Lisa had probably just sealed the deal."

"I didn't hate you," I say, dropping my eyes to my hands. "Far from it. I just knew I had to protect myself…you were too easy to fall for." I raise my eyes back to him. "I'm sure I wasn't fooling you."

He concentrates on his lap, his fingers absently fraying the edge of his vest. "I knew I hurt you," he says. His eyes flicker to my face before returning to his hem. "And I was filled with this overwhelming need to fix it—to make us okay. I was afraid I'd lost you and knew I'd never forgive myself if I did. I've never felt anything like that before." He looks up at me. "But maybe now you can see why I was reluctant to drag you into all of this?"

I study him, thinking through everything he's revealed to me. "Because Lisa's people are doing to me what Shar did to her—painting me as the seductress—but I don't have anything to gain from that."

"Exactly." His eyes are apologetic. "I wanted to protect you. It's not fair that you have to lose your privacy."

We fall silent. *I hate that people are judging me without*

giving me a chance to make an impression, but would I trade anonymity for Berkeley? What if I never met him? An image of bleak, lackluster days stretching before me with no promise of how alive I feel right now presents itself and I have my answer. *Who cares what people think anyway? Only the people who know the truth—like Blair and Parker, who love me regardless—matter. I can handle it. He's worth it.* "I know a thing or two about publicists and crazy schemes," I say, slowly. "And so far, they seem to have led me in the right direction." I lean toward him, letting my hand rest on his cheek as I find his lips, kissing him gently. He responds with passion, his hands sliding up my back, pulling me into him, plunging me into oblivion. It takes effort for me to slow us down. I soften my lips and pull back, looking into his eyes, our faces still touching. "Fixed," I whisper.

Tears spring to his eyes and he starts to say something. "I—"

"Hi, Berkeley." Even with my back to her, I know who it is. Reality descends and my spine stiffens as I pull away from him, preparing for a fight.

"Hi," he says. "Liv, you remember Lisa, right?" We both stand and face her. To my surprise, she's draped around the arm of a handsome young actor.

"Yes. Hi, Lisa," I say, unable to hide the apprehension in my voice.

"This is Oscar," she says to nobody in particular. "He's guest starring with me on the next episode of the show."

Oscar takes a tentative step back, looking around, seemingly wondering how he ended up in the middle of this triangle. I move to fill the silence. "That's really great. Good for you, Oscar."

"Thanks," he says, shifting his weight to his right foot, looking like he wants to bolt. "I'm excited about it."

We fall silent again. I would ask him about his role, but I don't want to prolong the uncomfortable conversation, and I look to Lisa to see if she's about to pounce. But she appears oblivious as usual.

Berkeley steps in. "We should be going, actually. I just got a text that our car is here. Ready, Liv?"

"Great!" I say too brightly as he pulls me away. "Nice meeting you," I say to Oscar. "Bye, Lisa."

"Bye, Berkeley," Lisa says as she looks up at Oscar.

"What was that all about?" I ask, as we exit the lounge.

Berkeley shrugs. "I don't know. I'm sure it's some sort of publicity stunt. At any rate, I don't think we need to worry about Lisa Greene anymore. I think she's moved on."

I hope he's right.

Chapter Thirty-two

OLIVIA BLOOM @BLOOMOLIVIA
IT'S OFFICIAL. MY TONGUE IS CURSED. #FUNKITUP

PARKER MIFFLIN @ISINDULGENT
@BLOOMOLIVIA AT LEAST YOU LOOKED FABULOUS SAYING IT.
AND HE OBVS CAN'T RESIST YOU. I SAY GET DOWN AND FUNK IT,
FUNK IT BIG TIME!

BLAIR HAMILTON @SUPERSPINSTRESS
@BLOOMOLIVIA PLEASE EXCUSE @ISINDULGENT HE'S A
LITTLE FUNKED UP. WE'VE OFFICIALLY INSTALLED A BAR IN THE
COURTYARD. PLEASE VISIT SOON!

MRS. BLOOM @PSYCHICMOM1

NOT CURSED, @BLOOMOLIVIA. IT'S OUT OF YOUR HANDS—AND
YOUR MOUTH. CHECK YOUR THROAT CHAKRA. #IKNOW

AMANDA CONRAD @BOOTSMD
@BLOOMOLIVIA YOU ARE FUNKING PERFECT JUST THE WAY YOU
ARE. #GORGEOUS

The next morning, the video from the premiere makes its way to YouTube. *E!* may have promised not to air the eff-up, but there's no way to stop the hundreds of phones in the audience that recorded it. In the end, Shar concedes and leaks an edited version of the video to some of the major media outlets. As it turns out, Berkeley's right—people find us appealing and it appears there's no better antidote to Lisa's poison than letting me make a fool of myself on international television.

The video doesn't exactly go viral, only getting a few hundred thousand views, so maybe my funk-up wasn't so disastrous after all. I still refuse to check what's being said on Twitter, though. As a former member of their ranks, I fear @BerkstinaFans may not be so easily swayed.

That evening I sit curled next to Berkeley on his couch as he presses play on the final edit. I'm not thrilled, of course, but I've finally agreed to watch it.

The scene opens with the two of us standing on the platform at the premiere. The sky behind us is a pale blue as twilight sets in and camera flashes glitter in the crowd behind us. I suck in my breath. It's not just seeing myself on camera for the first time that is overwhelming, it's seeing myself standing next to Berkeley that sends a pang straight to the bottom of my stomach. Having seen him on TV so many times before, it is surreal to see me (well—the prettier TV version of me) in the frame next to him. I can't help but notice how attractive we look next to each other—him standing a few inches taller than me, his sparkling blue eyes a perfect complement to my green. The camera pans my dress as I mention what I'm wearing and pulls in for a close-up on my face as the dreaded word escapes my lips. I want to shut my eyes and cover my ears to avoid reliving the horrifying moment, but as penance for my sins, I force myself to watch. Blessedly, the camera doesn't linger on my face after I say it. Instead, it pulls back to include Berkeley in the frame. This is something I've never seen before. Having been cocooned in my shame, I didn't contemplate his reaction, but now, through the beauty of the video, I watch it with intent.

After I say the evil word, surprise flashes across his features before amusement sets in and he reaches for me. As I stare at the screen, I realize it isn't my reaction in the video that's endearing; it's his. His words aren't audible as he whispers in my ear, but the way he looks at me, his expression an incomprehensible mix of protective and entertained—*it almost looks like he's…*I don't want to think about it. Abruptly the moment passes and his facade is back in place as he returns me to the camera. It pulls in for a close-up on him as he jokes about his girlfriend making headlines. A shot of Jillian laughing and Berkeley waving to the crowd ends the segment and the screen fades to black.

"So…what do you think?"

"It wasn't so bad…" I admit. "You looked really handsome."

He erases the latter half of my comment with a sweep of

his eyes. "Glad you think so because it's going to air on *E!* in about three minutes. Want to watch it again?" he teases, aiming the remote at the TV.

"I said it wasn't bad—but it's definitely not good enough to watch again." I lurch toward him and try to wrestle the remote away.

"Come on—I want to see it." He grabs one of my flailing arms and flips me around so he hovers above me. "If we're not going to watch it, I guess you'll have to distract me then..."

I'm about to submit to his kiss when his phone lights up and starts vibrating on the table. He pulls back and checks the display. "Hi, Shar." He activates the speakerphone and talks at it. "Liv and I are here."

"Wonderful. It turned out great, don't you think?" Her voice crackles through the device, but it sounds warmer than I've heard before. "That was a tough one. It's a good thing you two look so good on camera. I don't think we could have staged a better outcome." She's ecstatic, the complete opposite of the Shar from the limo.

"Good," Berkeley says. I can hear the relief in his voice, and part of me cringes for having worried him. "Maybe they'll leave us alone, now?" He sounds hopeful even though I'm pretty sure he knows better.

"No way. We have to decide who to give the first interview to...*Vanity Fair? People?* What do you think?"

He closes his eyes. "You know where I stand on this. I don't give those kind of interviews." His phone indicates there's another call coming through.

"Hey, Shar—my sister's calling on the other line—I'll talk to you tomorrow." He doesn't give her a chance to respond before he clicks over. "Hey, Mia," he says.

"I've been hearing some interesting things about you lately," I hear her musical voice tease before he clicks off the speakerphone and raises the phone to his ear.

"Really? What now? I haven't been paying attention," he jokes. "You saw the segment?"

He listens for a moment. "Yes, she is," he says, peeking sideways at me with mock superiority. He must know I'm dying to hear what she's saying.

I try to look uninterested as I perk up my ears to discern what the tiny voice on the other end of the line is saying. The only words I can interpret sound like they say, "This is different for you…"

"Hmmmm. How so?" He listens almost as intently as I do, but I can't deduce any more words.

"You're pretty observant," he says. "And you're probably right." He stands and walks around to the back of the couch toward the French doors that lead to the balcony, carrying her response with him.

He groans at whatever she says next. "Do we have to? Shouldn't that be *my* decision?" he asks.

A moment passes and he laughs. "I won't say it hasn't crossed my mind. I'll think about it. That's the best I can do for now."

He raises his eyebrows at her response, "We'll see. Bye."

Ending the call, he turns to me. "That was my sister," he says.

"I gathered that," I reply. I'm wanting to ask what "crossed his mind," but I don't know if he'll appreciate my prying so I keep my mouth shut. "What did she have to say?" I keep it general.

"She said you're really pretty." He smiles.

I roll my eyes. "I'm sure she did. What else?"

"She said you look great on camera…"

I give him a dirty look.

"What?" he asks, a playful glint in his eyes as he narrows them. "She's got great taste. I trust her judgment when it comes to this sort of thing."

"What else?" I ask, giving meddling one last try.

"That's it."

It's not it. He's hiding something, I can tell, but I'm unsure of how far I can push for the answer. I don't know his limits yet.

"Fine." I drop the subject (for the moment). "Where were we before all the phone calls?"

He moves back to the couch and lies down behind me so that I am horizontal in front of him. He wraps his arms around me. "Right about here," he says.

Twisting in his arms, I turn to face him, a question that has been plaguing me since the premiere on my mind.

"Can I ask you something about last night?" I ask, trying to be brave.

"Of course, ask me anything." The mischief leaves his eyes and he searches my face, suddenly serious.

"Well, last night after I eff-ed up, you turned me back to the camera, and said something I was wondering about…"

"I called you my girlfriend," he says.

"Right." I squirm a little, hesitating.

"Is that okay?"

"Yes, it's fine. It's great," I answer, stumbling over my words. "I just wasn't sure if you meant it or if you were just saying it for the cameras, is all."

"Do you have a preference?" He raises his eyebrows, and there is a smile in his eyes, but I detect an edge in his voice that tells me he wants an honest answer.

Anxious, I swallow. Technically he did say it first, but I'm still uncertain of his motives because part of me can't believe he means it. He must be mistaken. I feel like I'm taking a huge risk and putting my heart on the line as I say, "Well, I'd prefer you meant it... I would love to be your girlfriend."

A smile washes over his features, and I share in his relief as he says, "I was hoping you'd say that." He moves his hands to my face, cupping my cheeks as he pulls me toward him and kisses me. I giggle against his lips, unable to stop smiling. He laughs with me and kisses my cheeks, my eyes, my nose, before tucking me in his arms. Laying my head against his chest, I close my eyes, wishing I could stop time and stay here wrapped forever next to him, utterly content.

Chapter Thirty-three

BERKELEY DALTON @BERKELEYBRTSIDE
THREE DAYS OF RECORDING AHEAD OF US. FEELS GOOD TO BE
BACK IN THE STUDIO!

I wake with the sun and a deserted feeling. Rolling over, the emptiness is explained when I find Berkeley is gone. I crawl out of bed and pull on a sweater, searching the silent house for him. He's nowhere to be found, and I'm wondering if he left when I sense movement coming from the terrace. Peering out through the French doors, I watch him as he sips coffee while looking out over Los Angeles as she wakes. Picking up a pen, he writes something in a composition book. He looks peaceful, and I don't want to disturb him.

On tiptoes I leave him and head to the kitchen to pour myself some coffee. The dishwasher is running, and I search the cupboard where he keeps his mugs for a clean one.

Spying one on the top shelf I rise on my toes and strain to reach it. As my fingertips make contact and tilt it forward, the cup comes barreling out of the cupboard, and I dive out of the way, screeching as it almost hits me in the head during its free fall before crashing into a splintered mass at my feet.

Frantic, I try to clean up the mess as I hear the French doors open and Berkeley jogs into the kitchen. "Are you okay?" he asks.

"Yes," I answer, still on my hands and knees. "Your Hawaii coffee mug tried to attack me."

"Oh." He looks alarmed. "The Hawaii mug? That was my favorite one. I keep it on the top shelf so no one will use it."

My heart stops. I feel terrible. I just broke his favorite mug. Looking up at him from the floor, my eyes are wide with apology as I say, "I'm so sorry. It was the only clean one I could find…"

Looking down at me, he can't keep a straight face and starts laughing as he bends to help me clean up the mess. It dawns on me he's making fun of me. "You're not funny," I tell him, narrowing my eyes.

He cocks his head to the side, his smile widening. "I'm kind of funny," he says, raising his eyebrows.

He is delectable and I want to kiss him, but instead I shake my head. "Nope. Definitely not funny." I try to keep my voice dry, but I can't help it, a little giggle escapes my lips. "You got me," I admit.

"I know," he says as he drags me to my feet and throws the cup remnants in the garbage before wrapping his arms around me and brushing my lips with his own. "Good morning."

"Good morning. You're up early," I say, as he releases me. "Your bed felt so empty without you in it."

"I'm sorry. I couldn't sleep. I've had song ideas running through my head all night, and when I'm writing, I'm up at all sorts of hours. I got some good work done, though." He reaches into the cupboard and easily secures a clean mug, pouring me a cup of coffee before he leads me out to the terrace.

"Can I see what you wrote?" I ask.

"Yes. But not until it's ready. I've still got some work to do."

"Okay. It'll give me something to look forward to, then."

We fall silent as we look out over the city. I think about him out here working and am reminded I'm being negligent in *my* job. So much has happened, it's hard to believe it's only Friday. I've missed a week of work and the time has come. As much as I want to stay in the Hills (hills/clouds— same difference) I'm starting to get antsy. On Monday I'll need to return to my job. "I think I need to go back to work," I blurt.

"Me, too," he says. "I was just thinking about that. We're supposed to spend the next few days recording—actually, we start today. It's the beginning of the process. We start with recording the scratch track—it takes a while to set everything up and sounding perfect—but this is the first time I'm not there for that part, and it's making me a little nervous."

I look at him, surprised. "You should totally go. Why didn't you tell me?"

"Truthfully?" He smiles and takes a sip of his coffee. "I'm not sure I'm ready for this to end."

Inwardly, I smile at his revelation. "I know how you feel, but now you have to go. We can't hide up here forever," I say, shaking my head. "We have to go back to reality at some point, and I don't want to keep you from what you need to be doing."

"Well, it doesn't have to end today," he says. "Would you want to come with me? I have to warn you—it's pretty boring, you'll be stuck in a studio with a bunch of music guys who will spend hours debating where to put tape on the snare until it sounds just right, but I'd love it if you came."

Like I even have to think about it. "Of course I'll come," I reply. "I'd love to…but I can only come today. Tomorrow I have to go back to my normal life."

"I understand." He nods. "I'll drive you home after dinner."

We pack up my things and head to Conway Studios. There are fewer paparazzi waiting outside Berkeley's gate this time, and I join him in the front seat as we round the first bend in the descent toward Hollywood.

"We're only doing one song," he explains as we turn off Melrose into the studio's palm tree-lined driveway. "It's a digital single just to have something new to put out between albums so it should only take a couple of days."

"Are you sure it's okay that I'm here? I won't be in the way?" I ask, feeling a little nervous about being the only girl hanging with the band.

"I'm pretty sure I'm allowed to bring whoever I want," he says, laughing like I should know better. Grabbing my hand and opening the studio door he adds, "If anyone gives you any heat, you send them to me."

We step into the main lobby, and Berkeley greets the

unkempt guy who stands behind the counter reading a comic book. "Hey, man." The two shake hands. "Is everyone already back there?"

"Sure are," the guy responds. "They just started. Go on back…Studio C." He buzzes open a heavy-looking door and allows us to pass.

I trail Berkeley as he leads me down a hallway, past a room that houses both a pool table and foosball table, to a large kitchen. In a way, it feels like we're in a frat house, but my impression changes once we step out the back door on to a stone patio containing a large wooden table surrounded by lush gardens and tropical palm trees. Footpaths lead the way to three small Spanish bungalows. At the far end of the plot sits an expansive deck with lounge chairs, and adjacent to that is an open lawn covered with blankets as though set for a picnic. It's unexpected and charming; a rock-and-roll oasis. For some reason I feel at home and am certain that in some hazy, distant future Berkeley and I will be spending a lot of time here together. Maybe it's wishful thinking. At any rate, it's a bit Psychic Mom for my taste, and I quickly bury the vision.

I follow him to the deck outside bungalow C where the rest of the Brightside and some guys I assume are engineers sit chatting while lounging around a plastic table.

"Well, look who finally decided to show up," Mark greets us, grinning. "What's new?" he asks, his eyes intent on Berkeley.

Berkeley ignores him and introduces me to the guys at the table, "You all know Liv, right?"

I wave to Haynes, Mark, and Jeff, who I've met, and shake hands with the guys I haven't as Berkeley helps himself to bottled water from a nearby cooler and hands me one.

"Have we put anything down, yet?" he asks.

"No, they're still setting up, trying to decide if we should use the Telecaster or the Les Paul," Jeff says. "Do you want to go back? Ted's with them—"

Berkeley nods. "Yeah, I do." Directing his attention to me, he says, "Do you want to wait out here? It's going to be pretty technical for a little bit. I'll bring you back once we start recording?"

"Okay," I answer, somewhat unsure of what to do next.

"Have a seat, Liv." Mark motions to an open chair next to him.

Gratefully accepting, I make myself comfortable.

"So how are you doing?" he asks.

"Good, thanks. You don't have to wait with me if you want to go back," I tell him.

He makes a face. "I'll be back there soon enough. Believe me." He pauses before continuing. "So how's it been going, honestly? Things are a little nuts, right?"

I blush. "It's been a crazy couple of days. I feel like my life has been turned upside down."

"I don't think you're the only one... Last one to the studio? That's a first." The latter part he says more to himself. Smiling, he speaks louder, "Hey, I don't want this to sound weird, but if you ever need to talk—I've known him a long time..."

I cock my head to the side and try to comprehend what he's getting at.

"...and you seem like a nice girl. It's just that I know how chaotic it can be is all. I'm around if you ever need any insight."

I look at him for a moment, unsure of what to think. Is this some sort of veiled warning or is he just being nice? "Thanks, I'll keep that in mind," I finally respond.

"Good." He smiles again. "How's your friend Blair?"

"She's good," I say, wishing she was into him. It would be fun to have a friend around. "At least I think so. I haven't seen her in a few days…"

"You've been busy. Tell her I said 'hi.'"

"I will."

We fall silent, but not for long.

"Hey, do you wanna play foosball?" he asks, pointing back toward the main building.

It's random but preferable to hanging around not sure what to do with myself. "Sure," I say, standing and following him down the path.

When we return to the studio (he destroyed me at foosball), the engineers are just finishing setting up. Mark motions for me to have a seat on a row of couches behind the sound booth. "We're going to record the scratch track now. We all play together so we establish a tempo for the song," he explains. "Then we'll go back and record individual performances. Ted and I will record while listening to the scratch recording, that way we'll know, based on the vocals, where we need to fill in or bring more emotion. Then Jeff and Berk will record guitar and vocals to our tracks."

He leaves to join the band, and I sink into my corner, content to watch them work as they start sound-checking their instruments. Forty-five minutes later they begin to play, and I relish in my private concert. It would have been impossible for me to ever dream this. Listening to them, I allow myself to revert to my college dorm when I listened endlessly to their music while studying for finals. It's outside my realm to fathom this moment or all that has happened in the last few days. The fact that I still feel like I'm having an out-of-body experience pretty much sums it up.

"Lie, cheat, and steal. Running around on the rat wheel. Blood. Sweat. Tears. Been holding me down for so many years. And I can't pretend that it's something I want to do. We could be friends but it's better if you keep your distance. Now I'm reaching the end of the beginning of my life. Love. Faith."

I like watching Berkeley work. Even though he isn't performing for anyone, every time he sings it's impossible to mistake the passion in his voice—each rendition would bring a crowd to its knees. Over the next three hours, yet another layer to Berkeley's personality is revealed to me: Berkeley the professional. As I watch, I feel his hold on me tighten. I hope he'll never let go.

The song comes to a close and the band hits the last note. Stepping away from the microphone, Berkeley turns to Mark. "Was that the same bass line we've been playing all along?" he asks.

"Yeah," Mark replies, a defensive edge to his voice. "I haven't changed it. It's the same as it was last week."

"Are you sure?" Berkeley persists. "I thought it was more active."

"Do you want to listen to our last recording?" Mark asks, pulling his iPod out of his pocket and thrusting it at Berkeley. "*I've* been listening to it all week. Maybe *you* forgot what the song is supposed to sound like."

I try to make myself small, feeling as though my monopolizing Berkeley is causing grief in the band as Mark's words deliver their blow.

Berkeley narrows his eyes. "Yeah, let's listen back. If it's the same, though, I think we should talk about it. I still feel like it should be more active."

Jeff jumps in, "Berk, there's no need to tweak the song. It's fine how it is."

"But I don't want it to be fine. It has to be right. Good enough isn't good enough. It's got to be great—I can't sing it otherwise."

"Here we go." Mark groans, putting his bass down on its stand. "Let's listen back." He motions for the engineer to play the song back as Ted comes out from behind the drums.

The engineer punches some buttons and music fills the room. The Brightside listens, intent, to the entire song.

"One more time, please." Berkeley gestures to the engineer. Halfway through, he speaks into the microphone. "Stop! Play that part again?" The engineer does as directed.

"See? Right there. Listen," Berkeley says. "Wouldn't it sound better if it did this?" He picks up Mark's bass and starts to play.

Ted nods his head and returns to his drum kit. "I like it," he says as he jumps behind the drums, and he and Berkeley jam out a new rhythm for the song.

Jeff picks up his guitar and starts to play, nodding along in agreement.

Mark watches for a few minutes, shaking his head, until he finally concedes and walks over to Berkeley, holding his hand out, waiting for Berkeley to hand over the bass.

The band stops playing and Berkeley forks it over. "I

like it the old way, too, but I think this is better. It sounds more like us—we have to keep sounding like us."

Mark rolls his eyes.

"Hey, I know how you feel. I know. We are what we are, though, and I have to stand in front of this song and sing it, and I can't do that if I don't one hundred percent believe the fans are going to love it."

Mark nods in defeat as he puts the bass strap over his shoulder and starts to play. "What about doing it this way?" he suggests, playing a modified version of Berkeley's bass line.

Berkeley listens for a few minutes as Ted chimes in on the drums and Jeff plays the guitar.

"I like that A," Berkeley says, smiling, then he runs to his piano and starts to play. "Hit that A! I love it!" he calls out. The song jams on. "Yeah. Do that A with a little bit of C modulation on it... Yes! That's nice."

As the band plays, the energy in the room increases exponentially. Berkeley sounds out lyrics, changing the words to fit the changing melody. They are moving as one, all bobbing to the same beat. Looking at one another, they are smiling as collectively they move to the bridge, all sensing the need to change chords. Any animosity that existed is erased as they play, an overwhelming sense of joy overtaking the entire room. They finally bring it to a close, letting the final drumbeats resonate. "Yeah?" Berkeley asks Mark.

Mark smiles. "Yeah."

After a couple more run-throughs, they're satisfied with the changes and agree the song is ready to try recording again.

As the engineers begin adjusting mics that may have

moved during the jam session, the guys take a break.

Berkeley joins me on the couch. "Sorry you had to hear that," he apologizes.

"No, it's fine. It's what you were talking about the other night. I get it. Will you and Mark be okay?"

"Yeah, we're already fine," he says. "We're practically brothers—we've been friends for so long—we just have different processes sometimes. We've had the same argument in the other direction, too. Where I want to change something and he brings me back to center."

"I feel like it was my fault," I say.

He looks at me like I'm a crazy person. "Why? How could it possibly be your fault?"

"Because I've been taking up a lot of your time lately."

"Liv, this has nothing to do with you. You're not even close to a drain on my time. It's been worse before, believe me, and they're probably happy I didn't force them to rehearse all week."

It's been worse before? His words make me wonder about other girls he's brought into the studio. *Did Christina Carlton sit here? Was he even more absent from the band when she was present?* I don't like thinking about it.

"I hope it's not too boring," he says, changing the subject.

Snapping my focus back to him, I answer, "I'm not bored at all. I could never be bored watching you perform. And I know you do this all the time, but I think it's fascinating. Thank you for including me."

"Thank you for coming. It's so much more fun with you here," he replies. "Although…it's supposed to be an angry song, and I can't fake emotion when I'm recording. You'll have to stay away when we do vocals. Every time I look at you I can't help but smile."

"Or you could stop looking at me," I suggest.

"Not a chance."

He moves to kiss me, and I feel better as the man from the front enters behind us carrying a tray full of sandwiches.

"Come and get it," he announces as he sets the tray in a corner of the room.

Everyone inhales lunch, and before I know it, they're back recording.

Several hours later, the scratch track is deemed acceptable and drum recording gets under way.

I spend the rest of the afternoon next to Berkeley, watching Ted pound out drum fill after drum fill. It's an exhausting and tedious process. Often Ted will have to play the same note over and over again—trying to get the perfect sound. The glamour begins to wear on me as the day draws to a close.

Excusing myself to get some fresh air (and to escape the relentless drums), I wander outside to the deck. Dusk is falling, and it almost feels like summer. Taking off my shoes, I stand barefoot in the grass and allow the soft breeze to wash over me before I sink down onto one of the blankets and pull out my phone to dial Boots's number. I haven't talked to her since before the Grammys, save for the occasional text here and there. She's been busy studying, so it's not entirely my fault we haven't spoken.

"Hey, it's me," I say when she answers.

"Hi, you! I was wondering when you were going to call me. I wasn't sure if you were taking calls from us little people," she teases.

"I'll always take calls from you. I miss you. Especially

now."

"I miss you, too. I'd much rather be hanging out with you than this stack of medical journals, believe me." She groans before becoming chipper again. "So, I saw you have a new boyfriend…"

"I do," I say softly. "I'm sure you've heard everything."

"Oh, yes. And thank you for saying 'fuck' on national television. It makes me feel better about my life."

"Boots!" I laugh.

"You know I'm kidding and I've got your back. That Lisa Greene was being so mean to you! Don't worry. I let everyone here know you're not some floozy. I can't believe her. She's terrible," she says. "But seriously, at the James Bond movie premiere you were incredible—you guys look like you belong together and nobody can deny that. I'm not just saying it."

"Thank you. It feels right, but really I'm just trying to keep up. It's been an intense week," I say, downplaying my emotions, not wanting to address them here at the studio. "I'm so jumbled. I'm sort of looking forward to having a day to sort everything out, to be honest."

"Sometimes it's good to be able to step away," she agrees. "I know that was what I needed." She pauses. "It just so happens I have a new boyfriend, too."

"You do? Who?" I ask. "You didn't step away from school, did you?"

"No. I didn't step away from school, but I was starting to question if this is what I really want to be doing. I won't say I didn't consider it."

"Boots, really? That's a big deal," I say, feeling a pang for being so wrapped up in Berkeley that I wasn't there for my best friend's crisis.

"It was only a big deal for a second. I'm back on track now. Derrick made everything better."

"And Derrick is your new boyfriend. Where did you meet him?"

"He's the bartender at my favorite study bar. He's really cute."

"You study in a bar?"

"Well, I was feeling stifled in the library, and I needed to get away from all of the doctor types and have a normal conversation. I think that's why I was feeling so overwhelmed—too much brachial plexus and not enough esophageal libation."

"Boots, that's fantastic." I laugh. "Only you."

"Well," she replies, "let's just say when I start studying the brain, I may need to move on to someone else, but for now I'm acing anatomy."

I smile as I spy Berkeley walking across the lawn toward me. He looks worn out.

"I'm happy for you," I tell her as Berkeley sinks down next to me and wraps his arm around my waist, pulling me toward him. "Are you at the bar right now?"

"Oh, yes. Tonight we're learning about the gluteus medius."

"Nice. Well, enjoy." I giggle. "The band just finished recording, I think, so I should probably go."

"Tell Berkeley I said, hiiiiiiiiyee!" she sings.

"I will." I smile. "Derrick, too. Good night."

Clicking off my phone, I lean my head back onto Berkeley's shoulder and look up at his profile turned toward the sky. "It's such a beautiful night," I say.

"It is," he agrees. "Who was that?"

"My cousin, Boots. She's away at med school, and I haven't talked to her in a while. She's pretty much my Mark."

"We'll have to introduce the two of them." He smiles. "Are you hungry? They're setting up dinner."

"Starving."

Standing, he pulls me to my feet and, hand in hand, we head to the main patio for dinner.

I'm surprised to find the long wooden table filled with trays of sushi and set to include not only us, but White Lotus, who are recording in bungalow B. We find our places under the colored strands of crisscrossed Christmas lights glowing above the patio, basking us in an atmosphere decidedly more romantic than rock-and-roll. The bands are old friends, having come up through the same LA rock-scene ranks. Berkeley embraces White Lotus's lead singer, Jake, and as they reminisce, I learn Jake was Berkeley's mentor. A few years older than Berk, Jake showed him the ropes during his brief but torrid love affair with Mia. White Lotus gave the Brightside their start, allowing them to open for them at The Whiskey a Go Go, and tonight is a reunion, a rare moment when tour schedules relent and recording coincides.

The beer keeps flowing, and before the meal is done, plans are made to continue the party elsewhere, but Berkeley and I opt out.

As promised, he takes me home.

When we arrive at the Vicente, it's close to midnight. Berkeley walks me to my door. Having spent the last five nights with him, the thought of spending the night alone in my apartment is disconcerting and lonely. Once again I'm overtaken by the need to keep him with me.

"Do you want to come in?" I ask, hopeful, as I unlock the door.

"You need to ask?" It's more of a statement than a question, and he follows me in, locking the door behind us before we head to the bedroom to drop off my bag. Sitting down on my bed, he watches as I begin to unpack.

"This is pretty comfy," he hints, as I dump the contents of my bag into a hamper. "I like being in your room."

"I like having you in my room," I answer. "You *are* staying, right?"

"That depends."

"On what?"

"Can you guarantee you won't set off any alarms if I try to kiss you?"

Flushing at the memory of our botched first kiss, I pick up a pillow from the bed and hit him with it. Fearing retaliation I move to dodge him, but I'm not quick enough, and catching my wrist, he drags me onto the bed.

He holds me close as, giggling, I struggle to get away.

"I should have listened to the warning," he says. "You're impossible, Liv. Impossible to stay away from."

Giving in to his arms, I shake my head and look him in the eye. "That's certainly not true, but if it means you'll stay, I'll allow you to think it."

"There's nowhere else I'd rather be." He runs his thumb along my cheek. "Seriously, though, I think I can only stay tonight. We're pretty behind after today, and we don't have the studio booked much longer. I have a feeling tomorrow is going to be really long, and I need to concentrate on getting this song done."

"I understand," I say simply. I'm inappropriately sad

at the thought of a night without him and the official end to the whirlwind fairy tale. Normal life seems dreary in comparison, but I try to be logical. After all, we've spent the last week together and reality has to catch up to us at some point.

"Just promise me if you say you're going to call, you actually will?" It comes out of nowhere, this fear it will happen again; that he'll leave and never call.

He looks hurt. "Do you really think I could do that?" he asks.

I didn't mean to hurt his feelings. "No. It's just me—I'm being dumb. I guess sometimes it's hard to believe this is real, and I get scared."

His eyes hold mine. "I get it," he says. "To tell you the truth, this is the scariest thing I've ever done. Nobody has ever had more potential to hurt me than you."

It's too much. I can't (or won't) begin to grasp what he's getting at.

"I promise I won't," I say quietly.

"Good." He smiles. "Let's do this: I'll call you tomorrow when I get back from the studio, even if it's late and I only leave a message, and I'll take you to dinner as soon as we're done recording on Sunday."

"Promise?"

"Promise."

"Okay," I decide. "I think I'll be able to sleep now." I turn my back to him.

He laughs and pulls me closer. "Good night, Liv," he whispers in my ear.

"Good night," I whisper back as I try to memorize the feel of his arms around me—just in case.

Chapter Thirty-four

PARKER MIFFLIN @ISINDULGENT
@BLOOMOLIVIA JUST SAW *US WEEKLY*...YOU HAVE SOME
EXPLAINING TO DO!!?!? ARE YOU EVER COMING HOME?

OLIVIA BLOOM @BLOOMOLIVIA
@ISINDULGENT I'LL COME DOWN SOMEDAY, PROMISE. ;) MISS
YOU!

PARKER MIFFLIN @ISINDULGENT
@BLOOMOLIVIA YOU ARE A TEASE! IT IS ABSOLUTELY
HORRID OF YOU NOT TO COME DOWN HERE THIS INSTANT. I AM
DYYYYYING TO HEAR...

When I wake up Saturday morning, Berkeley is gone and I
don't recall him leaving. Crawling out of bed, I half expect to

see him drinking coffee in my kitchen and am disappointed when a quick apartment scan proves my aloneness. It's the first time I've been by myself all week, and I marvel at the emptiness in the pit of my stomach. This is new for me. I've always been someone who cherishes seclusion, craves it, even. But now, in Berkeley's absence, I long for him to be back by my side.

Moving to the coffeemaker to pour myself a cup, I notice coffee has already been made and the pot wears a little note written in Berkeley's hand:

"YOU LOOKED SO PEACEFUL I DIDN'T WANT TO WAKE YOU, BUT MAYBE THIS WILL DO THE TRICK. –B."

Smiling as I admire his penmanship, I'm instantly cheered by having a little piece of him to keep with me. I feel better and start to plan my day. I have plenty to do before my pending debrief with Blair and Parker.

Deciding to start with a run to clear my head, I slip out of the Vicente's gate and wave to Willis who greets me with a big "Welcome Home, Miss Olivia!" I run for an hour, letting all of the giddy energy that has built up over the last week escape as TV Olivia retreats and I begin to regain some focus on my normal life.

After my run, I take a long bath before dressing and slipping out to complete some errands to get myself ready for the coming workweek. *Oh reality, say it isn't so.* Upon return I pour myself a glass of sparkling water and settle in on my couch to call my mom. I've barely talked to her all week, and I'm sure she will be bursting with predictions given the newfound information she's privy to.

She picks up on the second ring.

"Hello, Liv," she says into the phone as though she's been expecting my call.

She isn't fooling me. Caller ID is a psychic's best friend.

"Hi, Mom."

"I'm so happy to hear from you. I haven't talked to you in so long. I miss hearing your voice."

"Well, things have been a little busy..."

"I *know*. It's so exciting. He's *so* interesting...very handsome and talented, of course, but I had Esme do his natal chart, and I found out his moon sign is Scorpio. The moon sign is important because it reflects your emotional self—"

"Mom!" I cut her off before she reveals any more. "Are you astro-spying on him? Stop it."

"I wanted to see how compatible you are, is all."

"Well, that pretty much ranks on the top of my list of things I don't want to know about," I retort. "We've been through this before."

"I'm just looking out for you." She sniffs. "You know how important your happiness is to me."

"I know. And I appreciate it, but my emotions are turbulent enough right now—I don't want to start analyzing if our Venus signs are in tune or not..."

"Don't worry. They are. You're attracted to his power, charisma, and intensity, and he can't resist trying to solve the mystery that is you. You hold back, you don't let everyone in, but you have amazing emotional magnetism that draws him to you. It's unbelievable, actually, the energy surrounding the two of you..."

"Enough!" I declare. "The oracle has spoken. Thank you.

I'm glad you're watching out for me, but please, no more."

She sighs. "Fine. But if you ever decide you want to hear them, I have some answers to questions you don't know you'll be asking yet."

"Wonderful. Thanks." I attempt to change the subject. "How's your Clairvoyant Certification Course going?"

"Ooooh! We're working on levitation."

"Have you gotten off the ground?" I ask.

"Not yet," she admits. "It's pretty hard to fight gravity at my age."

I laugh. "That it is. I love you, Mom."

"I love you, too."

We chat for a few more minutes before exchanging namastes.

After I hang up, I take some time to reflect on what she has just revealed about me holding back. The funny thing about being romantically involved with a celebrity is that you're not alone. When you're in a relationship with a normal person, you can usually bet you're the only one who has feelings for them. When you love a celebrity, you have to compete with other people's passion. Berkeley seems to be immune to the effect he has on people, but everyone wants to be close to him, and I can't fathom why he would choose me over all of the extraordinary people he meets every day. I feel so special that he picked me; I have to double-check that I really love Berkeley for Berkeley.

My mom did say I was attracted to his power and charm, and in the beginning I *was* intrigued because I was flattered. How could I not be? But now, I see him for who he really is and know him well enough to separate the person from the personality. And the truth is…*I love him.* Beyond the persona and the fame—if it all went away tomorrow I wouldn't care. My heart is on the table, and I have nothing left to hide. Feeling exposed and territorial, I'm terrified it will all end.

Hearing glasses clinking in the courtyard, I swallow my fear and hurry to join Blair and Parker for an early evening happy hour. The clear blue day is fading and the marine layer is rolling in, bringing with it a salty chill. As I step out, I see the courtyard is set for a feast. Parker has wisely prepared for my homecoming party by stocking up on snacks and (more importantly) wine.

"Could it be? Is it she? the Queen of The Hill has graced us with her presence," Parker says as I close my apartment door behind me. "Girl, come here and have some Pinot!"

I kiss Parker on the cheek and hug Blair before wrapping my sweater tighter around me and accepting a glass.

Teresa and Miguel, my upstairs neighbors, come downstairs wearing matching workout clothes, waving to us as they head out for their evening jog.

"Details, details," Blair begs. "All that PDA at The Bazaar... What was going on?"

"WHAT?" I almost spit out my wine. "Where did you see that?"

"It was in yesterday's issue of *Life and Style*," Blair replies. "You didn't see it? I have it upstairs. I'll run and get it." She jumps out of her chair and sprints up the stairs to her apartment.

"Loved your eff-up, by the way," Parker says. "So scandalous. What made you think to say it?"

"Parker. I didn't say it on purpose. I was *trying* to say 'funk' and it came out wrong. Oh my gosh, do you think people believe I *meant* to say it?"

"I did at first," he admits. "But don't worry about it—you looked gorgeous, and he looked madly in love with you. The whole thing was *hot*. Everyone is obsessed with you two. No one even remembers what you said."

Blair returns and hands me the magazine. "It's in the 'spotted' section."

I open to the page and am relieved to see it is just a small blurb next to two candid photos. The first is of Berkeley kissing me in the cabana and the second is of Berkeley, Lisa, Oscar, and I during our awkward conversation. The caption reads "Spotted: at the *007: Spy Another Day* after party, Lisa Greene tries to make Berkeley Dalton jealous with her buff new boy toy, but Berk doesn't seem to notice—he can't keep his hands off his new GF, Olivia Bloom!"

Interesting. If Lisa was in fact planted there to cause a scene, it seems to have backfired. Thanks no doubt to Shar's segment release, the press is clearly on our side.

"Shar wasn't kidding," I mutter as I flip the page. "There *were* cameras everywhere."

My stomach drops at what I see next. The following page pays homage to me and me alone. Pictures of me are everywhere: me sitting on a giant mushroom at Story Book Forest, me dressed as a flapper at a fraternity Halloween party, my college graduation picture. Where did they get all of these? My mom didn't mention anything. I read the brief bio about me attending Penn State before moving west that accompanies the pictures and the answer is revealed: Michael. The information is attributed to "a former boyfriend." Why did he do this? Blair interrupts me before I can make sense of it.

"I can't believe you've been hanging out with Shar Lambert. I'm so jealous," she says.

"Why would you be jealous? You think it's fun constantly being told you're pond scum?" I ask, setting the magazine down so I can concentrate.

"She's only Blair's idol," Parker says.

"What's she like?" Blair asks. "Working for her is my dream job. She's a PR legend."

"She's a tough lady," I reply. "And I'm pretty sure she hates me, but she *is* good at her job. I'll give her that. And Berkeley says she has a compassionate side; I just haven't seen much of it. If I get a chance to introduce you to her, I will." Blair has been so good to me, it's the least I can do if that's what she really wants. Besides, if Blair started working for Shar, it would be nice to have someone besides Berkeley on the inside looking out for me.

"Really? I would *love* that," she says, placing her hand over her heart.

"Why do you think she hates you?" Parker asks.

"My showing up threw a major wrench into a story she was spinning. She's warmed up a little since the eff-up video was a success, but in the beginning she definitely didn't like the idea of me."

"Do you think maybe she's secretly in love with Berkeley?" Parker suggests.

"Don't be so dramatic," Blair scolds him.

My stomach churns as I try to picture Berkeley kissing Shar. I can only imagine her wide, incredulous eyes glowering at him as if he's doing everything wrong. The thought is so ridiculous, it's laughable.

"Ew. Definitely not. Besides, she's at least ten years

older than him, and I think if that ever was an option, and I highly doubt it was, that ship has long since sailed. No. I just make her job a lot harder. She's used to him dating models and movie stars. I'm too ordinary for him."

"Don't be so tough on yourself," Blair says. "Any publicist is lucky to have you. I mean, you're an eff-ing Internet sensation. What more could she want?"

"I don't know—three more inches, a modeling contract, and the ability to say three words into a microphone without offending the entire viewing public?" I suggest.

"So basically she wants you to win the *Star Search* spokesmodel competition," Parker says.

"Pretty much," I agree.

"Did you seriously just make a *Star Search* reference? Is your ascot pulled too tight?" Blair asks with a glint in her eye. "I give you three and three-quarter stars for that."

He glares at her and changes the subject. "Okay," he says in his most reverent voice. "Enough business talk, tell us the juicy details. Is he a good kisser?"

I blush. "Yes."

"And?" he prods.

I laugh as my phone lights up with a text message. It's from Berkeley.

"Is that from him?" Parker gasps, grabbing the phone out of my hand. "'Just finished recording vocals, starting on guitar. Long night ahead—I'd rather be with you.'" he reads aloud. "So cute."

Another message comes in as Parker is reading. "'Good news—they're doing a rough mix tomorrow before we add backup vocals on Monday so I only need to come to the studio for a few hours in the morning. I'll pick you up for lunch?'"

"Too cute." Blair rolls her eyes. "Sorry. I'm antilove right now."

"What happened?" I ask as I snatch my phone back from Parker and respond to Berkeley with a resounding YES!!! "Things were going so well."

"I thought so, too. But apparently, I was alone in that notion." She lets out a dejected laugh. "It's fine. I'm over it. I think I was more impressed with the VIP treatment at all of his clubs and restaurants than I was with him anyway. And I'm not antilove, really. So tell us your story—starting from the Grammys, we've been *dyyyying* for details."

"Okay," I smile. "Here it goes…"

We spend the next several hours laughing over all the particulars, although I keep the private moments to myself, trying to keep the mood light. I'm not ready to let on how hard I've fallen.

"What a ride." Blair marvels as I finish my story. "So what's it like, being with someone so consuming?"

I suck in my breath, thinking she's alluding to the fact I've abandoned my life at the Vicente for the last week.

"I don't mean consuming in a bad way," she clarifies. "I mean as in passionate—powerful."

I nod, relieved she's not reprimanding me. "To be honest, it's a little scary. I love that he's so attentive—it's almost impossible not to be totally engrossed in him—but this little tiny part of me has been holding back."

"Why?" Blair asks.

"I think it's partly remembering what happened the first time. When he didn't call."

"Oh, we remember," she replies, her eyes solemn.

I smile my thanks at them for putting up with me. "But it's also how heartbroken I was when Michael cheated on me. This is so much bigger than either of those events. I can't imagine how blown apart I'd be if this came to an abrupt end. I'm afraid to feel that."

Parker and Blair look at each other, making "yikes!" faces and nod their understanding.

"So I've been protecting myself," I continue, "holding a little piece back. Until today."

"What's different about today?" Parker asks.

My answer comes slowly as I try to put my emotions into words. "I think I just needed a day away from him to gain some perspective. Being away from all the sensationalism and craziness has let me realize the only thing I care about is him. If we're not together, it's like half of me is missing, and even though I'm risking my heart, I want to know all of him, and for him to know all of me. So I have to jump. I'll regret it if I don't."

"You're in love with him," Parker says.

I remain silent. Having just fully admitted it to myself, I know the answer to the question.

Blair and Parker are waiting.

"No comment," I answer finally. I don't want to say it out loud. It doesn't feel right to say it to anyone other than Berkeley.

I pick up my phone as a means of distraction and realize it's almost one o'clock in the morning. "It's late!" I exclaim. "I have to go to bed, you guys. I'm expecting a phone call, and I have a date tomorrow—I need my beauty sleep. Good night." I make a run for it before they can force me to answer Parker's question.

"Come on! Stay!" they protest.

"Good night…" I wave and blow them kisses, trying to escape to my apartment.

"Wait! When do we get to hang out with him?" Blair asks.

I stop. "Do you want to?"

"Hello. Yes," Parker says. "He needs to come to dinner with all of us. I haven't given my stamp of approval yet."

"Parker. Isn't it enough that I like him?"

"It is. But we're your friends. He should get to know us. When are you bringing him over?"

I would love for Berkeley to get to know them. "Well, the Brightside is recording this week…maybe when they're done? I'll ask." I hope my consent will facilitate my release.

"Good," Blair says. "Just let us know when. We'll make a feast."

"Okay." I smile. "Good night." I close my door behind me.

I fall asleep before Berkeley calls and end up missing him, but that's okay, I'll see him in the morning.

Chapter Thirty-five

OLIVIA BLOOM @BLOOMOLIVIA
ALL RIGHT. ENOUGH WITH THE SURPRISES. @PSYCHICMOMI
WHERE WERE YOU ON THIS ONE???

I awake at nine Sunday morning, too excited at the prospect of my lunch date with Berkeley to sleep any longer. Setting my iPod to play *Dear Rose,* I crank the music loud and hop into the shower. It's the only place I allow myself to sing, and I belt the lyrics to "See Right Through Me" as I wash my hair.

"Yeah, I can't see anything from here, but I know one thing is clear, I can't hide anymore, can't hide anymore, can't hide anymore. Yeah, and the world is just a stage and deception's all the rage, I can't hide anymore, can't hide anymore, can't hide anymore…from you, 'cause you see right through me…"

Still singing as I exit the shower, I wrap myself in a

towel and walk out of the bathroom toward my bedroom to get dressed. A movement from the living room catches the corner of my eye, and I stop dead in my tracks, my voice catching in my throat. Peering around the corner, I allow fear to surge through my body.

Casually dressed in a T-shirt and shorts, Berkeley is lounging on my couch flipping through an old *Vogue* magazine. I take a sharp inhale. *How did he get in here?* Having not seen him in a whole day, I stare in stunned silence at how handsome he is. I don't give myself long to admire him, though, feeling the flush flood my cheeks as I realize he probably heard me singing. And not just singing any old song—singing *his* song—performing for the performer. My worst nightmare. In shock, I stand rooted to the floor.

He grins up at me from the couch. "You're pretty good," he confirms my fears. "We should do a duet sometime."

I close my eyes and allow the embarrassment to emanate from me before pulling it together and concentrating on him. "Are you sure you just heard that?" I ask, my voice tight. "You worked hard for your fans, you don't want to scare them away." Fighting the urge to run, I change the subject. "What are you doing here? How did you get in?"

"I couldn't wait to see you so I came over as soon as I could. Parker let me in."

"The key I gave Parker is supposed to be for emergencies."

"I consider not seeing you for a day an emergency," he says, coming across the room to stand in front of me. Engulfing me in a full embrace, he pushes me back against the wall and kisses me hello. "You really did sound good," he teases as we part. "You've been trained?"

I nod, thinking about the years of agonizing voice

lessons. At my mom's request, Esme started doing readings on me while I was still in the womb. During one prolific in-utero session, she saw me surrounded by musical energy and made the mental leap I'd be the next Barbra Streisand. The next fifteen years of my life were spent trying to coax my reluctant voice out of its hiding place. Finally, after my annual pitch-poor rendition of the *Star Spangled Banner* at the local Little League opening ceremony, my father put me out of my misery and banned all singing lessons. He actually received letters of thanks from the Little Leaguers' parents.

"Yes. But it's a long story. I'll tell it to you some other time." I don't feel like explaining my mom's fascination with the occult. It's definitely a topic for a later date. "I'm sorry you had to hear my concert, but I'm glad you're here," I say. "I missed you."

"Me, too…about the missing you part. I'm glad I got to hear the concert."

My stomach growls. "Where do you want to go to lunch?" I ask, ignoring the latter half of his statement.

He lets it go. "I was thinking we could ride our bikes up to the Farmer's Market—it's such a beautiful day," he says.

"Sounds fun," I answer. "But there's one little problem… bikes?"

"I already thought about that. I stopped on Pico on my way over and bought a couple. All we have to do is walk over and pick them up."

"You bought us bikes?" My voice is flat.

"Yeah." He shrugs as if that's a totally normal thing to do.

"Okay." I nod like I think it's a totally normal thing, too (it isn't). "Let me get dressed and we'll go."

Heading to my bedroom, I throw on a cotton T-strap top and some denim cutoff shorts. Slipping on strappy leather sandals, I pull my hair into a ponytail and drape a small braided bag diagonally across my chest.

"All set?" I ask, returning to the living room.

"You're adorable," he answers, grabbing my hand.

"So are you." My heart flutters at his words. "Let's go."

Hand in hand, we walk the short distance to the bike store. Outside the shop, two bikes stand waiting for us. Mine is a lemon-yellow beach cruiser with white racing stripes and a basket while his is a streamlined, fixed-gear messenger bike.

I smile, admiring his choice. "You picked this for me?" I ask.

"Yes. Do you like it?"

"I'm pretty sure if I had to pick out any bike in the entire world, I would have picked this one," I say. "Thank you."

"You're welcome. Somehow it reminded me of you… it's sunny."

I shy away from him, embarrassed by his compliment, heat building in my chest as he plants a quick kiss on my lips before getting on his bike and pedaling away.

"Coming?" he calls.

Jumping on my bike, I force my heart back into its place and follow his lead.

We zigzag our way through the neighborhoods leading to The Grove, an outdoor mall next to The Farmers Market at Third and Fairfax. The Farmers Market is a collection of food stalls, produce stands, and shops that have been a Los Angeles staple since 1934. It's known for its eclectic food offerings, relaxed atmosphere, and also its abundance of tourists.

Once we arrive, we park our bikes and head through the small corridor that leads to the bustling market.

As we stroll along under the green awnings that shade the stands, trying to decide where to eat, it dawns on me that people are staring at us. With every step we take, heads turn and people whisper. *What are they looking at? Do I have something on my face?* It takes me a minute to realize I'm meandering through a very public place with Berkeley Dalton, lead singer of Berkeley & the Brightside. To me, I'm just spending the day with my boyfriend *(boyfriend!)* who I haven't seen in a day and a half.

Berkeley seems to be having a similar wake-up call as he takes my hand and picks up our pace a little. "Shit," he says under his breath. "I totally forgot today's Sunday. I wouldn't have suggested this if I'd remembered. It's usually okay to come here during the week when it's more local people — people who live in LA tend to respect privacy more," he says. "But on the weekends all the tour busses stop here for lunch…we might need to change our plans slightly."

He brings us to a stop in front of Monsieur Marcel Market. "Do you mind if we just grab some food from here?" he asks. "I have an idea."

"Sounds perfect," I answer, feeling self-conscious as a woman at a nearby table takes out her camera and blatantly snaps our picture.

We hurry inside and make quick work of the market, filling our basket with cheese, bread, salami, and roasted pepper spread and rushing to check out. Despite our speed, when we exit the building, we walk directly into the center of a small crowd that has formed. "Berkeley!" one woman calls out, thrusting a receipt at him. "Can I have your autograph?" Others in the crowd follow her lead and begin rooting for any scrap of paper they can find.

Berkeley smiles and his lead-singer persona snaps into place. Charming as usual, he kindly signs the receipt before moving on to the next one and poses for a picture with a teenage girl.

"Will you sign it, too, Olivia?" the first woman hands me her receipt.

I'm floored. She knows my name? Feeling Berkeley's elbow connect with my rib cage, I realize I'm staring at the woman in shock. I look up at him as if to get his permission, and his eyes flash at me in amusement. "Get to work," he urges.

Fighting disbelief, I take her pen and sign my name. The others start thrusting their papers at me, and I try to be polite as I smile into their cameras. The growing crowd begins to close in on us and I sign as fast as I can, but it seems there is an unending amount of hands reaching out toward us. My breath quickens as the crowd presses forward, stranding Berkeley and I at the center of its frenzied nucleus.

Moments later, I spot several security guards headed our way and I breathe a sigh of relief.

"Hey, guys, it was really great meeting all of you," Berkeley says, spying the guards as well. "But we should get going…" Taking my hand, he tries to find us a way out of the circle as one of the guards comes to our rescue and helps to clear a path. Dragging me forward, we make our escape as the mob screams for one last autograph. Berkeley waves good-bye to the crowd with his free hand as he directs me up a flight of stairs and into an air-conditioned office. Slamming the door behind us, he turns and greets the receptionist.

"Hi, is Stan here today?" he asks, his voice pleasant and calm.

She stares at him, stunned speechless, before she picks up her phone and presses the buzzer. "Stan," she says in a daze, not taking her eyes from Berkeley, as if she expects he might evaporate. "Berkeley Dalton is here to see you."

"Thanks, I appreciate it," Berkeley says.

Stepping farther into the room, we look out a large picture window at the crowds below as we wait for Stan. We don't have to wait long.

"Berkeley." A tall man wearing a suit closes an office door behind him and extends his hand in a businesslike manner. He's probably fifteen years older than Berkeley, but his eyes are warm and he doesn't seem imposing. "It's good to see you," he says formally.

Berkeley shakes his hand. "Good to see you, too, Stan. This is Olivia," he introduces me, and I shake Stan's hand with a small hello.

"Sorry we caused a little disturbance out there," Berkeley says.

"That was you?" Stan laughs. "I was wondering why I was hearing so many security guards on walkie-talkies trying to treat hyperventilating women."

If I'm not mistaken, Berkeley's face flushes. It doesn't last long, and it probably would have been imperceptible to the average observer, but I notice it. At any rate he ignores the comment.

"I have a huge favor to ask. Do you think we could borrow the Adobe?"

"Of course," Stan confirms without having to think. "No

problem. Is it okay if I just give you the key? You can let yourself in?"

"That'd be great. We won't stay long—we're just looking for a private place to have lunch."

"Certainly," Stan nods his understanding and rummages through a nearby drawer before handing Berkeley a key. "There are blankets in the main hall closet if you'd like to use one for a picnic."

"Great. Thanks so much. We really appreciate it."

"Anytime. Feel free to leave the key on my desk in the Adobe office," he adds. "I'll have one of the guys return it so you don't have to worry about coming back up here."

"Awesome. That's perfect." Berkeley pulls me to the door.

"Say hi to your dad for me," Stan calls after us.

"I will." Berkeley replies on our way down the stairs.

"Keep your head down," he advises once we reach the bottom and he scans our path to make sure the coast is clear.

Avoiding eye contact with everyone we pass, we hurry out of the Farmers Market and make our way across The Grove to a wide wooden gate. Slipping inside, he secures the lock behind us. Safe on the other side, we find ourselves standing on an expansive lawn that leads up to an idyllic turn-of-the-century Spanish hacienda surrounded by arched covered patios and fruit trees.

"Where are we?" I ask, astounded that this place exists.

"The Adobe," he answers. "It's the Gilmore family's house. They've owned all of the land here for the last seventy-five years."

"Do they still live here?" I ask, trying to imagine living in the middle of a mall.

"No. It's actually in pretty rough shape. They use it as offices."

He guides me across the lawn and into the house. Inside, it is dark and cool and the air has a musty quality that comes with age. The rooms are grand with massive Spanish-tiled fireplaces, arched doorways, and vaulted ceilings. Wooden chandeliers hang from metal chains, and I can imagine the soft glow from their candles illuminating the spiderwebs that dangle from their arms. It's dark and romantic, but I can see what Berkeley means about it needing work. The ceilings sag and everything is coated in a thin layer of dust, obscuring the adobe's intricate wood details.

"This is incredible," I whisper. "Wouldn't you love to fix it up?"

"Yeah, it could be amazing," he answers as he pulls open a creaky closet door and shakes out a large blanket, engulfing us in a dust cloud in the process. "There's so much history here, it deserves to be restored, but where would you start?" Coughing, he pulls me out of the cloud, then disappears into an adjacent room, leaving the key on a desk just inside the door.

"Picnic?" He smiles upon his return.

I nod and follow him out a set of double French doors, across the back lawn, and into the shade of a lemon tree. Berkeley spreads the blanket and we make ourselves comfortable on the ground, taking out our lunch.

"It's beautiful here," I admire our surroundings. "Thank you for bringing me. How did you know about this place? Do you know *everybody*?"

"No." Berkeley laughs. "My dad worked on the real estate deal when they built The Grove so I've been here a few times with him and that's how I met Stan. And Mark and I used to hang out at the bar at the Farmer's Market when we were in college. Actually, we still do sometimes. I like it there; it makes this town feel small."

"Just not on weekends, right?"

"Right. I'm sorry that was a little crazy. I wasn't thinking," he says. "We shouldn't have come here. It's just I feel so normal around you I forget sometimes we can't always do regular things like spend a Sunday at the Farmer's Market. It's frustrating. You weren't scared were you?"

"A little at the end," I admit. "But I was more surprised they knew who I was."

"Really?" he asks. "Liv, your picture has been on the cover of every tabloid in the United States for the past week. How could they not know who you are?"

"I guess so... I just never thought about it that way. When I read that stuff, it seems like it's happening to someone else because all of that has nothing to do with this." I gesture between his heart and mine.

He looks at me with eyes brighter than usual. They actually look a little watery. "Thank you," he says simply. "That means a lot to me." He moves forward until his lips are on mine. My stomach constricts and my heart tightens until it feels like it might burst. I feel my core pull to him, and I can't get close enough. The only sound is my heart pounding in my ears as tears spring to my eyes as he breathlessly breaks the kiss.

Taking a ragged breath, he whispers, "I'm going to miss you so much."

Fear prickles through me as I search his eyes, trying to make sense of his words. "What do you mean?"

"I've been keeping something from you," he confesses in a quiet voice, not meeting my eyes. "Not because I didn't want to tell you, but because I was hoping to surprise you." He looks up at me, dejected. "I just found out it's not going to work, though."

"What are you talking about?" I ask, unable to hide the anxiety in my voice.

"We're going back on tour," he replies softly. "We leave this week for eight weeks in Asia, and I was trying to set it up so you could come with us, but it's not going to be possible. There's too much red tape, too many visas to get. The people at the label tried, Haynes tried, Shar tried, but they hired a company that has been working on getting all of us cleared for the last six months and there isn't time to push another person through."

My body clams up as he delivers the blow, and I try not to let the devastation show. "Eight weeks is a long time," I say, holding back tears. "Thank you for trying, though..." I trail off. I can't help but think about the last time he went on tour. *This is exactly what I don't want to happen!* But what choice do I have? I can't stop it. I should have known this is inevitable—that things can't stay this way—that his job will take him back on the road. I just didn't think it would happen so soon.

"It'll be different this time," he promises, as though he can read my thoughts. "I'll call you every day."

I nod, not totally believing him. "When do you leave?"

"Thursday."

"Wow," I exhale. "That's fast."

"It is. I don't know how I'm going to handle being away from you, actually. It's crazy. I'm totally freaked out that I won't be here to protect you."

"I'll be fine. You're the one doing all of the traveling. How am I going to protect *you*?" I ask.

His eyes cloud and he shakes his head. "Come here." He pulls me to the ground with him so that we are lying on our sides facing each other. Tucking a strand of hair behind my ear, he whispers, "It'll be okay. We'll make it work. Would you want to come visit at least? It's hard for you to travel with us this time, but let's pick a city where we're going to be for a few days and I'll fly you out."

"You don't have to do that," I say.

"I want to. It's no trouble. You'd be doing me a favor… as long as you want to come."

"I'd love to," I concede, exhilarated at the thought of being with him abroad.

"We'll figure it out. I just hope this doesn't ruin today."

I shake my head, willing myself to bury the news. "No. Nothing could ruin today. We should just enjoy the time we have and not think about Thursday," I decide, determined to make every minute count.

"Agreed," he answers, kissing me. "In honor of that, do you want to continue our bike ride?"

"Sure." Sitting up, I force a smile and push away the fear and doubt. "Where do you want to go?"

"Let's head north," he suggests.

Once we finish eating, we pack up the remnants of our picnic. Keeping our heads down, we stealthily reclaim our bikes and take our time working our way up to Beachwood Canyon.

It's nearing four o'clock as I follow Berkeley onto a pretty street lined with birch trees and large, gated estates.

He comes to a stop in front of one gate in particular and dismounts from his bike. I stop next to him.

"Everything okay?" I ask.

"Yeah. I just thought we could take a little break," he says.

"Sure," I say slowly, watching as he turns and punches a code into the keypad next to the gate. I narrow my eyes. He's up to something. "Berkeley, whose house is this?"

The gate slides open behind him as he turns back to face me. "My parents asked to meet you. We've been invited to a family dinner."

I feel the blood drain from my face, and I begin to shake. "You're full of surprises today, aren't you?" I look down at my outfit. It would not have been my choice for making a first impression. I can't believe he is springing this on me. I try to be calm as I ask, "You couldn't have warned me?"

"I didn't want you to overthink it and stress all day. Don't worry...they're going to love you."

I'm not so sure about that, but what choice do I have? Silently, I push my bike forward, following him up the long drive.

At the top of the hill sits Berkeley's parents' house, a sprawling estate with sunny windows surrounded by crisp white decks overlooking the canyon. It has a relaxed beach vibe despite its distance from the ocean, and even though the house exudes warmth, to me it is a fortress.

Leaning our bikes against a wall on the side of the house, he takes my hand as we make our way toward the front door. "Are you okay?" he asks, sounding concerned.

"I don't know. I'm pretty nervous." *And sweaty and dusty and disheveled.* I wish I could take a shower.

"I shouldn't have sprung this on you," he admits. "If it was the other way around and I was meeting *your* parents, I'd want some advance warning."

My mind flashes to an image of my mom reading Berkeley his Oracle Card and serving him roasted dandelion root tea while a Quick Spell "Activate the Spirit Within" candle burns in the background. "You have no idea," I mutter.

"I'm sorry."

"How long have you known about this?" I ignore his apology.

"Truthfully?" he asks. "Since Thursday. I wasn't sure I was going to go through with it though... I just decided today."

"Why?"

We reach the front door and he turns to face me. "This isn't something I normally do, Liv. There's never been a reason to. Christina and my sister never quite meshed so I usually avoided bringing her around, and there was never anyone else who was worth it."

My nerves tighten at the mention of his sister. Is she going to be here, too? Again I wish I had more time to prepare—to plot the perfect outfit for meeting Mia Dalton, whose quirky style consistently earns her placement at the top of best-dressed lists. Not to mention digesting the news that she and "America's Sweetheart" Christina Carlton don't get along. Despite what Berkeley says about her, the only Christina I'm aware of is the adorable peaches-and-cream version that adorns magazine covers. In her interviews she always comes across as a girl's girl, toothache sweet and funny. What's not to love? This is not looking good for me.

"What made you decide—"

I don't get to complete my sentence because the front door opens. Standing on the other side is a woman who can only be Berkeley's mother. A statuesque brunette with light blue eyes, her hair falls loose in unruly waves around her face. She is casually dressed in cuffed jeans and a white tank top layered under an oversized, striped men's shirt accessorized with chunky jewelry.

"Are you planning to stand out here forever?" she asks brightly in her heavy South African accent. "Come inside this instant. I never get to see you, and I won't let you stall another minute." She pulls Berkeley inside and catches him in an embrace.

"Hi, Mom." He hugs her back.

"And this must be Olivia." She releases him and sets her sights on me. "Come inside, dear, we've been waiting to meet you."

I smile and take a timid step through the doorway, extending my hand. "Nice to meet you, Mrs. Dalton."

She ignores my hand and hugs me hello. "Please call me Jodi," she says. "Come on in, you two. Dad and Mia are down on the tennis court."

I cringe internally at the mention of Mia's name. I think I'm more nervous about meeting her than Berkeley's parents.

We follow her into the house. It is comfortably furnished with white, overstuffed couches, blue-and-white pinstriped pillows, white wicker tables, and vases filled with seashells. Framed family pictures cover almost every available surface, and colorful portraits adorn the walls. I'm surprised at how homey it feels. I guess I expected something sterile and glamorous, but I'm pleasantly surprised to find that family

seems to be the center of the Daltons' world, and they
don't seem so different from us ordinary people. Aside, of
course, from the fact that Berkeley's mom is a best-selling
author, his dad is a major real estate developer, his sister
is an Academy Award-winning actress, and they're all
devastatingly beautiful, their home seems pretty normal.

Berkeley's mom leads us through the kitchen and
outside onto a large deck with sweeping canyon views. "I
thought we could have some hors d'oeuvres out here. Make
yourselves comfortable. I'll be right back with some wine."

"Mom, relax," he orders. "You don't have to wait on us.
Let me help you."

"Yes," I agree. "Is there anything we can do?"

"No. I've got it all ready. Just give me a minute," she says
before she disappears back into the kitchen.

Berkeley shakes his head after her. "She's a total
perfectionist," he says as he walks to the edge of the deck
and looks down toward the tennis courts. "I think she wants
to make a good impression on you."

"She's not the only one worried about making a good
impression," I reply, while inwardly I laugh at Berkeley
calling someone else a perfectionist. I'm interested in
observing where he got it from.

I sit down on an L-shaped couch as he waves down to
his dad and Mia. "Hello," he calls.

"Hey, stranger." A deep voice comes up on the breeze.
"We're coming up!"

My heart begins to pound. Berkeley's mom seems
sweet, but I have a feeling my biggest test is yet to come. At
the sound of their footsteps on the stairs below, my palms
begin to sweat. I stand awkwardly as Berkeley's dad's head

appears above the deck railing.

"Hey, Dad." He greets his father with a brief hug. They are similar in height but Berkeley's dad, though trim, is rounder. Physically, Berkeley takes after his mother, but it's clear to me his presence and intensity come from his father. Though his father's eyes are kind, I find him intimidating and imagine his ability to command a room is imperative to his success in business.

An instant later a second head appears above the railing, and my heart almost stops in fear. The moment I've been dreading is upon me. Mia Dalton, clothed in a tiny tennis dress, her dark hair perfectly framing her face and accentuating her brilliant blue eyes, surfaces and immediately fixes Berkeley with a giant hug. "I missed you! You never talk to me anymore," she scolds him.

"Sorry. I've been a little distracted." He hugs her back. "Dad, Mia, there's someone I'd like you to meet," he says as he steps back and reaches for my hand. "This is Liv. Liv, this is my dad and my sister."

"Hi," I extend my hand to his father, hoping he isn't too put off by my bike-riding attire. I am somewhat comforted by the fact that they've just come off the tennis court. "Good to meet you."

He shakes my hand. "Hello, Liv. Very happy to meet you."

Swallowing my nerves, I turn to face Mia and again extend my hand with a quiet hello. She meets my eyes and bats her impossibly long fringe of dark eyelashes at me. "Olivia Bloom," she says, taking my hand. "It is *very* nice to meet you. I've been *so* curious about the girl who has entranced my brother. It's not easy to do."

Berkeley rolls his eyes as I blush. "Mia," he says, giving her a warning look, "leave her alone."

She winks a sweet smile at him and turns back to me. "Come on, let's sit and get to know each other. It's not often I get to meet a girl my brother's interested in. He never brings anyone home. In fact, the shoe is usually on the other foot. It's usually me subjecting *my* dates to him, which, as you can imagine, is *always* fun."

In an instant I feel sorry for anyone she brings home. I imagine for guys, meeting Berkeley Dalton must be intimidating. He would never be impolite, but I'm pretty sure if he doesn't think someone's good enough for his sister, he won't engage them in conversation, either. That could lead to a long evening, and I have a feeling I am about to pay for Berkeley's sins.

I make myself comfortable (at least as much as my nerves will allow) on a couch as their mom appears with a tray filled with bruschetta, hummus, pita, and pistachios. "Mia, will you bring the wine and some glasses?" she asks.

Mia sighs and stands, giving Berkeley a look that indicates she isn't done with us yet.

"So how are album sales?" his dad asks him in a businesslike manner. "I saw *Up All Night* made it to number one on the charts."

"Yeah. It was there for a few weeks. Sales are good," Berkeley answers. "The album's been getting some good reviews, and we've already sold out five of the shows in Asia."

"Good. Good. Sounds like it's all working, then," his dad says.

It's interesting, listening to them talk about the business

side of Berkeley's world. He never mentions his successes to me, and I learn more listening to the brief conversation with his father than I have in all the time we've spent together.

Mia reappears with a chilled bottle of Sauvignon Blanc, and Mrs. Dalton (I mean Jodi) follows with a tray of glasses. She sets the tray down as Mia plops the bottle in the middle of the table. "Here, honey, use this coaster so it doesn't leave a ring," Jodi says as she flings a large cork coaster across the table toward Mia. The lightweight disk catches on the breeze and before I have a chance to react, it sails across the table and hits me square in the forehead.

"MOM!" Berkeley and Mia exclaim at the same time.

"Eish! Olivia! I'm so sorry," Mrs. Dalton exclaims, her hands flying to her face to cover the flush that rises in her cheeks.

My blush matches hers and I can't help it, I start to laugh. *Of course*, I think. *Of course. If anything is flying through the air…*

"Please don't worry," I soothe through my giggles, hoping she isn't too embarrassed. "It happens *all* the time. I promise. I'm like a magnet for flying objects."

"It's true," Berkeley says, putting his arm around his mom. "It's all I can do to keep her out of trouble. She reminds me of you in that way."

"Well." She composes herself, joining in my laughter. "That's one way to break the ice."

I smile back at her. She's right. I feel more comfortable already.

Berkeley joins me on the couch and kisses my forehead as his dad fills our glasses and Mia fixes us with a stare. "All right," she says. "How did you two meet?"

"Mia," Berkeley says, "can we do without the third degree?"

"No. As a matter of fact, we can't," she replies. "You never tell us anything, and frankly I think you owe us the story. After all, we're your family. It's not fair for us to have to read about it in a magazine."

He nods and sighs, taking my hand. "You're right. We met in January at a fashion show Liv was working at, and even though we only exchanged a few words, I couldn't get her out of my head. I never thought I'd see her again, so I was shocked when Mark brought her backstage at the Santa Barbara Bowl a few months later—she and Mark have a friend in common and he'd invited them. After that I relentlessly pursued her until she agreed to go to dinner with me."

"Don't you mean invited yourself to dinner at my house?" I interject.

"Berkeley! You couldn't even spring for a meal?" Mia admonishes. "Have I taught you nothing? I can't believe you went all 'rock star' on her."

Berkeley mock glares at me and gives Mia a dirty look before he continues with the edited version of our story. "As I was saying, until she agreed to go to dinner with me. After that dinner, I couldn't shake the feeling I had to hold on to her, but the timing was bad with us on the road. A month went by before our paths crossed again. This time I wasn't going to let her get away, and I surprised everyone, including myself, by inviting her to the Grammys. I think you know the rest…" He grows quiet as he looks at me, a hint of a smile on his lips. He squeezes my hand, and I lose myself in his gaze.

"I think we do," Jodi says quietly a moment later,

breaking the spell.

I notice they're all staring at us, and I compose myself as I turn back to face them.

"Well, that pretty much says it all," Jodi says. "This calls for a toast, I think. Cheers." She raises her glass to us. "Welcome home, Olivia." She smiles.

I smile back and raise my glass, my heart pounding at her meaning. As unexpected as it is, I do feel right at home.

Later that evening, I retreat with Mia and Jodi to the Daltons' large family room. The room is light and breezy with its white-washed, open-beam ceiling and bank of wide paned windows that overlook the front garden. A built-in bookshelf encompasses the entire far wall, and it's hard to tell if more books or family photos adorn its shelves. Berkeley and his father excuse themselves shortly after dinner, retreating to his father's study and referencing some contracts they need to look at. Normally I would balk at the idea of being left alone with the female half of his family, but I've been feeling oddly comfortable all evening and figure talking with his mom and sister will be more interesting than whatever business he and his dad have to discuss.

I walk over to the bookshelf and pick up a black-and-white photograph of Berkeley and Mia sitting on a cobblestone wall in a vineyard. The Berkeley in the photo is around fourteen years old with longish hair and a thin build. His face is softer, his jaw less defined, but there's no mistaking his eyes. He's holding his guitar and looking off into the distance while Mia smiles prettily into the camera. It looks like it came straight out of the pages of *Life Magazine*. Normal people don't look like that when they're teenagers. I push away a recollection of my own frizzy hair and braces with a shudder.

"Great picture," I say aloud.

Mia peeks over my shoulder. "Ugh," she says. "I can't believe how pudgy I was back then. And Berkeley was just learning to play guitar. I remember that summer at Pap and Ouma's," she continues as I follow her to the couch. "He wouldn't talk to anyone. He'd just lock himself in his room and play constantly—the same chords over and over until he got it right—for the whole rainy summer, which is really winter in South Africa,."

"Mia, I'm sure your brother wouldn't appreciate that," Jodi says. "He was always the shy one," she tells me. "He was a loving child, but quiet. He never told us anything. Maybe that's my husband's fault. Thomas always took something of a hands-off approach when it came to Berkeley's teenage years. He wanted to let him figure things out for himself. Thomas always said, 'If he does something wrong, I'll get a phone call. As long as there's no phone call, I trust him.'"

"Until he got a phone call, that is," Mia says.

"Really?" I ask, trying to imagine a time when Berkeley was reckless. It is hard to fathom that even at a young age he would have allowed a crack in his outward persona.

"It could have been much worse, believe me." Jodi shakes her head. "When Berkeley was sixteen, one of Thomas's coworkers was out at the Gig, and when the last band came on around one in the morning, there was Berkeley singing and playing lead guitar. The coworker called us the next morning to let us know he'd seen our son in a bar the night before and he must have had a fake ID because they wouldn't allow anyone under twenty-one into the club. He also said the band was terrible, but he thought Berkeley had potential." She laughs.

"Did he have a fake ID?" I ask.

"Oh yeah," Mia says. "I got it for him. I was hoping he'd use it for something more intriguing than sneaking out to play music, though."

Jodi's eyes snap to look at Mia. "*You* got it for him?" she asks, blinking her eyes and awaiting explanation.

"Oh, ummm," Mia falters, at a rare loss.

"Hmmm." Jodi narrows her eyes and regards Mia, her expression a perfect Berkeley replica.

"It was a long time ago, Mom."

"But the truth always comes out," Jodi replies. "Anyway, Thomas and I were shocked," she continues, letting the subject drop and returning her eyes to me. "Berkeley was so quiet, we never pictured him as a performer. Mia was always dancing and singing—she never minded being the center of attention, but Berkeley was the opposite. He kept to himself. We couldn't believe he would get up on stage, let alone sing in front of a crowd."

"He didn't even get in trouble," Mia complains.

"No?" I ask.

"That's not true!" Jodi exclaims. "He was in *huge* trouble. He had all of these crazy ideas about touring with the band that summer, which we forbid. And we forced him to invite us to his next show, which he was not happy about—I believe he felt inviting his parents did not qualify as 'rock and roll.'" She smiles. "And we took away his fake ID and told him he was only allowed to play places we approved of."

"Where was his next show?"

"We let him play Froggy's in Topanga on a Sunday afternoon—an acoustic set. As soon as I saw him up there, I knew he was where he belonged. I felt like the stars were aligned and this was what he was meant to do." Her voice cracks at the memory, and there is no mistaking the pride behind the tears in her eyes.

She and Psychic Mom might get along after all...

"Okay. Enough you two," Berkeley's voice sounds from the doorway behind us. "I'm taking her away before you can spread any more rumors."

He stands behind me, resting his hands lightly on my shoulders as I look up at him.

"Ready to go?" he asks me.

"I'm just getting started," Mia threatens, a glint in her eye. "I owe you."

He shakes his head at her. "Next time. I promise. We have to ride our bikes back to my place, and I want to go before it gets too late."

I stand and join him. "It was wonderful meeting all of you. Thank you so much for dinner—and the dirt," I add with a smile.

I hug everyone good-bye—even Mia—and follow Berkeley out the door.

"See, it wasn't so bad, was it?" he asks as we mount our bikes.

"Not at all. I had a wonderful time."

"They all liked you—even Mia. It may not seem like it, but she's actually on my side. She doesn't joke around with just anyone. She was being real tonight—that means she was comfortable around you."

"I'm glad. I'd hate to be on her bad side."

"Yes, you would. It's not pretty," he teases.

It may seem like he's joking, but I have a feeling he means it, and Mia's opinion matters to him. I'm glad I seem to have passed the test.

"Do you want to go to my place?" he asks. "It's closer. If you don't mind getting up early, I'll drive you home so you can get ready for work tomorrow."

"I'd love to... I could use a shower."

"That can be arranged," he promises, and we head through the Hills.

Chapter Thirty-six

PARKER MIFFLIN @IsIndulgent
CAN'T WAIT FOR *PROJECT RUNWAY* TONIGHT! YOU KNOW HOW I
LOVE A PROJECT.

BLAIR HAMILTON @SuperSpinstress
@IsIndulgent AND YOU KNOW HOW I LOVE A COCKTAIL.
WHAT'S ON TAP?

PARKER MIFFLIN @IsIndulgent
@SuperSpinstress PROJECT-TINIS? WE CAN USE SEWING
NEEDLES INSTEAD OF TOOTHPICKS!

OLIVIA BLOOM @BloomOlivia
@IsIndulgent @SuperSpinstress WISH I COULD JOIN!

STILL AT WORK…REMEMBER WHEN I DIDN'T HAVE TO SAY
THAT? AH THE GOOD OL' DAYS… #YESTERDAY

OLIVIA BLOOM @BLOOMOLIVIA
@ISINDULGENT @SUPERSPINSTRESS PS IT'S ALL FUN AND
GAMES UNTIL SOMEONE SWALLOWS A NEEDLE. PROJECT-TINI =
#DANGEROUSDRINK

Monday morning rears its ugly head, and Berkeley drives me back down the hill. We linger over our good-bye, as I won't see him until tomorrow night when he's set to come to dinner at the Vicente. The Brightside needs to finish recording before they leave on tour, and he thinks tonight will be a late one. We've decided that after dinner Tuesday night he'll stay with me, and I'll stay with him Wednesday night so he can make sure things are in order at home before he leaves for Asia on Thursday.

Arriving early at work, I slink through the halls trying to keep a low profile. I make it to my office, unseen, and turn on my computer. Examining the overflowing samples on my rolling rack, I'm wondering where I should start when Gemma accosts me.

Under her slim blazer she's wearing a sheer white T-shirt tucked into rust-colored, wide-legged pants paired with wooden platform sandals. She tips forward on them as she pulls me down into the guest chair. "You're back!" she squeals. "You *have* to tell me everything."

I try to disentangle myself from her. "I don't know where to start—with last week or with this rack." I gesture helplessly toward the mass of babydolls.

"Oh, that's the new line. I'll let Lillian tell you about it. Start with last week."

I stand up and walk around my desk. Taking a seat in my chair, I groan at the six hundred e-mails in my inbox. I'm never going to get through all of this. I'm so behind! "Well, I think you probably saw most of it..." The truth is there isn't much information about my time spent holed up with Berkeley I want to share—especially here at work where I'm sure the walls are listening. "Kay Pritcher dressed me for the Bond premiere, though." I figure Gemma will appreciate that information.

"NO!" She sucks in her breath and exhales her excitement in a rush. "I'm so jealous. I love her! Was she a bitch?"

"No, actually. Quite the opposite. I was surprised, too." I laugh.

"Liv—" a voice announces its presence through my speakerphone. "It's Lillian. Do you mind coming to my office for a minute?"

"Sure!" I respond, trying not to convey the blast of fear that just spiraled through me. "On my way." As my phone clicks silent I look at Gemma and whisper, "Do you think I'm in trouble?"

"No." She smiles. "You're definitely not in trouble."

"How do you know? I just ditched out on work for a week."

She shrugs and moves to my door. "Go see what she wants," she says. "And I want all the details at lunch."

I follow her out the door and head down the hall toward Lillian's office. Poking my head in, I try to sound upbeat as I say, "Hello!"

"Liv! Welcome back. Could you close the door please?" she requests in a pleasant voice.

Uh-oh. Closed doors are never a good sign. "Sure," I say nervously as I tug her door softly shut behind me.

"Take a seat." She offers me a plump purple chair and makes herself comfortable across from me on a gray suede couch. "So, that was quite a week you had," she says.

I feel myself blush. It doesn't feel appropriate talking about such intimate things with my boss. "It was... Did you see I mentioned Jonquil?" I ask, drawing her attention to the effort in hopes of saving myself.

"I did as a matter of fact. It would have been impossible not to notice because our sales jumped four hundred percent across all stores thanks to your mention."

"They did?"

"They most certainly did. But that's not why I requested you here. We're grateful for the mention, of course, but Liv, do you know why I hired you?"

"Umm...no," I say, preparing for the worst.

Lillian sits back on the couch and studies me. "It wasn't for your design skills."

"It wasn't?" I'm sweating.

"I thought you had lovely taste, and the sketches in your thank-you note were beautiful, but we had applicants who were more technically qualified than you who may have been a better fit on paper. No, I hired you because you seemed eager—driven—like someone who'd roll up her sleeves and do the dirty work. I always hire the person I want on my team. The skills come with time."

"Thank you for taking a chance on me," I say, waiting for her to say I've disappointed her. An eager, driven person doesn't disappear for a week…

"I'm glad I did," she replies. "You see, I also found you inspiring. Did you see the new line hanging in your office?"

"Yes," I say, rushing with the sudden hope that I'm not getting fired. "It's really cute."

"Thank you. I think so, too. It's part of a new line I've decided to develop. I *love* a good love story," she says wistfully. "And watching you this week made me realize I should be designing for *you*. Everything we do here is beautiful, of course, but it's elegant and sophisticated. You made me see I need to be designing a line that's young and fun and flirty—things you and your friends would wear. It's based on some of the ideas you and Gemma came up with for Nordstrom, and we've been making samples all week. I'm really excited to show it at market."

"That's wonderful," I say. "I think it's a great idea."

"Well, I definitely want you to have design input on this line. Every piece needs to be something you and Gemma would wear. Are you up for that?"

"Of course." I smile.

"And," Lillian continues, "I'd love for you and Gemma to come to New York when we launch the line to be the line ambassadors."

This is getting better and better. I should have closed-door meetings more often.

"Really?" I ask, my excitement growing. "I'd love that."

"Well, there's one catch," she says.

"Okay…" I say slowly, a tinge of fear creeping through me.

"I'd like to call the line In Bloom, after the girl who inspired it, if that's okay with you," she reveals.

Tears spring to my eyes. She's naming the line after me? My voice catches in my throat as I respond, "I think that's a perfect name. I'm honored."

"Good. I hoped you'd say that." She beams. "I love the name, too. I think it's going to be a huge success."

"I hope so," I say, as I stand and move toward the door. I'm feeling like I want this meeting to end as quickly as possible so I can escape to my office and jump up and down for five minutes straight, but I manage to keep my feet on the ground. "I should probably get to work on illustrating, then."

"Oh, take your time. We have a month until the next market and there will be design changes. I was just so motivated this week I wanted to get the line started as fast as I could. It was a good week for you to be gone. It was a quiet one."

"Well, thank you for being so understanding. I feel very blessed right now."

"So do I." Lillian nods with a smile as I close her door softly behind me.

The rest of the day and the next fly by as I weed through the pictures from the photo shoot, choosing my favorites and retouching them while filling Gemma in on the previous week's details. Surprisingly the rest of my coworkers keep their distance and don't pry. Perhaps they aren't interested, or maybe they don't pay attention to *TMI*. Either way, I'm grateful for the anonymity.

Berkeley keeps me updated on how recording is going with frequent texts, and I can't wait for our Tuesday night dinner at the Vicente. As I plow through illustrations for the new line, I try to focus on that, and not his impending departure.

When Tuesday afternoon finally draws to a close, I shut down my computer and practically float home to the Vicente in anticipation. We've decided to keep dinner simple and are planning to barbecue in the courtyard.

Blair is hovering over the grill, basting artichokes in lemon and olive oil and turning the tri tip, while Parker stirs his famous potato salad and I set the table.

When Berkeley arrives, I'm impossibly happy to see him after our almost two-day hiatus, and it's all I can do to resist flinging myself into his arms. Somehow managing to contain myself, I take the wine he's brought and set it aside, shyly pulling him into the courtyard. For some reason I'm jumpy with nerves. I know I shouldn't be, but these are three of the people I love most in the world, and I want so much for them to get along. I'm concerned that I won't be a good hostess, with me being so easily tongue-tied and all.

Berkeley is in show mode, his persona in place. He greets Blair and Parker, graciously asking them about work as they finish cooking the meal. We hover around, making small talk. We need to loosen up. What this party needs is wine.

"Hey, Berk," I say once there's a lull in the conversation. "We need to open this bottle—come with me to the kitchen for a minute?"

"Sure," he says, allowing himself to be dragged away.

The truth is I might explode if I don't get my hands on him soon.

He seems to have similar ideas, and as soon as we round the corner to my kitchen he wedges me against the refrigerator and kisses me a proper hello. "I missed you," he whispers into my lips as his persona dissolves. He's back to being mine again.

"I missed you, too." I run my fingers down his chest and claim his lips again.

We're dangerously close to not being able to leave the kitchen when Parker walks in. "Oh! I *love* it!" he exclaims as Berkeley and I leap away from each other and my hands fly to straighten my top. "You're my favorite couple, seriously. So adorable," he says, any pre-Grammy wolf-pack protector teeth baring erased as he morphs into a playful puppy.

"We were just on our way back out," I say, scrambling to cover our tracks, even though I know I'm not fooling anyone. I start moving toward Parker. "Did you need something?"

"I came to get the pepper mill, but I wasn't expecting to find such a fine grind." He grins.

Inwardly, I groan, but I can't help letting a giggle escape. "Ugh. Parker!"

"I'd say it was more of a coarse interruption," Berkeley comes back at him as he catches my hand and hands me the wine opener. "Don't forget what you came for." He smiles.

"Scandalous," Parker declares. "I like him."

"Well, he's taken," I remind him, trying to keep my voice stern. I can't contain it, and we all dissolve into laughter as we head back to the courtyard, the ice broken.

After filling our plates, we gather around the table as the last of the sun sets. I pour everyone some wine and we relax into dinner.

Taking charge, Parker drills into Berkeley. "So talk to me about groupies. You must have to beat them off with a stick!"

"PARKER!" Blair exclaims while I choke on my wine.

"Mr. Manners," she scolds him.

I can't believe he just asked that and I stare at him, eyes bulging. Not that I'm not curious myself…it's a topic I've been too afraid to broach, but it's a conversation I would prefer to save for a more intimate environment. I shift my eyes to Berkeley. *Must change the subject. He'll never answer that question—he's too private.* To my surprise, however, he seems okay with it. He lets out a little laugh and his eyes graze my face.

"You don't have to answer," I tell him. "Parker sometimes forgets we're not filming a reality show and most normal people don't want to share every past dirty detail with the entire world," I explain for Parker's benefit.

"It's okay, actually," Berkeley replies. Turning his gaze to Parker, he lets his guard down and fields the question.

"There aren't as many opportunities for groupies as you would think. Honestly, we're usually exhausted after a show. Touring isn't very glamorous. We travel through the night and we keep pretty tight security, even on our days off. Haynes—you've met him, Liv—has strict orders not to let anyone back to the busses or after party unless they've been cleared through him. I won't say that girls *never* make it back, after all I'm not alone back there, but I will say it's been years since anyone has made it back on my invitation."

Despite Blair and Parker's presence, I know this answer is meant for my ears alone, and I allow relief to flow.

"Years? So you're not saying it never happened," Parker digs deeper.

Jumping to Berkeley's defense, I kick Parker under the table. "Parker," I grumble, "can't we change the subject?"

"This is information you should *know,* sweetie, and I

know you'd never ask yourself."

"It's true, Liv," Berkeley surprises me by siding with Parker and takes my hand. "And I don't mind. I don't have anything to hide, and it's not like you couldn't Google it anyway. I'd rather you hear it from me."

"Well, just so you know you don't need to answer," I say. "And you guys can't breathe a word of anything you hear, either." I glower at Blair and Parker.

Blair looks offended. "Of course not. Rule number five. Who do you think we are?"

"I know, I know. I'm just being safe…" I trail off and my eyes meet Berkeley's curious ones. He wants an explanation, but I'm definitely *not* explaining rule number five to him.

Parker saves me, encouraging Berkeley onward, "So?"

Berkeley tears his eyes from my face and addresses the table with a sigh. "I won't say it never happened. I'm a different person now than I was at twenty-two. In the beginning, when everything was so new, girls were certainly part of the scene, although they were never why I chose to pursue music," he says. "I loved music more than anything else in life, and I guess in some selfish way I wanted to keep that part of me to myself—I never wanted to share it with anyone—to have anyone get close enough to understand me. So, having access to girls who were disposable, that weren't going to stick around because the next day we'd be on our way to the next city, was convenient. I'm not proud of it, but at the time I didn't want to care about anything other than making music. And in a way, I had an image to keep up. That's what I was supposed to do. It was almost expected."

We're all hanging on his every word.

"So you were kind of a dick," Parker clarifies, breaking

the silence and ignoring the daggers I shoot his way.

Berkeley laughs, though I detect sorrow behind his eyes. "Yes, I guess you could say I was kind of a dick," he confirms.

"When did that all change?" Blair asks.

"A few years ago." He cocks his head to the side, his focus far away as he continues. "I started to feel shallow. The band was doing really well, but with that success came responsibility and the pressure of having so many people's livelihoods depending on me—of always being the party. It was an unbelievable time. We were riding a tidal wave of good fortune, but the rare moments I was alone started feeling empty. I didn't know why at first, but soon I realized what was bothering me: when all of those people finally went home, they were going to something. And there I was, already home, but I had nothing. No one. I've been trying to find my way home ever since."

I feel his eyes on me, and I raise mine to meet his, my heart pounding out the recognition that I'll always be home as long as I'm with him.

Parker wipes a tear from his eye and says, "Love! I'm so totally taking notes. It's so romantic I might vomit. I believe. I believe in romance, damn it! And to think you almost didn't go out with him, Liv. It's a good thing you were following your butterfly guides."

"Parker!" I tear my eyes from Berkeley's and shoot Parker a warning look. Enough is enough. Groupies are one thing, but Psychic Mom is a category I refuse to discuss. How can I explain to Berkeley that every day since birth my mom has tried to predict my future—has tried to infuse my path with magic? He'll think I'm insane.

"You're really on fire tonight, aren't you?" I say to

Parker.

"Flaming." He grins.

Berkeley is studying me, his eyes questioning, waiting for elaboration. "Your turn." He smirks, raising his eyebrows.

After all he's just revealed, I suppose he's right. It *is* my turn in the hot seat. He's been so honest, it's my duty to reciprocate.

"Fine." I give in. Here it goes. "My mom has always had a fascination with the supernatural, and she has a tendency to read into things—to find insights into the future. Everything is a sign to her. *Everything.*"

Berkeley watches me with a smile as I struggle to explain, stumbling over the words.

"Do you agree with her?" he asks.

"No. In fact, I avoid her predictions as much as possible. It's not that I think they're true—I don't—it's that I prefer not to know. I'm always afraid that knowing something will taint my decision process and will therefore change my path either toward the vision or away from it. I'd rather let fate follow fate."

"Except for that one time," Parker reminds me, as if I could forget.

I give him a dirty look. "Except for that one time," I agree grudgingly.

"The picture…" Blair urges me along.

I roll my eyes and continue, "Yes, yes, the picture." I almost spit the word as I stare at my lap. "This is so ridiculous," I mutter, shaking my head and peeking up at Berkeley. "But after we talked at the Lakers game and you invited me to dinner the next night, I made up my mind I wasn't going to join you. I was dead set against it, actually. It wasn't that I didn't *want* to go," I add, fearing I may have hurt his feelings. "I was flattered and curious and every ounce of me wanted to go, but my brain was protecting my heart, and it told me no."

"What made you change your mind?" he asks gently, his eyes warming me.

"Well, believe it or not, it wasn't your relentless charm," I tease, trying to keep the mood light. "After I left the game, Parker and I drove home in my car with the windows rolled down and this envelope I'd totally forgotten about—my mom gave it to me when she came out for a visit—flew forward into Parker's lap. And he opened it." I exhale, staring at my thighs. *I'm grateful Parker opened the envelope. What if he hadn't and I'd stuck to my plan not to go to dinner?* I guess I wouldn't have known the difference—never would've experienced what could have been—but having brushed so closely to missing out on Berkeley sends ripples of fear through me.

"What was in the envelope?" Berkeley interrupts my reverie.

Elation overtakes fear as his voice reminds me I made the right choice and he's here next to me. Looking up at him, I cannot mask the tears forming behind my eyes as I answer softly, "A picture of you with a note on the back from my mom that said 'no regrets.'"

Berkeley shakes his head, disbelieving. I knew he'd think I was crazy. "That's very strange." He squints his eyes, trying to work it all out in his head. "What picture? Did she get it from a magazine?"

"No!" Parker asserts. "That's the best part. It was a photograph she took in Pittsburgh. It looked like you inadvertently walked in front of the camera just as she snapped the photo."

Berkeley turns pale, and I see rapid recognition reflected in his eyes. "Was the photo taken at…that overlook with the incline…umm…Mount Washington?" he asks.

"Yes…" I confirm.

"Wow." He sits back in his chair, shaking his head to himself, his eyes lighting in delight, contemplating.

It feels like several moments pass as we wait for him to elaborate. Finally, Blair can't take the suspense anymore and begs, "What? Wow, what?"

Berkeley looks up at her before focusing on me. "I think I have a message for you…" he says. "I totally forgot about this. When we were on our last US tour we had a day off in Pittsburgh and were doing some sightseeing. We went up to Mount Washington, and I did mistakenly walk in front of this lady's camera."

"Stop it. You don't remember this happening," I say as my body explodes in goose bumps. "You don't."

"But I think I do," he replies in an astonished voice. "I apologized, saying it was an accident, and she got this big smile on her face and looked up at me and said, 'There are no accidents.'"

Oh boy. That definitely sounds like Mom. I stare at him, trying to remain skeptical as he continues.

"And then she hugged me."

Of course she did. Yep, that seals it. Undeniably her.

I drop my head into my hands and let out a whimper before looking back up at him, covering my mouth with my hand. "I'm so sorry. This is crazy. You must think I'm crazy," I mumble through my fingers. "My mom is definitely crazy…"

I add as I look to the heavens for an answer.

"No, I thought she was endearing, actually." He laughs. "When she let me go, though, she told me something that at the time I thought was just some sort of cryptic saying." He sounds out the words as he recalls them, "'If you ever meet the girl you can't bear to live without, tell her you're glad she listened to her mother.'"

I scoot my chair back in one swift motion and leap up from the table. Turning my back on the courtyard, I retreat into my apartment, cursing my mother and the fact she has used Berkeley as a means to get me to listen to her prophecies. *Where does it end?*

"Wait, Liv!" Berkeley calls after me. "There's more!"

"I don't want to hear it!" I yell without looking back as I kick open my apartment door.

"But we do!" Parker says.

"Liv! Come back!" Blair's voice completes the trio.

I slam the door behind me in response. Flinging myself onto my couch, I try to calm down. I don't believe in this stuff. It's not real. It's not true. It's just a coincidence. A really weird coincidence.

A sliver of light slices through the room and basks me in a triangular glow as Berkeley enters carrying the remnants from dinner.

"I don't want to hear anymore," I warn him.

"Okay. I promise I won't tell you anymore," he says, closing the door behind him and plunging me back into darkness. He heads to the kitchen and sets our plates down in the sink. "You have to agree it's pretty fantastic, though."

"No, I don't. I think it's all a random sequence of events that happens to coincide," I reply.

Joining me on the couch, he pulls me into a sitting position, dragging me into his lap so we're face to face, my legs straddling him.

"Don't you believe in magic, Liv?" he asks, seeking my eyes.

"No," I say with childish stubbornness. "Do you?"

"Yes. I do."

"I guess we're going to have to agree to disagree, then."

"Or I'll have to prove you wrong," he replies.

Before I can argue, his lips are on mine, coaxing my mouth open and sending me into a whirl that whips any semblance of coherent thought straight out of my head. He's getting good at distracting me, and as my body resorts to its virile nature, I let him have the last word. For now.

Chapter Thirty-seven

Mrs. Bloom @PsychicMom1
Oooh, the hairs on my arm just stood up!
#almostlevitating

The next day flies by and we cling to the dwindling moments of our dream, knowing all too soon, we'll have to wake up. Life as it has become is about to crash to a halt. The night before Berkeley is to leave, I sit cross-legged in my pj's on his bed, watching him pack for the next eight weeks on tour.

"Are you excited?" I ask as he folds shirts into a duffel bag.

"Yes and no." He pauses before he clarifies. "I always look forward to playing for people who've never seen us before, and we've never toured this extensively in Asia, so from that viewpoint, I guess I'm excited."

"They'll love you," I assure him.

"I hope so." He zips his bag shut and moves it to the floor. Standing at the edge of the bed, he gives me his full attention. "But from the perspective that for the next eight weeks my life is going to consist of waking up, eating breakfast, waiting, doing an interview or personal appearance, waiting, eating lunch, getting shuttled to a venue, waiting, sound-checking, waiting, playing the show, waiting, getting shuttled to a bus or a train or a plane or a hotel—if we're lucky—and traveling to the next spot and doing it all over again the next day, I wouldn't exactly say I'm thrilled."

"Sounds exhausting."

"It is. I've traveled all over the world, but I've never been anywhere. Pretty much all I see are arenas and hotel bars." He moves onto the bed and pulls me down next to him. "And combined with the fact that here, safe at home—safe in my bed—is you, well, I can't think of any place I'd rather be."

"I don't know, hotel bars and shuttle buses sound pretty appealing," I quip in a halfhearted attempt at levity.

Neither of us feels like laughing, and the room falls quiet save for the sound of crickets outside the window as we lay on his bed, staring at the ceiling.

"I wish you could come with me." He breaks the silence. "I'm going to miss you so much."

"Me, too. Maybe next time," I suggest with a sad smile.

"Definitely next time. When I get back, I'm never leaving your side." He gathers me against his chest and kisses my forehead. "And just think—in a month you'll come meet me in Bangkok. It'll be here before we know it."

"It still feels like an eternity," I say, leaning my head against him and inhaling his clean scent as I've become so accustomed to doing. My thoughts turn to what it'll be like without him. We've decided that halfway through the tour, I'll fly to Thailand and meet him in Bangkok. The band has three days off there, and we've been able to secure my visa for that time. He'll be gone longer than we've been together, though, and I can't help but think that when I arrive in Thailand we'll be strangers. Allowing a single tear to escape, I struggle not to believe it's all going to end tonight.

Noticing the tremble in my lower lip, he wipes the tear from my cheek. "Hey, look up here."

I follow his gaze to the ceiling where a shadow-puppet gorilla is lumbering along. Berkeley contorts his fingers and the gorilla morphs into a giraffe eating leaves. He has amazing hands. They can do anything.

Next, a swan ruffles her feathers and floats by. I can't help but giggle. "You're a nerd. Call up *TMI*; this is *news!*"

He glares at me playfully. "How about this one? What's this, Liv?"

I return my eyes to the ceiling.

The shadow above us is of a hand with its thumb, index finger, and pinky raised.

I catch my breath as the meaning behind the symbol registers. Tearing up, I turn to look at him. His eyes haven't left my face since he asked the question, and as I return his gaze, I am lost.

"I love you," he whispers.

My heart hits my toes and a glorious warmth spreads over my skin as an unseen force tugs me to his core. "I love you, too," I release the words that have been on my lips for so long. It's a relief to say them out loud.

His eyes brighten in response, and he doesn't try to mask

the joy that shines through. He rolls over so he is above me, his fingers brushing my hair from my face, his lips finding mine, lingering, sweetly sampling, as he holds me tighter and tighter.

I can't get close enough to him. Every nerve in my body is awake, alert. Breaking the kiss as a soft moan escapes my lips, my mouth traces the roughness of his jaw, and one of his hands slides under my shirt, discovering my breasts. His mouth moves to my neck and a powerful surge flows through me, overwhelming me. I run my fingers down his chest, moving lower until I find him, gripping him outside his pants. With a low growl he pulls away, his eyes dark as he rids me of my clothes. I return the favor, tugging at his pants until he is exposed. Once we are both naked, he puts on protection and drags me forward, his fingers circling my hips, positioning himself to nudge me open until I'm burning for him. Neither of us can wait much longer and he slides into me in one swift motion. Nearly bursting against the pressure expanding inside me, I arch into him, pulling him down on top of me. Every inch of my body is pressed against him, and wrapping my legs around him, I hold him closer still, unable to get enough, not wanting to let go. Our breathing heavy, he fills me to overflowing as we both cry out and tears spring to my eyes. His skin is bathed in a thin layer of sweat as I move my hands down his back, and he collapses over me, placing his forehead to mine. We lay still, clinging to what we know must part.

After a moment he exhales, gently rolling us over, unlocking us in the process. He doesn't let me go for long as he arranges himself around me, positioning me in his arms, and covering us with a sheet. "Let's get some sleep," he suggests.

"I don't want to. It'll make tomorrow come that much faster," I whisper my complaint.

He smiles down at me. "I'm not going to let you go."

"I wish I didn't *have* to let you go," I say as I pull his arm tighter around me. "And I don't. At least not for tonight."

"No. Not tonight," he promises as he turns out the light and gives me a squeeze.

I burrow into him, fitting my body snuggly against his, determined to stay awake, memorizing exactly how this feels.

My eyes flutter open at the earliest beginnings of morning light. The filtered, white rays bring with them the day I've been dreading. Rolling onto my side, I watch Berkeley sleeping next to me. In his slumber, he looks softer—more like the boy from the picture I saw at his parents' house, his lips relaxed in a soft bow. I want to kiss them. Unable to resist touching him, I reach out and brush his hair from his forehead. He stirs and opens his eyes, instantly recognizes me, and smiles.

"Good morning," he murmurs.

"Bad morning." I pout as I flop back onto my pillow.

Berkeley laughs. "The worst," he agrees. "Did you sleep okay?"

"Yes," I answer. "But I didn't mean to." I'd tried to stay awake as long as possible, but in the end the heaviness behind my eyes overtook me and I fell into a deep, dreamless sleep. Somehow it ended up being one of the best night's sleep I've had in a long time. "Did you?"

"No. Too much on my mind."

I wait, but he doesn't elaborate.

"We should get ready before Shar gets here," he says.

Grimacing, I drag myself out of bed and into the bathroom. I haven't seen Shar since my eff-up, and that's fine by me. Though I'm in no rush to leave Berkeley, I wouldn't mind avoiding her.

The band's chartered jet is scheduled to leave for Tokyo at 12:55, and Shar has volunteered to drive Berkeley to the airport. He sees her offer as less an act of kindness and more an opportunity to lecture him on cultural customs so he won't accidentally offend anyone, thereby making her job more difficult. I offered to drive as well, but he declined saying he didn't want me to be late to work. *I* have a hunch his refusal has more to do with the scene a public good-bye could cause at the airport, should there be any paparazzi lurking, than it does my tardiness. But what can I do. I understand.

As he showers and shaves, I change for work and silently apply my makeup, my heart grows heavy while I watch him out of the corner of my eye. Once I am presentable, I gather the smattering of my belongings that have become fixtures in his house and begin carefully folding them into my overnight bag. My movements are slow and deliberate. I'm stalling because once I zip the bag closed, I'll have no reason to stay.

As I am putting the last piece into the bag, I feel his presence behind me. His arms circle my shoulders and he holds me against him.

"I wish I could stand here and watch you forever. I don't want to leave…" His voice is quiet in my ear.

"Then don't," I half joke.

He turns me to face him with a wistful smile. "Promise you'll wait for me." His tone is light, but the eyes that search mine are earnest.

I gaze back. He's always doing that—saying things it makes no sense for him to say—as if he's the one who has to worry, as if it's going to be humanly possible for me to move from this spot and not stand here pining for him for the next four weeks. "Of course," I say, "the *only* thing I plan on doing is waiting. Just *you* promise not to forget me."

His expression shifts to reflect both amusement and sadness. "Impossible. You have no idea…" Lowering his face to meet mine, his kiss starts gently, and energy shoots straight to the pit of my stomach. His lips persist as I kiss him back, and the tension between us elevates to incessant. His fingers find my hair, and he pushes me back onto the bed as the front door slams.

"Berkeley!" Shar's acid voice rips us apart, and Berkeley pulls away, staring down at me as we both try to catch our breath. She's certainly taking the cake with this one. I'm not usually a violent person, but I'm pretty sure if she walks into the bedroom right now, I'll find a way for the bedside lamp to connect with her skull. The vision brings me great joy.

Berkeley frowns and runs his finger down my cheek by way of apology. "I love you," he whispers with a conspiratorial flash in his eyes before he rises from the bed and tries to compose himself.

I, too, stand and straighten my dress.

Walking out into the living room, he greets Shar before retreating to the kitchen for coffee. I make my entrance a moment later.

"Oh good. Olivia's here, too." She smiles, her eyes

lighting up as I come into view. "How are you?" She greets me with a full embrace, like we're long-lost sorority sisters.

My eyes widen over her shoulder. I'm confused by her change in attitude. Sure she was pleasant the last time we spoke, but this is totally unexpected. Is eff-ing up on national television all it takes to be accepted into her good graces? Or maybe she sees Berkeley is happy, and that's all she's *really* wanted for him all along so she's decided to acknowledge me as one of her own? Hmm. I'm skeptical.

She lets go of me and stares in that invasive way of hers. "Hi!" Her voice is breathless. "I'm *so* glad I get to see you."

"Good to see you, too," I say, trying to sound genuine and keep the bewilderment from my tone.

"I've been meaning to call you," she continues. "I wanted to talk about what you should be doing while Berkeley's gone. I think it's best you keep a low profile and not talk to the press....not that they would care about you anyway with Berkeley not around..."

Ah. That's more like it.

"But just in case... You know what I mean?" She blinks her eyes at me in rapid succession as if that will aid my comprehension.

"I know exactly what you mean," I confirm. "You don't have to worry about me. I actually prefer to keep to myself anyway, and I know how important privacy is to Berkeley. I would never do anything to jeopardize that." I keep my tone innocent and sweet, even though for the second time that day I want to throttle her.

"Good. Glad we're on the same page," she says as Berkeley reenters the room. "We make a great team, don't you think?"

"Great," I agree, hoping to put an end to the conversation.

"Well, Berkeley, are you ready to go?" Shar turns her attention to him. "I've got a bunch of things to go over with you. I made sure Haynes has a list of all of your appearances and interviews, and I'll be in constant contact with him since I won't be able to meet up with you until Hong Kong…"

As she speaks, I pick up my bag and start making my way toward the door.

"Shar, will you put this in the car for me?" Berkeley asks, cutting her off and gesturing to his own bag. "I'll meet you there in a second."

"You want me to do *what*?"

"Just give us a minute, okay. I'm going to lock up, and I'll meet you outside."

"Fine," she says, grabbing his bag and brushing past us. The front door slams behind her.

Berkeley ignores her exit and picks up my bag. "I'll walk you to your car?" he asks.

It's time. "Sure," I say, trying to be strong.

As we head outside, he locks the door, and I trudge behind him to the top of the driveway where my Volkswagen is parked, just out of Shar's view.

Setting my bag in the backseat, he turns to face me. "I guess this is it," he says, sounding distracted.

"Have a good trip," I reply, fidgeting and fighting back tears. There's so much I want to say, but for some reason the words won't form on my lips.

"I'll try." He avoids my eyes, and we stand apart, not sure what to do next. "Hey, come here." He finally focuses on me and pulls me into his chest, hugging me tight for a full minute before letting go. "It's not good-bye, Liv. I'll call you as soon as I get to Japan," he promises as he releases me, his gaze searching my face.

I nod as he steps backward. "Miss you already…" I manage.

He half smiles before he turns and jogs toward Shar's car.

Watching after him, I see my Berkeley retreat and public Berkeley snap into place. He may as well already be in Japan. His leaving me behind while he goes off on this new experience alone, an experience that will shape and change him, makes him feel like a stranger to me. This is the exact opposite of "Team Adventure," and even though I know it isn't his choice, it sure feels like good-bye to me.

Trying to push the negative thoughts away, I get into to my car and turn up "Leave My Mind" by Berkeley & the Brightside until the windows rattle. Driving out Berkeley's front gate, his voice in my ears, I head down the hill toward work. I'm already late.

"I can't rest my mind until I set the record straight, let this be the line I had to cross to escape a lonely fate, yeah, everything I ever got from you is nothing that I can leave behind, I'm still waiting for you to leave my mind…"

When I get home from work later that night, Blair and Parker are lounging in the courtyard armed with Irish coffees.

"Are you okay?" Blair asks.

"No. I'm miserable. I feel like I've been ripped in two."

"I'm sorry, honey," Parker says. "Just think. It's not forever. And if you were never apart, you'd never get to be reunited. I can see it now…you step off the plane in Bangkok, scanning the crowd for him, but you don't see him at first. You start to panic. What if he's not there? But wait. Out of nowhere he appears behind you and wraps his arms around you. You turn to him and he covers you with kisses, and the crowd cheers!"

Parker regains his focus as he realizes Blair and I are staring at him.

"I'd stick to writing reality, if I were you," she says.

"It's true," I agree. "That would *never* happen. He kissed me once in public and we all know how that ended up…"

"Fine." Parker huffs. "I thought it sounded romantic."

"It did." I soothe him. "Thank you. And you're right. There's no point moping around for the next month." I am trying to be logical about the situation. It reminds me of when I first moved to LA and had to force myself to keep a positive attitude. "I just have to keep busy, is all, and it's not like we aren't going to talk. It'll be fine." It's the same pep talk I've been giving myself all day. I'm not sure I believe it.

"It *will* be fine," Blair says. "And it'll be good to have you around again for a little while. We missed you!"

"I missed you guys, too—"

"Oh! Do you know what we need?" Blair asks, cutting me off. "A spa weekend. Let's head to the desert and revive."

"I'd love that." A weekend poolside with Blair and Parker sounds like exactly what I need. It will give me something to look forward to and hopefully make at least this week go by faster.

"Just promise me we won't end up at some ghetto hotel pool," Parker says. "I don't even *want* to know what is floating in the water at those places. That could end up requiring a whole different kind of 'treatment.'"

"I'm sure someone can loan us a house," Blair assures him. "I'll make some calls."

Twenty minutes later, Blair's boss has offered up his

three-bedroom, golf-course-adjacent, private-pool condo (for free!) and we're good to go.

Later, around midnight, my phone finally lights up and I answer even before it can begin to vibrate.

"Hi! You made it."

"Hey—yeah—we're here. We just got to the hotel and we're getting ready to go to dinner." His voice is clear. It's hard to believe he's on the other side of the world, and I allow myself to believe he's at the studio instead, only to be crushed by reality a second later.

"I'm getting ready to go to bed. Dinner sounds more fun."

"I'm not so sure about that. Bed sounds pretty good to me right now, but we have to try to stay up and adjust to the time. The first show is tomorrow night so at least we have a few hours to get used to it."

"You'll be fine."

"Yeah—once I'm on stage, the adrenaline will get me through. But until then, I'll be homesick. That usually happens when we first get on the road, but this is the worst it's ever been... I miss you already," he says, his voice quiet.

"I miss you, too."

We both fall silent. Again I'm struck by the inability to form sentences. Feeling distant and tongue-tied, I try to think of what to say next.

Fortunately Berkeley steps in. "Sorry this morning was so weird... I'm not very good at good-byes."

His revelation unknots my tongue, and I relax. "It's okay. I much prefer hellos myself..."

I can hear his smile. "Before you know it, I promise."

"It can't come soon enough."

"No it can't..."

I hear muffled voices in the background. "Hey, I'm going to have to let you go. Everyone's waiting on me. But I'll talk to you tomorrow night?"

Disappointed at losing him so quickly, I concede, "Sure. Have fun at dinner…"

"Tomorrow, I promise we'll have more time. Sleep tight, Liv. I love you."

"I love you, too. Good night…."

As I hang up the phone and drift off, I smile, wrapped in the cocoon of his voice. Maybe this won't be so bad after all.

My work life is chaos. Market week is rapidly approaching, and we're busy putting the finishing touches on the new In Bloom line. True to her word, Lillian tells Gemma and me to book our tickets to New York for the launch (using Lillian's company credit card, of course). I'll return from the trip the day before I'm to leave for Bangkok. What is this crazy jet-set life?

As brand ambassadors, Gemma and I want this line to be extra perfect. I'm up to my ears in illustrations and costing. Plus, production for the Nordstrom babydoll we designed arrives, and to my chagrin, it has the Jonquil label sewn into the bra cup instead of the back of the garment. Even I, with my limited design experience, know a label doesn't go in a bra cup and am certain it isn't my fault when Tina calls me into production and the fingers start pointing.

Turns out, I'm wrong. As keeper of the tech-pack, label placement is my responsibility, I learn.

Tina sits me in the middle of her lair, pacing back and

forth, trying to sweat the truth out of me.

"But I didn't say to put the label in the bra cup!" I try to defend myself against the production team's pitying stares.

"Did you say where to put the label at all?" Tina asks.

"No. I didn't know I had to."

"Well, now you do. You can't leave these sorts of decisions up to the factory. You need to be specific. The original sample must have had the label in the bra cup. That's the only explanation. If we send a garment over there with a ketchup stain on the front, we'll get production back stained with ketchup, guaranteed. Where was the label in the original sample?"

"I don't remember, but I doubt it was in the cup."

"Did you take a picture of it?"

"No…" Again, didn't know I had to. But I'm learning now. *Document everything.*

"You've made a mess. Now we have to rip out all the labels and resew them in the correct place. You're lucky it's only a thousand units. It'll still take a couple days to fix if the girls work overtime, though, and we need to ship by Friday."

"Can I help sew?" I'll do anything to fix it.

"I think you've done enough. Just be more careful next time. If there's a next time," she replies. "You can go."

I scramble to get away from the interrogation and hurry back down the hall, feeling my mistake will set into motion a series of catastrophic events: the order will be late, Nordstrom will cancel, we'll lose thousands of dollars, everyone will hate me, resulting in my ultimate demise. I should start looking for a new job now. At my next interview my reputation will probably precede me, though. I imagine greeting my potential new boss: Yep. That's me. Olivia

Bloom. Ending the world, one G-string at a time.

Shoot me.

On the bright side, Berkeley dutifully calls me every night (my time) and we talk until I fall asleep. We fall into a comfortable rhythm, and bedtime becomes my favorite time of day. He checks in from places like Busan and Seoul, mostly sounding exhausted as he tells me about interviews and stages and hotel rooms. I try not to dwell on the fact that our lives are heading in two different directions and concentrate on learning as much as I can about life on the road. Hearing about his adventures is not the same as experiencing them with him, though, and listening to his voice every night doesn't replace the emptiness I feel when I wake up alone every morning. The intensity of our short time together is blurring around the edges. Sometimes I can't believe it really happened. It seems like a fantastical dream I saw in a movie once.

Feeling rooted in my real world, I focus on spending time with Blair and Parker. I'm thankful they allowed me to tumble into the Berkeley-hole and resurface weeks later without mentioning my tunnel vision. They are my champions. Knowing exactly what I need, those martyrs cart me off to Palm Springs for a poolside weekend with the only necessary "treatments" being sacred hot-stone massages, tanning, and copious amounts of margarita.

The week following our trip flies as I concentrate on getting ready for New York and Thailand. Not to mention this weekend we're planning a dinner party in the Vicente courtyard. All the residents of the building are in town for once, and Blair has even consented to put up with Lance for a night in the name of the party. As head chef, menu planning is proving to be a modest distraction as well.

Berkeley continues checking in from Taipei and Manila, but the farther he travels, the more he reverts to being wrapped up in the band. As we share less and less, a distance between us grows. I try to ignore it, try to pretend it isn't there, but it can't be denied. It's becoming hard to believe I'm going to fly to Bangkok to see him. It doesn't seem real.

The last I spoke to him, he was in Hong Kong, and he said he probably wouldn't be able to talk for a couple of days because of the band's travel schedule to Jakarta. I'm disappointed, of course, but I said I understood, and I'm looking forward to his next phone call as though it's a mini-homecoming.

Saturday afternoon before the party, I run out to Whole Foods to get some last-minute dinner supplies. Standing in the checkout line, I'm half double-checking my list and half scanning a rack of magazines when a bright yellow headline catches my eye: "Berkstina: We're Team Adventure."

The freight train strikes without warning. I snatch up the magazine and open to the article as tentacles of fear twist inside me. There, splashed across two pages, is a picture of Berkeley looking intently at Christina Carlton as they share an intimate drink at a bar in Hong Kong. There's no mistaking him. I recognize those eyes.

Across the top of the page, a title reads, "Reunited At Last." In dizzying disbelief, I collapse, taking a rack of granola bars down with me as I pass out and hit my head on the floor. I don't know how long I'm out, but when the blackness dissipates, I can't catch my breath—suffocated by panic and sorrow—and the only thing I can do is lay in a helpless heap. Gravity holds me prisoner, and I stay still for a few minutes, my cheek against the cool tile, trying to gain composure, until a grocery checker comes to my rescue. Ashamed and disoriented, I try to help her clean up my mess as the hipster Whole Foodies look on in horror.

Leaving the store in a daze, my groceries forgotten, I wander on foot back to the Vicente. I fight the image of Berkeley and Christina that's searing itself into my brain, erasing the Berkeley I've come to love in the last five weeks, but I'm no match for it. The dark thoughts surge forward. *I'm an idiot. I should have known better. Who am I to think someone like him would be interested in someone like me when he could have her. I'm nothing. Nobody.* My thoughts flash back to conversations we've had about her, and I can only remember Berkeley saying he had liked Christina *a lot*—that he didn't break her heart, she broke his.

As I walk, a glorious numbness overtakes me. In order to protect me from the rush of pain, my body ceases to feel. By the time I reach the Vicente, I'm desensitized. I'm oblivious, and I can't comprehend what has just happened. *Hello, denial.*

I begin to shake.

In an attempt to distract myself, I turn on the TV. Big mistake. Huge. As my TV blazes to life, there is Christina standing on a street corner in Hong Kong being interviewed on *TMI*. A new rush of awareness overtakes me. She looks dewy and fresh, her blond hair blowing softly in a breeze. I'm no match for her perfection. How could I have thought I could compete?

"In a recent tweet, America's favorite actress, Christina Carlton, announced her reunion with rocker Berkeley Dalton, when she tweeted, 'We're Team Adventure!

#BerkeleysBack,'" Felix Sheridan's voice informs me.

"Doesn't Berkeley have a new girlfriend?" a reporter asks Christina, as a still of Berkeley kissing me at the Grammys flashes on the screen. I close my eyes to the blistering pain of having one of the most thrilling, intimate moments of my life displayed for all to see. When I reopen them, the image has been replaced with a smiling shot of Christina and Berkeley at a similar event a year earlier. Seeing them standing next to each other in all of their flawless splendor is like a dagger to my soul, but instead of swiftly slicing me open and putting me out of my misery, it just keeps poking me, inflicting tiny flesh wounds, and allowing the pain to slowly mount.

"You can't believe everything you read," Christina informs the reporter. "Berkeley and I should *never* have been apart. We just had a small misunderstanding is all. I'm so happy! It feels like serendipity that we're staying at the same hotel in Hong Kong. I'm here to film a shampoo commercial, and I was at the front desk checking in when all of a sudden there he was. We've spent every minute together ever since. It's so cute. We've even decided to call ourselves 'team adventure' because we never want to go anywhere without the other person ever again."

"Berkeley has been quoted in the past as saying he didn't think he'd ever get married," another reporter jumps in. "Is that still the case, or do you think now that you've reunited, that's a possibility for you two?"

"Oh, *that*. It was all so silly. He never meant it. I know for a *fact* he's changed his mind. I think all this time apart has made him realize what he really wants… I mean, I really can't comment, but…" She glances down at her left hand and gives a little laugh, winking at the reporter.

I can't listen to any more. Swallowing the bile that rises in my throat, I click off the TV and let the tears roll down my cheeks. When we spoke last, Berkeley made no mention of running into Christina. Is that the real reason he can't call for a few days—because he wants to be alone with *her*? How can he? And worse, how can I have been so dumb? This must have been how Lisa Greene felt. Maybe there *was* more to their relationship than Berkeley let on. Maybe it was this feeling, this awful feeling, that made her drag my name through the mud.

I add "ashamed" to the list of emotions swirling inside me and, surrendering to the pain, I curl into a ball and cry. Praying to be delivered from ex-girlfriends and trying not to think of the two of them together laughing at my naivety, I fall into a fitful sleep.

At some point I hear Blair's and Parker's muffled voices in the distance as they enter my living room, but they leave as quietly as they came. Blair must have seen the news; she gets *TMI* text updates with all breaking celebrity news.

I register that dinner will be canceled.

I don't know how long I've been lying here, but twilight is falling as I awake to my phone buzzing next to me. "Shar Lambert" the display reads. I throw it across the room, begging it to shut up. It falls silent. A moment later it alerts me that I have a voice mail.

Standing unsteadily, I cross the room and pick up the offending object from the floor. Not wanting to listen to her orders, I power off the phone. Turning to my computer, I set my e-mail to return all messages anyone tries to send me.

I know what I have to do: consider him erased and avoid the media.

Chapter Thirty-eight

CHRISTINA CARLTON @CELEBRIGHTLY
BEST SHAPE OF MY LIFE YOU GUYS. DON'T CALL IT A COMEBACK
LOL. LOVE TO YOU ALL! FEELING SO SERENE, SO INSPIRED!!!

I sit despondent on my couch.

Blair and Parker have stayed by my side all day. Physically ill, I can't eat or sleep. I cut off all communication with the outside world (even with my mom and Boots because I can't risk turning my phone on and having him call — I hope they'll understand why I'm not talking to them) and sequester myself inside my apartment. Within an hour of the *TMI* report, the paparazzi comes to camp outside of the Vicente, waiting for me to emerge and play my role of scorned lover. It's not going to happen. I lack the ability to form a complete sentence, let alone brush my hair or make myself presentable. It's a waiting game. Ultimately, I figure they'll go away if I stay in hiding long enough.

"Don't you at least want to check your messages?" Blair nudges my phone toward me. It isn't the first time she's mentioned it. "There must be some explanation. Maybe he tried to call?"

I shake my head. "No." I'm prone to one-word answers these days. Somewhere deep inside I know she's right, but I'm afraid. I'm right back where I started. Everything I knew—or thought I knew—has changed. And this time is so much worse. I opened my heart and allowed myself to trust him, only to have it bludgeoned once again. If he *did* call, there's a chance he'll try to explain and tell me it's all a giant misunderstanding. That's what I want to hear. However, I'm not immune to the possibility that he'll tell me his feelings for me have changed—that as soon as he saw her, he knew he had to have her back. The truth is, the only thing keeping me from completely snapping is a small glimmer of hope, obscured beneath the torment, that he really does love me. I desperately cling to that unlikely notion, and if it's ripped from my already weak grasp, there's no telling how far I will sink into the waters of despair. I can't risk it.

"Liv, there must be some reason Christina is doing this. I told you these things are never what they seem. Maybe you should check your e-mail...something?" Blair says.

"I can't imagine she's doing it for any other reason than they're meant to be together. What could possibly be in it for her?" I ask.

"Press?"

"Well even if she's just doing it to get her name in the papers, I still can't deny something happened. They at least had a drink together, and he didn't tell me about it. And

'Team Adventure'? Why would he give her that? That was *ours*. It was private and now it's tarnished. Now it's *theirs*." I can't get past this betrayal. The fact that he shared something so intimate is proof to me he's chosen her.

"True. Okay," Blair concedes quietly. "No e-mail. You know he's been tweeting at you, right?"

"Please, I don't want to know."

She ignores me. "He doesn't say much…just 'please talk to me.'"

"I can't." Fat tears roll down my face. I'm lost. I know I said I didn't believe in magic, but I now know I was lying. He made me believe—only to have everything disappear in an unceremonious *poof*—and I'm not interested in giving him a third chance. Conjuring the image from the magazine, I remind myself I don't belong in their world and close my eyes.

Parker bursts into the living room, slamming the door behind him. "It's getting crazy out there. The paparazzi are *everywhere*. I almost couldn't get in the gate. I hope they got my good side…" He trails off. "I brought chocolate croissants." He gestures his peace offering toward me.

I attempt a smile and ask, "When will they go away?"

"They're not budging," he says. "In fact, I think they're multiplying. They're hounding every person who walks out their door for information. Lance has elected himself secret service for all of us at the Vicente—earpiece and all—and he's escorting everyone to their cars. Willis is just about the only person they're leaving alone. He keeps waving Betty in the air and yelling 'no riffraff!' whenever someone comes near his porch. I think he might finally crack."

I'm trapped. And what's more, the entire neighborhood

is being held hostage because of me. It isn't fair. They didn't ask for this disruption any more than I did, though I *deserve* it for taking the supreme risk of dating an A-list celebrity. Picturing Willis sitting on the porch that has been his perch for sixty years being badgered by heartless photographers shakes me to the core. *This isn't his fight, and I have no right to ask him to stand up for me. I need a plan.*

"What do I do?" I ask. "This can't go on. I just want things to go back to the way they were. Before him. Before this crazy dream began."

Parker sinks down next to me, and Blair squeezes my hand in understanding.

"I wish I had some expert advice," I continue, vocalizing more thoughts than I have since seeing the magazine. "I know what Shar would say—'don't say anything.' But given the circumstances is that what I *should* do?"

Blair turns toward me, smiling. "Honey, the good news is you *do* have an expert. You *know* I live for this stuff, and personally I *don't* think silence is the answer in this situation. If this whole Berkstina thing is true, I'm sure they'd prefer for you to disappear as well, but as *your* publicist, I think it's high time you make a statement. The only way for the paparazzi to stop caring about you—and for your life to go back to normal—is for you to elegantly say farewell, and stop being news."

"It's true," Parker agrees. "The longer you hold out, the more it's going to build, and eventually the balloon is going to burst. It's probably best for you to put a piece of tape on it and stick the pin in on your own terms."

Through my clouded judgment, what they're suggesting seems to make sense. Filled with a longing to put an end to my misery and move on, I nod my agreement. Making a statement seems to be the quickest path to normal. "Okay. How do we do this?"

"I thought you'd never ask." Blair smiles. "Parker, call the hair and makeup people. I'll get to work on the statement."

The next morning, I call in sick to work, apologizing for abandoning everyone during crunch time and promising to return tomorrow. Lillian is understanding, though I imagine she thinks less of me, adding to my anxiety. Everything will go back to normal soon, though, and once it does, I'll work extra hard to prove myself.

Slowly showering, I dress in a fitted black Elizabeth and James skirt and pair it with a pale pink spaghetti-strap top and white ballet flats. Sitting in perfect stillness as Parker's team makes sure the circles under my eyes are camouflaged and gives life to my hair, I allow myself to reflect on the last few months. Somehow finding the ability to watch as a quiet observer, I say good-bye to the memories I know will be too painful to think about for a long time. Some of them make me smile in spite of myself, though, and those precious few I vow to meet again. Someday. Filing those keepsakes away, I begin to dwell on the last Berkeley image I possess: the image of him and Christina in Hong Kong.

A fresh stab of pain surges through me, and I close my eyes to the vision. If I'm going to get through this, I have to focus on why I'm doing it: to return to life as I once knew it as quickly as possible. It's a survival tactic, and as far as I can tell, the fastest way to the finish line is to eliminate everything that reminds me of him, starting with the biggest one: the throng of photographers lining the street beyond the Vicente's gate.

"Are you ready?" Blair asks as the makeup artist tips my chin up and finishes applying a hint of gloss to my lips.

Looking up at her sideways and taking a deep breath, I nod as my stomach twists. It's strange. My nerves are pulled to a breaking point, but it's not speaking to the media that's making me anxious; it is my desire to get it over with. I'm ready to move on, to put an end to this chapter.

Running her fingers through my sleek hair one last time, the makeup artist grants her approval and I stand.

"Now remember, keep it simple. Don't say more than we discussed. Short and sweet and get out," Blair coaches me as we walk to my front door. "You'll be fine." She squeezes my hand.

"I'll be fine," I repeat, more for my benefit than hers.

I hug Parker, who has been calling the paparazzi play-by-play all morning (Oh! The horror! They're eating mini-mart corn dog rollers. Where do you think they go to the bathroom? They must be so sweaty waiting out there in the hot sun for Liv to emerge. We should invite one in for a shower…maybe *that* one…).

Giving my appearance one last check before I step into the courtyard, I make sure TV Olivia is in place.

"See you in two minutes," Parker says.

"Or less." I attempt a smile as I open the door.

Rule #4: Just breathe—you can always decompress later. Exhaling, I arrange my features in a facade of calm as I cross the courtyard. Before I can lose my nerve, I open the Vicente's gate and walk with purpose to the middle of the street.

An excited cry careens across the crowd and a surge of flashbulbs ricochets against the cloudy morning sky. There are more photographers than I realized, and for a moment I falter, my knees giving out. Fighting the urge to turn on my heel and run, I bite the inside of my cheek and force myself to stay rooted in place. Running isn't an option.

Clearing my throat, my voice cracks as I begin. "Good morning. I'd like to make a statement." The paparazzi fall into a hush as they all lean forward, expectant.

My voice rings out over the street, sounding foreign to my ears as I strain to keep it steady. "I just want you all to be the first to know, I'm very happy for Berkeley and Christina," I say. "Clearly they were meant to be together, and I wish them all the best. Thank you for your time—that's all I have to say at the moment." With that, I turn and start back toward the courtyard, my poise in place (for once!).

The photographers yell for more, but that's all I have to give. At least until I hear one voice rise above the others. "Olivia! So it's all true? You talked to Berkeley?"

I stop in my tracks as Berkeley's promise to always be honest with me floods my ears. I cringe. *He told me I could ask him anything. That he'd been portrayed a million different ways...*

It takes every ounce of acting ability I possess to keep my eyes vacant and the despair from my voice as I turn to face the inquisitor. "No," I whisper without elaboration before, betrayed by a single tear, I disappear inside the Vicente's gate.

Safely on the other side, I lean against my front door, gulping in huge gasps of air. *I've done the wrong thing. I took a vow of silence… Didn't I promise not to jeopardize Berkeley's privacy? What was I thinking talking to the media? I should have talked to him first.* Fear grips me until I picture him with Christina, enjoying their "Team Adventure" cocktails. *No. His message is clear. And I don't have a choice. I can't keep a neighborhood hostage. This needs to end.* Frustrated tears smother me as I struggle to put it behind me. What's done is done. I have to make peace with my decision.

Eventually my sobs subside into a dull ache and the photographers dissipate—with the exception of a few stragglers—accepting that my statement will be all they are going to get.

Harmony is nearly restored.

That night, the news hits the media. I try to ignore it, knowing my moment of celebrity will blow over, and soon I'll be just another forgotten face. It won't be long now.

Focusing on putting it all behind me, I set my sights on getting back to normal.

Chapter Thirty-nine

Mrs. Bloom @PsychicMom1
@BloomOlivia Channeling Usui-Sensei and sending
you Reiki. Unblock your head and listen to your heart.
#TheForceIsStrongWithThisOne

Blair bursts into my living room.

"Turn on your computer," she orders. She's so bossy sometimes.

I'm sitting on my couch trying to read while holding a blue-crystal lotus flower that showed up on my doorstep this evening. A gift from my mother. It came with a note telling me the stone had been Reiki cleared and that I should put my intention into it—it will bring me clarity and peace. My insanity is solidified as I give it a shot. I'll try anything.

This morning the street outside was silent, and I ventured back to work. Arriving before anybody else, I closed my office door, indicating the need for privacy, and started illustrating. Thankfully my coworkers kept their distance, except for Gemma, who I allowed inside. The tears I'd been swallowing overflowed as soon as I saw her. She did her best to comfort me, hugging me as I hiccupped about ruining the In Bloom line — the last few days haven't exactly lived up to its fun, flirty vibe. In the end I cried myself out and pulled it together, shifting my focus to work. I tried to look professional in front of Lillian, and we were so busy, it ended up being a modest distraction.

At home, however, distractions are less readily available and I'm trying to read. Putting down *The Keystone* by Hailey Kattaden, I look up at Blair. "No," I say, trying to keep my voice calm. "You know I'm avoiding all forms of media right now."

"Tough. I just got an alert about this article on my phone and you *have* to see it." Plopping into the chair next to my computer, she opens the Internet and pulls up *TMI*. "Get over here and read this. I don't feel right reading it to you."

I resist moving and instead make a show of settling farther into the couch.

Defiant, she glares at me and begins to read out loud, "'Olivia, You're happy for us? I hope that's not true. I don't know how else to get in touch with you because you won't answer my calls or e-mails...'"

Electricity shoots through my veins. Stunned, I close my book. "He didn't."

"He did."

Time stands still as I rise and cross the room to the computer. "He wouldn't. He's so private, he would never do something like that."

"Well, maybe love makes you do crazy things," she says as she makes her way to the door. "You have to read it."

Nodding, I sit down and take in the headline on the screen as she closes the door behind her, leaving me to read alone.

EXCLUSIVE
Berkeley Dalton:
Olivia or Christina?
His Choice Has Been Made

Berkeley Dalton, the notoriously private rocker, reaches out to *TMI* for help in an e-mail entitled "Please Post This."

Always happy to help a friend in need, we've posted a link to Berkeley's letter to Olivia. See below…in his own words…

I begin to scan the letter, my eyes brimming as I go.

Olivia,

You're happy for us? I hope that's not true. I don't know how else to get in touch with you because you won't answer my calls or e-mails. You've left me no choice other than to revert to the thing that is driving us apart.

First, let me tell you that I am so sorry I've put you in this situation. Admittedly, I never should have had a drink with Christina. I assumed that because I didn't have feelings for her any longer, we would be able to have a civil conversation. Clearly, I was wrong because for some reason she has spitefully decided to tarnish what is true, and the truth is, I talked about YOU the whole time. She has robbed us of our reality and publicly tried to make it her own. For that, I hope you can forgive me. I should know better than to speak personally to someone whose need for publicity is so consuming. It is my hope that after this she will leave us alone, because the only thing I want from life right now is to be alone with you.

As you know, I usually like to keep this part of my life private. In this case, though, I think I need to set the record straight so that in the future you won't be subjected to lies because you'll know the truth, and so will everyone else. So here it goes:

You've had a profound effect on me, and I'm better for it. The first time I saw you I was sitting in a corner backstage at the fashion show, trying to write. It was another event in the endless sea of parties I was *supposed* to attend and I was bored. I was having trouble concentrating when you caught my eye. As I watched you work, I got the impression you were different than everyone else, innocent but determined. I found inspiration in you and was compelled to talk to you, so after the show, even though it was completely out of character for me, I followed you to the restroom.

Usually people assume they know me, and I've given up trying to convince them otherwise. I've come to accept the "good side" people present to me, but you, you were different. You didn't waste time with pretense and you didn't pretend. You may have noticed I have a tendency to take things too seriously, and in that brief meeting, I knew you had the ability to make me laugh at myself. I found you refreshing, and you left quite an impression, to say the least.

By the time I saw you backstage at our show in Santa Barbara, the idea of you had been on my mind for some time, but I never thought I'd see you again. Suddenly, though, there you were. You looked different than I remembered, so put together. It scared me because I was sure that Hollywood had gotten the best of you, and I felt like I'd missed my chance. After the show, I tried to put you out of my mind, but you wouldn't budge. Finally, I decided I had to know for sure if I'd lost you so I had Mark invite you for movie night. When you came into the room that night, my fears were confirmed. I was positive you were gone—you seemed so cool; you wouldn't even look at me! Now I know better. Now I know that in a room full of people trying to stand out, you're the one trying to hide. I've always been looking for you, and you're the only one I want to see. It didn't take me long to figure that out—as soon as you introduced yourself to me in the kitchen, I knew. Anybody else would have expected me to remember them. I was so happy; it was all I could do to resist pulling you into my arms and kissing you right then and there. It's an urge that has come to haunt me, as you well know.

The night before I left for Japan, I watched you sleep, trying to memorize your face. It's the first thing I think about when I wake up in the morning and the last thing I see before I go to bed, and I can only hope you'll forgive me for putting you through this so I can see your face again.

You're so much more than I expected.

I love you, Liv.

—B.

He loves me. He loves me. He loves me. A cascade of chills and shame explodes through me, and I read it again. And again.

I feel awful for making him resort to this. It's my fault for not trusting him and for not believing in myself. I guess, having been through this with Michael, I automatically assumed the worst. I know better than anyone not to believe what I read, but when it comes to matters pertaining to my own heart, I obviously can't be bothered with reason. Overcome with self-loathing, I hope for a second chance, vowing to be better for him.

I have to call him. I have to talk to him right away. Scrounging for my phone, I turn it on. My voice-mail box is full.

I dial his number and it goes straight to voice mail. After hanging up, I check the tour binder that contains information about every planned moment of their trip, and try his last hotel. He's already checked out. He must be traveling to the next stop on the tour. I call his voice mail again and leave a message.

"Hi. It's me. I saw your post on *TMI*. Are you crazy? You are, you know. That's why I love you. Call me as soon as you get this. I promise I'll pick up." I hang up the phone, then e-mail and tweet at him for good measure.

Feeling I've done all I can, I lay back on my couch and start listening to my messages.

First message:

"Liv, it's Shar. I'm sure you've heard the news by now. Sit tight and remember, don't say anything! The last thing we need is you making things worse than they already are. I have a few things to clear up here in Hong Kong before I meet Berkeley in Jakarta, but I'm on it. Don't even think about a thing. This will all blow over. Bye."

Don't think about a thing? Sure. No problem. Delete.

The next message is from Berkeley, and my heart stops

at the sound of his voice:

> *"Liv—it's me. I'm sorry I didn't call sooner. I've been on a bus for the last day and a half without cell reception. I just heard the news. Please, I'm so sorry. None of it's true—I don't know why she's doing this, but I promise you're the only one. I love you so much—I wish I was there with you. Call me when you get this."*

I take a deep inhale and let it out slowly, closing my eyes and cursing myself for not listening to my messages sooner. Save.

Next message:

> *"Liv, it's me again. Please pick up or call me. I need to know you're all right. I'll try you again in a couple hours after the show. I love you."*

Ouch, I wince. Save.
Next message:

> *"Hey, Liv. Your phone is going right to voice mail so obviously you're avoiding me. You have every right to. I'm so sorry. I don't know what else to say and I don't know how to fix this. I hate the thought of you going through this alone... Please call me..."*

His voice echoes the same anguish I felt. It makes my heart sick, and I swallow my disgust at myself in retribution. Save.

Next message:

> *"Liv, please let me talk to you. I've tried everything—*

you can't just disappear. I need to talk to you—to be with you—I've never wanted anything more in my life. Please call…"

A steady stream of tears slide down my cheeks and collect in a pool at the base of my neck. I brush them away with the back of my hand, smearing black kohl across my face. Save.

Next message:

"Liv, my brother's an idiot, but he's not that much of an idiot he'd ever give her the time of day. Don't listen to it. I've never seen him look at anyone the way he looks at you. Believe me. I know him better than anyone, and even if he doesn't know it himself yet, he would do anything for you. And so would I. You can call me if you need to talk."

Ugh. She definitely hates me now. There goes that chance at friendship. Save.

Next message:

"Hey, Liv, it's me. Mike. Hey. It seems like you've had a lot going on… I can see why LA is so much more exciting than back home." Sigh. "Anyway, sorry about those pictures ending up in that magazine. A guy called and said he was from Penn State and they were putting together a web page for our year so I gave them to him. Guess I'm not very Hollywood, but I'm here if you decide to come home—"

Delete. Not a chance.

Next message:

"Liv...I'm not going to give up. I love you too much. I'm going to fix it..."

His voice breaks at the end, and my insides recoil. I try not to think about how easily *I* gave up. Save.

Next message:

"Liv! It's me. I took my head out of a book for five minutes and turned on the TV... What the heck? What a mess! Are you okay? Call me if you need me. Even if I'm in the middle of a breast augmentation I'll take your call. I'm here. Anytime. Loved your skirt by the way."

I can't help but smile at Boots. Hearing her voice always cheers me up. Save.

Next message:

"OLIVIA! I CAN'T BELIEVE YOU DID THAT. DIDN'T I TELL YOU NOT TO TALK TO THE PRESS? I FINALLY GOT CHRISTINA UNDER CONTROL ON THIS END AND THEN THERE YOU GO MAKING A MESS OF EVERYTHING. NOW THIS WILL NEVER DIE. WHAT WERE YOU THINKING? I. AM. BESIDE. MYSELF. I CAN'T BELIEVE YOU. CLICK.

Oops. Delete.

Next message:

"Liv—it's me. I just saw your statement. Mostly I'm glad to see you're okay. It was good to see your face—you looked so beautiful, it made me miss you

that much more. I really hope you didn't mean what you said. I don't think you did. I have an idea... Hopefully I'll talk to you soon. I love you."

I *would* talk to you soon, if *you'd* just pick up! Save. Next message:

"Hi, Liv, it's Mom. I just saw you on TV and I thought I should tell you something—you're just coming out of a Saturn Cycle and—" Click.

"Voice mail is full."

Perfect.

I wait all night for him to return my call. He doesn't. He must be on a bus or something. Poring over the tour schedule, I try to figure out what city he could be traveling to, but the schedule has the band planted in Indonesia for the next three days. Something must have changed.

Fitfully, I try to sleep, and as usual my mother inserts herself into my dream, but this time it's different:

We meet at the base of a tree, twilight beginning to glimmer around us. A cool breeze ruffles our hair and lightning bugs burn.

"Do you want to hear my prophecy?" she asks in an ominous tone.

"Yes. I *do* want to hear your prophecy," I reply.

She takes a breath before she reveals her secret. "He's holding out," she whispers.

What does that mean? I'm unable to ask. The words won't vocalize. The only thing I can say is—

Me: "Namaste."

Her: "Namaste."

Then she turns and climbs the tree. "Ooooh...there's a party up here!" she calls down.

The next day at work I can't help but check my phone every fifteen minutes. Nothing. No calls. No texts. No tweets.

I can't understand it, and I begin to worry. Why isn't he calling? Cyberstalking offers little relief. The Internet is void of non-Christina-related Berkeley news; even my statement and Berkeley's letter seem to have disappeared into the ether. Averting my eyes from the endless photographs and hopeful blog posts celebrating their reunion, I console myself, noting that at least there aren't any mentions of bus crashes or anything.

Pretending to stall under the mound of work we still have to do before we go to New York, I stay in my office as late as possible. It's after dark when I finally leave.

My phone remains silent.

When I arrive back at the Vicente, I've just begun unloading the groceries I picked up on the way home when a voice rings out from across the street.

"Miss Olivia! Miss Olivia!" Willis yells, hurrying to the end of his porch. "Intruder! Intruder! Don't go into your house through the side door like you normally do!"

Thank you for announcing my routine to the entire neighborhood, Willis.

"I just saw a man back there! Don't go in," he continues, his voice growing more agitated.

Unsure of what to do, I hesitate. Could it be a member

of the paparazzi? Should I call the police? No. At this point, I'm old news. Maybe I'm being naive, but I don't think there's anything to worry about. I'm pretty sure Willis is mistaken. In the time I've lived at the Vicente, there's never been an incident on our street, and I feel very safe.

Willis waddles across the street, Betty clanking in his pocket.

"I'll go with you," he says, arriving breathless at my side and giving her a tap.

I think for a moment, eyeing his pocket. "Okay." I sigh, figuring Willis is mostly harmless, and if there *is* an intruder, at least there's safety in numbers.

Together, we walk to my front door. As I insert my key into the lock, out of nowhere Willis decides to take over. Moving with surprising agility for a ninety-year-old, he whips Betty from his pocket and kicks my front door open, guns blazing.

"Come out with your hands up!" he shouts.

The door swings open and my heart lands in my throat as I realize someone has, in fact, broken into my apartment.

Construction paper hearts, moons, and stars dangle from ribbons that cover nearly every inch of the ceiling, while paper chains swing in the doorways. Colorful pinwheel bouquets cover every available surface, and interspersed between them warm, flickering candles cast their spell on the room.

Clearly this is a welcome intruder.

I hardly have time to take it all in as my groceries crash to the floor and I attempt to tackle Willis from behind, struggling to wrestle Betty from his grip. "Don't shoot! Willis! Don't shoot!"

In the midst of our tussle, Berkeley steps out from the kitchen, an acoustic guitar in his left hand and his right hand raised to chest level. He stands in awe as he takes in the scene before him.

Willis and I freeze and stare, Betty's nose trained on the ceiling. "It's okay, Willis. I know him," I whisper, my eyes unable to leave Berkeley's face. As our eyes connect, I detect a glint in his that sends a bolt straight through my stomach and tells me he's enjoying this.

"Are you sure?" Willis asks.

"I've never been so sure of anything in my life."

Still poised for action, Willis slowly lowers Betty to his side. He gives Berkeley a once-over before saying, "Well, all right. I was just making sure there was no riffraff 'round here."

"No riffraff," I confirm, not taking my hands from him. "Thank you for looking out for me, though."

"Anytime, Miss Olivia. Anytime." He grants us a toothless grin as he returns Betty to his pocket. Surveying the room as he moves to leave, he adds, "You enjoy this, now. Enjoy it."

"Yes, sir," I answer.

Wishing Willis good night, I gently close the door behind him and allow my forehead to rest against its smooth grain for a moment before I turn to face Berkeley.

Chapter Forty

Mark VanCleer @BrighsideBP
Don't worry guys. We'll reschedule @BerkeleyBrtside doesn't stay quiet for long.

"Hi," I say.

"Hi," he responds thickly with raised eyebrows and a smile behind his eyes. "That was quite an entrance."

I blush. We have everything to say to each other and none of it matters. I don't know where to start. "Did you do all of this?" I ask as I take in the paper fairyland surrounding me. "It's beautiful."

"I've been pretty busy," he confirms. "As soon as I saw your statement, I knew I had to come home. I got on the next plane out."

"But aren't you missing shows?"

"Not yet. The next one is tonight. Haynes is canceling it.

And all the rest."

His words shoot through me with a loathsome pang. "You're canceling the tour?" I ask, feeling responsible. I know how important the band is to him, and my lack of trust has ruined everything. Thinking of all the sold-out shows and disappointed fans, I bite back tears as I say, "I'm so sorry… I know how hard you work to please your fans, and now I made you let them down. The guys must hate me."

The pained look in his eyes makes me want to reach out and hug him. He looks miserable.

"Stop it. This isn't your apology to give. It's mine," he says with force. "And it's more important to me not to let *you* down."

He stares at a point over my shoulder and seems far away as he says, "I should have learned by now." Refocusing his attention on me, his eyes burn as he quietly continues, "I'm sorry. This is exactly what I didn't want to happen…" His voice trails off, allowing the words to hang in the air. The atmosphere weighs on us, and I want to interject and beg his forgiveness, but before I can, he lightens the mood. "And please don't worry about the band. We've been touring for almost two years straight and they've wanted a break for a while now. My guess is they're at a bar somewhere in Jakarta toasting you…or me… They'll toast to just about anything."

I let out a laugh. "Nice move. It was getting entirely too serious in here."

"I learned from the best." His eyes scald me.

I try to ignore his stare. "I was pretty worried when you didn't return my call," I say softly with a smile to keep the sting from my words.

"You called? I'm sorry, I didn't know. I was in such a

hurry to get to you I left my phone charging in my hotel room in Indonesia."

"Well, it may be selfish, but I'm glad you're back." I don't try to mask the relief in my voice.

"Me, too."

We stare at each other for a moment, letting gravity take over. I want him to hold me and never let go.

Instead, he takes my hand and leads me into the living room. "Have a seat." He gestures to the floor a little nervously. "I have something I want to say to you."

Lowering myself to the floor, I crisscross my legs as he sits down on a chair and moves the guitar to his lap.

"Remember how I told you I was still waiting to write my first album?" he says. "Well, I've been writing this song since the first time I saw you, and it might be a keepeh…"

I bite back a smile at the South African slip as my stomach tightens with anticipation.

His eyes flash to mine in shared acknowledgment as he strums the guitar and begins to sing.

"There is love and there is pain, there's a song I've been singing through the rain…"

I sit, mesmerized. All of his talent and charisma are concentrated on me as he plays. He's intense and beautiful, and as his song washes over me, I'm captivated.

"There is anger and there is fear. There's the reason that I'm holding you so near. Hey hey hey…"

Closing his eyes, he holds the note before he repeats it as he plays into the chorus.

"No one knows you like I know you now, No one needs you like I need you now, and no one loves you like I love you now…

He opens his eyes, but they are far away as he strums the guitar and I'm drawn to him, hanging on his every word.

"...but I'm holding out..."

Holding out? That's familiar...it takes a second before it registers. Psychic Mom. She is inserting herself into my dreams! No. That's crazy. I dismiss the thought and return my full attention to Berkeley.

"There are countries and there are oceans, there are places where we hide our emotions. There's frustration and there's confusion, someone told me that it's all an illusion... hey hey...No one knows you like I know you now, no one sees you like I see you now, no one loves you like I love you now...but I'm holding out... I'm holding out..."

As he plays the last note of the song, he focuses the full force of his eyes on me. Setting his guitar aside, he lowers himself from the chair and joins me on the floor, kneeling in front of me.

Gently, he runs his fingers down the side of my face, and I shiver with warmth, as the energy tightens between us.

We lock eyes.

"Everything we've been through the last couple of weeks has forced me to do a lot of thinking," he says. "And I've come to a decision. I don't want to hold out anymore. I know what I want to keep. It's you. I want to keep you next to me, forever."

He presses something round into my palm and leans toward me, his breath brushing my ear as he whispers, "Liv, will you marry me?"

What? My eyes widen and the breath leaves my body. I'm at once shocked and terrified. The earth spins on its axis, my mind in overdrive as I look wildly about the room, registering only streamers and candles. It's all happening so fast—I didn't see it coming. Pulling myself out of the spin, I force myself to focus on a simple question: is Berkeley who I want to spend the rest of my life with?

As soon as I bring my eyes back to his, I know there's only one answer on my lips. "Yes," I whisper.

"Yes?" he verifies.

He looks so happy I can't resist. With a smile, I grab his face and kiss him.

And it is magic.

Epilogue

Impatiently, I tug the door to my apartment closed with my pinkie as my hands are full with precariously placed champagne glasses and bottles. (One bottle is never enough here at the Vicente.) Skipping down the stairs into the center courtyard, I spin around and yell at the top of my lungs, "CHAMPAGNE!"

Parker emerges from his apartment, carrying a bottle of pomegranate juice in one hand and fresh raspberries in the other.

"It's French mimosa o'clock!" he sings.

"I'm coming!" Blair calls as she runs down the stairs from the upstairs balcony. "I've got the ice bucket!"

"Oooh… The good stuff! What's the occasion, moneybags?" Parker asks, eyeing the champagne.

"Well…" I say, shaking slightly as I make a show of opening the bottle so they are unable to miss the ring. "I got a new toy…"

"Oh. My. God," Parker whispers, grabbing my hand. He

is always reverent in the presence of rare stones. "Three-carat, old European, hand-cut, center diamond in a platinum art-deco, Tiffany-style setting... You trollop!"

Blair and Parker look at each other before turning to stare at me as if I've just shown up wearing last season's Louboutins. "Berkeley," Blair mouths, her voice barely audible.

The knot that has been forming in my stomach contracts, effectively exploding my body in goose bumps at the sound of his name. "Berkeley," I repeat, my breath catching in my throat and my brimming eyes threatening to overflow.

This defies the rules. It does not fit into a genre or scheme. To say it is a miracle is the understatement of the millennium. I watch them trying to wrap their heads around the enormity of what has just happened. Both (for once!) are at a loss for words, their faces contorted into masks of absolute bewilderment.

I begin to giggle at the awe on their faces. This is a treat! My giggle evolves into outright laughter, and soon Blair and Parker join in until we are all shrieking uncontrollably. My emotions have been pulled so taught they snap and come tumbling out as I laugh and cry and laugh some more. The release leaves my body limp as our mirth subsides. Crumbling into a courtyard chair, I take a deep breath. "Would you pour the champagne already?"

"I'm going to need something stronger than that," Blair says, "but we'll start with champagne. After all, we've got a wedding to plan..."

"A toast!" Parker croons as he tops off each of our glasses. "To breaking The Rules, to Mrs. Berkeley Dalton to be, and to *us*... We *deserve* this!"

And our glasses clink.

BONUS CONTENT

**WHAT *REALLY* HAPPENED AT THE *SPORTS ILLUSTRATED*
SWIMSUIT FASHION SHOW? LET'S FIND OUT FROM BERKELEY.**

I set down my composition book in frustration and scan the hangar. Around me, the space is bustling with stage hands and set designers. Watching them with half interest, I settle into the leather couch in the makeshift lounge that will later house the after-party, cursing Mark for dragging me here. He got me out of the house by suggesting I needed a change of scenery—that maybe the reason the words aren't coming is because I need to be around people. And what better place could inspiration be lurking in than a room full of swimsuit models?

Midscan, I spot Mark across the room acting out an animation for a girl with her hair full of curlers who is trying to hold steady as a makeup artist shellacs her face. Shaking my head, my eyes return to my lap and the words I've been staring at for a week.

There are countries and there are oceans,
I turn the page.
There are places where we hide our emotions.

I am foolish to believe there is magic in these pages. Two weeks ago, when my mom unloaded the contents of my high school closet on me, I found my old composition book. It used to be my constant companion, but I'd nearly forgotten about it. As I thumbed through the pages, I thought maybe my sixteen-year-old self knew it all; that if I could find him again maybe I'd be able to write. But no such luck. It's the same old song, and the words are as elusive as ever.

Crossing my ankle over my knee, I stare blankly ahead,

only half cognizant of the stage being set up behind me to resemble an under-the-sea fairy tale. I already feel like I'm underwater as the ocean of rolling racks, lights, and people barking orders float around me. *How did it all come to this? What is the point anymore?* In the beginning I wanted to write great songs that meant something, that changed people's lives, touched them in some way, and here I am sitting at the *Sports Illustrated* Swimsuit issue launch and everything is about fame and money. It's ridiculous; a farce. *How did I end up so off course?* Sixteen-year-old me would be disappointed, I know it.

Glancing back at the row of models having lies painted on their faces, I bite back my frustration, though part of me has to laugh. Young me wouldn't have totally minded the swimsuit model part.

As I look away from the models, my eyes come to rest on a girl across the room. Wearing cropped black pants and a sleeveless black top, she sits on her knees, feverishly steaming a heaping pile of sequined shorts. The hair from her ponytail falls forward into her eyes, and when she pushes it away I see panic on her face. She seems young, too young to be here, too innocent to get caught up in this delusion, and my first instinct is to save her—to tell her the truth—to tell her to run.

She grabs another pair of shorts and starts smoothing the sequins. Her eyebrows are furrowed in concentration, and I sense her determination as she bites her lower lip— there's more riding on this for her than just making sure some model's clothes are in order. It reminds me of a lost time when every moment counted, when every step was leading me somewhere. One eye still on her, I pick up my composition book and write, *there's frustration and there's confusion, someone told me that it's all an illusion...*

"Berkeley," Mark yells, snapping me back into reality. He's approaching with a half-dressed model in tow. "This is Alexa." He smiles, presenting her to me. "I was thinking the two of you might want to join me and Irina." He nods across the room toward a tall, blond Russian model who is standing still while a swimsuit is being painted on her body, before he continues, "And get some dinner after the show."

Silently I ask Mark why he is putting me in this position, and he widens his smile, telling me, *because you need to stop moping around.* He's not giving me a choice.

My eyes move to Alexa, and she strikes a pose as though she is auditioning for a role. Her eyes roll back into her head, resembling a shark's right before he takes a bite, and when they return they are full with promise.

She's probably very talented, but I'm not up for this. For one, I promised Shar I'd lay low, and if I know one thing for certain, it's that Alexa has an agenda. If I go out with her, I can expect our pictures to be plastered over every gossip website by morning. She'll most likely use my name as a stepping stone to build her celebrity, to help catapult her career. I don't blame her for it—it's the way the game works—it's expected. But I'm tired of playing, not to mention uninterested. I've known many versions of Alexa, and even if she *is* different from all the other models in LA, it seems tedious to have to dig through all of her deceitful layers to see if there is anything worthwhile underneath. Looking past her, my eyes find the girl again. She is snapping Polaroids of the shorts and scribbling on the pictures with black marker, and I find myself being sucked into her, her hopeful dedication making me smile, lifting my spirits.

"Let's go to Dan Tana's. It's on the way home," Mark says, naming an old-school Italian restaurant in Hollywood, knowing I can never pass up their eggplant parmesan a la Berkeley Dalton—they put my name on the menu after it—and bringing my attention back to the model at hand.

Somehow the girl across the room has softened me, warmed my insides with a sense of anticipation and promise that I haven't felt since my first days playing with the Brightside. It's a feeling I've been actively seeking, and it's as though a fog has been lifted. Everything looks brighter, and for a moment the "on stage" façade I usually keep in place to protect my image slips. Alexa is very pretty, and in my suddenly buoyant mood I decide I've probably misjudged her. Plus, knowing Mark, he won't take no for an answer, so I nod my acceptance.

Alexa breaks into a seductive smile, and when she speaks her voice is deeper than I expected it to be—she kind of sounds like Sylvester Stallone. "Great. I can't wait."

Out of the corner of my eye, I see the girl hanging costumes on a rolling rack, and there is no comparison between the positive energy that radiates from her and the drain that is Alexa, confirming my initial perception. They're both hungry, but for different things, and I have no intention of allowing Alexa to take a bite out of me. Instantly, I start dreading dinner and begin trying to think of an excuse not to go. Shar, perhaps? I dismiss the thought. Shar will be pleased. Alexa is a perfect candidate for "the seductress", provided she keeps her mouth shut.

"I should go finish getting ready now... See you after the show?" Alexa asks.

"Yeah," I say, resigned, as she heads off in the direction of the stage.

Mark takes a seat next to me. "How's it going? Writing good?"

"It was until you brought Man Voice over," I reply.

"It's not that bad." Mark laughs. "She's really sweet, I promise. Besides, I thought you were trying to be more optimistic about things these days. Here's your chance."

"I am optimistic," I retort. "I thought of her as half dressed when I first saw her, not half naked."

"Either way works for me," he says. "Hey man, seriously though, everyone needs a rebound after they get out of a two-year relationship, and what better way to bounce back than with a swimsuit model? Swimsuit models are the best. They're the only kind of models that have boobs!"

"Mark," I complain, laughing because it's true.

"I'm just kidding. You don't have to go to dinner if you don't want to. I just thought I'd offer in case you did want to go but didn't know it yet."

"Thank you. I appreciate it. And we'll see. You're probably right. I should get out... I just wish I could concentrate on writing right now."

"We're about to go on tour—you'll have plenty of time to write on the road. Don't force it. It'll come."

"I know," I sigh, giving in and closing my composition book.

A guitar starts to play over the sound system, and I recognize it immediately as Ted's drums start and my voice fills the hangar. The show is beginning and apparently *When You Need Me* is kicking it off. My own words slam into me, and as many times as I've sung them over the years, I'm not sure they have ever rung more true.

All this longing to be free has got the best of me... Baby, you've got to give me a break, I've got my own smile to fake, Got enough on my plate, Without the lines you want to feed me...

"Come on." Mark drags me up. "We don't want to miss the show."

"No, no we don't," I reply, tucking my book under my arm and following him to the stage. As we go, I peek back to where I'd seen the girl steaming the shorts, strangely hoping for one last glimpse of her, but she's gone. Combating the sudden hollowness in my stomach, I shake her out of my head, unsure of what it is I think I'm missing.

We take seats in the last row, and I lean back and watch with half interest as the models clomp down the runway in varying stages of undress, each segment of the show depicting a new under-the-sea phenomenon. The show moves quickly, and before we can grow bored, the music changes and the models appear in a single-file line—each encased in a swirl of chiffon and sequins, wearing seashell bras for the grand finale. Alexa takes her turn at the end of the runway, striking a pose as she finds me in the crowd, and blows me a kiss. Dodging her affection, I find myself more interested in the sequined shorts she is wearing and how the girl I'd been watching succeeded in making them look like mermaid scales, but I push the thought away as quickly as it comes, chiding myself for allowing her to pop into my head for a second time in the last fifteen minutes.

The show ends and waiters carrying trays of champagne appear as Mark drags me backstage to find Irina and Alexa. When we walk up to them, they are already drinking champagne and have yet to change out of their sequined mermaid outfits.

"Great show," Mark says, kissing Irina as she throws her arms around him with glee.

"It vas so fun!" she exclaims in her thick Russian accent as she releases him and claps her hands over her chest.

"I just wish I had more changes." Alexa pouts. "I only had three looks. I hardly got to be out there at all."

Irina starts to console her, and I tune them out as I spy the girl from earlier. Somehow, even in this sea of people, my eyes go straight to her. Half hidden by a potted palm tree, she is standing alone, sipping a glass of champagne, looking like she's trying to blend in to the plant. Her effort makes me laugh because it would be impossible for her to blend in anywhere. Her presence is so strong, it's as if only she is in color and everyone else is black and white. Something magnetic is drawing me toward her, and troubled by the unfamiliar sensation, I try to turn the poles and repel her. Focusing back on Alexa, Irina, and Mark, I tune back in to dinner plans.

"I'm going to get changed, and then we can go," Alexa says. "I'll be right back." She walks off in the direction of the restrooms.

"Oh, me, too," Irina says as she removes her seashell bra and takes her time choosing a dress off a rolling rack, not caring who sees her swimsuit painted breasts.

Averting my eyes, I turn away from Irina's display and give in to the pull, again looking for the girl, the effort to resist already too much. It's like I have a sixth sense that is watching out for her, and we are doing some sort of dance where I am in constant awareness of her every movement.

I'm compelled to get closer to her. Feeling like a hunter, my eyes easily find her as I scan the room. She is on the move, and without a word to Mark and Irina, I chase the rabbit down.

She squeezes through the crowd, her thin frame easily slipping between groups of gossiping models as she heads toward the bathroom. I barely have time to wonder if I've lost my mind as I follow close behind her to the end of the dimly lit corridor. *What am I doing?* Maybe I'm chasing a feeling, a lost part of me that I want to get close to? I don't know. One thing is for certain: I have no idea what I'm going to do if I catch her. Yet I persist. This isn't like me, but curiosity has me by the throat.

I reach the end of the hallway and, leaning against a wall, watch as she fumbles with the restroom doorknob. It is locked. With a sigh, she turns to face me, and for an instant her clear green eyes meet mine. And then she jumps, obviously expecting to be alone. She looks away, but in a flash her eyes reconnect with mine, and this time they reflect recognition. There it is. No use trying to pretend I can talk to her without *me* getting in the way. Trapped, the rabbit shies away, her slight figure tensing as she shrinks into the corner, eyes focused on the dirty tile floor.

"I always wonder why they don't have more restrooms at these things," I say, keeping my voice light while inwardly I groan. *Great opener, Berk.*

She looks up, unable to hide the shock in her expressive eyes, and again I am struck by how fresh faced and innocent she seems. I watch the emotion she can't control play across her face, and when she finally speaks her voice is so soft I strain to hear it.

"Yeah. Tell me about it. You'd think they'd plan it better." I lose her to the floor again, but before I can vie for her attention, she continues, this time in a stronger voice, her eyes meeting mine. "So, I know you're Berkeley Dalton, and you know I'm—well, actually, you don't know—so let's move on. You're taller than I expected."

I bite back a laugh as I study the horror seeping over her face, her eyes looking wildly around as if she can't believe the sound of her own voice.

She is adorable.

My instinct is to pull her against my chest and hold her there, but I refrain, my thoughts rapid firing with adrenaline. *At least the introductions are out of the way. She knows who I am. But that isn't exactly fair...*

"Um, thanks? I think?" I say, and I can't help it, for some reason I'm desperate to win her over, so I let stage Berkeley—who is guaranteed to seduce the toughest crowd—shine behind my eyes for a moment as I hit her with a small smile. "Maybe I *should* know you?"

Just then the bathroom door slams open, and Alexa invades, glaring at the girl and stomping her into submission as she scrambles to get out of the way. The model's makeup-caked face obscures her features, and her eyes light up as they focus on me.

Damn it. Nice timing.

"Oh, Berk," she slurs, stumbling forward on teetering heels as she wraps her arms around me like we are intimate friends instead of recent acquaintances. "You waited for me. So sweet."

Her dress leaves little to the imagination, and I ignore the body beneath it as it presses against me, having eyes only for the rabbit that is trying to make her escape.

"Let's get out of here. I'm starving," Alexa demands, tugging me forward.

A pang shoots through me as I realize I don't know the rabbit's name. But what can I do? I don't want to let her go, but I know I can't keep her. I've already acted like a lunatic, stalking her to the bathroom, and I don't know what is wrong with me but I should definitely go before I make a fool of myself. Still, I'm reluctant to release her, and resisting Alexa's pull, I lean toward the rabbit. "It was nice talking to you," I say, catching her eye before allowing Alexa to drag me back down the hall.

The rabbit grants me a brief, disbelieving smile as she retreats.

I can only hope she knows I mean it.

WHAT HAPPENED DURING LIV'S FIRST WEEK IN LA *BEFORE* SHE
RAN INTO BERKELEY AT THE FASHION SHOW? READ ON TO FIND
OUT.

MRS. BLOOM @PSYCHICMOM1
@BLOOMOLIVIA I HIGHLY SUGGEST YOU KNOCK BEFORE
OPENING ANY DOORS.

I can't sleep. Tomorrow is my first day as a costume intern
on a real Hollywood movie set; my childhood dream come
true—though the dreams I'm supposed to be having right
now elude me. Rolling onto my side, I burrow deeper under
the bed sheets, squeezing my eyes shut and praying for sleep
that doesn't arrive. After a few frustrated minutes, I flop
onto my back and stare at the ceiling. *What if I'm not good
enough? What if I'm late? What if they don't like me?* The
night drones on, anticipation growing inside me, splinters
of doubt pricking at my brain. *What am I doing here? What
made me think I could do this? Maybe I should have stayed
home, tried to salvage the life I was supposed to lead...* My
nerves threaten to snap, and as the clock ticks to four thirty,
I give up and get out of bed.

In an attempt to brighten my thoughts—to remind
myself I have to try and all I can do is my best—I shower
away the doubts. Dressing in slim jeans and a long tunic I
won't mind getting dirty, I pull my hair into a bun at the
nape of my neck so it will be out of my way, hoping I've
struck balance between casual and professional. Stretching
my lips into an approachable smile, Edith and Cecil give me

a mental pep talk as I head out the door.

And so it begins.

I arrive on the "set" at six forty-five. Actually, it's not so much a set as it is someone's house, but even at this early hour it's buzzing with activity. This is an indie film, and despite obsessively Googling the names of the director and cast, I still don't recognize many of them. Even the head costume designer who hired me, Meg, listed her biggest credit on IMDB as a National Lampoon movie that went straight to video. Still, despite the low budget, I'm impressed with the size of the production. All around me the crew is busy running miles of cable up and down the hill to the house to provide power for the lights and cameras while a camp of Star Waggons and trailers line the sidewalk before me.

I have a 7:12 a.m. call time, which at first I thought was a mistake because it was so specific. 7:12? *Do I have to be there at exactly 7:12?* It turned out it wasn't a typo, though. Meg explained in her last email that call times on this set run on a six-minute interval in order to save money: when times are written in they are rounded to the next six-minute period rather than the next half hour or hour. Apparently this is normal, but in this case it doesn't matter because I'm working for free anyway.

Trying not to trip over the wires, I walk past a row of trailers and come to a stop behind a U-haul truck with a WARDROBE sign hanging on the outside. My stomach squirms as eagerness and fear collide. I knock on the metal truck frame, startling the girl inside who is frantically ironing a pair of suit pants.

"Hi. Are you Meg?" I ask, sounding more confident than I feel.

"No. I'm Carrie. I don't know where Meg is. Are you the new girl?"

"Yeah. I'm Olivia," I say, walking up the ramp into the truck. "Can I help you with anything?"

She doesn't pause to think. "Yes. See the racks behind me? Each group of hangers has a name on it. Those are the wardrobe changes for the day for each actor. Take them to their trailers and hang them inside in the order they'll need them. Nobody should be around—they're probably all at craft services eating breakfast. Here's the call sheet with today's scenes and a script with what outfit goes with what scene listed. And hurry back. They moved up the bar scene, and I need to go buy leather outfits for the hookers."

Suppressing panic, I try to process the amount of information she just dumped on me. *Where are the trailers? How do I know which trailer belongs to which actor?* But sensing the need for urgency and wanting to come off as capable, I don't ask questions and speed into action.

Taking the script with a nod, I drag the flimsy rolling rack forward, its wheels grating against the metal ramp and jarring several of the costumes off their hangers onto the ground. Biting back frustration, I retrieve the costumes and hang them up, hoping I've put them back in the correct order, before heading toward where I'd seen the Star Waggons, the rack fishtailing behind me and sending costumes flying as I go. When I finally arrive at the first trailer, I am presented with five doors, each with its own set of metal steps leading up to it, and I'm relieved to spot a piece of masking tape across the front of each door with an actor's name scribbled in black Sharpie.

I knock tentatively on the first door and wait. No

answer. Opening the door and poking my head in, I take in the small space—a sink, a toilet, a cushioned bench along one wall—and confirm the dressing room is empty. Relieved I'm not disturbing anyone, I quickly hang the wardrobe on a hook on the wall, carefully smoothing it so it is perfect and triple checking that the name on the Polaroid attached to the hanger matches the name on the front door, and make my exit before the "star" returns from breakfast.

Pretending I'm a wardrobe elf, I effortlessly hit three more trailers, each time rapping against the door and calling out "wardrobe" before stepping inside and depositing the costumes. When I reach the last Waggon, only two outfits are left on my rack. This trailer is the same size as the others, but has only two doors. *It must have larger dressing rooms. Maybe it's for the "big" stars.* At this point assuming no one is home, I forgo knocking and burst through the first door, stepping into a small living room with an L-shaped couch, only to be confronted with one excessively hairy, naked man locked in an intimate embrace with a decidedly less hairy, half-naked woman. We all three scream. Dropping the clothes, my hands fly to cover my eyes as I begin backing out of the trailer, knocking over a potted plant in the process.

"Sorry. Sorry. I'm so sorry." I moan as I remember the costumes and blindly start to feel around the floor for them.

"Olivia? Just leave it here. I'll take care of it," the woman orders.

Oh no. I think I just found Meg. Not a good way to meet your new boss. Definitely different than the connection I thought I'd be making. *Oops.*

I tiptoe back to retrieve my next set of orders from Carrie, not taking my eyes off the ground. "I found Meg.

She's busy."

Carrie rolls her eyes. "I hate when she does this. Well, you're going to have to be the set costumer and do continuity, I guess."

"What's that?"

"You can't be serious." She looks at me like I am an annoying flea she wants to flick away. "Here's the continuity bible," she says, thrusting a giant, three-ring binder at me. "Go up to set and take a Polaroid of every actor in costume, including close-ups of any accessories they have on, and put it in here. That way if we have to recreate the costume later we don't forget anything," she explains. "Take good notes. You stand behind the director. When they call for 'last looks' make sure the actor's clothes look exactly the same as they did in the last take. Hair and makeup will do the same. You both have to sign off that nothing has moved before they call action. It makes it a lot easier when they edit the film."

Go up to set! Wow. The power of those four words erase the mortification of the previous moments, and I float away in a dazzling daze of optimism.

I spend the rest of the morning watching the actors perform. *What must it be like to play make-believe all day and get paid for it?* It seems like so much fun, like it shouldn't be a real job. *Of course, how different is it from playing dress-up all day?* I'd like to find out.

Not having much to do other than nod my approval that the actor's costume hasn't moved, I mindlessly watch the action around me. At first I'm enthralled with studying the lighting technician's work and learning how the cameras move, photographing the same scene at many different angles. But by the time the "quiet on the set" call is passed on telephone style from PA to PA all the way down the hill to the Star Waggons for the fifteenth take of the first scene, I realize this is pretty boring. I know this is part of a costumer's job, and maybe if I was getting paid I'd find it more interesting, but I doubt it. So far I'm not feeling like much of a "designer".

My afternoon is spent in The Valley (read Hot as Hell!) in the back of an air-conditionless station wagon, wedged between a hair stylist and a makeup artist, all of us trying to maintain personal space and not brush sweaty thighs. We are following a car containing two actors that is being towed by a truck with a camera on the back. Every few minutes, between each take, we stop, get out of the car, and look at the actors to make sure nothing has moved. Then we get back in the station wagon and start following them again. The other girls ask where I'm from and inform me I made the right decision choosing to live mid-city and not in the Valley, but we run out of things to talk about after two hours and ride on in silence. My mind begins to wander and my thoughts turn to Hairy, the man from the trailer with Meg this morning. Picturing him screeching, I stifle the urge to laugh and beg my brain to let me un-see that. My brain does not comply. I pass the time, tweeting, "Seriously do not know if I can handle one more last look. Not one thread has moved in the last 3 hours" and texting the story to Boots.

Seven hours later, we roll back to set.

Deflated and exhausted, I approach the wardrobe truck. Meg is smoking a cigarette. "I quit smoking three years ago," she says on exhale. "This movie is driving me back to it—I'm not getting paid enough for this. Here's tomorrow's call sheet. They've moved up the gnome revolt. We're going to need to bloody and distress thirty-five pairs of midget overalls before the 6:36 call tomorrow morning."

Edith and Cecil would be so proud. My visions of lacy petticoats and seamed stockings fade as I pick up a cheese grater and a pair of overalls and get to work. I try to console myself. Even though the wardrobe in this movie leaves much to be desired, at least I'll have something to put on my resume. What did I expect anyway? Nobody starts at the top. With renewed energy, I pour barbeque sauce on the overalls and start rubbing, hoping the dried effect will resemble caked-on blood. If I have anything to say about it, these gnomes are going to look *exceptional.*

At two a.m. when I finally return to the Vicente, exhausted from the day and previous night's lack of sleep, I drag myself across the courtyard and into my apartment where I crawl into bed, trying to ignore the visions of dancing gnomes in my head.

Three hours later I wake to my phone buzzing next to me.

"Hello?" My voice cracks, though I try to sound like I've been up for hours.

"Olivia. It's Meg," a raspy voice reveals. "I have bad news. Apparently one of the investors on the film backed out so they're shutting down production. They may pick it up again in a few weeks, but I don't know when. I'll let you know, but for now, the show's over."

And just like that, I'm unemployed. Show business. There's no business like it.

Acknowledgments

To Jennifer Pooley, who the universe gifted to me in a shot of magic I'm still not certain I deserve: For your unending belief, for your prolific editing, for the joy you exude in everything you do, for the magic that manifests in all that you touch, for being an EMMA, for being a force that changes lives for the better… I am eternally grateful our paths crossed. I wish for you the stars. MAGIC! Fairy tale ON!!!

To Jason Lautenschleger: My other half, my best friend. You're the funniest person I know, a rock star, and a renaissance guy. Thank you for believing anything is possible, holding the vision, taking chances, and for putting up with all of "us." I promise I'll come to bed soon…

To Diane Samandi for being the mentor I wished for every day but didn't see coming. I am forever grateful you took a chance on me. You have opened my eyes to the world and taught me how to *give*. I am in awe of your open-mindedness, your acceptance of all people, your capacity for love, and your never-ending thirst for understanding. This WORLD is so lucky to have you in its corner.

To Alexandra Anderson Conrad: For playing medical Mad Libs with me. You are hilarious. For being an example of a strong, talented, compassionate, powerful woman that girls should look up to. I know I do. For being someone whose book I'm *dying* to read and know everyone will adore. Can't wait for you to write it.

To Miss Amanda Gilarski Mancuso. I'm so glad we're still friends. I'll trade with anyone who has a Jacuzzi! Hugs.

To Barry McLaughin, Dawn McCoy, Rich Kelly, Kirby Howell (aka Jessica Alexander and Dana Melton, authors of AUTUMN IN THE CITY OF ANGELS—go get it!) and the aforementioned Jason L. and Alex C. for putting up with crazy color-coded spreadsheets and playing the characters on Twitter. How lucky am I to have such incredibly gifted, generous friends?

To The Remainers: Nate Bott, Frank Staniszewski, Jason Lautenschleger, and Kaumyar. For the use of your prolific lyrics and kick-ass songs. I'm a huge fan. Their EP *Formal Fridays* is available on iTunes and Amazon.

To Sara Bareilles: For being so kind and supportive early on and tweeting to Liv. You are an inspiration, and believe me, when not listening to Berkeley & the Brightside, Liv was singing along to "Gravity" and "Gonna Get Over You" and "Brave" all the way (and so was I!).

To Shad McFadden and Kathy Chamberlain for being early readers and always being so encouraging. Love you guys!

To Kristilynne Savage and Hanna Johnston: I don't know you personally, but you both took the time to write and tell me you were enjoying this when it was a blog, and I was baffled that anyone was reading it. Your kindness kept me going, and I am forever grateful that people like you exist. I will pay it forward. Namaste.

To Maria, Jessica, Danielle, José, and all the folks at The Bonita. Thanks for the loan.

To everyone at The Bent Agency—especially Jenny Bent, Victoria Lowes, and Kasey Poserina. What a classy group! I'm humbled to be on your roster.

To everyone at Entangled Publishing—Liz Pelletier, Heather Riccio, Brittany Marczak, and especially Karen Grove and Nicole Steinhaus—for reading IN BLOOM over and over (and over again!). For their thoughtful editing and attention to detail. Thank you for weeding out all those adjectives, bearing with my first-timer ignorance, and for the smiley faces.

To everyone at MGT—especially Jeff Mirvis, Sandy Strahl, and Mike Brooks for standing by while I figure out this website thing—I'm so grateful for your support.

And finally,

To Mum and Da: For red wigs, dresses that spin, and seeing rainbows in prisms (and lotus flowers). For butterflies (all kinds). For reading to me (CAPS FOR SALE!). For loving stories. For fostering that in me. It all comes from you. I'll love you until you're yellow like butter. Mmmm butter.

And for remembering to always Leave. The. Door. Open. (except that one time... Click. Click. Click. What the H?)

About the Author

Katie Delahanty is a fashion designer turned novelist. She holds a BA in Communication Studies from UCLA and a Professional Designation in Fashion Design from FIDM. It never occurred to her that she was a writer until an economic-crisis-induced career shift from lingerie designer to e-commerce webmistress led her to start the company blog. Not being an expert in lingerie, she decided to write the blog as a fictional serial starring a girl named Olivia Bloom who worked for the lingerie line. And that's when Katie fell in love with storytelling. She hasn't looked back since. Katie lives in Los Angeles with her husband.

To contact Katie visit her website at www.KatieDelahanty.com

43396612R00236

Made in the USA
Middletown, DE
24 April 2019